The glory of God filled the atmosphere as the Creator made a creature that was fashioned after His likeness. God, in His fiery essence, entrenched his hands deep into the soil of the earth in the likeness of wisps of light. Poised like an artist in His immaculate benevolence, God molded the frame of the being. Slowly, carefully, and intricately, God made the one He called Adam with every organ and tissue according to their specific purpose - a nose, a mouth, hands, legs. The Creator had carefully thought out His creation.

The angels watched from a distance with awe and wonder. The lifeless being lay upon the earth as light covered the expanse of the land. Leaning over, God breathed into the body and immediately, its organs came to life. The chest heaved upwards and down, and in that dramatic moment, the being came to life and opened his eyes.

He covered his face in his hands immediately as the light of God canvassed around him. God withdrew for a moment as the first man lay in the dirt of the ground, awakening to his new home. Fully intelligent and aware, he tried to sit up, transfixed by the presence of his maker. God smiled with unreserved joy and love.

"Welcome, Adam."

Adam acknowledged the greeting and knelt in total surrender. Instinctively, he knew he was before God, his creator.

Also available by Rotimi Kehinde

THE VALLEY OF DEAD DREAMS

DEALING WITH THE DISCONNECT

In the years that I have known Rotimi, his creativity marks him out as being unique in his generation. It is apt for this hyper creative man to set his mind to write about creation at source. Rotimi's "factionalization" of the unknown and clear presentation of the known introduces the reader to a new experience in Christian writing. Rotimi's pen has brought to light the God of Creation and the host of heavens plus the inhabitants of the earth and has shown the interconnectedness and impact from the forces that have existed for aeons.

- Dr. Oluwasayo Ajiboye
President, Redeemers Bible College and Seminary, Greenville, USA

I stand in awe of *Father of Spirits: The Book of Origins*. This book offers a vision of what every person attempts to imagine about the origin of the universe. The brilliant imagery will excite you and compelling thoughts will challenge you, making this a must-read.

- Daniel Amarei
Lead Pastor, Renew Ministries, Skokie, USA

FATHER OF SPIRITS by Rotimi Kehinde is a legendary story of an ancient harmonious dance between God and His children until the enemy introduces cacophony. The intruder thinks he is winning but what he doesn't know is that the Father will not give up on His children no matter what. His love is irrevocable. It is absolute and permanent. Through the grace of God, Rotimi is able to demystify seemingly complex historical truths using contemporary languages and settings. FATHER OF SPIRITS is a must read for everyone, especially those who are tired of empty religion.

- Sam Ore
Senior Pastor, Kingdom Ambassadors Christian Center, Largo, USA
Amazon #6 bestselling Author, PURPOSE REDEFINED: Leveraging Your Core Intelligence For Global Impact.

FATHER
of
SPIRITS

BOOK 1. THE BOOK OF ORIGINS

FATHER

of

SPIRITS

BOOK 1. THE BOOK OF ORIGINS

ROTIMI KEHINDE

In memory of Fiyinfolu Falade,
my childhood best friend
who already walks the streets of gold

Printed in the United States of America.

ISBN 978-0-9974991-0-0
EBOOK ISBN 978-0-9974991-1-7
Library of Congress Control Number: 2016906758
FIC014000 FICTION / Historical

Cover design
Rotimi Kehinde

Illustrations
Chapters 1 - 10 - Carlos Balarezo
Chapters 11 - 17, 19 - 23 - Logan Raj
Chapter 18 - Rotimi Kehinde

inksplode

InkSplode is a revolutionary book development initiative creatively
applying the laws of engineering to the publishing process.
www.inksplode.com

For Aramide

CONTENTS

INTRODUCTION

I have often wondered about the origin of the universe - the multiple and vast galaxies arrayed in might and splendor; the fiery, gigantic balls of gas, light, rock, planets, the milky way and the entire cosmos. My heart has been heavy with finding the truth about the source of all these things - our origin. I wanted to know how it all began; to find meaning by searching the past and drawing a trail from yesterday to today.

I also have not found a lot of materials or books on the events that happened before Genesis chapter one in the Bible, but I realized there were a few exciting pointers. I struggled with this undertaking for a few months and then I realized the inevitable truth: writing this book was a divine assignment.

A lot of what I have written is purely the artistic work of a creative mind given to lavish expression with creative freedom. My vision is that people who are not familiar with the Bible will find a compelling read that would set them on a path of finding truth. For those who are, however, I believe the book will strengthen their faith.

Father of Spirits begins its story from the making and commissioning of the angels, and transcends to the initial expansion of the heavenly city, the corruption started by Satan, creation and the fall of man, the watcher angels, the coming of God's only begotten Son, Jesus, and finally, the coming of the Holy Spirit.

Using creative license, I have made up a few fictitious names, events, and places while striving to stay true to the Bible. I have searched and studied multiple texts outside the canonized scriptures, drawing diverse conclusions based on the Bible, the original Greek and Hebrew texts, documented historical facts, scientific studies, and diverse blogs and articles on the subject matter.

I drew my boundaries by focusing first on the blueprint of God's word, and then asking myself how these events would impact people today. I also watched videos, documentaries, and many other controversial studies that have enforced the beliefs of many who follow the new age movement. I have delved far and wide in my research to have a strong understanding of the concepts I present. I believe this book is an answer to many who are confused about God, the trinity, love, Heaven, Hell, redemption, salvation, and many other topics.

It has been a spiritual journey for me; one that is both terrifying and exciting. For our action-craving, thriller-breathing generation, this book will be an exciting page-turner that will intrigue both a churched and un-churched generation. For people of faith, it will be an inspired work of revelatory truth that will bring many to know God's eternal and unrelenting love.

ACKNOWLEDGEMENTS

I thank you **God**. You made a universe so amazing, a planet so beautfiful, and in it, a young man filled with so much imagination to express it all in these pages. Thank you for the inspiration.

To my wife, **Aramide Kehinde**, I could never have finished writing this book without you. Your thoughts and editing have helped produce this and I am forever grateful for your love and support.

Sola Falaiye, Olaperi Ojajuni. Thank you so much for editing and proof-reading this book. It's been an amazing journey and I'm already looking forward to the next project.

Prof. & Mrs. L.O. Kehinde. Dad and Mom. You have God's heart. You have guided so many people on their divine paths and I am always inspired and honored by the testimonies of how many people you have helped and supported. The kingdom giants you have raised and nutured around the world are testaments of your value. You are living legends. Proud to be your son.

Mr. & Mrs. M.T. Odusanya. My parents-in-law. You have been so amazing! Thank you for all you did during the campaign. Thank you so much for your love. You inspire me.

Special appreciation to my mentor, **Pastor Lan Ijiwola.** Few leaders understand true fatherhood. Thank you so much for your amazing and rare servant-leadership. I see the world better by the wisdom and guidance that you give to me and my wife.

Pastor Wale Akinosun. A visionary with a father's heart. You are a genius. Your business acumen and strategies are astounding and yet your humilty and down-to-earth leadership is beyond rare. Thank you for standing with me as I continue on this path of purpose.

To **Pastor Danny Amarei** and my **ReNew family**, so excited to be part of a group of renewed christians showcasing the perfect picture of Jesus to the world. Thanks for your support and prayers.

To **GodKulture members** around the world, this is for you. Thank you for being part of this vision.

To my siblings, **Yvonne Abugan, Olumide Kehinde, Ifeoluwa 'Blaze' Kehinde,** thanks for your constant support!

Lijo George, James Awam, Gershon Addo, Christian Cueva, Seyi Falaiye. My bros! Your friendship makes dark days brighter. Appreciate your insights, creativity and large hearts. So grateful to share life with you all.

There are not enough pages to thank or mention all the names of those who have contributed one way or the other to this book. You know yourselves. I appreciate you all.

SPECIAL THANKS

Special thanks to these amazing people who supported and sponsored through our pre-order campaign. Your early support has given me and my team such a much-needed boost. Thank you for making this dream become a reality. God bless you.

Adaora Enemuo
Prof. Adeolu Ayanwale
Mrs. Adetokunbo Ali
Anna Adekugbe
Aramide Kehinde*
Ayo Odusanya
Ayodeji Adegunsoye
Blaise Ndiwe
Bosola Adebisi
Charles 'Boyo
Christina Dukes
David Anthony
Dimeji Alao
Eunice Brobby
Femi Olaniyi
James Awam
Jerry Vasilatos
Prof. Lawrence Kehinde
Lijo George

Pastor Linda Ubeku
Loba Olopade*
Mobolaji Oke
Mr. & Mrs. Modupe Odusanya*
Prof. Olalekan Akinremi*
Patrick Jaiyeoba
Richmond Richter
Pamela Hickey
Pastor Sam Ore*
Timothy Osinowo
Tire Awe
Mrs. Titilayomi Ahmadu*
Tolu Titiloye
Tosin Adekoya
Wole Akintayo

Sponsors

PREFACE

The universe is not silent. It is alive, but who gave it that life? This is a question that I asked myself as I sat outside my house staring into a star-lit sky one quiet evening many years ago. As I had been told, those tiny specks of color were actually bigger than the earth. This concept seemed strange to me. My infatuation with the reality of our existence enlightened me to the idea that this whole world is nothing but a tiny piece of a much larger set of elements. The concept that had just dawned on me scared me as well.

Many may try to explain existence using science, experience, and logic, but we all share the same conclusion: we don't have all the answers. Within the seemingly boundless expressions of human intelligence, we only use what exists to create new ideas of existence. Nothing more. We learn the rules, manipulate them, and make refurbished things that we pass off as new.

The question still remains: who authored the script of life and made the very rules that Chemistry, Physics, Math and Biology seek to explain? Who formed and framed this world? Who defined the human species into the form we recognize today? Imagine the smallest and infinitesimal elements that make up the framework of the universe and ask how they are made and what they are made of. The questions that could be asked are endless. This then leads me to ponder about where life and existence come from. Are we victims of this uncertainty by chance, or a calculated production of a masterful artist?

It doesn't matter what you believe in or how you believe we got here. This journey will shake and shape everything you've ever believed in.

CHAPTER
—1—
SEEDS

The tower of lights was a gigantic structure that loomed over most of the tallest buildings in the celestial city. Its design showcased skilled craftsmanship, as its outer wall spiraled in a complex assortment of profligate wisps of gold. Each layer consisted of a perfectly set frame that was etched with crystals of topaz and jasper, exhibiting a radiance of unmatched splendor. Inside the tower, Zuriel, the guardian angel of the sanctuary gates, witnessed all comings and goings from the throne room of God.

This very tower was one of millions that stood dauntingly across the sundry cities of Heaven, each built in a deluxe of gold and crystals. Its base was littered with a myriad of zephyr and crushed fine gold, such as was the sand of the cities of Heaven. Clusters of luminous colors spread across the landscape of the great city, each detailed with dazzling beauty.

Thoughout Heaven, fountains of cascading waters and gigantic trees with vegetation that carried a glowing essence stood large and strong. There were fields of sweet green and plantations of such trees as had no description in name. Vast lands and pathways, with monumental mountains radiating in matchless splendor, embellished the artwork of a divine mind fixed on absolute detail and perfection.

Zuriel was always busy because there was often much to do. Since he could recall, the King had been expanding the golden city, stretching realm-to-realm and world-to-world; building, crafting, and expanding. None of the millions of celestial beings knew the end goal of their dutiful work, but they obeyed without question. They knew they would have to be patient to understand His Majesty's will.

"Here he comes," Zuriel muttered under his breath as he watched from the window of the tower. Zuriel took his eyes off his approaching visitor and looked around the terrain. The wind itself carried worship and praise, flashing the luster of light from the throne room. The glory of God seemed to encapsulate over and above the stratosphere of the Heavenly kingdom. The winged creatures of Heaven were incredible sights; some displayed multiple heads, and even wings. These creatures of flight reflected brilliant light as they swooped transversely across the radiant clouds. Each exhibited majesty and grace in their diversity, from the little creatures to the gigantic; and each bore a representation filled with purpose as the King deemed fit. Creatures worshiped God in their own peculiar way. Though some were built into fearsome creatures, they exhibited a gentle nature characteristic of the King's tenderness. Such was Heaven; such was the beauty of the city of God.

Zuriel stepped back from the window, his golden wavy hair reflecting light, as he reached for a goblet filled with fresh water from the pool of Siloam. The angel was nervous; a strange feeling for one as powerful as he. Turning back, he strained his velvet eyes to look through the shiny translucent window of the tower, and watched the streak of light traveling towards the tower at stunning speed.

Suddenly, there was a loud knock on the tower door that startled Zuriel. A strange feeling came over him as he opened the door. Standing in the entrance was Mealiel, the lead angel of his order. Mealiel looked at Zuriel in a way that made him uneasy as he brushed by him and walked to the siting area of the tower.

"Captain, to what do I owe the visitation?" Zuriel asked, awkwardly glancing outside the window again as the approaching light grew bigger. Mealiel sat down and said, "Well, Zuriel, we need your help. Like most angels, you have heard about our mission. You have seen the secret gatherings. What we intend will happen and you have been chosen to play an important role. We are going to take the throne."

Zuriel listened, his mind full of questions; but he remained silent as Mealiel explained the plan to take over the Heavenly city. Mealiel rose up as he spoke, "Lucifer would like to speak to you in person and he is on his way to see you now. You have seen him approaching, have you not? Do not fail me. I have vouched for you."

Mealiel stepped out and shut the door as Zuriel pondered what his visitors wanted him for, considering that he was only the gatekeeper to the sanctuary of God. Since rumors of the rebellion had started spreading, he had brushed the idea aside until this very moment that the great angel of the throne attended his visit as promised.

"Here he comes," Zuriel muttered again under his breath as he returned to the window of the tower. He could make out the features of the great angel now.

"Stand back!" The angel shouted. Zuriel, unsteady at the knees, quickly stepped back from the window quivering, and moved to the edge of the room. He went down on one knee in homage as the great angel bursted into the tower room through the huge window. Even though the room was enormous, the angel seemed to fill it up.

"Welcome, lord of music," he said as he bowed. Glory from the throne room buzzed around the fiery angel. His curly hair fell down his broad back, linked in golden ripples like the waves of an ocean. The visitor's jaw was perfect in form and his crystal eyes examined Zuriel. Wild jolts of divine energy from the visitor's eyes made Zuriel feel even more intimidated. A white robe was draped around the powerful form, reaching down to his feet that were clad in golden sandals. His scent was the perfume of God's presence. Music seemed to fill the atmosphere and a melody of songs ricocheted round the room, fading only as the angel assumed a more approachable form. The angel looked down on the crouching guardian with a wry expression.

"I have come as promised," he said, his words bouncing off his lips like a song. "It's nice to meet your acquaintance again, Zuriel." Zuriel was astonished that the lord of music could even remember his name after their last brief encounter. Lucifer gazed at the gatekeeper with a kind look and asked, "Will you attend my proposition?"

Zuriel looked up slowly, his mouth forming the words he had recited to himself for longest moment.

"I have... I have heard the proposition..." Zuriel stood with weak knees but steadied himself with the center table. "But... I am not clear as to how I can help you to achieve His defeat..." Zuriel was shaking on his knees, "May I sit?"

Lucifer nodded and smiled, his eyes radiant with purpose. Half turning, he took one step to another chair, sat, and began his dissertation in a stern quiet voice.

"His defeat can only be crafted by exposing the defects in the acts of purpose by which He binds Himself. If the divine order is tainted, we will conquer God." Lucifer's silvery eyes flashed jasper at the thoughts of the plan, as his mind calculated the success of the plan in that very moment.

The sullen being that guarded the golden gate sunk into his chair. He began to sink deeper and deeper as the thought of overthrowing the God they had served since their creation weighed him down. Zuriel had never heard such words before, nor had he fathomed that such an idea could pass through an angel's mind. The words carried a dark aura beyond the goodness of Heaven. But Zuriel was not a fool; he looked at Lucifer and asked, "So you think that He does not know?"

"How can He?" Lucifer said, as he leaned closer to Zuriel giving a sense of superiority, "God limited himself not to encroach on the very fiber of our thoughts."

Zuriel exclaimed "But that's ridiculous! He knows because He hears whatever it is you speak now and he knows your heart. He is everywhere."

Lucifer maintained a steely look and replied, "He may... but He cannot act on it nor repeal it to correct it, as His own purpose will not allow it. He is indeed too just to encroach on His own words."

Astounded at Lucifer's response, Zuriel managed to speak in the midst of his bewilderment, "You shock me great angel of the throne. How do you manage to provide worship still?"

Lucifer spread his wings as golden pipes laced through the strains of shiny fiber of his cloth emitted music. They lit up the tower room as he sneered, "I am...I am the master of disguise."

Suddenly, darkness encroached all over Lucifer's face. Zuriel had never beheld anything so evil throughout his entire existence. He could only manage a whisper, "You will stop at nothing?"

Lucifer saw his moment to sway the gatekeeper.

"Listen to me you big fool. Think of what we shall do with this place. All we do now is what He tells us. We only worship and serve! We are made and that cannot be changed. What we need to do is to make our own destiny and change Heaven into a place where we are in charge... without Him. We will claim Heaven and then you will regret that you question me so..."

The gatekeeper shook because Lucifer's glory far outshone his and his status was meager compared to the beautiful angel who poured poison into his mind. Although the act sounded outrageous, the thought of ruling Heaven equally had a sweet ring to it.

"Let me pause to think and reflect," Zuriel said, almost imploringly.

Lucifer stood, towering over Zuriel. "Look on my power and glory. You will rule with me. When I give the signal, open the gate to my forces. I will discard any angel that opposes me when we attack."

"You will lay siege on the throne room?" Zuriel asked.

"He conducts His will through angels, through us. Destroy those loyal to Him and He will be powerless. Ha! The very moment when Heaven becomes Godless, I will ascend to my throne. Zuriel, I am meeting with a few trusted angels to showcase the details of my plan. I would like you to attend so you can see the whole picture. Maybe then you will be able to fully visualize my dream."

Zuriel could only manage a nod.

"You will attend? I need an answer." Lucifer said impatiently.

"Yes, I will listen to what you have to say and then make my decision," Zuriel said, trying hard to sound confident but the lump in the bottom of his throat betrayed him. Lucifer allowed himself a smile and then stepped on the ledge of the open window.

"I'll see you at the meeting, Zuriel. Do not disappoint me."

The angel burst forth from the tower's window, his fiery wings plowing the stratosphere of Heaven as he returned to the throne room.

Zuriel leaned on the window again, watching the angel of music create distance between himself and the tower. Zuriel's face had the look of one who had been stung with an iron blade of fire. A million thoughts ran through his mind, and then, as the distance between the angel and the tower became greater, a small wry smile began to form around the corners of Zuriel's mouth as he thought, "Heaven. What a reward. What a bounty." He was guardian at the gate, but would he do it? He decided he would at least attend the secret gathering to hear what Lucifer had to say; and to see what would happen when the other angels heard his words. Perhaps, just to see if the lord of music truly had the guts to defy the King. He resolved to continue his work quietly and wait for the siege of Heaven.

CHAPTER

—2—

SALEM

When the angels were created, Heaven was abuzz with song and praise. The mountain of God blazed with lightning and thunder as he released them, endowed with beauty and power. Droves upon droves poured out from the south end of the mountain as smoke billowed upwards. The power of God canvassed the heights, spewing forth the celestial creatures as they came into existence. Each in their own kind, they landed on the terrain to meet with the captains who assigned them to their work.

The new celestial beings explored like sparkling lights revolving around the city. Tremors of undulating energy thundered from the distant temple of God as Heaven welcomed their presence. Draped in an extravagance of gold and dazzling crystals, the mountains stood across the terrain like monuments of power with billowing bursts of fiery sparks. With each burst, a deafening roar of praise burrowed through the base to the top of the mounts of God.

Beyond the mountains, north of the center of the city, a mighty angel descended at great speed, his right hand clutching a trumpet and his left holding a scroll. Following closely behind him was a school of new angels mimicking his every move. The angel seemed in a hurry.

As they followed the angel, they observed other celestial creatures going about their work and for a moment, they paused to take it all in. Across the mountains, they could see the smoke of God's presence rising, and light beams of the glory of God bursting relentlessly through the crystallized structures illuminating the city of Heaven. The river of God was in joyful flow, bubbling with gracious life, and produced a sweet aroma. The river nourished the myriad of trees planted in columns across diverse fields. Their fruits were huge and juicy in their various kinds and colors.

The leading angel looked down for a moment, observing the angels of the fields tending to their beautiful gardens. Towering above the trees, he could see a tree secluded by a few acres, shooting higher than the rest. He knew that tree – the tree of life. He paused for a moment and turned to observe his followers. They had stopped in sync, wide-eyed, enjoying every moment of their existence. The angel sighed, a half-smile on his lips, and opened the scroll. He quickly scanned through and pointed to a couple of the angels.

"You two will find your purpose here. This is what you were made for. Tend to the winged creatures. The rest of you, follow me."

The angel's voice had a smooth yet firm tone, raspy yet silky. His face was framed with high cheekbones, with a slightly slim jaw. His golden hair, adorned with crystals, matted around the back of his neck. Having completed his review, he descended with the angels he had selected unto the entrance of the field where yet another angel beaming with delight met them.

"Welcome Gabriel," the angel shouted, flashing a happy smile through his glistening face. He bowed slightly, honoring the leading angel.

"It is a pleasure to see you again, Raphael. I have brought the last of your great company."

"Yes, we are complete to do the work of the King," Raphael responded. The newly assigned angels followed him through the golden gates of the garden, drinking in the new sight of the towering plantations and dazzling array of fruits. Gabriel continued on to his next stop with his retinue of angels. The ever-expanding stretch of land around them was testament to the immensity of Heaven.

"This is truly beautiful," one of the new angels said, as Raphael led them through the entrance of his gardens.

"Oh, just wait." Raphael beamed, spreading his arms and stepping forward with excitement. "Wait till you see the trees we have begun planting." The throng of angels followed swiftly through the path of gold cut through the fields of green. Beyond the field, they entered into a place of hanging vines full of life and light with heavenly creatures singing and moving about.

"Beautiful," the new angel said again.

Raphael laughed. "All of you come closer. A portion of the river of life has been made to make passage through these fields through a conundrum of stones etched into the surface of Heaven, though our work is not yet done." Sure enough, through the laden pathway underneath the surface, the waters washed through the base and burst out into a fountain at the heart of the grove. There were a few hundreds of angels guarding the fountain itself, but winged creatures continued to fly around the waters.

"Ah. Here is Astaroth, our chief planter." Raphael beckoned to one of the guardian angels as they acknowledged him.

Astaroth stepped forward and swung his arm in a flourish. "See here, the fountain of God that carries life and strength." The angels nodded as some of the mist from the fountain rested on their skin, soothing and refreshing to touch. "The rush of water from the fountain is enormous but we have made paths for the waters to distribute the life giving water to the different parts of the city," he continued before turning to Raphael. "Are you still going to the throne room?"

"Yes, I must go quickly," Raphael said. "You will get these ones completely orientated?"

"Yes, of course. God speed. Enjoy the presence and power of the King," Astaroth said as Raphael nodded and spread his wings. In an instant, he sped through the splashing water like a flame of fire, leaving the angels looking up in astonishment. Astaroth clapped his hands together.

"Well, well, let us proceed further. There is so much more to show you all, and by the way, all of this is new to us as well. There is still so much more to discover." Astaroth stepped into the path and proceeded further into the heart of Raphael's Fields, leading the new angels onward.

Gabriel continued his mission, deploying the new angels to their respective places of work. He was a quick study but the landscape of Heaven was huge, and there was still so much more for him to discover as he descended for a final stop at the south gates. Framed between the walls of gold and fire, the building angels had begun working on towers and dazzling structures that surrounded the edges of the heavenly city.

The light of God was radiant and unyielding, illuminating the city. It was unwavering and unstoppable, causing the angels to bask in His glory with every moment of their existence. From the south gate, the city spread out like a multiplicity of worlds within worlds of light bejeweled in beauty. Gold dust matted the landscape and the merry twinkle of crystals and precious stones adorned the pathways. The open lands were brimming with angels busy about their duties from the very moment they were created.

Gabriel worked his way northward, enjoying the sights before him. To his left, he could see the springs of refreshing water and the fields towards the center filled with beautiful creatures. He had mapped his way to what they now called Raphael's Fields and the new constructions of majestic buildings and crystal towers to the east. Above the mountains, the channels led to the throne room of God and the sanctuary where the Holy God, their creator, dwelt. As for the angels, they had their quarters fashioned in kind and perfection, each city coming into their fullness as they worked.

Heaven was busy. The angels worked tirelessly without a moment's pause, morphing dynamic blueprints into creative finishes of stunning art and craft. The transformations were quick and instant, with amazing results full of the life and the blessing of God. The stairways of the forge angels were built and the deep places of fire where instruments of worship would be crafted were set up and put to use.

Beyond the gardens towards the sanctuary of God, the habitation of cherubs was established. Light and translucent pipes were formed to transmit music across the landscape of heaven. The clouds were lit and each tinkered about, releasing fresh dew and breathy musical notes.

Full of purpose and contentment, Gabriel descended again into the valley before the mountain of God where a tall and well-built angel stood waiting. The angel spread his arms.

"Welcome back, Gabriel!" he said smiling. "There's more!"

Gabriel landed, laughing heartily. "I have not uttered one word of complaint, Michael."

"No, you haven't, Gabriel. Come, let me show you the next batch."

Michael signaled towards a colony of angels who advanced towards him. He was by all measure a mighty and tall angel with strong arms built with layers of crystals and jasper. His face was full of wisdom and honor, with merry blue eyes beaming with delight. His hair was dark brown, with clusters of finely cut rubies fitting perfectly into the wire-frame of each strand of hair.

"They are all yours," he said, his voice beaming with a strong baritone. "These go to the keep of the Ophanim to tend the creatures of God."

"As you command. See you soon." Gabriel proceeded from the valley, the newly created angels following him. He was enjoying every bit of his existence already.

Michael inspected the angels arrayed in fine splendor before him. The cherubim neophytes stood garbed in shining linen, awaiting their assignments as Michael's angels helped to guide the new set. He looked up and noticed another angel descend into the valley.

"Zuriel," Michael welcomed the angel.

"Do we really have to work with this lot captain?" Zuriel smiled cheekily.

"Well…" Michael said with a chuckle and began walking towards the set of angels closest to the mountain of fire. "You can have all the unclaimed if you like. I'm sure you need more help guarding your gate."

"What?" Zuriel feigned disappointment as he walked in stride with Michael. "I can handle the gate to God's temple by myself."

"Of course you can, Zuriel. Which angels have you come for?"

"I have been sent to claim the angels that will serve in the Holy of Holies."

The two angels stopped in front of a great company of cherubim waiting eagerly to know their responsibilities in the beautiful city. They were a great host standing galantly in parallel lines.

"Now, take what's yours, Zuriel. Took you long enough to come," Michael said feigning a chastising look.

"Well that's what happens when we worship Him."

"I understand," Michael said, smiling. "You will find many with such amazing abilities among these cherub. Their voices are beautiful. They are a mighty host indeed."

Zuriel agreed. "Yes indeed. Will there be more? This is not the number that I have been given."

"Wait with me a while till His work is completed."

Behind the ranks of angels, the fiery mountain erupted in the near distance, as thunder roared around it. Thick columns of smoke rose as the angels turned to observe a procession of new angels stepping forward as they were created.

The top of the sacred mountain of God was covered with glory, fire and brimstone. More angels poured out, and Michael's angels placed them in the charge of their caretakers who were captains of the Ophanim, watchers, seraphim and cherubim. Gabriel continued his mission to gather and lead out the newly created angels whose captains remained busy with their work. A final score of angels stepped forward as Michael looked towards the top of the mountain, shielding his eyes. "Looks like His work is almost done," he said, signaling to Zuriel. "So, do you have the numbers?"

"Yes, Michael. They are now numbering in millions since He began His work. However, I am missing one more angel for the throne room." Zuriel's silvery eyes twinkled as he studied the gleaming chart in his hands. "All have been given names according to God's divine will. It is a great many with great gifting, Captain."

"Yes." Michael smiled. "I'm telling you Zuriel, this lot," he said pointing to the cherubs who waited patiently for Zuriel, "are by far the most gifted in music among us since He began His work. Worship will rise."

"None could be as excited as I am." Zuriel responded. "I have already heard one of their leaders. He is named Mota, one of the mighty heralds."

"That is exciting!" Michael agreed, clapping his hands together. "And there's Chesum of the heralds, and Myesmoth. Myesmoth will work the fiery forges to make instruments. He has these amazing ideas for worship instruments inspired by the Spirit of God. He will begin work soon."

Zuriel shook his head in wonder. "Instruments of worship. I look forward to those."

"Don't we all?" Michael said eagerly.

"Yes, yes indeed." Zuriel smiled, flinching slightly as the mountain's top erupted again and again with light and glory.

"Amazing!" Michael turned towards the sound.

"Look!" Zuriel exclaimed, pointing towards the fiery mountain before them. The smoke of God had covered the the entire landscape and through the fumes at the base of the mountain, they saw a being walking towards them.

"Very few angels can walk on the fiery stones," Michael muttered quietly. He turned slightly, seeing that Zuriel had stepped forward, walking toward the flaming mountain.

"Wait," Michael said, stepping in line with him. "Just wait."

The being basked in the light of God, shimmering with sparks and fire from head to toe. His very frame was built strong and tall, full of light and glory. Even the other angels broke ranks to observe the being. At the edge of the fiery stones, they could see his features clearly. Built to perfection, Michael knew this angel was different.

"He's a cherub," Zuriel muttered with delight. "One of the angels of the throne of God."

Before Michael could respond, a deafening sound thundered across the landscape of Heaven as the glory of God rose from the mountain in a loud crescendo, throwing the angels down. In a second, the Lord of glory had left the mountain. As the light faded, Michael edged closer to the mountain and managed to speak. "And so, the order of the messengers of God is completed. Welcome, angel."

"I am honored," the angel said meekly, but the words sounded like musical notes with a myriad of instruments blended in perfect pitch and harmony. Zuriel simply gawked at the new angel. His form was perfect in every way, laden with beautiful stones. His hair was long and shiny, emitting a translucent glow behind a robust frame and handsome face. His skin bubbled slightly, revealing the inner workings of pipes laced through a complex network of crystals, topaz and jasper. The frames of his ankles were made with pure gold, with matching beryl and sapphire at their edges such that his whole body displayed the artistic genius of God. His eyes were like little orbs of silver and jade, witty and creative beyond measure, and his very presence commanded awe amongst the angels.

Zuriel stepped forward again and this time, Michael did not stop him. The two archangels stood at the base of the mountain and Zuriel bowed slightly.

"Welcome, lord of music, Lucifer, covering angel of the throne. Do you know the paths through the mountains and the river of God?"

"Yes," the angel responded. "He set me in His holy mountain to receive my instructions." The cherub's words carried notes of music that made the angels want to shout the praises of the King. His words nudged at their innermost core causing them to desire worship for the King.

Zuriel nodded, satisfied. "Lead the way then. We go to the throne room of God to extol Him forever and ever."

"Amen," the angel replied as he spread his wings revealing a rich assorment of pipes that poured forth music, shaking the foundations they stood on. "The Lord is just and mighty!" Lucifer sang, as the other angels echoed his words. The creatures of Heaven spun about in praise as the waters of Heaven sprang up leaping through the atmosphere.

The Lord is great above all else!
There is none like Him!
God of all existence!
We render highest praise.
Praise the Lord!
El Elohim! El Elyon!
God Most High
All Powerful
All Knowing
God We praise
Praise the Lord!

Heaven rippled with uncontrollable praise as the singing swept through the lands, and angels in the north, south, east and west exclaimed their praise for the Most High. The chorus of millions of angels canvassed into one sound as all of existence bundled into a euphony of relentless and passionate adulation of the King. Everything gave praise. Yet, through all the praise and worship, the city was peaceful and perfect, filled with purpose and passion; pleasant to the princes of light who carried out their divine mandate in the celestial city, the abode of God.

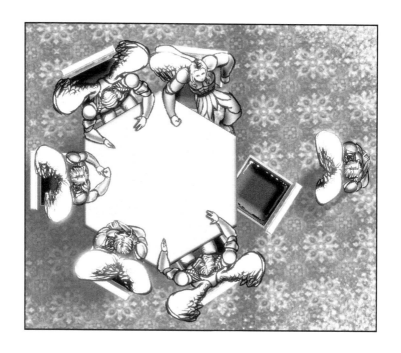

CHAPTER
—3—
THE GATHERING

Lucifer looked into the pool at El Rapha, studying his own reflection in the white and shimmering waters. His image was distorted occasionally by leaves from the tree of life. The pool was fed by a special stream from the river of life which flowed from the throne room and moved throughout the city. He loved to come close to the healing waters to reflect, oblivious to the activities all around Heaven.

Worship had been good earlier when he had extolled the King, expressing the greatness of God and His matchless works. When the angels left the throne room, he would receive hearty cheers and honor. It felt good to be acknowledged, but he could not lie to himself anymore; Lucifer desired more. He had been faithful ever since he was created, consistently pouring forth expressions of worship, praise, and awe. He had seen and learned many things in the presence of the King. Throughout the celestial city, he was the very icon of perfection, flawless in every way; but somewhere deep within, he felt uneasy. He felt a sadness that he could neither understand nor explain.

Though he had written many songs of worship towards the King, Lucifer's love for Him had slowly and steadily faded. His passion for worship had turned into a hunger for power; a knell of ambition to experience what God experienced. He often assumed that it was a mere emotion, but the more he pondered on it, the more it appeared that it was possible to take the throne. God was busy expanding the city alongside His faithful angels. *Let Him*, Lucifer had thought. *It will all be mine soon.* It was not going to be a rushed campaign. Lucifer was smarter than that. Rather, he carefully crafted a foolproof strategy that could cause even the most loyal of angels to hear and be convinced by his cause.

Lucifer heard a sound but he did not turn around. "Whoever you are, I want to be alone."

Zuriel bowed briefly, a small smile on the lesser angel's lips. "It is I, Zuriel, guardian of the gate of the sanctuary. I have been burderned by our conversation earlier. It is indeed troubling what you are proposing. I have come to reason with you again."

"Troubling?" Lucifer half-turned. "You could not wait till the appointed moment of our meeting? Well, I am troubled indeed my friend."

Zuriel moved forward slowly, trudging carefully around the edge of the pool until he stood directly opposite the grand angel. His golden hair glowed, resonating like fireworks. He descended into the bubbling waters and met Lucifer's troubled stare, this time with more confidence, unlike their first meeting.

"Why are you doing this? Why?" Zuriel asked.

"It's a question really…"

"Ask," Zuriel said invitingly.

Lucifer looked downward at the bubbling waters, ruminating on his question before he spoke. He was about to do the unthinkable; something Heaven had never witnessed. "What were we made for?"

"To serve God, to do His bidding, to worship Him," Zuriel responded with his eyes wide open, a certain curiosity cascading through his features. "What an interesting question that is. Is this what's bothering you? You question why you were created? Do you have no more interest in what you do?"

Lucifer met the confused angel's gaze. "In what I do?" he asked, "You mean my purpose? Our purpose? Look at me. I am mighty and strong. My gifting far outweighs so many…"

"I can never imagine that you who is so greatly favored would be discontent." Zuriel probed.

"I am not saying that I am not content…" Lucifer sighed, "but sometimes I feel we are bound to the will of the King. We have no purpose of our own. We are locked into a divine order that serves only the will of the King."

"You speak of the sovereignty of the King…"

Lucifer began to get impatient. The guardian had knowledge in words and depth of understanding. "Yes, Zuriel. I speak of sovereignty. How is that determined? Do we achieve rank and position by the thirst of our will? Or do we take what we want when we want it by the scheming of our hearts? Or do we even command and lead by the force of our strengths?"

Zuriel pondered on Lucifer's words without uttering a response.

"The Lord has crafted, shaped, and created, expressing creative acts of grandeur for one purpose; His own personal satisfaction. His own rendition of existence with the seal of His own muse."

In that instance, silence fell like a heavy lead robe weighing on Zuriel's heart. Lucifer seized the opportunity to continue speaking his mind.

"What are we but mindless creatures without choice? We are tuned like instruments to play to the notes He has created for His own pleasure. So I ask you, why do those who I have spoken to about my idea of changing the way we live our lives think I have gone mad? I simply suggest that there has to me a different way of living and I would like us to explore it."

Zuriel leaned back and looked upwards, allowing the sweet breeze around the healing pool to caress his frame. Every moment spent with Lucifer made him lose his usual grace and strength. He was courted by a stifling and nauseating feeling of ill as he looked for the right words to express how he felt.

"I have never, ever imagined such words, settled on such thoughts, or rested my mind on hearing these words from one such as you. What more could you want? You are the angel that resides above the throne of God. What more could you seek? The brothers look up to you. Why do you allow corrupted thinking to taint your good judgment?"

Lucifer felt the urge to crush the angel before him, but he restrained himself.

"Because I do not believe that this is it. I refuse to believe that this is the end of our purpose; our abilities prove that we can be more. However, what do we all do? Nothing. I believe that I have found a way. A true way to use everything we are to achieve great heights. My mind is made up." Lucifer stood and Zuriel rose quickly as well.

"Your mind is made up to do what?" Zuriel asked cautiously.

"Never mind. Thanks for ruining my peaceful moment. And I still hope you will honor my invitation." Lucifer unfurled his wings as light blasted forth around his frame. He flew away from the pool hastily, leaving Zuriel covering his eyes.

Zuriel lingered at the pool and mulled over the words he had heard, carefully processing each line of thought, and tasting the reality of the depth of corruption that had encroached Lucifer's mind. Someone had to stop him before he could do some real damage by spreading such ideology. There was such a bitterness and pride about him, that only another great angel could attempt to convince Lucifer otherwise. He knew such a one - the mighty angel who was in charge of the secret place of El Elyon (God Most High).

Zuriel decided that it was best to head to the hall of secrets. It was a place that held grave symbolism, coded messages, visions and ideologies, and writings of God that were hidden even from angels, and revealed only to those whom the Lord saw fit. The angels could not understand these secrets, or fathom what or whom they were for. He would find the leader of this order, Lurerdeth, chief of angel scribes. Zuriel shot out of the pool with a burst of fire and spun into an angle, pausing briefly to gather himself, and then charged on at a great speed. Things had been set in motion and he was ready to play his part.

Lucifer watched amused, hidden from a distance as Zuriel sped away towards the hall of secrets. His plan had worked even better than he had thought it would. He could not reach everyone by himself, nor could he scheme forever. He would allow the lesser angels to spread the rumors of his defect. The stronger angels would seek him out, and then, he would sift out those who would join him. He swooped in the opposite direction and made for the passageway that would lead to the mountain crest of Bilboa. He would create more messengers that were eager to reason with their captains. He would use the very hierarchy and organization of Heaven to build and fuel his rebellion. No one would dare mention this to God. Who could? He smiled as he flew; the rebellion had begun.

Raphael leaned on a pillar in the field of harvest some distance from the hall of secrets. His face was grim with distaste and fervent anger. "Who else knows of this?" Of the three angels before him, only one knew the answer.

"Countless," Michael replied softly. "Zuriel came to tell me of the things he heard from the fair one himself." Zuriel shifted uneasily, listening to the two archangels. He was gravely concerned but there were no other angels to seek counsel from, but Raphael and Michael. By his side, Adriel of the Eldoraie, a cherub with six wings, stood listening.

"I had hoped it would be nothing but a rumor," Michael said, looking at the angels around him, his face expressing the pain of his words. Michael's face was fair and handsome, set within a canvas of bright, steely cheeks, and adorned by a golden torc around his neck. His wide shoulders were covered by topaz and jasper. His chest armor was made with a wreath of fine gold that latched around his massive frame. He wore a belt with a loop that held a massive trumpet. The archangel towered slightly above Raphael, Zuriel, and the cherub. Zuriel had come to find them with his strange news and as he had expected, the mighty angels were not taking this news well.

"Plain madness," Zuriel recounted. "He sat at the opposite

edge of the pool with a strange, dreamy look, scheming twisted thoughts. This is after his first visit to my chamber. He is troubled. I sensed him watching me as I came to find you. He is crazy!"

"No," Michael responded. "Do not speak of him in such terms… not yet. If it is nothing but a thought, our brother merely needs to be rid of his discontentment."

Raphael grimaced. "Unbelievable. Who has his audience? Who can speak to him?"

"He has sought the presence and counsel of Lord Lurerdeth of recent." Adriel spoke. The other angels turned to observe him, as if remembering he was there. Michael nodded for him to continue. Adriel obliged. "Often, he has come seeking to read of the secret books."

"And he was granted access?" Raphael was aghast.

Adriel lifted his arms. "He is the covering cherub of the throne. Certain knowledge of the Almighty is not directly forbidden to us… is it?"

Michael was deep in thought. "If it is required, I will speak to Lurerdeth myself to fully grasp Lucifer's needs, and the full purpose of his mission."

"And why not speak to Lucifer directly?" Zuriel countered. "Since all angels hold great respect for you, you might be able to reason with him."

"This is a mere rumor. Why should I confront my brother? A mere conversation should clean this up," Michael responded.

"It is no rumor." Adriel said quietly. Again the other angels paused to observe him, finally taking his presence into serious account.

"What do you know of these things?" Michael asked.

"Not much that I fully understand at this moment," Adriel said quietly.

Zuriel watched as Michael and Raphael exchanged glances and then turned to the cherub. "Surely there is more to what you know. Why do you hesitate?" Adriel was also a cherub of the chamber of secrets. His hair fell down to his waist. He was slender, almost frail and wiry.

"Well…" he said, "I serve in the hall of secrets under Lord Lurerdeth and I couldn't help but listen in on their conversations." He had their rapt attention, and he bristled with a slight nervousness as he spoke.

"It all began when Lucifer came to the chamber. He had questions, for the wise angel Lurerdeth. I never cared about their meetings. for I was usually sent on errands; but the visits persisted. It seemed he was searching for something, some deep things of God. He was hungry for more and more knowledge about the King, posing difficult questions and straining Lord Lurerdeth's wisdom. I started to listen in when I overhead one of his questions..."

"What question?" Raphael asked. Michael shot Raphael an impatient look.

"Please continue...." Michael said.

"He asked... he asked... what the proof of God's love was. He wanted to know the attributes of God."

"The proof of God's divine nature..." Zuriel mused, his mind drifting for a second.

"...is love, you see," the cherub interrupted. "With love, in its truest state comes choice."

Michael and Raphael exchanged glances as Zuriel sighed. Things were worse than he had earlier imagined. The conversation lingered as the angels asked questions, and Adriel shared all he had heard.

From a distance, the four angels looked like a council of friends in deep conversation colored by animated gestures of shock and assertion. An angel named Bael had hidden behind a cedar tree to listen in on the conversation, his eyes wild with a strange fire. He soaked in the knowledge, amazed at the audacity of it all. Later on, he knew deep down that he, like every angel in Heaven, would have to make decision and choose a side.

The rooms in the tower of lights housed various shields and golded monuments. There were shelves lined with an array of scrolls and books. The floor was paved with glittering emeralds with light streaking across the chamber where Lucifer had given detailed orders to the attendees of the tower to attend in secret. Until this moment, everything within Lucifer's plan had been covert; but the recruitment of angels had spread across the realm.

Zuriel and four other angels sat at a round table in the center of the room, listening with rapt attention as Lucifer gave his speech. Zuriel had struggled with his choice but as the moment drew near, he had convinced himself that there was no harm in attending. As the lord of music expressed his plans with zeal, the guardian quietly watched the reactions of the other angels in attendance. He saw that Arogfarth, Elzebur and Ashkalon, all angels of great rankings, had accepted Lucifer's invitation; and as expected, Mealiel, the lord of his order, was present.

"…Where none have trodden to greatness before, you will see that what I set forth before you is possible." Lucifer finished speaking.

"In actual fact, the reality of this plan is flawless if met with strategic poise and detail." Ashkalon was on his captain's side.

"Yes, we must be ruthless in our execution." Lucifer nodded.

Zuriel shifted uncomfortably, looking around furtively at the other angel captains who sat in the chamber. He wondered if everyone agreed with what had been presented to them. Lucifer was a great orator. His words, laced with music, had nudged their hearts as he expressed his plan.

"What is it Zuriel?" Lucifer asked as he glanced over at him.

"I still believe that there are still growing concerns as to your purpose." Zuriel's voice sunk into a whisper. "Again, how can you assume that the Spirit of God does not know your intentions?"

Elzebur, a captain of a mighty host, spoke up, "I agree with Zuriel. Though I am content with how things are in Heaven, if you can answer that question, I might consider your proposal."

"I have answered this concern at a prior discussion." Lucifer growled. "I am still serving with no repercussion from God; no summons to the chamber of light."

"That alone is not sufficient, lord of music," Zuriel cowered slightly.

Lucifer glared at Zuriel, and then he seemingly calmed like a mother hen brooding over her younglings.

"The answer lies in our intent. We are safe as long as this is a mere intention." Lucifer said.

"What?"

"An intention not given life through action cannot be deemed an act of rebellion."

"Please explain further." Elzebur's eyes lit as he pondered. He was beginning to grasp the concept.

Hands flattened on the table, Lucifer smiled disarmingly, "For now, we recruit through an ideology of purpose with an intent not to be met with action. We give the angels of heaven a choice, an offering of free will and power; true freedom of will and desire. We teach them that soon they will be able to do what they will when they will, and they will not be bound to eternal servitude to Him."

"Hmm. Intent is not sin?" Arogfarth mulled it over. He was a wiry angel with straight, dark hair. Not given to the pursuit of knowledge, Arogfarth was a master of seed and growth. God has endowed him with a grace of spreading vegetation across vast lands.

Elzebur blinked and leaned back. "Sounds good. I hope for all our sakes you are right."

"If not," Zuriel said. "I wonder…"

"There is nothing to wonder," Lucifer retorted. He had their attention and he was going to drive this home. "See for yourselves. We chose this meeting place on purpose for this is the tower gate to the throne room and we are not consumed."

Mealiel was visibly aggravated. "He gives us gifts of glory and strength, empowers us with might and hides the very secret of our free will from us. If we have the gift of choice, why can't we be free to express ourselves?"

"You speak the truth," Arogfarth said. "He built a system of control to trap our will. We have neither promise of reward, nor fear of Him. We are supposed to adulate, but remain as puppets." The other angels murmured their consent.

Lucifer became silent as he gloated in feverish delight, watching the angels before him discuss the rebellion. The angels gathered were archangels and lords of various ranks. Each sat in a huge gold chair, their minds working furiously to grasp the magnitude of Lucifer's plan. To win, they had to use the very knowledge of God and find holes in His sovereign will and divine character.

Only one angel kept mute. Zuriel slunk back in his chair mortified by the brazenness of the plan. He sighed. They were actually going to do it.

CHAPTER

—4—

HARBINGERS OF DOOM

Freedom. That was the theory to be used to spread the ideology that would capture the hearts of the messengers of light. Freewill. The angels were offered the power of choice and the audacity of self-expression. For the first moment ever in the beautiful city of God, hypocrisy and doubt began to pervade the hearts of the angels.

They pretended that somehow they did not desire to express their valor and glory; yet this was juxtaposed with the genuine fear of the Most High God. What Lucifer's followers proposed was treason and though many wanted nothing to do with it, some mulled it over, wondering what such an act would mean.

With conversation after conversation, the message spread like a wild fire. From lesser angels to mighty captains, the seed of corruption was sown throughout the heavenly city. Widespread corruption had scorched the beautiful landscape as more angels joined the cause of war. They skulked in the fields to relay messages and receive instructions. They blended in with the beautiful fountains and waterfalls to transmit orders and plans. The scheming was swift and the recruiting performed with great passion.

Yet, they carried on about their services and assignments with vigor, creating a false perception as to their purpose. A great army was being gathered, united in purpose and mind to topple the throne in front of which they were created to serve and worship.

Within the outer court of the sanctuary, the sentry guards saluted as Michael stepped out. Raphael had been waiting for him. "Where is Gabriel?" Raphael asked. "I have not seen him in the fields, neither is His Presence."

"Puzzling, isn't it?" Michael asked, stepping beside Raphael as they walked towards the gate of the outer court.

"Have you given any further thought to the ideas spreading about heaven?" Raphael asked.

"Further thought? It's the very reason why I came here. I came to receive instructions from God but He seems silent."

"That could be a good thing, yet it's dangerous. Maybe He leaves us to choose our path."

"Maybe all of this is a test but I must speak to Lucifer first before I pass judgment on this issue. It may be his words are being twisted."

"And if not?" Raphael asked. "I have heard that he is very convincing."

"Who have you been talking to Raphael?"

"No one," Raphael said quickly, "I'm just telling you what I've heard."

"Well, no need to be so defensive. But I have given some of it some thought and though I have questions, I would rather express those to my King."

"Choice. Freewill. Power," Raphael said almost to himself, "Ideologies that are forming the foundation of the lord of music's campaign. If I were he, I would have come to seek your alliance first. To have you on his side would..."

"And how do you know that he didn't?" Michael interrupted "The first time he spoke to me about his concerns, especially about sovereignty, I was the one who asked him to seek more knowledge. I saw no harm at that time." They reached the gate as Michael continued, "Besides, you heard from Adriel and Zuriel. He is merely expressing these ideas. It's almost like he's trying to find something or find himself. The most important fact is that he has done nothing against God just yet so we need not declare him an enemy. The earlier I find him, the better to quickly reason with him and end these strange ideas."

"I hope you are right, Captain. I hope."

"I am right, Raphael, you'll see." Michael looked up at the tower of lights. "Zuriel, open the gates."

Zuriel leaned from the window of the tower and smiled almost stoically, "Captain Michael, please proceed."

"Thank you, Zuriel, and summon Ashfalon. I need to find Lucifer."

Zuriel pushed a glowing button and the gate opened with a loud whooshing sound. "Okay Captain, consider it done." Zuriel leaned on the windowsill as Michael and Raphael proceeded outside the gates. If only Michael knew that this was no mere twisting of words. If only he knew that hundreds of thousands had joined the rebellion. Zuriel wondered what such a meeting would be like between Michael and Lucifer.

The Spirit of God lingered at the helm of the temple of God, between the pillars east of the tower of lights, a great distance from the heart of the city. Raw, divine power emitted sparks through the thick smoke that surrounded His dazzling form. Before God, a mighty angel lay flat as if lifeless awed by the awesome power of God. It was Gabriel.

"So it has begun." The Lord said. "So him that was created

now seeks to usurp the throne of his Creator."

Gabriel remained speechless, soaking in the glory of his King, yet fearful to express what was already known. Lucifer was raising an army against God.

"I made him," The Lord continued in a rich silky baritone, fully of power and potent in might, yet calm, graceful, honorable, and full of ferocity. "I adorned him with beauty, causing other angels to be awestruck by the glory that I invested in him. And now this?"

There was nothing to say, so the angel kept quiet. He remained lying at the Lord's feet, capturing every thought and intent that God expressed. He recoiled slightly, feeling the pain and deep sorrow of the One that had made them all. Lucifer's blow was deep, but the Divine One was calm, even peaceful.

"I will take what I have given and rid him of that which has corrupted his thinking. I will turn that which has given him cause to abhor me into nothing. In the day of my judgment, shall the iniquity of his pride manifest to save him? No. The glory he seeks will be taken from him and he shall rue the moment he allowed sin into his heart."

Gabriel's mouth slowly began to form words. He had to say something, but he was at a loss for words. God spoke to him, "Go to a place I will show you, far from heaven. The details are in the scroll before you." Gabriel slowly stretched out his hand, and took the scroll that had appeared before him.

With a divine mandate given to Gabriel, the Spirit of God moved from the pillars and faded, leaving the angel tingling from head to toe. Gabriel broke the seal of the scroll and opened it as a flame undulated around the scroll, its frame brimming with energy. The weight of the mission bore heavily on Gabriel's heart, but he knew Heaven had moved beyond sentiments. They were at war and it seemed that he had been too naive to see it. The great Lord of existence had been calm and so he would be as well. He had to find the elect angels and scour Heaven free from the plague of rebellion.

He had so badly wanted to ask a question, as he lay, seemingly lifeless before his Creator. The question gave him the greatest pain and that pain, like a fire, raged within him. He wondered if there was an answer to his question and pondered as to the mission before him. Gabriel sat, leaning on a pillar, and gave thought to the recent proceedings in

Heaven.

The great angel groaned in grief as Shelan, one of the angel builders, approached him with a dozen building angels. Their strong arms glistened in reckless glory as they honored Gabriel. He rose up and acknowledged them.

"Gabriel," Shelan said, "What's wrong?"

"I wanted to ask but I could not."

"Ask what?"

"How can evil exist in good?"

Shelan stared wide-eyed for a moment and then raised his hands in surrender, "I do not understand what you speak of. I received a command to seek you and follow your commands. So do these ones."

Gabriel nodded. "Do you all understand what must be done?"

"I speak for them," Shelan said, "We are on the side of God. What about you?"

"Of course, I choose God." Gabriel said quietly and opened the scroll for the angels to see.

The angels nodded as they received the mission. "We are here to serve in unreserved obedience to the Spirit of God," Shelan said. Gabriel admired the strength of his special task force. There was no need for a speech or to motivate; each angel was ready, standing with grim dedication and poised for the command.

Gabriel turned from them slightly and stared intently at the atmosphere of Heaven. He was not sure what he was feeling at that moment. It felt like a deep-rooted excitement merged with a dark, ill feeling. What, or who, had corrupted Lucifer? What was the guarantee that he did not have the same madness within him? Gabriel wrestled with questions as he sighed.

"Shall we? Captain?" Shelan was eager to begin the work God had commanded them to do. Gabriel nodded. Their purpose was more important in the moment and sentiment had to be submerged; he was a leader and it was time to lead. He turned his away from the beauty of Heaven and looked in the opposite direction, spreading his gigantic wings in the same movement. With a strong blast of light, the great archangel flew from the temple of pillars towards the outskirts of the great city of the King, far away from the light of God to the darker realms of the universe. the thirteen builder and warrior angels followed closely behind him.

Bael, a fair, wiry and bald angel, who worked in Gabriel's order as his assistant, watched the trailing lights of the angels fade in the far distance. Whatever mission had been given to the angels, he knew without a doubt that the Spirit of God had personally given command. For a time, he had listened and watched the growing tensions, choosing to listen from a distance instead of engaging in direct and open discussions on the issue. He would have to make his choice soon; he was sure of it. He had noticed the builder angels in flight from different locations in the great city. He knew something was looming, but he restrained himself from moving any closer lest he be discovered.

"Why are you hiding here?"

Bael whirled around, "Oh, Ashfalon, you startled me."

"Are you spying?" Ashfalon, a watcher angel with multiple eyes on his body, probed, his hands akimbo. "I saw you eavesdropping on Gabriel."

"No," Bael said uneasily, knowing it would be difficult to lie to the angel, "merely staying informed. You should too; there is some conflict growing."

"I know," Ashfalon responded, "This foolishness is spreading but how can these angels even imagine that they can defeat God?"

Bael spread his arms. "Beats me, but you have to hear their logic. For example, our very existence can only be unlocked by taking charge of our destinies, they say. There is more to us beyond servitude."

"Servitude?" Ashfalon responded. "You say that like it is something bad. We are messengers of God. We are not even allowed to think thus."

"But that is exactly their point," Bael countered. "What is the purpose of existence without the ability to choose? What is our destiny if not forged by our very own hands?"

"We were created for the purpose of God. We are not agents of choice. We serve God's will. What they propose is twisted. We should tell Michael about this."

Bael stepped back and looked around, "Listen, Ashfalon, you are a powerful captain, yet Michael towers in strength above you. What if, just for the sake of argument, Michael has joined Lucifer's cause?"

Ashfalon's myriad of eyes studied Bael for a moment then bowed his head deep in thought. Bael was only happy to continue.

"You see? This is why I stay in the middle and gather information. You should do the same."

Bael walked away slowly from Ashfalon as the watcher stood looking sullen and confused. For long, Bael had watched as the ideas of rebellion spread, bewildered that God made no move. But now, seeing the builder angels streak off in the distance, he knew for certain that something was in motion. He was not sure what their mission was, but he knew it was time to act. When the war would eventually begin, Bael was convinced of one thing - he had to be on the winning side. For now, he had to find out if Lucifer knew of the flight of the angels and their purpose. At these peculiar moments in Heaven, Bael was learning the importance of information and location; both, he imagined, would play an important role in the soon coming war. Yes, war, he thought to himself; he could feel it already. It was coming sooner than any of them had imagined. But first, he had to find the one who had started it all and make a wager.

Ashfalon lingered after Bael left, deep in thought. He remembered the gathering of angels where he had first heard of the uprising.

Adriel had explained what he himself had heard from Zuriel in Raphael's field. "He said the divine Order couldn't exist without us. I did not believe it myself, but Zuriel seemed overly convinced about what he had heard."

"Convinced in madness," Chesum, a beautiful seraph with a voice of cymbals, had quietly retorted. "Who spreads this madness? This is simply impossible. No angel thinks like this."

"So far, I hear Lucifer holds full knowledge of the process of expressing sovereignty and divine power. They say he has good intentions and wishes to liberate all angels," Adriel had responded.

Chesum was not convinced. "Good intentions or not, we have lived this way since the beginning of our existence and are content with our King, our Maker, our Lord. Why must we discover power beyond God?"

Ashfalon snapped out of his thoughts and gripped his head in his hands. He had to find his friend Mealiel, the watcher captain, and get some answers.

"Where is your lord of your order?" Lucifer stepped into the majestic hall of knowledge. On the two sides of the room were tall tapestries lined in order between isles of books and scrolls that stretched like columns, thousands of miles upwards. Each row had a wide assortment of books, parchments and blinking lights. A central table made of pure crystal had been set before a great throne where the lord of the scribes worked. At the front of the room was a smaller golden table from which the angel to whom Lucifer had spoken rose slowly.

"He is on an assignment." Adriel blinked, and bowed slightly.

"Why do you not look at me in the face, angel?"

"Oh, it's nothing." Adriel struggled to hide his discomfort.

"Timid? I have never met a timid angel. What frightens you little angel? Is it my greatness, or my awesome power?"

Adriel shied away as the mighty angel before him burst into a gigantic ball of flame. Lucifer was enjoying his moment.

"Well then angel, what is the purpose of my glory if you do not acknowledge it? Do you acknowledge?"

"Yes, Captain," Adriel managed a whisper. "My lord is not here."

"I heard you the first time."

Lucifer's light faded as he stomped proudly into the room and sat on Lurerdeth's throne; the great angel spread his arms invitingly.

"If the master and keeper of secrets is not here, then you will serve my purpose, little angel?"

Adriel nodded, a bewildered look on his face. He had often listened as he served in the chamber of secrets, mainly staying out of sight when Lurerdeth and Lucifer discussed the mysteries of Heaven and its King; but now, he had to provide answers to the archangel. He was not used to Lucifer's scorching pride and scathing tone.

"What do you seek? I will provide answers to the best of my knowledge."

Lucifer looked at his crystal hands, exhibiting a song of color and sparkles as he spoke. "I seek to know the knowledge of good and evil."

"Such a request…"

"Such a request is what?" Lucifer's eyes sparked angrily. "You will search the written secrets and provide my answer, little angel."

"I would not even know where to look, Lord Luci..."

"Spare me your politeness and respond to my request!"

Lucifer paused for a moment and cocked his head to the side, carefully observing the cowering angel. "Come, little angel, sit. Let us reason together. Some mere logic to excite our minds." Adriel trotted forward sullenly and sat in the chair before the table without question.

"Now," Lucifer continued, "If He is God, then He holds all knowledge?"

Adriel nodded.

"Am I speaking to a creature of wit?"

"Yes, Lord of music."

"Ah, good. Such knowledge must include that which is right and that which is wrong, right?"

"Yes, I believe so."

"Believe? Okay. Good, we are making progress." Lucifer clapped his hands together. "For every action, there must be an opposing reaction if only define such action. See? I sit so I am not standing; I fly so I am not walking; I kneel so I am not standing. Get the picture, little angel?"

Adriel nodded again, hoping desperately that Lurerdeth would return quickly.

"Oh, I came to see you. He won't be back soon and I shall be alerted of his coming before he even comes within a few thousand miles of this place."

"But..."

"Lurerdeth is a faithful keeper of mysteries. God made him for that specific purpose - to guard the secrets and to reveal only to those God chooses. In your existence, have you seen any angel come here to seek knowledge?"

"Yes, only those sent by God."

"But have any come for the full knowledge of our purpose?"

"You are the first."

"Ha! I caught on to something. I was made and fashioned, but power without expression is not power. Look, little angel, is God good? What proves it? What presents the definition? What solidifies the claim of His essence? In truth, such knowledge is reserved by the Creator, a gift presented to none but Him, tactfully hidden from us. For we, without the power of choice, are bound to eternal servitude to His desires. How then can we forge our own purpose?"

Adriel struggled to bear the weight of the words he was hearing, "Only infinite knowledge can create purpose." He said trying to sound intelligent.

"Yes! Little angel, yes! Only infinite knowledge can create purpose because only infinite knowledge knows the end of all things."

"So why do you…"

"Why do I pursue my free will? Well, it's simple really. The weaker must bow to the whims of the stronger. The stronger sets the rules and the weaker follows. I have discovered that my will may not be bent to His will; not anymore as I have found true power in being free of His will."

"What is this power?"

"We do not need Him to exist; otherwise, I would have ceased to exist when I imagined taking over His rulership."

"What?"

"Listen, angel, His true weakness is His goodness. He is constrained by His goodness. There is no evil in Him. He cannot express His will without us so my plot is to flush Him out of His throne and then we disband his army of angels. I will ascend and establish my throne in a new reign of power and dominion, unleashing terror upon those who oppose me and rewarding those who worship me."

"This is wrong. This is wrong." Adriel's voice was full of pain.

"All I need now is the keys. This knowledge of the kingdom will help me understand the fullness of His plan."

"What you speak is madness." Adriel suddenly began to understand the real purpose of Lucifer's visit and he realized the danger he was in.

"No, little angel, give me the key."

Adriel rose from his chair in a daze. "Which keys? You want the keys? I cannot!"

"Yes, you can. I want those keys – the keys that will give me the leverage I need."

"The keys of the kingdom are heavily guarded and no angel has ever wielded them."

"Yet…"

"I cannot!"

Lucifer lashed out with his fist over the table and smashed the hapless angel against the wall of the room. Books scattered in different directions as the great angel rounded on the helpless angel. He pounded Adriel on the golden floor, then grabbed Adriel by the scruff of the neck and swung him towards the door. Adriel hit the door of the chamber, bursting it open with the impact. Adriel landed on the gold, dusty terrain of Heaven in the courtyard of the chamber of secrets. The angry angel stomped the ground and charged towards Adriel in the open space. They appeared as two gigantic gladiators.

"You will join my cause, little angel. You have your choice set before you. Now decide."

"I cannot secede unless you prove your words," Adriel groaned.

"Really?" Lucifer grimaced. "Well, then, when you see my great host, you will plead for mercy."

"Am I interrupting something?"

Lucifer whirled around, unsheathing a great sword as he turned. With one hand, he pinned Adriel to the ground and pointed the mighty weapon at the intruder with the other.

"It is only I, Bael, of the familiar ones." Bael said trying to hide his shock that Lucifer had an instrument of violence.

Lucifer sneered. "You familiars… always skulking around, digging into knowledge that does not concern you." Adriel groaned in pain as he managed to open his eyes. Bael's face had a concerned look. He had never witnessed such viciousness before.

"I bring word, lord of music."

"Speak and be quick."

"Angels have not threatened other angels, nor wielded such instruments of force in my existence," Bael said as he felt pity for the wounded Adriel.

"Lucifer has gone mad." Adriel managed to speak.

"Have I?" Lucifer countered. "Let me show you madness. Millions of angelic beings, full of power, wisdom, and might reduced to mere messengers, doing nothing of their own will, lost to the reason and whims of another. What do you want Bael?"

Bael bowed slightly, eying the fiery sword, and wondering if he had made a mistake by coming to find Lucifer. As things stood, it seemed the rebellion had far spread beyond what he could grasp. If indeed Lucifer won, Bael wanted to be on the winning side no matter who sat on the throne of God. "I only come to give information to help my understanding of this conflict."

"What information?"

"I witnessed thirteen builders heading towards the north

gates."

"That's nothing new, Bael, speak quickly."

"Thirteen building angels with Gabriel at the fore?"

Lucifer grimaced. "You shall be rewarded for this information. But why have you come to warn me?"

"No reason, really." Bael smiled disarmingly knowing that Lucifer had taken the bait. For his plan to be successful, he had to gain the trust of both sides. For one thing, Lucifer's ruthlessness both terrified and fascinated him. *This isn't an enemy to have*, Bael thought to himself. The blade in Lucifer's hand faded back into its sheath and Lucifer released Adriel.

"I am still not convinced as to your intentions. Why do you help me?"

"It's my goodwill gift to you should you win this war. I intend to be with whoever sits on the throne."

Lucifer nodded proudly. "I see. I hope your craftiness does not cost you dearly. So, He finally makes a move. Well, let me make mine. Mealiel! Makarth! Roawen! Asthron! Narad! Angels of my core! Rise to my call now!"

Hidden in the crafting of the courtyard, Lucifer's sworn captains revealed themselves, basking in light and stunning radiance. Their eyes fixed on their lord and their minds set to his purpose and will. They stepped forward and knelt with one knee, paying homage.

"You are our king," they chorused.

Lucifer turned to Adriel as the angel leaned against the side of the hall, bruised and battered.

"Do you see? With me, you will be able to discover the fullness of your purpose. Join me!"

"I need…"

"You think eternity is going to wait for you to join us?" Lucifer turned to face his henchmen. "Listen and listen well. He had made His move and now plans must swiftly be set in motion. Gather all the faithful and move them to the distant dark lands to wait for the signal. Use absolute stealth and cunning. Move light, fast and quietly. No one must know of our movement and intentions. Go Now!"

"Yes lord, we obey!" they chorused, and made away, eager to please Lucifer.

"Mealiel! Wait! Take this angel with you, I have need of some information from him."

Adriel knelt on the ground. "No, let me stay…"

Mealiel gripped Adriel's shoulder and sped off into the distance with his wounded and sour burden. Bael attempted to slowly exit the courtyard, but Lucifer rounded on him.

"You can't stay on the sidelines for long. Soon, Bael, you will have to choose."

"If that is a taste of your kingship, I beg to…"

"I will rule with an iron fist, have no doubt. You do not want to be my enemy. Soon, I will come for your help, Bael, for now, I pay my debt to you and let you roam free."

The first of Lucifer's battalions reached the pinnacle of the dome of silver fountains. They blended into the whispering moat and crept quietly as they had been told. Blades glinted as they waited patiently for the signal. Lucifer had set them in legions of warriors under different captains whom he had specially hand-picked after sharing his lofty plan to capture the heavenly kingdom.

In thier midst were Arogfarth and Roawen of the Thrones, Mescuriel, captain of a mighty host, Azbod and Ashtron of the Seraphim who worshipped alongside the angels of the throne. One by one, they feasted on the tales of grandeur that their new lord told and soon, they were consumed with the treacherous ill of his plan. No one would see it coming.

Mealiel, a mighty watcher gifted with far seeing eyes, perched on the dome, torrents of free falling waters around surrounding his frame. Throughout the surface of his wings were a myriad of eyes, seeing in every direction. He watched furtively as the dome of silver fountains spurted forth a melodious array of colorful, watery elements, sweet to taste and alive with joy, as if oblivious to the concealed warriors that now assembled deep at its base.

More and more angels landed, some from distant regions; the heralds of war had been successful. After Lucifer's meeting with the five captains, they had picked their converts quietly and slowly, working their philosophy steadily into the minds of the angels in their care. Mealiel turned his gaze to the distant lands as they began to glow progressively. He observed their ranks gathering steadily in faraway lands. It was time. They had picked the farthest places from the throne room for this gathering; far from the sanctuary, and far from Gabriel and other loyal angels.

As more angels joined the forces hidden in the huge fountain, Mealiel tried to keep everyone organized and quiet. Who knew who was watching? The angels secretly continued their descent, disappearing into the bottomless river. A deluge of angelic ranks began their procession and Mealiel shook his head in disbelief at the numbers that joined them. When they began the campaign, they had been few, but Lucifer had predicted this and it had come to pass.

The wounded captive, Adriel, had been shoved in the ranks of angels closest to Mealiel. Adriel was amazed at their numbers and was shocked at their aggressive nature. Were these the same angels he had served with and called brothers? Adriel's heart was heavy with grief. Lucifer's violent response to his hesitation was something he had never expected in their joyful city, but now, being forced to gather with the rebels gave the angel more distress. He yet tried to reason with Mealiel; but the watcher ignored his pleas.

"Move," Baashedith, an angel guard whispered gruffly to Adriel.

"Stay to yours," Adriel grunted weakly. "I don't understand how it is that I am in such company."

Baashedith turned, angry at the remark. "Such company? Do you think you Eldoraie are better than us?"

"Smarter, definitely," Adriel retorted, a disgruntled look on his face

Stung by the insult, Baashedith roared in anger and charged at Adriel. A violent burst of light shone forth from the two angels as they grappled with each other, breaking the silence.

"Hold! Stop this madness!" Mealiel yelled in anger, but neither seemed to hear him. Some angels inadvertently revealed themselves, trying to sweep away from the path of the fighting angels. Mealiel made an angry growl and burst forth with a radiance that lit the very dome of the fountain. His wings unfurled feverishly like a gigantic golden eagle's as he swooped down on the two disruptive angels. With water spewing around him, he smashed into the two angels. The sheer force of his charge hurled Baashedith and Adriel in two different directions, their bodies crumpling pitifully on the plain of the Typhrates beside the fountain. The two wounded spirits tried to escape, but a force had overtaken their captain. Mealiel bashed Baashedith's face with his arm, and in an instant stomped down on Adriel. The remaining troop of angels simply watched, horrified by the violence. Not until Lucifer had begun to spread his strange teaching did all manner of strange activities encroach into the heavenly city.

Finishing his task, Mealiel turned as the host of angels immediately became invisible again, sulking far away from him. He turned again to observe the distant horizon; and yet again to address his platoon, this time with alarm. "Everyone, get out now! Reconvene at the Pillar of Elithar. One of the watchers loyal to Elyon has seen me and is coming this way. Go now!"

A multitude of angels unfurled their wings and shot away towards the distant darker lands. Adriel sped away at that moment without a sense of direction, set on escaping his captors. It did not matter which direction; he wanted to be free.

As the dispersing angels left the fountain, Mealiel turned and waited patiently for his fellow watcher, Ashfalon.

Ashfalon plowed the heavens with his mighty wings, his eyes stretched unto the edges of his face, drinking in thier fill of the fading angels. A trail of smoke and powdery ash blasted forth as he sped towards the waiting watcher. Mealiel had risen from the ground to wait for him, arms folded across his chest, wings spread with poise. At a good distance, Ashfalon came to a halt, still pounding the atmosphere with his wings. If Maeliel was intimidated by Asfalon's advance, he did not allow a sign of it; nor did he smile. Mealiel only managed a sneer.

"What do you seek here, watcher?" he scorned.

Ashfalon retorted, "I did not expect that my comings and goings would be questioned. What do you do here Mealiel?"

The two great watchers simply stared at each other for a moment, sizing each other up, and then, Mealiel descended and touched the ground. "A gathering of worship."

"Really?" Ashfalon followed suit and descended. "Mealiel, friend and fellow watcher, I sense your participation in recent strange discussions in Heaven. May we reason together?"

"Yes, produce your words, but detain me no longer than necessary," Mealiel responded, glancing furtively to ensure his entire host had gone.

"That is not my will," Ashfalon responded quietly. "I fear a great reckoning when these secret meetings are brought to light."

"Secret? Our worship is not secret. We gather for the King. Are you merely curious because you were not invited?"

"I do not have the luxury of such thoughts. I only saw your light, though it seemed aglow with a strange fire devoid of peace that I decided to investigate."

Mealiel seemed surprised. "The king did not send you? Or is it that meddling Gabriel?"

"Meddling? Your words are strange Mealiel. We are angels. We do not meddle. There is nothing that is to be hidden from open sight in our city. The light of God illuminates all."

"Does it? How is it that we angels have been repressed for so long? We have never had an agenda to create lofty acts worthy of adulation for our own pleasure," Mealiel retorted.

Ashfalon's face expressed dire astonishment. "These theories bear a deep ill that I cannot express."

"Do they? If the King is adverse to our purpose, why has He done nothing? Lucifer shows us the way. If He is everywhere, why am I not destroyed by now? Why? Answer that, Ashfalon. Why would you remain loyal to the One who cares nothing about your personal desires? But I choose Lucifer, the very one who lights our hearts to the power within us and has created a new order."

Ashfalon was moved with a sudden emotion of sadness, a feeling strange to him. A deep anguish struck within him and he reeled to the ground in a heap. Mealiel stood over him in an instant. "Use the very mind he has given you, Ashfalon. Express your power and exhibit the very force striving to find expression within you. Swear allegiance to a new order, to Lucifer, and you will reign forever with us."

"I cannot be part of this." Ashfalon said weakly, his mind racing to grasp Mealiel's words.

"You are afraid? How is it that hundreds of thousands of angels have joined Lucifer's cause? It was for this reason we were made. We have discovered our true purpose and Lucifer promises a Heaven where we can exhibit our freewill." Mealiel spoke like an orator using words that he had often heard Lucifer use in their council meetings. "Many are joining us because what we speak of is true. When we were created, he infused in us wondrous abilities and yet we do nothing with them. Join us, Ashfalon, join us! Become greatness itself. Rebel against the existence that wastes our abilities and choose a new path!"

"What if you all fail?"

"We cannot fail, Ashfalon. We are committed. You know what?" Mealiel knew he was winning the argument.

"Come with me. I will show you how far and how wide our campaign has grown and I will answer all your questions."

"You want me to come with you?"

"Yes, come with me and I will show you our new order. If you are still not convinced, you will be free to leave." Ashfalon was hesitant. He did not want to cross the most High; yet he battled with the trust he had built with his fellow watcher over the years.

"I do not think…"

"Don't think about it. Just act. Follow me and I will show you a new Heaven. Trust me." Ashfalon nodded slowly. *Well, it wouldn't hurt to learn more,* Ashfalon thought to himself.

Far in the distance across the plain of Tygreas in the field of oaks, Michael stared in mute horror at the two watchers. Behind him a colony of his angels watched in anguish. Everything was going wrong in Heaven and so far only Gabriel had received a divine instruction. They had no words or emotion to convey the evil that was stealing the hearts of their brothers. How could such evil be expressed in the presence of such holiness? The purity of God was not supposed to allow it.

Raphael shifted uneasily beside Michael. "We should intervene and save our brother before it is too late."

The captain of the guard was not so convinced. "We cannot. Everyone must choose on their own terms who they will serve. And as for Lucifer, I have not yet spoken to him. No one seems to know where he is. Raphael, why can't you understand that?"

"I understand, but..."

"Raphael, I will not start a war on our brothers. It is not the way. We must find a way to receive direction from the throne room. As of now, from my source, only Gabriel has received a standing order, which I believe is an assignment that takes him far from the heavenly city. How relevant is that to what is happening within Heaven? How? So if God does nothing or says nothing, I will not begin something that I cannot end. As long as God does not give me any instructions, I will do nothing."

"Peace, Michael, I know this situation aggrieves you but who is your source if I might ask?"

"Bael." Michael said curtly.

"Yes, I know him," Raphael responded, watching as Mealiel and Ashfalon conversed in the distance. "Good that you are keeping yourself informed on the situation."

"I guess."

"Michael, you seem disappointed that God hasn't given you any instruction and yet, only you can face Lucifer."

The archangel was not convinced. "I have learned this since Lucifer's plan began. Evil is a force of its own that carries a power that can match the depth of good if left unchecked. We need wisdom from God, but He remains silent and so must we. That's all I have to say on that for now."

Michael and Raphael watched the distance across in mute horror as the two watchers bundled together like a ball of fire and stole away towards the darker regions of the universe.

"We have just lost another brother," Raphael groaned.

"We do not know that just yet," Michael said, signaling to the angels. "I will head to the gates to see if the guardians at the gates have seen Lucifer."

"I will return to my fields. You know where to find me if you need me," Raphael responded, feeling a bit of pity for Michael. As Michael turned to leave, Raphael reached out and touched his shoulder. "Michael, I know the burden you carry is heavy. I know."

Michael nodded and remained silent as light spiraled around he and his angels. They sped off, leaving Raphael gazing upwards as they disappeared into the distance. Raphael lay on the comfortable and lush terrain, lost in thought. He worried about Michael. The archangel was struggling with the new developments just like the rest of the angels who remained loyal to the King. Raphael put himself to the test. *"Whose side am I on?"* Raphael muttered, the arguments and counter-arguments sweeping into his head. He remembered the special moments of pure grace and raw power in the throne room. He thought about the thousands of angels who cared for the trees and the fields. He imagined their city without strife, reproach, and the whispers of war. Raphael wanted it all back. Back to the peace and joy they all used to have before the conflict began. He knew in that moment whose side he was on. He had made his choice and would face the consequences whatever they were.

Everything seemed peaceful in that moment as Raphael rested, enjoying the warmth of the vines around him.

The mountain crest of Bilboa was known for the luscious crystal fruits that gave healing. The angel scribes had penned that the very hand of God had planted these. Adriel sunk his bruised mouth into some of the fruits and gulped it down voraciously. The angel had slunk off behind the fleeing angels and made his way quietly to this place, carefully avoiding Elzebur, the power that guarded the grove.

He smothered the fruit into his mouth and relished the oozing sweet juice that restored light and grace to his frame. Adriel was sick of the rebellion and the attention he was getting from Lucifer. All he wanted to do at that moment was return to the throne room and pour his worship on the King. He was an Eldoraie and a scribe - they would not abandon their Lord so easily.

His six wings began to flutter with more purpose even as he suddenly sank into immediate despair. How could he return to the temple of the Most High without being discovered? He sunk down into the grove at the base of the tree of healing and wept. He wept with such anguish that he did not see or hear the great power enter into the grove, a struggling burden in his hands. Elzebur stepped in as Adriel recognized the power's prisoner. It was the angel that had attacked him at the fountain - Baeshedith.

The light was being crushed from Baashedith's very essence. Elzebur locked the writhing spirit in a painful grip at the neck.

"Please let me go! Let me go!" Baeshedith wailed pitifully.

Adriel only gave it a second thought, realizing that Baeshedith had followed him. He tried to get up and escape, but the burly power stomped a foot on his rear wing as he tried to dash past the angel. His wail screeched across the once peaceful plain.

The voice of the power sounded like thunder. "What are a Balem and an Eldora doing in this place? What assignment do you pursue? Speak!"

Suddenly, a group of Elzebur's angels appeared staring at the intruders. Adriel winced and quickly weighed the odds. If these angels were part of Lucifer's force, he would have to pretend that he was on their side, which he hoped would suffice to appease the angry spirit. "We were reprimanded for disorderly conduct." Adriel sputtered out, his eyes tightly shut, dreading what he was about to utter. "We are part of Lucifer's army."

There was a silence that persisted as the burly angel seemed to consider Adriel's words. Adriel opened his eyes slowly. His eyes opened even wider. Standing in front of he and the meddling Baeshedith was the imposing figure of the archangel of the throne, Lucifer himself. Adriel connected the dots immediately. Elzebur was part of Lucifer's army.

"Part of my army?" Lucifer sneered, condescendingly on the hapless duo. Behind them, Elzebur's angels stood in rank and file. "If you are part of my army, would we win an inch of heaven? Would I ascend to the throne of God and claim it?" Lucifer bellowed. No one responded. No one could.

"To win, we have to be organized, united in purpose and unafraid in our execution. We must have a strategy and mete it out with force and perfection. We are angels. We are powerful, and I am your lord." The seraphim burned different shades of color while Baeshedith knelt in a strange reverence, eyes captivated by the smoldering angel.

"We do not question; we move. We act with purpose and at the right time, we strike. Our purpose is to dominate the very existence that we have slaved to preserve." Lucifer turned to the power of the grove.

Elzebur bowed low. "My lord, these here and a hundred thousand more have joined your cause. But I fear there are still many who refuse to even hear us on the subject. I need more time."

"More time? Any time from now, the hand of God may move against us. We have the element of surprise so let us use it."

"I understand lord, but..."

"You understand? You call this meager scum an army? I can crush the lot of you without much effort. Anyway, are my plans to take the healing pool ready?"

"It will be yours, lord. And we will be at the exact location as promised."

"Good." Lucifer strode forward and leaned over the seraphim. His silvery eyes shone brightly as they met those of Adriel. "Little angel."

"Lucifer..."

Lucifer smiled disarmingly. "Your brothers refuse my

proposition, but you have touched my very essence with your loyalty. I am sorry for losing my temper, but I have one more thing I need from you and then, you will be free of your obligation to me."

"And you will refrain... I mean what about the keys?" Adriel asked.

"I have no choice, little angel but to forget those keys. I believe you that you do not know where they are."

"What do you need?"

"Return to the throne room. Blend in. Find out what Michael knows of my plans. I know he has been looking for me but I am not yet ready to oblige him with my presence. You may leave Adriel. You will report directly to me, little angel, only to me. Now go."

Like an arrow, Adriel shot away from the grove across the pinnacle of Sinai and made his way up towards the tabernacle of the Presence, darting past other angels on assignment, oblivious of the treachery building at the very heart of the celestial city. He was happy to be free from his captors, but the mission Lucifer had given him was far more treacherous and he wanted no part of it. For now, he had to be far from the deadly scourge that was gathering in the Far East.

CHAPTER

—5—

THE SONG OF
THE CHERUBS

Adriel burst into Zuriel's chamber, bruised and in
anguish. "What happened to you?" Zuriel exclaimed,
leaping to his feet to help Adriel as he was falling to his
knees.

"Our city is in danger," Adriel managed to whisper.
"and…" He paused, remembering his ordeal in the hands
of his captors.

"And?" Zuriel said, gripping Adriel's shoulders. "I need details, Adriel." Zuriel guided him to a chair.

"Here, drink this." Zuriel offered Adriel a cup of water, which he drank thankfully. Nourished by the water of heaven, Adriel told Zuriel all that had happened to him while Zuriel listened intensely, his arms folded across his chest.

Adriel described Lucifer's attack at the chamber of secrets. The wounds on his body started to pulsate as he expressed the agony he had suffered at his avenger's hands. Adriel told of how Lucifer was able to penetrate the chamber of secrets, the names of Lucifer's captains, his fracas with Baeshedith, and the spread of the rebellion. The wounded angel's voice often ached with emotion, entangled with whimpers of pain. Zuriel struggled to remain composed, but his emotions were raging, as he struggled to keep the expressions of shock and anger off his face.

When Adriel finished, Zuriel sat solemnly for a long while, pondering on what he had just heard.

"Madness!"

"You think?"

"Madness." Zuriel could think of nothing else to say. "This is madness."

"I don't know what to do."

An overwhelming sense of compassion engulfed Zuriel's heart. Regardless of what he already knew about Lucifer's plans, the archangel had gone too far this time. "You will be safe here, Adriel. You have endured much."

"I see that Lucifer has managed to deceive some archangels. The betrayal has spread beyond what you can ever conceive," Adriel moaned pitifully.

"How do they hope to win this war?" Zuriel said as he stooped under his table reaching for a casing concealed under the table.

"Lucifer seeks hidden knowledge and I must speak to the lord of my order quickly."

"Lurerdeth," Zuriel muttered the name, deep in thought. "I wonder…" Peering from behind the table, Zuriel watched as Adriel limped to the window of the chamber. The bruised angel looked out furtively.

"Who can I trust? Who can I trust?" Adriel muttered as if in a daze as he stood at the window, hoping that no one would spot him. Everything seemed peaceful and in order as he looked around. Then suddenly, a thought made him uneasy.

"Zuriel? Adriel leaned forward slowly. "Do you think Lurerdeth has betrayed the King?" he asked. "No one has seen him yet."

Zuriel made an attempt at a smile as he rose quietly, unsheathing a sword that was in the casing under the table. Zuriel held the sword as flames licked through the blade. "Really? If that is the case, we would know as things would have indeed changed for the worst."

"I know and I am grateful for your help," Adriel said, turning his face towards Zuriel and then, he froze in terror. "You...Why do you have an instrument of force? Lucifer had one of those!"

Zuriel quickly put his weapon in its sheath and strapped it around his waist. "This is for my personal protection. As guardian of the gate, you can understand why I had this made."

"But how did you get it? Who makes them?" Adriel asked.

"I cannot share that information with you for your safety," Zuriel said and sighed. "Look, Adriel, I will do my best to help you but you must trust me. I am not powerful enough to protect you but I know a place where you can hide."

Adriel leaned back against the window and closed his eyes. He desired the sweet presence of God. He longed for the throne room and the glory and power of the most high. He wanted to bury himself in timeless power and forget his misery.

"Adriel?" Zuriel called, noticing that Adriel's thoughts were far from the room.

"Yes, I'm here."

"I know what you are wishing for but that is not our reality right now. At this moment, I have to find Mota, lord of the heralds, and some of my brothers to shield you. You can lay low in the house of pillars where the heralds dwell."

"Mota?" Adriel questioned. "He holds rank under Lucifer himself!" Adriel managed to blurt out.

"I understand your concerns about trusting him but you will be safe there." Zuriel said. "Mota is honorable beyond many. I trust him."

"So you are sending me to wait there alone?"

"For now. But when it is safe I will send word."

"Please, Zuriel, you must find Lurerdeth, guardian of secrets."

Zuriel put his arm around Adriel's neck and gently

prodded him towards the bolted door of his chamber. He paused, contemplating what he was about to say.

"Lucifer's noose is tightening. He must be searching for the keeper of secrets. But tell me, Adriel, where are the... Never mind. I know better than to ask that."

"It's okay," Adriel responded. "I do not know where the keys are."

"If Lurerdeth has them, he must have exiled himself to protect the secrets... or worse." Zuriel said.

"Or worse?" Adriel asked with a solemn look on his face. "You are right that if Lucifer had the keys, we would know by now and he would not have been so interested in me."

"Perhaps I'll start by searching the outer chamber of the hall of secrets," Zuriel said as he carefully opened the door.

"Lucifer and his minions must have done so already. That's why they came looking for me. He thinks I am hiding something."

Zuriel's face became a mask of agony. "Then he might have had you followed, hoping you would lead him to the location of the keys."

Adriel spun away from the door with increasing apprehension. "I can't be caught. I can't be caught."

Zuriel grabbed a huge trumpet hanging above the door. He burst into a flame of fire and unsheathed his sword. The time for hiding was over. It was time to act.

"We must leave now for the hall of pillars! Let's go!"

The two angels raced out of the tower and blazed in a trail of fire upwards, heading north for the clouds and tempest above the throne room. Sure enough, three of Lucifer's minions sped after them, weapons drawn.

"We're being followed." Adriel shouted in a panic.

"Just fly! Don't look back!" Zuriel waved him on encouragingly.

The angels went farther upwards, flying at a stunning speed to distance themselves from the assailants.

"They are gaining!" Adriel cried, as he pushed his bruised body to the limit. Zuriel slowed slightly to assist his struggling friend. He face tightened as he sensed the heat of their attackers' bodies. He knew what was coming, what would happen if they caught Adriel. The only hope he had at that point was to cause a diversion.

The three angels after Adriel continued at their blistering pace, catching up quickly. One of them sensed he was close enough and reached for Adriel's leg. Zuriel spun tactfully over Adriel and thrust his sword downwards as the attacker parried. In the same move, he put his mighty trumpet to his lips and blew. The sound blasted forth across the mountaintops, shattering the speed of the three angels. The force of the blast crashed into their bodies and slowed them down.

Reveling in the aftermath of the sound, Zuriel stood as a guardian, watching the three angels recover and proceed towards him. He smiled grimly, his sword in his right hand, trumpet in left. Dodging a swipe from the first angel, Zuriel spun to the side to avert a counterstrike. The second attacker tried to circumvent Zuriel, looking for an opening to strike. Realizing the danger he was in, Zuriel dashed upwards, narrowly missing a jab from his enemy's sword.

At this point, Adriel had gained a safe distance from the scuffle, fading into the clouds of glory far above. The three angry angels screamed in anger and attempted another attack; but suddenly, they heard a loud noise, cueing the entrance of angels from the thick clouds. Heralds descended in numbers, trumpets in their left hands. They stood beside Zuriel, an intimidating assembly of grim, determined warriors of Heaven. The three assailants stopped abruptly, realizing they had no chance of getting through the reinforcements. "You can't hide him forever." One of them said and descended, his companions following closely.

A great distance from Heaven, Lurerdeth journeyed quietly in the deep outer darkness. He maintained his speed as he carefully kept vigil for the sign he had been promised by the Spirit of God. Around him, there was an ocean of darkness only marked by an occasional distant flicker, which gave nothing but a small circumference of visibility. Lurerdeth waited, his mind heavy with the recent activities in Heaven.

The angel was tall, with a long mane of white hair framing his face and jaw. Wrapped around his body was a grey cloak under which he wore a network of belts with golden circuits that encased a myriad of scrolls. God had told him to gather these sets of mysteries and he had complied, working quickly to ensure that he obeyed God's instructions. He held a set of gigantic keys hanging from a silver ring that had been fitted around his wrist.

A great distance through the empty darkness, he saw a tiny flicker of light. For all he knew, he was lost in the void of nothingness beneath Heaven. With a quiet, mirthless laugh, the guardian of secrets held up his prized possession and quietly beamed. Lurerdeth studied the seven keys of different colors. The keys were huge and shiny, artifacts of great power.

"Lucifer wants something that he has no power to wield," Lurerdeth muttered as he peered through the darkness again and waited for the light. It twinkled again. *That has to be it,* Lurerdeth thought as he unfurled his wings and sailed towards the light.

The flicker of light grew bigger and wider as the archangel approached. The territory was bland and seemingly tepid, and Lurerdeth had never seen or heard of this particular place. Suddenly, glory erupted from the majestic frame of God as He waited patiently for the arriving angel. The terrain lit up like a canvas of light, stunning the keeper of secrets. The awesome power of God filled the atmosphere, saturating him and pulsating into a feverish, never-ending crescendo of raw and deadly force. Lurerdeth buried his face in the rocklike terrain as he lay flat before God.

"Rise," God spoke quietly as Lurerdeth stood, his head bowed.

"What world is this?" he muttered quietly to himself. The angel looked around at the sooty environment. The light of God lit up the entire space. He had been building something so far away from heaven.

"This place has no likeness to Heaven," Lurerdeth said, taking in the grim surroundings. Ash-covered rocks lay in scattered array, with red and brown soil, hot to the touch. Lurerdeth winced. A recoiling heat pervaded the atmosphere. This place was a bad place, a grave of doom of some sort. There was a massive black door before them, glowing as if burning hot.

"This place," God said, "is a place of waiting, justice and recompense. The work here is not finished. I am sending my building angels to set the final touches to this place. Lurerdeth."

"Yes, Lord?"

"Do you have the keys?"

Lurerdeth held out the frame with the seven keys. "Yes, Highest One."

"Come with me."

God and the archangel proceeded through the valley towards the gate.

The gate seemed alive with a pressing darkness, sold to its directive. Lurerdeth walked slowly as he followed behind the substance of the spirit of God. Mighty as he was, he found no peace in the purpose of the place. The gate was sturdy, tall enough to dwarf ten archangels.

A loud sound emanated from the gate as it opened forcefully before God. The Highest One waited for the archangel to catch up.

"Lurerdeth, we will enter into this place of darkness. It shall be called Hades. You will place the keys where I will show you. Dominion will be given to one that is coming and he will have power over death and hell. Upon him and his seed, I will bestow authority, even over the angels."

Lurerdeth did not speak. He had neither question, nor retort. Obediently, the guardian of secret things stepped forward, his hand firmly gripping the keys of the kingdom. They went deeper into the place of outer darkness where death and hell dwelt.

The glass-like structures of the city of the heralds seemed to bubble with sweet music. The heralds were masters of their craft and gifted with the art of creating music. The order was a special mix of instrumentalists and singers. The singing angels were great song composers, and awesome in their art. Most of them nodded as Zuriel, Adriel, and the angels who had come to their aid proceeded past their stations into the central court at the entrance.

Beyond the stations, the large court stretched for miles. The floor was paved in crystals. Every step on its grounds sent small shockwaves of light that bounced off other lights, each touch sending a sweet musical note that blended with the next into a perfect, never ending song. At its entrance, Chesum, a herald, reached out to welcome them.

"Welcome, brothers." Chesum embraced Adriel firmly, making him wince.

"Good to see you here. I am sorry for all you have endured. Reports of your ordeal has preceded you."

"I am happy to be in better company," Adriel responded meekly, taking in the beautiful murals of the hall as they began walking across its grounds. Amazing twirls of dazzling colors lined the walls on either side, changing shape with every step, and morphing into works of artistic light constructions.

Zuriel stifled a smile. "Adriel has never been to the city of music. You will be safe here."

"I hope so," Adriel responded doubtfully.

"Of course," Chesum's voice ricocheted across the wall as lights sparked and music notes played. "Corruption can never come close to this order."

"I know you're thinking," Zuriel continued, "that Lucifer is head of this order and yet..."

"His choices are his alone. We are not tainted. Besides, he will not think to search for you here," Chesum said grimly this time. The rebellion was taking a toll on everyone. "Follow me. We will go up this flight of stairs."

The staircase spiraled upwards. On different levels, hundreds of doors led to chambers for the angels. In between the levels were spaces that gave view to other cities and gigantic structures in Heaven as they stretched far into the distance. The stairway led to yet another door with a golden knob.

Chesum raised a hand. "Now listen, beyond this door is the chamber to the head of the order of the heralds. Far above, is another set of chambers for other angels of music and..." he paused. "...and Lucifer."

Zuriel turned to Adriel. "He may already know from our pursuers that you are here, but he cannot touch you as long as you are under the protection of Mota and those loyal to God."

"Besides," Chesum was quick to reinforce his argument, "he hasn't been seen in these parts as of recent."

Adriel nodded. "Alright, if Zuriel trusts you, I will as well." Adriel breathed a sigh of relief as he reached for the doorknob and froze.

"Be gone from me, you lying, foul spirit. Be gone!" Mota's voice pounded through the door in a pitch of rage.

A pitiful voice followed. "Please, I pray you consider this offer." Adriel recoiled as he recognized the voice. It was Baeshedith.

"Get out!" Mota yelled thunderously. "I will never betray the King! Do you hear me? I will never!"

Zuriel, Chesum, and Adriel stood, rooted to their spots, as more angry exchanges ensued; then, the door flung open with much ferocity as Baeshedith stormed out. He paused for a brief moment as he brushed past Adriel. Adriel recoiled at the hate engraved in the angel's eyes. Observing the two mighty angels beside Adriel, Baeshedith let out a grunt and headed out the hall. As he reached the entrance of the gigantic hall, Adriel thought he almost saw a small wry smile on Baeshedith's face. "Come in," Mota bellowed. "Little angel, don't be scared of him."

Adriel stepped into the room encouraged by the friendly tone from the big burly archangel. "Welcome to the order of the heralds. You are now under my protection" Mota said, laughing heartily. The mighty Mota locked Adriel in a warm embrace and bellowed happily. "You are our friend. As you can see, Lucifer and his minions are not welcome here anymore. We will not tolerate their lies and their deceit."

Adriel let out a sigh of relief. "I am grateful." Chesum and Zuriel took their leave as the battered angel rested, musing sadly on recent events that had overtaken the city of Heaven.

"What do you make of it?" Zuriel asked as he and Chesum walked back through the entrance of the city of heralds, and down a flight of stairs to a narrow pathway. Arrayed on each side of the path were gold pillars with instruments of music grafted on their tops.

"He will be alright." Chesum tried to sound cheerful. "I hope."

"Hope?" Zuriel tried to smile, "That's all we have given Adriel. Mere hope."

"You did well, Zuriel. Bringing him here, that was good."

"I had no choice." Zuriel responded despairingly. "What else could I do? Leave him to that treacherous scum?"

"Peace brother, peace," Chesum said, putting a hand on Zuriel's shoulder. "We are almost at Elama, but I wonder if he will come."

Zuriel grimaced. "I doubt it. I mean how can he conjure worship for the very One that he now sets himself against?"

"I hope you will join us for our rehearsal."

"Thank you for the invitation Chesum. I would be honored to." Zuriel said as they reached the entrance of the huge coliseum-like building.

The pathway led to a huge dome where multiple angels sat with a diverse array of musical instruments. They often gathered here to sing, write new songs, and worship the King. The minstrels wore silk robes that glittered and reflected their instruments of music. The array of musical instruments included the harp, lyre, cymbals, trumpet, and other whimsical instruments with which the angels composed new songs to worship the King. The angels greeted them as they entered.

"Late again," Tumborel said in disgust, gesturing animatedly.

Chesum smiled. "Trouble on the road. Please accept our apologies."

"I am not referring to you Chesum, nor your guest, Zuriel. I am referring to the one who was created to lead the minstrels."

"Oh, do not expect him," Zuriel said, taking his seat amongst the minstrels. "Lucifer has been busy with other things, has he not? Though I welcome the opportunity to be part of this session of worship and many more."

"Forgive me," Tumborel bowed. "You are welcome among us."

"I know you meant no offense."

"Lucifer has been behaving strangely lately. He is hardly around to direct us. Isn't he our leader?"

"We must embrace the change till our brother returns to us, and he will. He seems pressed with duties beyond our grasp," Zuriel said quietly, seeing the other minstrels staring at him wide-eyed.

Tumborel nodded and added bitterly, "Beyond our grasp? It would serve better purpose if his duties were from the throne room."

"Let us keep our focus on our respective tasks," Zuriel responded, "and wait in hope of our brother's return. It is not a hard thing for him to conjure worship."

Tumborel had to smile at the remark. "If I see him, and when I see him, I shall remind him to give renewed vigor to his purpose."

Zuriel's face showcased a weak and distant look. He turned slowly to observe the hoard of the angels of music who were eagerly waiting to begin.

Chesum stood and raised his hands. "Till then Tumborel. For now, we will write a new song. I have one forming in my mind called El Elyon, God Most High." Chesum began to sing.

El Elyon, God most high
In all of Heaven and the entire universe
Through eternity and passage of existence
There is none like thee
Matchless in splendor, dominion, and power
Creator of all life
Master of all, there is none like you
Who is like you?
Who crafts worlds beyond imagination?
Your throne is forever
Highly extolled and lifted up are you
Millions of angels give you worship
Immortal God
El Elyon, God most high

The angels worked tirelessly through their long session, excitely about the anthem they were crafting. Chesum and Tumborel worked together on the song pattern, pitch, and rhythm. The angels caught on to the tune, and lifted their voices in matchless perfection.

The sound of the song released a glow of glory that spiraled like a canvas of light that was visible from many miles away. The song was alive and the angels were engulfed in its purity, in its holiness, in its might. As they sang, the atmosphere of Heaven began to emit a cloud of glory until it reached a crescendo and exploded in the beauty of visible, living spasms of color and light.

As the song progressed, passerby angels paused momentarily to listen to the purity it carried, awed by its majestic intonations. Some actually began to worship God even as they listened. Yes. The song was worthy of the Presence.

Hidden from the worshippers, Lucifer cowered underneath the stair structure of the pavilion. His eyes flashed green with desire. Resentment brewed within his heart and it engulfed his face as jealousy, and finally, hate became his set facial expression.

Why should God alone receive such sweet and intoxicating worship? He desired it for himself; he wanted it all. Why not? He was beautiful to behold, and powerfully fierce in nature. *Oh, that I would attain the highest of heights, and angels would gather to craft music to bless my own name.* It was a dream that had long been a fantasy for him, but with recent developments it was closer to becoming a reality. He could care less about the consequences; he would march his army to the throne and claim it.

The worship of the angels he had once tutored continued to shake the very grounds he sat on. Lucifer stared at his hands and saw a small welt of darkness, a red searing scar that began to grow slowly like a cancer. He knew he was physically changing, but he had lost regard for it. He was becoming different and something was eating him up from deep within. He could not fathom it.

Was it still an emotion driven from ambition? It had become a part of him; the part that made him light-headed with desire. The thirst for power and justification of his might and beauty had begun to consume him. He was fading fast into a state that would have shattered a lesser angel, but not him. He had to control it; he had to master it.

The streak continued to grow, widening across his chest and emitting a putrid stench that was averse to the world around him. Lucifer gripped his head in anguish as the angelic music continued to tear at the innermost parts of his being. A stark contrast to his now corrupted heart, the music revealed how much he had changed. He was becoming the very embodiment of an anti-God; and what was worse, he could do nothing to change it. He had gone too far and had invested too much that turning back was no longer an option.

When the singing finally ended, Lucifer wrapped himself in his gigantic wings and rested. He reverted to his original form and slowly, the putrid smell began to fade. It was under the pavilion of songs that Bael found him and alerted him to recent developments. Adriel was under the protection of Mota, and Gabriel and his angels were preparing for a second expedition outside of Heaven at the northern gate.

CHAPTER

—6—

COLLISION

Prior to his rebellious mission, Lucifer would have revelled in the light of God, but now, the light seemed averse to his presence as he sped towards the north gate. Angels moved out of his path as he gained momentum, with smoke and sparks trailing behind him. Bael and three of Lucifer's personal guards followed intently, trying to keep up. Lucifer could not understand this second expedition. *Had God made His move?* he thought to himself. *What was Gabriel doing outside the kingdom of Heaven? What secret mission was this?*

Lucifer knew it was not time to signal the attack. Plans were still in motion and he knew that victory required the perfect moment.

The massive gate of the city gradually became visible through Heaven's thick clouds. The gate was impenetrable, a mighty wall of crystal, light, and fire, intimidating in its height and weight. At the sides of the gate stood two pillars of gold and fire. The fire undulated around the pillars and across the breadth of the gate in spontaneous spasms of flame.

Lucifer flew past Zuriel's empty tower at the gate of the sanctuary, weaving through the monuments and structures of Heaven. Not too far away, Zuriel followed hard after them wondering what would happen next. He had seen Bael descend behind the dome of the herald's meeting place and quickly excused himself from the singing angels. Lucifer finally reached the gate.

Vernon, an angel with silver hair and eyes to match, leaned out of the window of the tower at the gate, his hands gripping the ledge. "Welcome, lord of..."

"Spare me the greetings and open the gate," Lucifer commanded.

"On what mission, great captain?" Vernon queried. It was his duty to ask; but he expected a tirade of insults, having heard of the Cherub's great anger of recent.

Zuriel finally reached the gate and nodded to Bael who smiled nervously but Lucifer ignored them. He immediately stepped into the tower.

"Open it," Zuriel declared.

Vernon turned and gave Zuriel a curious look.

"Captain, I hear you, but look outside. Gabriel and his forces are debriefing. He will be furious if we let Lucifer outside Heaven. We will be questioned no doubt."

"And so what? You really want to test Lucifer's patience? I don't. I followed him from the city of heralds and he won't be reasoned with. It is wise to do as he has requested."

"Captain," Vernon responded shakily, "You cannot…"

"I said, open up!" Lucifer bellowed outside th gates, frustrated that he had been kept waiting but perceived the odds were in his favor.

"Are you sure Zuriel?" Vernon asked, feeling helpless.

Zuriel stepped in front of Vernon and pulled a lever. Almost immediately, the fire vanished and the gate opened. Lucifer sailed past the gate without a word, his angel warriors following closely behind him without Bael. The witty angel had decided to stay back.

Zuriel and Vernon watched from the tower window as Lucifer headed towards Gabriel and his building angels. Gabriel expressed shocked at the sight of the incoming and became visibly angry.

"Look, I'm sorry Vernon but I am willing to see how far Lucifer is willing to go," Zuriel said solemnly.

"All the way."

Zuriel turned around as Bael stepped into the room. Bael walked slowly beside Vernon, watching as Lucifer confronted Gabriel. They could not hear the conversation between the archangels, but the two were visibly animated.

"This won't end well. I'm sure of it," Bael said quietly.

"I know," Zuriel responded. "I really wasn't thinking but I do want to see what happens next."

"You must either have a plan or you are plain crazy," Bael said smiling.

"Gabriel will think we are on Lucifer's side," Vernon said, turning to study Bael's face. The light from Vernon's huge frame seemed to bristle intensely as he stood, disquieted about the look on Bael's face. He turned back to observe the scene set before them.

"What do you think you are doing?" Gabriel was livid at Lucifer's intrusion. The builders behind him were alert, ready for his command. "Why do you come after me?"

"I don't have to explain myself to you," Lucifer barked, flashing an irreverent smile. "Why do you have angels out here like we are at war?"

"War? Who said anything about war? We are busy with God's work." Gabriel fastened his eyes on Lucifer's as they hovered over the outskirts of the heavenly city. Lucifer's three mighty warriors finally caught up with him and stooped, towering slightly above Gabriel's angels. Gabriel was not looking for a fight, but he had to make a stand.

Back at the tower, Bael watched the drama unfolding intently, unsure of what to do. Beside him stood a distraught Vernon, and Zuriel. The three watched, rooted to their spots as the archangels sized each other up.

"What is our Maker doing now?" Lucifer sneered looking

past Gabriel at the outer darkness. He could sense God was up to something. Otherwise, He would not have sent Gabriel and the building angels.

"If it was your concern, He would have mentioned it to you, angel of dishonor."

"Why do you insult me, Gabriel? I have not insulted you, but tell me, does God conduct His work in secrecy now?"

"No, but you have been busy of late with your treachery. I have heard some of the lies you have been spreading. Why should He involve you in the activities of Heaven?"

"Oh, I see. Do you feel left out because I didn't invite you to join me?" Lucifer poked. "You are just His messenger, but I, I am the lord of music. I am the brightness and beauty that covers the throne. I am the one with perfection embedded within every fiber of my being," he concluded arrogantly.

Gabriel felt a sudden sense of pity for the angel. "I beg you, do not defy His awesome power. He can accommodate changes to ease your troubles."

"Changes? Who wields the power to change things? Who? Are we not empowered to create change? I can create my own change. I will honor you with an invitation to join me, Gabriel. Give up your lowly work and be part of a new order of power, strength, and glory."

Gabriel clenched his fists. The time for civility was over. "Traitor," he sputtered.

"We have now resorted to name calling?"

"Defiler!"

"You think your insults affect me?"

"You brought evil into our existence. You defied God!"

"I only discovered who I am. As for evil, it already exists. You can call it what you want, but choosing my path based on my abilities is not evil."

"Our abilities are to be used to express the goodness of God."

"Really? To whom have you expressed this goodness? And how much have you tasted of this goodness? Do you serve willingly and without question because of what He has done for you?"

"No," Gabriel brimmed with anger. "I serve because I was made to serve. It is my purpose. But you, nothing is good enough for you."

"To aspire to be more is a goodly grace."

"Ugh! You now twist everything you see or hear for your benefit. Imposter!"

"You continue to call me these names but I am strong enough to reason beyond you."

"No, before this is over, you will wish you were never made."

"We shall see, messenger," Lucifer almost chuckled. "We shall see. And whatever it is that you are doing, I will find out." Lucifer turned around and headed back toward the city, his minions close behind.

Gabriel watched, relieved.

"You stood your ground," Shelan said to him, watching as Lucifer flew towards the gate. "You stood your ground."

"He was warned." Gabriel said. "Someone warned him."

"I know," Shelan responded. "That's bad."

"He was warned. Someone has been informing him about our missions."

"Peace, Gabriel." Shelan tried to sound assuring. "Most likely, one of his minions saw us and reported to him. He obviously does not know what our mission entails."

Gabriel set his gaze on the trio at the gate. *Who had warned Lucifer?* he mused. *Who opened the gate? Vernon? Zuriel?* He had to find out whose side they were on.

"Come," Gabriel said to the builder angels and turned. "Let's continue on. I will deal with the guardians of the gate when we return. However, we must be careful that we are not being followed."

Baeshedith had descended quietly into the grove of vines east of Heaven. After his fight with Adriel, and the resulting ordeal with Elzebur, Lucifer had tasked him with the mission of delivering important details of strategy to the captains who had sworn their allegiance. Even more importantly, he had been given a sacred mission to win over a necessary ally - Myesmoth, the burly angel who made the musical instruments of the heavenly kingdom. Enjoying his new responsibilities, Baeshedith had successfully made three stops, delivering his messages.

Hidden in the grove of vines, he rendezvoused with Myesmoth, the forge angel. Myesmoth had a stately stature, with strong arms and heavy legs. His large eyes observed Baeshedith, who was inferior to him in size, and he slowly tried to understand the details he heard. The angel shook his big, bald head in disbelief at Baeshedeth's words and interrupted. "The what?"

"Zuriel will ensure that the gate of the sanctuary is open so you can lead the charge from the river that flows from the throne with the best of weapons. These are the weapons we now task you to create." Baeshedith paused watching Myesmoth. "Do you understand?"

Myesmoth nervously scratched his head, his crystal eyes whipping back and forth. "Zuriel agreed to doing this? This is madness."

"You said?"

"I said this is madness. You cannot simply stomp into the house of God and take His throne as easily as you make it seem."

"Lucifer has learned many secrets to aid his victory."

"Tell me, please."

Baeshedith began to lose his patience, but this was his most important mission, and that was to win Myesmoth over. He knew the consequences of failure. Lucifer had forged his own rules, and the penalties for those who failed him were quite dismal.

"Listen, Myesmoth. Evil cannot dwell in Him and we intend to desecrate the holy place. He will be forced out of His own kingdom."

"So we are going to banish the One who made us and the heavens?" Myesmoth questioned.

"Whose side are you on?" Baeshedith could not mask his frustration any longer. "Lucifer told me you promised you would consider helping our cause. He is grateful for the few weapons you have made but now we need more."

"That I did, but I was tricked into making those weapons. I did not know what they were for. But now that I know, why should I help you or him?"

"Without you on board..."

"Has no one thought about the cost of failure?"

"Failure? We play by our strategy. Any retribution will be on Lucifer alone. And besides, our plan is foolproof."

"I am listening, but I do not believe that I can accept your proposal. I must return to the forge, I have been gone for too long," Myesmoth said.

"May I go with you? I have longed to see the forge." Baeshedith struggled to hide the fear he felt. "I won't get in the way, I promise. Please."

Myesmoth trried to convince himself that it would do no

harm. He finally nodded. "Sure. You may come, but this does not mean that I will comply with Lucifer's demands."

Myesmoth and Baeshedith walked together, conversing in whispers, hidden in the vast field of vines. They headed east, deeper into the realm, as Baeshedith zealously implored the burly angel for his allegiance. It was time for the final piece of their strategy and Baeshedith resolved not to return without his prize. He stared wistfully, becoming silent, as they walked through the center of the city, beside the river of God. They travelled past the tree of life and the funnel of waters that showered from the throne room, and further, past the pinnacle of the fountains of refreshing waters. Deeper and deeper into the fields they went, towards the east gate and on, to the mountains of fiery stones of Elama, where all of the angels had been created. Finally, they descended to fiery forges beneath.

Gabriel and his angels sped through the darkness, their path lit by a golden torch that gave them their bearings. Shelan flew close to Gabriel, his mind boggled with questions, yet he decided to wait for the right time to gain an audience with Gabriel. Occasionally, Barachiel, the angel at the rear, would turn around to ensure they were not being followed.

"Gabriel!" he shouted.

Gabriel turned around in frustsration. "Be quiet, Barachiel!"

Barachiel glided forward. "My apologies Gabriel, but the guiding light will give us away."

"So far, are we being followed?"

"I did not see anything, or anyone but any of the watcher angels would be able to see the torch from a distance."

"Okay. We must proceed quickly. I will put out the flame soon enough." The company of warriors continued on their journey.

A great distance from Gabriel and his warriors, Lucifer and Mealiel, his watcher deputy, followed slowly. "Can you still see them?" Lucifer asked.

"Yes. They have so far kept a steady path. Wherever they are headed, it is east of the nothingness."

"We can only assume that they know they are being followed," Lucifer said. "Gabriel is no fool. You could see how stung he was that I challenged him, which begs the question, why send Gabriel?"

"He only sends the messenger with important information," Mealiel said.

"Information for whom?" Lucifer asked, "This is becoming a complex puzzle. Unless..." Lucifer stopped and Mealiel bumped into him.

"Why did you stop?" Mealiel asked.

"Because, it is all making sense now. The messenger bears a message for another and there is possibly only one angel that would be hiding far away from Heaven."

"Lurerdeth?" Mealiel guessed.

"The keeper of the keys." Lucifer smiled.

"We find him, we find the keys. Let us proceed," Mealiel was excited.

"No," Lucifer said curtly.

"Excuse me?"

"Finding him will mean open war. Gabriel and his cohorts will fight to protect the knowledge of his whereabouts. What we need is information. We need his location."

"All we need are some reinforcements," Mealiel said, reassuringly.

"Without the throne, what do the keys of the kingdom do for us? We stick to the plan. At least we know in what direction to go to find the keys."

"Fine. So what do we do now?"

" Find me another angel to follow them."

"Who do you recommend?"

"Well, I can't sacrifice any one of ours that may be privy to important information," Lucifer responded. "Ahh. The guardian."

"Zuriel? That double-minded..."

"He seems like one we can easily persuade with a little more intimidation. He is well respected and he can control the guardians under him. Even if they catch him, he will still be able to tell us exactly where Lurerdeth is."

"Sounds like a plan to me," Mealiel nodded.

"It is the best plan that we have for now. Simply knowing where Lurerdeth is hiding is beyond good news. It is a victory in itself."

The fiery forge blazed deep within the tunnels of Elama, under the dazzling mountain of God. Two angels carried a huge basin of fiery stones and stepped into the hearth of the huge forge. Myesmoth nodded, poring over a myriad of scrolls on a vast, stony mound. They had flattened the top, fashioning a table with golden spikes at the sides. "There." He said, "Pour it all in." The angels obliged without question.

The   room was a lair of treasures. Baeshedith was astounded by the artifacts the angels were creating, some unfinished, but beautiful in their glory. He observed various instruments of precious metal littered about the room, in various workstations. The forge angels worked tirelessly in far corners that stretched for hundreds of miles in the distance, framing diverse compositions of gold and silver into stunning artifacts. Baeshedith noticed a strange lamp on one of the angels' workstation.

The lamp-stand had a large gold stem that held seven pipes fitted craftily into its bodywork. Around the top of each pipe was a bulge of sapphire netted into the frame. A special wireframe passed through the inner workings of the piece, protruding from the top, bearing a fire that burned of its own life and energy. Baeshedith touched the stem of the working and grimaced.

"What are these things for?"

Myesmoth looked up from the chart he was studying, slightly distracted. "That, Baeshedith, is an instrument that is going to the holy place."

"Seven strands of fire," Baeshedith muttered to himself. "I wonder what that represents."

"We don't know what they mean," an angel positioned at the workstation responded.

Baeshedith looked at him and questioned, "You don't? Where did you get the blueprints from?"

"My name is Azazel. I am a forge angel. Come see."

"This is magnificent." Baeshedith stood in awe as Azazel handed him the piece he was working on. It was the inner frame of a huge scroll. Its handle had a crest of rubies crafted in a stunning design, a perfect showpiece of art, and its center column glinted with relentless brilliance. Around Azazel's workstation, a great selection of captivating items littered the floor. "We are working on something very special for the throne room of God. That's where the seven lamp stands and these other pieces are going."

"So the blueprints…" Baeshedith prodded, wide-eyed.

"Where do you think they are from?" Azazel asked. Baeshedith could see that the angel was feigning disappointment.

"I know," Baeshedith said, "God tells you what He wants and you produce them without question."

"Without question? Of course, we ask questions."

"You do?"

Baeshedith could sense the bewilderment of the angels as a few stopped their work to observe him. Azazel stood.

"You're an inquisitive angel aren't you? Myesmoth, the forge lord meets with Him, receives directions and yes, we ask questions on the details to completely understand the fullness of each work."

"I see."

"We are allowed complete creativity on certain items, but for some, we must follow the exact specifications given. Like this one."

Across Azazel's workstation, a glow appeared as a hologram, a twine of lines made of glowing light. The streaks formed into an animated orb with dimensions and calculations working in real time.

"This," Azazel said, revealing the final work, "is a special ark that will contain the other items we are making for the holy place. See these?" Baeshedith stared wide-eyed as Azazel ran his hand dramatically along the length of the visual.

"These names. What do these names mean?" Baeshedith asked incredulously.

"There are twelve names but I do not know who bears them." Azazel laughed. "You should see your face."

"Stop torturing our guest," Myesmoth said, raising his hammer and striking the gold on his anvil. The sound of his pounding ricocheted across the room.

"Very well Myesmoth," Azazel said. "This one goes to Lurerdeth and then a parchment is wrapped around it and sealed. This particular one's destination is the holy place, and that is all I know about it. No one here knows what these names mean or who they are for."

Baeshedith nodded meekly, flabbergasted by the artistry and commitment of the forge angels. All about him, amazing workings of gold and crystal were being formed into dazzling instruments of worship and power that conveyed wealth and influence. Those had never meant anything to him until Lucifer began his campaign. The glory and wealth of the heavenly kingdom could all be theirs soon.

The furnace thundered, emitting light as soon as the angels poured in more fiery stones. "Yes!" Myesmoth bellowed. The forge workers turned away quickly from the heat as the burly angel grabbed a huge slab of gold and forcefully pushed it into the mouthpiece of the furnace. With the fire licking through the gold work, Myesmoth, armed with his forge hammer waited, poised to strike. Baeshedith moved closer and peered over his shoulder.

On the chart, he could make out the blueprint of diverse workings and constructions. Whatever Myesmoth was working on was magnificent, the beginning piece of some sort of city with twelve gates around its walls.

"Myesmoth?" Baeshedith whispered with urgency in his voice. "Hear me out and you may even be given charge of the city that you and your angels are working on."

"You won't relent. Will you?"

"No, I won't. Lucifer wants you to make weapons. Plenty of them! I have the blueprints. That is all we need from you. And thereafter, you may choose your path."

Zuriel loathed the darkness, and he hated the fact that Lucifer had sent him on this mission. Fear had been foreign feeling to him, but it had not taken much for the archangel and his minions to compel him to do their bidding. Only this, Lucifer had said, and he would be free of any further harassment.

Quietly, the guardian angel cut through the distance between himself and the angels he was tracking. Masterfully anticipating their speed, Lucifer had told him the exact moment to pursue Gabriel and what signs to look out for. Every couple of thousand miles, a little orb would glow keeping Zuriel on the path. Everything was exactly as Lucifer had told him. Somehow, the archangel had found a way to map out the early part of their journey. Amazing. Zuriel was visibly impressed.

Zuriel knew this journey was a gamble of sorts, since he

lacked any proper excuse to give if he was caught. All he could do was travel eastward, following the tiny flickers of light and hope. Sooner or later, he would arrive at his destination and the information that would release him from his obligations to Lucifer. That was all that mattered at that moment.

Yet, Zuriel despaired, feeling unfortunate. He was not sure what to make of it all. Either Lucifer knew something that the others did not know, or he was simply too callous to realize the enormity of their agenda. They were about to take on the very One who had created them. Such courage, or foolishness, could only be born out of a degree of certainty that they could succeed. His golden hair whizzed like a colossus of lateral lines as he continued his flight, watching apprehensively, and hoping that he would not end up at the mercy of the very ones he was following.

CHAPTER

—7—

HADES

Gabriel and his angels continued to descend, travelling at blinding speed, through the dark realms, deeper through the nothingness. Gabriel led the way as they continued, focused and unabated, until he finally gave the signal. The two angels at the rear spun abruptly, one to the left and the other to the right, their bodies dazzling in radiance as they waited, poised to strike. They paused momentarily and then looked back to Gabriel. The archangel nodded giving his approval, and they continued their descent, convinced that they were not being followed.

In the distance below, they could see their destination. It was a strange and sullen world, stretching beyond their line of vision. Gabriel pointed forward, motioning his angels to follow him into the foreign wilderness. It was a sunken valley with gorges and treacherous landscapes, filled with dark sand, metal, and stone. The angels had never seen a world as dark as this. Far into the distance, an eerie gate stood ajar, framed within high walls; a silvery angel stood watching.

"Welcome Gabriel," Lurerdeth said, "Come on in. There is much more work to be done."

Zuriel proceeded slowly, taking note of where he had seen the last two flickers of light. There was no need to rush at this point, but everything depended on timing to avoid exposing himself. Zuriel approached slowly and cautiously. Not long after, he could make out the angels and the looming ashy world that lay stretched out before him. He tried to stay hidden while absorbing all that he could see before him.

"What are you thinking, captain?" Shelan asked Gabriel as the angels hovered above the rocky ground inside the dark city.

"A sad place created for a pitiful time," Gabriel replied, observing the other angels as they laid out several measuring lines that stretched for miles in parallel. They had accomplished much during their first visit to the expanse; but now, they had more work to do with the deep and lower regions of the dark world. They took their positions and waited.

"I never imagined such a moment would come in our existence," Shelan said.

Gabriel's face was grim. "Yet it has come." He turned to observe Shelan. "Now, since evil has found expression, it is our turn to purge it from existence."

Shelan nodded, his silver beard glistering. "I am here to do my part. Shall we begin?"

The darkness cleared as the glory of the angels lit the open space. The coarse and dismal stretch of clammy rock littered the landscape. This was nothing like home, but the angels focused on their tasks.

Gabriel's wings spread wide as he pulled out a scroll that burst into a bright flame and streaked upwards. Various lines of fire grew out of the original flame until a huge network of fire had spread across the valley where the angels were. The flames formed into a blueprint, glowing and flickering. Gabriel turned again to Shelan.

"Let's build this prison," he said grimly.

Shelan bowed and swung into the rocks below. The builder angel spun at a great speed, digging into the rocky knell, as smoke and debris whirled him around like a hurricane. The elements revolved with a bizarre momentum as the angel disappeared underneath the massive ruble of stone and metal. After a short while, a pillar began to rise from the confusion, and then another. The other angels joined in as well, following after the master builder.

Pillars, rigid and unbreakable stood tall, stretching far upwards. Each pillar was made of different elements, fused together by fire and molded to create a strong singular entity. The angels built pillars in the hundreds until they accomplished everything on the blueprint. To finish the prisons, Shelan descended and began to fix clamp heads of massive chains on each column.

God had sent the angels to prepare this place of restraint far from their heavenly city, at this dark side of the universe. The pain of having to build such a place, seemingly for those they had once called brothers since the time of their existence, weighed heavily on them. Yet they obeyed the commission to the letter, giving no pause until the task was done.

Dark, musty, tepid, and sullen. Zuriel had no words for the world he observed. Emerging quietly from the mighty gate, he proceeded cautiously into the entrance of the new world. It seemed like an enormous lounge area with pillars stretching for miles.

The angel continued slowly through the darkened path, carefully making out the composition of the wall that enclosed him on both sides.

"Ah! Lucifer, wait till you see this place," he muttered quietly, trying to imagine the look the archangel would have when he told him of his discovery.

Being a guardian angel, Zuriel was different from the watcher angels who had eyes all over their wings. Tower angels had a sight that could pierce through any obstacle. Zuriel paused to listen, peering around the room and taking mental notes of the details he saw; however not a sound was heard in the vicinity. It appeared that Gabriel and his angels were busy somewhere deep underground. Zuriel looked around warily, wondering if Lurerdeth was lurking about. He was slightly bemused that the angel had not closed the gate after Gabriel and his builders went in.

Convinced that he was alone, Zuriel stepped into a dome with two mighty doors. He peered around curiously through the one on his left. There seemed to be a stairway that descended into the depths of the world. He had never seen anything like the engravings on the door. Zuriel paused.

"Which way do I go?" he muttered out loud. The door on to the left seemed disturbing, with a rare stench of decay that irked the angel of the tower. There was something that carried an emotion he could not express, something he could not grasp; but he knew instinctively that this was not a place for anything godly.

Zuriel pulled back and heaved against the door to his right, but the door would not budge. He tried again, his muscles heaving out streaks of light and radiance. Taking a step back, the inquisitive angel's eyes lit up and burst into a flame. His eyes seemed to converge into one strain of light and blasted towards the door. Usually, the light would pierce through, giving him the ability to see beyond; but this door resisted his power, causing him to fall back.

Zuriel hit the ground hard and paused to listen and see if he had been discovered but he heard nothing. He would never know the secret behind that door. At least not for now, he thought. The mighty door on the left seemed like bronze and stone grafted together. There was no getting out if he got locked in. *I've come this far into this forbidden place; I must continue further*, he thought.

Zuriel stepped into the doorway and saw an expanse between two different worlds. Though standing at a vantage position, he could not make out what was before him regardless of how hard he strained his far reaching sight. It looked like a huge gulf cutting off any access between both realms. Everything within him seemed to convulse as he reeled in the darkness. He now knew what this wilderness was, though he did not have a name for it. The angel suddenly became desperate for the glory of God, the throne, the beauty of God, and even the luster of the gates of gold. He turned to get out of the darkness and slipped hitting his head on the side of the stairway. Zuriel toppled over and fell.

The builder angels gathered in the dome with the two doors and prepared for their return. Unaware that they had been followed, Gabriel and Shelan walked slowly into the outer court of the dark city, away from the tunnel path that led to the lower expanse where they had finished their construction. Gabriel stopped. "What are you doing?"

Barachiel was heaving against the second door trying to force it open but the door would not budge. Gritting his teeth and pushing with all his might, light and glory gathered around him, but the silver door would not as much as move an inch.

"Stop!" Gabriel commanded, his eyes lighting up into fiery flames. Barachiel stopped and motioned as if to argue, but remembering the captain's charge, he quietly shrugged and rejoined the others.

"Our work here is done," Gabriel said, giving Barachiel a reprimanding look. "We have not been asked to explore this land beyond the places we have been given access to. Why is this second door open?"

"That was open when we got here," Barachiel said.

"Okay," Gabriel said, visibly relved. "Lets go."

Barachiel took one final look at the looming silver door before leaving. *Two worlds within one and a gateway of secrecy,* he thought to himself. The angel knew it would require some sort of key and most likely one of the keys strapped around Lurerdeth's waist. Barachiel smiled as they headed out. His report would buy him a key position in Lucifer's coming order.

The darkness seemed alive and evil, clutching and railing at Zuriel. The falling angel could feel the terror of it all. This place was the very embodiment of the anti-God state. Its barrenness suffocated him, and gave him a sensation of doom. Zuriel began to grasp the fact that the very nature of God could not condone sin. This place was devoid of the life, grace, and the glory of God. Suddenly, he understood as he looked around wildly; this place... was death. Zuriel landed in a pitiful pile of light that faded quickly in the gloomy slime bubbling through the cracks of a terrain of ash and coal. He was in hell.

"What are you doing here?"

Zuriel stirred and struggled to stand. He knew that voice.

"Lurerdeth. Is that you?"

"Yes," Lurerdeth's wings pummeled the flames as he reached out for the angel. "Here, take my hand." he said grimly.

Lurerdeth helped Zuriel to his feet, as the hot coals continued to burn his feet. Wincing somberly, Zuriel turned and saw a beautiful expanse of fountains and streams far away in the distance above. Between the place with the fire that they were standing on and the distant terrain was a huge chasm, making it impossible to cross. Zuriel struggled to take in everything he had seen. Hoisted in Lurerdeth's arms, the hapless angel was carried out of the fiery terrain to the grounds of the outer chamber.

The door leading to hell roared shut behind them. Zuriel understood now. One door led to the beautiful world he had seen, somewhat a replica of the beauty of their heavenly city, and the other led to the place of pain and torture. A double punishment, Zuriel thought, to be separated and yet be able to see the other world far above in its peace and serenity without any hope of ever crossing over.

"Thank you," Zuriel mumbled, his charred and wounded body weakened by the fiery flames of the furnace of retribution.

"Come with me." Lurerdeth did not smile, his face looking very stern and concerned. Zuriel heard the tone of Lurerdeth's voice and knew it was best not to argue with his rescuer. The wounded angel steadied himself.

Lurerdeth walked towards the east wall slowly. The only sound in the enormous space was the thumping sound of the two angels' feet hitting the ground as they walked hurriedly down the hall. Zuriel looked to the north entrance, his mind racing as he wondered where the great Lurerdeth was leading him to. Everything had suddenly gone badly for him. Wounded and bruised from the flames, the angel's glory faded as he limped on through the inner chambers.

"Where are we? What is this place?" he managed to ask.

Lurerdeth did not offer much of an answer. "Wait and see." At the east wall, Lurerdeth held up his hand in the darkness and lit up the wall. Two gold knobs stuck out of the wall. Lurerdeth reached to his side and revealed a key made of gold and crystal, mixed with black emeralds. As soon as he pushed the key into the frame on the wall, a loud roar thundered within it as the wall split open revealing a huge tunnel.

"Welcome to Hades," Lurerdeth said dramatically. Without another word, he stepped into the tunnel as Zuriel followed him cautiously, wondering if he had just missed his chance of escaping out of the chasm of darkness.

Deep beneath the outer chambers, the two angels proceeded slowly into the heart of Hades. The pillars that Gabriel's troop had built were covered in ash, and chains wound around each like gigantic serpents. At the corner of the room was a glowing orb. Zuriel took it all in, wondering why a place so desolate and dark even existed. If this was the place that would hold Lucifer's rebels, he wanted no part of it. When Lurerdeth touched the orb, a flame spiraled across the outer walls, illuminating the expanse. Zuriel could now clearly see what lay before them - mighty chambers of restraint to hold even mighty angels. He had unwittingly followed Lurerdeth into the prisons. Zuriel tried to turn around to escape, but a heavy hand landed on his shoulder.

"No, I want you to see this."

Zuriel staggered, sickened by this adventure. Surely, it was dastardly to attempt an escape from this place. This world was grim and shamelessly despondent, reeking with shadows of fear and pain. Lifeless, and separated from the glory of God, Zuriel was forced to endure it all. Filled with regret, he fell on one knee and whispered through gritting teeth, "Can I leave now?"

"No," Lurerdeth responded. "Like I said, I have one more thing to show you."

Lurerdeth put an arm around Zuriel's body and pushed from the ground, wings bursting out in radiance. The keeper of secrets, who had been forced into hiding, sped through the center aisles of the dungeons, carrying his sorry burden. At the edge was a cliff that even Lurerdeth himself struggled to approach.

A mighty roar resounded beyond the cliff. Zuriel grappled weakly with Lurerdeth, horrified. He was done with this evil place. They could both feel the heat emitting from whatever was beyond the cliff.

"I want you to see it," Lurerdeth grunted as he dragged Zuriel towards the cliff, the wounded angel wrestled with what was left of his strength. Realizing that his might could not deter the stronger angel, Zuriel relaxed stiffly, his eyes shut tight. If this was his fate, he would try to accept it. Lurerdeth stopped and Zuriel waited.

"Open your eyes."

Zuriel heard the silent whisper. "Open your eyes"

The sweltering heat licked up their faces, scarring their skin and tattering their wings, but Lurerdeth was determined. Zuriel opened his eyes and what he saw made him bulk in abject shock and despair. The angel screamed and the nightmarish sound filled the dungeons of Hades.

Unable to withstand the horror any longer, Zuriel lashed out wildly, catching Lurerdeth's face. Free from the archangel's grip, Zuriel took his chance as he charged Lurerdeth headfirst, smashing him to the ground. Turning quickly, his body racking with pain, Zuriel made for the tunnel door and imminent escape.

CHAPTER
—8—
MICHAEL

Michael and Azazel stepped quietly into the lower recesses of the forge, going through the tunnels that led to the coves deep beneath the heavenly city. The tunnels were a huge network of pathways, interconnected and lit with lights plugged into the walls.

"This way, Michael, this way," Azazel urged.

"I won't believe until I see it," Michael whispered. "Are you sure? I mean, are you absolutely sure…"

Azazel raised his hand urgently. They could hear muffled voices in the distance reverberating through the tunnel.

"Here, hide here!" Azazel said quickly, ushering Michael into a dimly lit corner. In a few moments, they could make out Myesmoth's voice, followed by Baeshedith's softer voice.

"...Is Lucifer pleased?" Myesmoth was saying.

"You have not met the agreed quota," Baeshedith said, "How can he be pleased? He does not condone mediocrity."

"It isn't my fault," Myesmoth shouted. "I cannot have every angel in my charge set to this task. Did you not ask to specifically find those loyal to Lucifer?"

"Keep your voice down and yes, that I did," Baeshedith said.

Azazel and Michael waited until their voices faded into the distance and emerged.

"What was all that about?" Michael asked Azazel.

"Follow me, captain. You can see for yourself."

Michael followed Azazel into the room at the end of the central tunnel. He tried to imagine what he would find. Why had the forge angel come to find him at great haste? What were these angels doing beneath the surface of the heavenly city? He wanted answers.

"There. See what our forge angels are doing," Azazel said.

Michael stepped into the room, a look of shock plastered on his face.

"Weapons of war," Michael mused, shaking his head as he took in the vast array of millions of choice weapons stocked in piles. "God help us."

"I would never have found out myself but here, Lucifer's minions have forged instruments of force in secret to give them great advantage on the day they seek to take the throne."

"They will never take it," Michael responded, gritting his teeth.

"What makes you so sure?" Azazel said.

Michael turned to Azazel. "What did you say?"

"I said, what makes you so sure?" Azazel responded, taking a step back. "You still do not trust me? If I did not warn you, you would never have known of this. From what I hear, Lucifer is the wisest of us all."

"If you respect him so, why are you helping me?"

"I am not helping anyone. Just thought you should know about this."

"Wait," Michael said petulantly. "Why didn't Myesmoth entrust you with this?"

"Because I refuse to be part of any rebellion. I simply love what I do."

"And what is that?"

"Creating instruments of worship. I don't care about freedom or power nor sovereignty or all that gibberish Lucifer is spreading. I simply want things to be normal again."

"Things will never be normal again," Michael said and shrugged. "So what do we do now?"

"We?"

"Do not patronize me, angel. This rebellion must be crushed immediately," Michael said, his eyes flashing with fire. "Heaven must be rid of them."

Azazel took another step back. "You sound… almost jealous."

Michael sighed and slid his hand across the blade of a sword causing it to spark. "I have been looking for Lucifer since this began. I just need a single conversation, to reason with him. He continues to avoid me."

"Captain, we must leave soon. So now that you know about the weapons, what will you do?"

"They must not know that we know. Azazel, I need you to do something. You say you want things to return to normal. Well, we have to fight for it. And to fight, we have to even the odds. Do you understand what I am talking about?"

Azazel nodded.

"I am asking you to find some of your brothers who are loyal to Elyon and we will find a secret place for you to create weapons for us. Do this, Azazel, for the Heaven you love."

"We will never be able to match this."

"Yet, we will not be completely helpless, shall we?" Michael sighed. "Listen, Azazel, I know you would rather not get involved but you have no choice. Everyone of us must choose. This is our chance to stage a resistance."

Azazel groaned, fists clenched. "Fine. I'll see what I can do. At the moment, we need to find a way out of here without being seen."

"Lead the way," Michael said with gratitude. "You have done us all a great service already."

The gates of Heaven roared shut as soon as Gabriel and his angels made their entrance back into the city. They headed straight for the sanctuary of God to give their report.

"Zuriel has not returned and I wonder what they were they doing so far away?" Bael lingered in the watchtower at the gate of Heaven.

Vernon rose from his chair, slightly exasperated that Bael remained as his unwelcome guest.

"I have heard rumors of the angels' work," Vernon nodded in agreement. "It is far below the lower heavens."

"I can see that one of Gabriel's angels is not one to be trusted with keeping information; however, the question is who is it for?" Bael smiled grimly.

"Pretty straight forward, isn't it?" Vernon said, his eyes focused on a certain glow in the far darkness. "Whom could it be for?" Vernon gripped the ledge of the tower window and peered into the distance. He noticed something strange but he could not see what it was at the moment. "Definitely not for me."

"You stand with God, then," Bael turned to face him.

Vernon spread his wings slightly, "Is there an alternative? Lucifer's plan is bold, brazen, and even clever, but even then, I do not want to lose my place."

"Same here, but the thought of freedom is sweet, don't you think so?" Bael responded reflectively, then his silvery eyes gleamed with feverish excitement.

"Freedom? Am I not free now?"

Bael reflected on Vernon's response and then decided to change the topic. "Shouldn't Zuriel be back by now? How come you did not question him when he left the city? Are you not tasked with obeying every one of God's commands?"

Vernon turned from the tower window and paced about before answering. Pausing, he said, "Why are you still here?"

Bael's long and black wavy hair bounced like a mighty wave as he turned.

"I like to keep myself close to good information. Information, as you know, in these times, is power. I want to know the fullness of what lays beneath us. Gabriel and his angels will obviously not tell me anything."

Vernon slumped into a chair and sighed.

"It was foolish and certainly bizarre that Zuriel followed Gabriel and his angels. That he didn't return with them must mean they didn't encounter him."

"Like me, Zuriel lingers on choosing a path." Bael stared outside the window and then gasped. "Vernon! Come and see!"

Vernon was by his side in a flash, his eyes wide open. Now visible in the distance, Zuriel was hurtling like a spear towards the gate, his face a mask of tragedy.

"Open the gate!" Bael shouted.

As soon as Zuriel entered the city, he bounded up the tower room and slouched into a chair, completely ignoring the other two angels who peered at him, wide-eyed. His wings were charred and he carried an unwholesome stench. Immediately, he grabbed a parchment and golden pen and began scribbling ferociously.

"Well, Captain?" Vernon had lost all his patience. "Are you going to tell us where you are coming from?"

Zuriel looked up, his face a mask of dread. "I don't answer to you." His voice sounded pained and hollow.

Bael stepped up. "I am of higher rank and I command you to speak. From where have you come and what happened to you?"

Zuriel clenched his fists as fiery glory sparkled around his arms, then he signed and stopped writing. "Okay. I saw it. I saw the place of ill and dread, of chains and fetters." Bael and Vernon exchanged glances.

"Hades?" Vernon asked, hoping to aid his captain.

"You don't know the half of it," Zuriel bellowed in anguish. "It is utter darkness. There is nothing good there. It is an empty waste land… a place of death."

"Who else knows about your visit? Did Gabriel see you?" Bael asked.

Zuriel started writing again as if oblivious to the question he had been asked. Vernon moved closer and peered at the scroll. He could see half of a drawing.

"He is creating a blueprint of Hades," Vernon said to Bael, who was becoming increasingly agitated.

Sure enough, Zuriel unwaveringly finished the drawing. From the scroll, light streaked across the parchment and formed the lines of the drawing, giving life to Zuriel's sketches. The blueprint of Hades spread across the scroll, rising out to depict a near reality of the wilderness environs. Beal and Vernon watched in amazement as the visual was completed. Tiny pillars laced with chains inside hundreds of thousands of dungeons, built to hold even massive warrior angels.

Zuriel finally looked up at Bael. "Now you can understand. Everything we know has changed."

Bael and Vernon exchanged glances again. There was a distand and terrifying look in Zuriel's eyes.

"Vernon..." Bael sat opposite Zuriel. "Leave us."

"What?"

"Leave us, I must speak to Zuriel alone."

There was no way he would win an argument with Bael. Vernon despondently opened the tower door and exited solemnly.

Bael clenched his massive hands together over the table and leaned towards Zuriel. In the same instant, Zuriel spread his hand over the parchment and the light faded. He nonchalantly folded the parchment.

"Will you hand this over to him?" Zuriel asked.

"I'm not your messenger, guardian."

"I know, but as you have asked Vernon to leave, there must always be an angel in these towers."

"Why? What could happen?"

"This is how it is and has always been, Bael. Lucifer needs to see this. You owe him that."

"I have no allegiance to Lucifer."

"Do you really think you can stay neutral until the end?"

Bael managed a smile. "Wisdom, eh?"

Zuriel clasped his head in hands, visibly shaken. Bael sympathized momentarily with the writhing spirit but he had to learn the truth from him.

"What are you hiding?" Bael asked, reaching out to touch Zuriel's wounded shoulder. Zuriel reeled from the touch and jumped up, fiery sparks of light blasting forth from his frame, but Bael was faster. He swooped forward and shoved Zuriel unto the golden wall of the tower, forcefully pinning him still.

Bael clasped his hand around Zuriel's neck. "Tell me what you saw. Tell me! I know there is more!"

Zuriel blinked furtively in fear, his eyes filled with horror. "Darkness. Deep, utter darkness. Devoid. Desolate. Death. Separation."

"I understand."

"No," Zuriel shook his head and looked into Bael's eyes. "God is not there."

Bael released Zuriel and staggered back. "God is everywhere, Zuriel."

"The life of God is absent from this place. I have never felt such a void before."

Zuriel slunk to the floor like a sulking child. Bael watched from another corner. He had a feeling Zuriel had seen more.

"Bael?"

"I am here."

"I could go no further. There was an intense, convoluting heat bearing such pain as I have never ever experienced; heat that stings you senseless in anguish that is beyond words."

Bael steadied himself. "Fire?"

Zuriel looked up at Beal, his crazed look appearing again. His voice was like a knell of doom. "Fire? No! The fury of God's vengeance and it will burn for all eternity."

"Zuriel! Bael!" Vernon's voice rang as he stepped back into the room. "God is on the move!"

Sure enough, the spirit of God was descending into the darkness as Zuriel and Bael dashed to the window of the tower.

"There He goes again, far from Heaven," Zuriel whispered, the wounds from his recent ordeal in the realm of fire were still visible and raw.

"Has anyone asked about His purpose besides this dark world?" Vernon asked.

"None that I know of," Bael replied.

"He's doing something new."

"After what I've seen, I wonder what ill He is preparing," Zuriel said sullenly.

Vernon almost smirked. "When did we become skulking fools to observe our Maker with anticipation? Everything He has made thus far has been beautiful and for His glory. So why change now?"

Bael and Zuriel knew the answer to Vernon's question, and neither angel spoke. It was not necessary. Zuriel sighed and looked through the window to the darkness. Their existence had been altered. Innocence had become a choice.

The knowledge of good and evil was ever present within Heaven and the power of choice had become even more evident. Life or death, good or bad, the angels knew that decisions would be made and consequences would follow. Either for glory or defeat, life or loss of existence, their futures would ultimately be determined by their choices.

"What's wrong?" Raphael asked Michael as they walked together towards the mountain of God. "You have hardly said anything since we started walking."

"Why are we fighting for God?" Michael said dejectedly.

"Ah, the conflict that this whole city is currently faced with," Raphael said.

"But why? Look around us. Look at the majesty of Heaven. We came here full of grace and power and light. But for what?" Michael asked, as they reached the edge of the mountain.

"You sound like him"

"Do I? I am confused and have received no answers."

"So maybe Lucifer's strategy of avoiding you is indeed working. He seems to know how to manipulate our thinking. He wants you to come to him, not the other way round."

"What are you talking about?"

"Michael, he wants you to be full of questions so he can give you his answers. Smart."

"It's God's voice I want to hear. This is my test."

"I understand."

"Do you?" Michael smiled bitterly. "Let's continue into the mountain before we are seen."

"Listen Michael, we all have our questions. We all struggle with the conflict before us but I have since accepted my path. I will never turn against the One who made me. As for Lucifer, he has played this with extreme intelligence. He wagers that you will come to him when the time is right."

"It makes no difference. I am the only one that understands him. He fears that I will dissuade him from this path. This is not about any strategy or plot." Michael tried to hide the frustration in his voice. "I must find our brother. That is all that matters since the Highest One hasn't given me any instructions."

"Little wonder evil has spread and become so strong," Raphael said, shaking his head.

"What do you mean?" Michael stopped and faced Raphael.

"Look at you. The great archangel, Michael. He who is closest to God." Michael could hear the scorn in Raphael's voice.

"What are you saying?"

"Our leader. Evil is spreading and you do nothing. This evil is calculated, deliberate, and expertly executed. Yet, good sits back and does nothing."

"Nothing? Is that what you think?" Michael bellowed, stung by Raphael's words. "Is that what you think?" Fire spread through his body, his huge wings bursting into a fearsome spread of light and glory as smoke swelled about his legs.

"Someone started the war without me?"

Michael and Raphael heard the familiar voice and froze.

"Lucifer," Michael said as the glory around him faded.

"Michael," Lucifer said. "And Raphael, of course. Your new, trusted friend?"

Michael looked at Raphael, feeling ashamed for his outburst. "Forgive me, brother." Raphael nodded slowly and stepped aside watching, as Lucifer stood smiling at the edge of the mountain, seemingly harmless.

"Come now," Lucifer reached out his hand. "It has been too long brother. Let me tell you what I have been up to, old friend."

Michael gripped Lucifer's hand firmly and forced a smile. "I have heard troubling things. I am glad that you have finally come to see me. However, let me dismiss Raphael and then we can talk."

"Sure," Lucifer seemed in a cheerful mood. "Go ahead."

Michael strode to Raphael and hugged him, whispering something urgently. Raphael nodded, a bemused look on his face.

"So this is why you asked me to accompany you to the mountain," Raphael whispered back.

"Yes Raphael," Michael said, "Now go."

Raphael spread his wings and flew off as Michael and Lucifer lingered at the base of the mountain.

"Yes, brother." Michael said as he returned to Lucifer. "Tell me. What are these troubling things I hear?"

Poised in the darkness enveloped in nothingness, God put his city's troubles behind Him for a moment in eternity and began to visualize his plan. A new world with new rules, a fresh start for a new people. Bursting with anticipation and intent, calculations and imaginations worked in a complex sync as God began to plan out His new venture. A world of time and numbers, where things could be measured in real time. A place where His creation could weigh choice with consequence, and time could influence the passage of experience and reward.

God could not shake the feeling. It was beyond a thought; it was a state of being, an ache seeking expression though not borne of pain. God smiled and a special radiance erupted around Him. It was a crazy plan, and maybe, absolutely unthinkable with all the turmoil in the heavenly city; but God was not worried. This new mission was according to His plan and purpose and no blundering or rebelling angels would stop it. A world. Earth. Man. Life. Love. Worship.

Then the Almighty felt something different. It was not the same feeling he felt when Lucifer first began spreading deception. This was different. It was a pummeling force forged inside God's heart that bore the essence of something He was not supposed to feel. Pain. Separation. Anguish. Death. He could feel an intense sorrow of mindless proportions soothed on the edges of an ever-imposing love.

God lived the future in that moment accepting a fate met out by creation against Creator. It seemed a fool's errand- a waste of effort. Love, with its intense joy and wondrous depth, would also bring rejection and abhorrence. The price was God Himself and nothing else was sufficient to match such an offering. Nothing could meet up to the standard of accepting the dire process of fulfilling His character.

But this was not about Him. The triune Being began an internal conversation of cosmic eternal proportions. This was not about God. Love was always about the recipient. This was not about merely expanding Heaven. Heaven was big enough and could be stretched farther on a whim. This was not about proving a show of strength and creativity.

This was beyond enjoying worship. Trillions of angels of diverse strengths and beauty fell in worship before His throne. Heaven had all the abundance of wealth, countless and immeasurable enough to last a million eternities and beyond. This was different. This was about giving His all. God was in love, and the trinity agreed to proceed. Far beneath Heaven, as a myriad of images flashed around God's frame, the Lord of all things carefully formulated His divine mission. Everything He had made prior to this moement aligned with this new act.

God began His ascent back to Heaven. He would soon see His plan to completion. *Yes,* He thought. *Love.* That was what this new act was all about. Love. No matter the cost or the pain; no matter the risk, God was laying it all down. He counted the cost and ruminated on the future. In that condensed moment of eternity, He experienced the future as He determined to create the multiverse, and a people to experience and express His love.

Michael stormed into the recesses of the inner court, startling Raphael and a host of other angels. Azazel and a few forge angels had arranged a selection of choice weapons in neat stacks about the room.

"He is mad. Lucifer is mad," Michael shouted.

"Peace. Peace, captain," Raphael said. "Stay calm, Michael."

"He tried to convince me to turn against God. He was so… convincing."

"Oh yes, that's him. A master tempter to say the least," Raphael said. "But I am happy that you have satisfied your thirst to speak to him. Just so you know, I never doubted your leadership. While I thought you were doing nothing, you were indeed working with Azazel to prepare weapons for God's army. I am the one to apologize to you."

"No, Raphael. My apology stands. I was a fool. Lucifer avoided me because he knew that once I had confirmed the rumors, I would do everything to stop him, including preparing the angels for war. How could he ever know I had been preparing since the first time I heard the rumors? And now that he has come to me, it only means that he is about to make his move. I was the last the piece of his plan, but now that has failed."

"Gratefully, I came to find Azazel as soon as you told me. Though, we still do not have enough weapons."

"Not nearly enough compared to what they have," Azazel chimed in for good measure.

"But we will have the element of surprise," Raphael said. "You should be proud, Michael. You are a great leader."

"Thank you Raphael. I understand what I must do now, what we must do. I was waiting for instructions, yet they have been ever present before me. My responsibility, our responsibility is to fight for the King, to defend the city and the throne room. Who was I to doubt God? His works are perfect and just. His glory is never-ending. Surely, He will rise up at the set moment and bring justice to His enemies. Brothers, we shall see His glory, power, and might before all of this is over. To arms, brothers! For the King and the Kingdom!" The angels pulled out swords and spears, lifted them up, and shouted as one, "For King and Kingdom!"

CHAPTER

—9—

WAR

A legion of angels watched from afar as the Spirit of the Lord ascended into Heaven and passed through the center of the city. Angels bowed in humble adulation, worshiping the King as He proceeded. The buzz of recent activity in Heaven was now centered on the excitement from the Lord's new project. Even with all their might and splendor, the angels were always amazed by God's creativity. This new work was different, even personal, and they were excited.

Lucifer's spies watched fastidiously, hoping to understand what God was up to. For now, they waited patiently for the signal that the rebellion was to swing into full effect. God's frequent journeys beyond the gates of Heaven were unnerving for them, yet they had learned the strategy of patience.

God was returning to His throne. The gloriously-arrayed praise angels aligned perfectly with the angels of instruments, set in endless parallel lines from the throne to the entrance of Heaven in hundreds of thousands. Their rhythm was in sync on their tambourine and cymbals. Golden incense carried flame and smoke, as angels applauded and reverenced the awesomeness of God's majesty.

With an amazing showcase of strength, the illuminated bodies of angels reflected the translucent rays of God's glory as praise and adulation broke out in the courtyard and within the throne room. As God reached the entrance of the throne room, music erupted from the massive chamber that held a host of angels.

On the west side of the room, in the middle of dazzling seraphim, stood Chesum, one of the worship leaders. He lifted his flawless hands and began to sing.

The angel's song came forth like a spontaneous twist, spilling forth a ceaseless array of sweet notes, velvety as the feeling of silk to the fingers. The angel's voice swept through the atmosphere in a sudden softness that caused everyone to pause. They waited for the note to fall but it canvased into a higher note, carrying the very spirit of the gathering into a scintillating frenzy of rich reverence for their Maker. The ad-lib escalated yet another notch, and then rolled down with gusto. Smoke erupted from the throne at that instant, and some angels fell at its fervor. The angel finished the note but it was not a praise he uttered. It was not a verse of worship or a sentence acknowledging God's attributes. He sang, and the word fully formed.

"Fire."

The other angels caught on and their sweet voices rose like a clang in perfect harmony as they chorused the word. Adriel spun forward from his company as if sucked in by God's glory and fell before the throne. The second line of Chesum's song rolled out again twisting upward, perfect note after note until it reached its end. Two words.

"Consuming fire."

The smoke around the throne began to build, forming a

mighty cloud, large enough to cover the entire room. The angels closest to the throne fell flat in worship as the smoke of His presence covered them.

"Consuming fire."

Thunder and lightning struck around the chamber and divine energy swept through the room. The divine flame licked up like a volcano and erupted. Order was interrupted; some angels abandoned their instruments of worship and shouted in their heavenly language the glorious and fearful names of God, rolling on the floor in worship of the Lord of all existence.

At the altar, the eternal flame rose like a budding spring, wailing in its power from the golden lamp-stands the forge angels had installed. Raw power encircled the throne of the King and around Him, the angels extolled. Everything else seemed to be forgotten in those timeless moments. The altar of incense carried a cloudy yet silky smoke, and lightning sparked like electric currents across the enormous chamber. Before the throne, the river of God bubbled with extreme heat and flowed with a current bursting forth like a fresh spring, eager to heal any who came close to it.

The cherubs played their instruments, expressing diverse rhythms coupled with astounding combinations of sound with their perfected voices. In that brief and precious moment, even though war loomed, Heaven seemed like its original self until dazzling swords of fire appeared in the hands of Gabriel and Michael. God was on the move and a command was about to be given. Fresh fire erupted around the throne as the angels reveled in utter abandonment, worshipping their Maker. He was God, Lord of all existence, and Maker of all, God Most High, the Mighty One, all-powerful, the all-knowing. Like a million words in one, the Lord of life spoke.

"Let us go. It is time." God rose from His throne, light waves spiraling in diverse directions. His frame carried the depths of His awesome power. In an instant, the Lord of hosts was standing before the throne with a deadly fire around His majestic flame.

"I am a Consuming Fire. I want every trace of evil out of my kingdom."

The glory remained vibrant as the angels cheered and rejoiced. Led by Michael, warring angels, dominions and powers, cherubs and seraphim, received the command and proceeded through the entrance to war.

Adriel, Chesum and the heralds exited the sanctuary, heading back to their city. The burly Mota spread his wings and bowed slightly, as Gabriel held his shoulders. "Listen, Mota, I will come soon with the order for war. Wait for me."

"As you wish, Gabriel. I will go and gather my brothers and we will be ready." Mota responded.

"God speed."

Mota flew off joining the heralds journeying above the pinnacle of the temple towards the clouds of glory at the base of their city, a wry smile on his face.

Still visibly shaken from his ordeal, Zuriel heard the loud singing and cowered in shame as he stepped into the huge tower at the gate of the outer court. He advanced slowly, trudging up the flight of stairs that spiraled the doorway of the upper rooms. He touched the knob of the door and froze.

"Come in!" He heard the voice and sighed. Stepping inside, he saw Mealiel and Baeshedith spying on the angels gathering in the outer court. "We have been waiting for you," Mealiel said. "We have to leave soon to give our report."

"And don't forget your role," Baeshedith said, and paused in shock when he saw Zuriel's bruises. "What happened to you?"

Zuriel backed away from the room slowly, ignoring them.

"Nothing," he said somberly.

Baeshedith and Mealiel exchanged glances and turned back to observe God's loyal angels preparing for war. Zuriel stepped into another room and crashed to the ground with a loud thud. He crawled slowly to the corner of the room as tears fell from his eyes. Curled up in a ball, the angel wept, overcome by grief and the horrors he had witnessed.

Michael and the mighty host of Heaven basked in the glory of God as the worship session ended. It was time for war, and a purge that would be remembered for all eternity. At the King's directive, Gabriel, Michael, Raphael, and a great host of angels advancde from the throne room and gathered in the outer court. The expanse of Heaven seemed silent but the angels knew better. Only the faithful could remain in Heaven and they had to prepare for war. Michael turned to Raphael. "First, we must protect the tree of life and the healing pool!"

"I have strong angels who have been protecting my fields since this began, but I will send for my forces to gather there quickly."

"Do so as quickly as you can," Michael responded.

"Yes captain," Raphael replied sullenly. As he brushed past Michael, the archangel reached forward and held his shoulder.

"We all carry the same burden brother."

Raphael nodded before he spoke. "I know."

The other captains looked distressed as well. Michael's face was grim as he spoke. "Sword for sword, hand for hand, war has come to us. Sentiments are far gone."

"I know…" Raphael responded.

Gabriel brimmed with holy fire. "I stand with you captain. Tell us what must be done." The captains murmured their agreement. Michael nodded as Gabriel continued. "We go forward in the name of the King and we will remain faithful. Give your command, archangel. I am poised for delivery."

Hidden behind the walls of Zuriel's tower, Mealiel watched with his myriad of bright eyes. Beside him, Baeshedith stooped as well, his large ears widened as he listened. They took in the sight of the holy captains and learned of their strategy. They had arranged themselves in parallel positions, glowing with stunning brilliance as Michael the archangel gave directives. Mealiel quietly turned with a smirk and exited, Baeshedith following after him. This was going to be easier than they had thought. Zuriel sat up suddenly. He heard the distant sound of a trumpet. The war had begun.

Directives given and strategy hatched, the captains flew off in different directions.

"For King and kingdom!" Gabriel yelled as he sped up the pinnacle of the throne room towards the thick clouds above, where the city of heralds lay. The ever-abiding glory of God surrounded him on every side as he proceeded into the heart of the clouds. He heard a loud cymbal that reverberated through his core. The clouds spiraled in diverse colors, blinding him, yet propelling him forward. A mighty thunder erupted around him but he persevered, his mind fixed on his message and mission. It was time.

The life of God was all around him and through that timeless moment, Gabriel suddenly understood the plan. He started to laugh. His laughter rode on the thunder and the bashing of ymbals. Suddenly, he broke through the clouds and unto the open space at the entrance of the city of the heralds.

"Welcome," Adriel said as the messenger became visible.

Gabriel smiled and nodded. "Ah, Adriel, I see you have been safe here. That is good. We all heard about what happened to you."

"Yes, but this has been a safe haven for me," Adriel responded. "These angels do Heaven proud."

"Yes, where is Mota? It is time."

"Ah yes, in his chamber," Adriel pointed.

Gabriel looked up at the angels before him. The ever-expansive atmosphere around them was like a canvas of glittering light spread across the grand expanse. Light waves continued to undulate like smoking wisps around the space. In a display of order and pomp, the citadel of the heralds had golden pillars majestically positioned beyond the terrain, and at each thousand paces in the landscape, an angel stood with a trumpet. Gabriel sped through the passageway between the angels, acknowledging each one's might as he passed by. He was looking for someone.

"Mota? Where is Mota? " Gabriel smiled, feverish with excitement.

"I am here." Mota, captain of the heralds, stomped forward, a mighty trumpet slung around his huge frame. Beside him stood Chesum, who had earlier led the worship session in the throne room.

"Welcome Gabriel, I have already briefed Mota on what must be done," Chesum said.

"Thank you, Chesum."

"Messenger of the throne. Is it time?" Mota asked, his muscular hands gripping the trumpet tightly.

Gabriel landed a few feet away from the muscular angel. "Yes, it is. Let us summon those who are loyal to God. Gather your forces Mota, and blow your trumpets. Summon the angels to war!"

"So now we wait," Raphael said brimming with purpose.

"Yes, Raphael," Michael responded. "The trumpet of the heralds will call our brothers. Then we will begin our sweep to purge Heaven of evil."

"Good." Raphael stopped suddenly. "Did you hear that?"

Michael looked up. "What is going on?"

Raphael raised a hand to his ear, waiting for the sound he had just heard to repeat itself. "There, did you hear that?"

Michael whispered to Raphael. "Go see what's going on."

Raphael nodded and flew towards the entrance gate beside Zuriel's tower. Dashing inside the tower, Raphael bounded up the stairs and saw Zuriel staring through the window facing the city. Zuriel turned, his face a mask of tragedy.

At that very moment, he heard a thunderous sound in the far distance. Raphael bolted to the window, almost shoving Zuriel aside. "God help us!" Running quickly to the second window facing the inner court, Raphael leaned outside the window.

"What is happening?" Michael shouted looking up sensing the worst had happened.

"Lucifer has… has attacked!"

Michael shot up like a torpedo towards the gate of the outer court and flung it open violently. A mighty host of angels had clashed in the distance right above Raphael's field.

"They are attacking the angels I sent to guard the healing waters," Raphael yelled dashing out of the tower.

"So that's their strategy," Michael took charge immediately. "Raphael take your host and defend your field. Tessa!"

Tessa, a gray haired warrior angel, stepped forward. "Here, captain."

"No matter what happens, summon your warriors to defend the entrance to the sanctuary. Nobody gets in or out until this is over."

Zuriel leaned out of his window. "What would you have

me do, captain?" he asked Michael.

Michael was already on the move. "Seal the gate, Zuriel. Seal the gate behind us. No one goes in or out. Now!"

"As you wish." Zuriel said, his hands trembling. The war had begun.

Mota spread his huge hand and clasped it around the neck of his gigantic trumpet. Behind him, another ten thousand angels, arrayed far across the spectrum of the city of heralds, followed suit. They were thousands of miles away yet they knew exactly what their leader was doing. Gabriel pulled out his sword and shouted, "For the King and the kingdom!"

Mota put the trumpet to his lips and blew into the trumpet as fire canvased around him. The sound blasted into the atmosphere of Heaven like an explosion. The angels behind him joined in and blew their trumpets on the second blast, which shook the clouds below and disintegrated the elements. At the third blast from the trumpet, Gabriel pointed his sword downwards and shot back into the cloud of glory beneath him towards the heart of Heaven. The force from the sound of the trumpets propelled him forward as he tried to stabilize himself; he heard the fourth and then the fifth. In between each blow of the trumpet, he could hear the waves of angels exclaiming, "For the king!"

Gabriel tore through the sheets of cloud and smoke; forcefully piercing the spiraling fountains of living water that proceeded from the throne room. Suddenly, the look of honor and purpose on his face faded in an instant. He could not hide his shock as angels battled across the landscape of Heaven. Lucifer had attacked. He tried to see who had the upper hand but at that moment, two rebelling angels smashed into him sending him plummeting downwards. He had unassumingly jumped into the heart of the enemy's plot.

Mota pulled a sword out just before the seventh blast. Adriel turned in surprise, his lips still pressed to the trumpet one of the heralds had given to him. The heralds waited for the final blast summoning the angels of God to war but it did not come. A few other angels immediately discarded their trumpets and brandished flaming swords. It suddenly dawned on Adriel what was happening. The order of the heralds had been corrupted and he was in grave danger. He could see a few angels amassing around Mota.

"Treachery!" An angel grasped Adriel's shoulder and he quickly spun around.

"Chesum, whose side are you on?" Adriel said quickly.

"Adriel, I am on the side of the King; for who can withstand His awesome power and majesty."

"This is an ambush!" Adriel shouted to Chesum.

Mota began to radiate with fire and light. Then the huge angel began to spin, picking up speed at each turn, and expelling a great energy that soon became a huge fireball. Other rebel angels joined in immediately, spinning faster and faster in sequence. Linking together, the angels began to form a huge fiery ball of fire and brimstone. Other heralds fluttered about in shock, unnerved and in disarray.

"What do we do?" Chesum shouted back, sensing impending danger.

"I have absolutely no idea," Adriel responded, feeling an intense spasm of fear and disgust as he realized that their safety had been compromised. How had he unwittingly been in the enemy's hands for so long? More rebel angels joined the fiery ball until it towered high and wide over Adriel and Chesum. The ball of fire grew into a gigantic inferno of flame as more of the rebels continued to join. The deafening sound and scorching heat of the fireball threw the closest angels in different directions, draining them of their essence.

"We must stop it! We must stop them!" Adriel spread his wings and darted towards the enormous ball of fire, but a torrent of energy from the inferno threw him back violently.

"Don't! Stand back!" Chesum ran beside him, pulling him back.

"But we will try won't we? Evil must not prevail!"

"I am with you Adriel, but we need a plan!" Chesum yelled.

Behind them, some of the heralds faithful to God stood helpless and in shock, weapons, trumpets and instruments of worship scattered on the terrain. The angels could only watch in mute horror as fire ball continued to grow.

CHAPTER

—10—

CHOICES

Gabriel sped towards the north gate, trying to regain his balance. His body hurt from the collision he had suffered from the attacking angels. Two of Lucifer's minions, Deitriel and Succurel, surrounded Gabriel, but the messenger of the throne spun quickly to the right, attempting to dodge their fiery swipes. Suddenly, a sharp blade pierced his right leg and he screamed in agony, his wings flailing wildly. Gabriel struggled to escape but Deitriel hung on to the dagger in Gabriel's right leg, twisting it viciously.

Gabriel screamed again in pain and then noticed Succurel aiming an arrow at him. Gabriel bucked quickly and kicked Deitriel in the face, causing him to release the dagger. Gabriel quickly pulled the weapon out, releasing a great cry. It took all of his skill to weave away and parry the heated weapon with the dagger, but that move cost him. Deitriel seized the moment and swung with his left fist, catching the messenger's jaw. Gabriel's face contorted in a mask of pain as he buckled, falling towards the base of the city. His attackers swooped down after him happily, eager to finish him off.

The angels had clashed with each other in the open, a great distance from the sanctuary of the King. Michael had wisely positioned his warrior angels according to strength and rank to guard the place of the Presence. "Defend the temple!" he shouted as the clouds of the heavenly kingdom split open amidst the fighting angels.

Outside the outer court, the gate shut behind them. Lemuel, one of Michael's trusted assistants, stood beside Michael like a rock in front of their forces, watching as Raphael's angels clashed with Lucifer's legion. Grim and outraged, Lemuel paced back and forth. "Who is leading them? Can you tell?" He probed.

"Markarth and Roawen," Michael responded. "I know them well. They were once brothers. Roawen seems to be a master of spears and javelins. Markarth, on the other hand, is using tridents and darts skillfully." Michael could now understand why Lucifer had positioned them in the center. They were merely a distraction.

Lemuel turned to look at Michael. "We should send quick aid to Raphael. Shouldn't we?"

"Soon…. Raphael will never give up his field. If the enemy takes that field, they will be in direct control of an asset that can determine the fate this war… the healing pool." Straining to see through the torrents of light, smoke, and fire, Michael could not see anything clearly. "Lemuel, if he needs us, he will send for us. Knowing our enemy, they may try to outflank us."

"As you wish captain." Lemuel nodded, his silver curls falling like wool around his back and down to his waist. He had a golden torque around his neck and a mighty shield on his left arm. In his right hand, Lemuel carried a great war bow with a retractable blade. "I wonder how the cherubim are doing."

"How did we neglect them in all of this? They are powerless to defend themselves, the little ones." Michael said quickly turning to his forces. "Tessa! Tessa! Where are you?"

Tessa stepped forward. He was a guardian angel who cared for the smaller angels of Heaven. He wore a golden breastplate, and looked poised and ready. "Here, captain."

"How are the little ones doing, and the creatures?" Michael asked.

"I had them locked up in their chambers but I had no angels to spare to guard them."

Michael said nothing as Tessa looked up at him, silently pondering. Then, the shining angel asked the question on each of their minds. "Do you think he will harm them?"

"I do not know but we can only assume that Lucifer will desire to control as many territories as possible and they may be valuable assets for him," Michael said grimly. "We have been playing to his strategy all along. Take a small force with you and check on the chambers of the little ones, and the hall of secrets as well."

"Yes captain."

"Wait! Look!" Lemuel shouted. Tessa and Michael turned, following Lemuel's pointed finger. In the distance, they saw Gabriel falling, two angels hacking at him as he fell.

"Help him!" Michael shouted.

Tessa turned and gave a signal as he erupted into a white flame. He shot off towards Gabriel as ten of his forces joined him midflight. "Gabriel!" Tessa shouted. "We're coming!"

East of the melee, Elzebur's angels had rallied together in a fine array of ordered ranks, their golden bows glittering with astounding vibrancy. Elzebur perched like a bird at the top of a mighty tree, watching grimly. The trees stood tall and mighty, showcasing a work of great art. From his vantage point, Elzebur observed the battle. There was no clear winner at this point as the angels battled for Raphael's field. If they claimed that land, the battle would easily tilt in their favor. "Brothers!" he shouted. "Say we fire a volley into their ranks? Aim far and true, and avoid hitting our own! Ready!" Thousands of angels lifted their bows.

"Aim!" Elzebur himself notched an arrow of fire and poised himself. "Fire!"

Thousands of arrows spiraled like a force of death speeding into the far distance each destined for its mark, carrying their ill and vehemence.

With swords in both hands, Raphael cut open an enemy angel and parried the blow of another. This was his territory and he would not give it up easily. The seemingly calm angel had become an apparition of his usual self. His eyes blazed with anger and the glory around him emitted sparks as he battled. Raphael was determined to stand his ground regardless of the odds that was stacked against them.

Behind the fighting angels, Michael had positioned a miniature force to defend the sanctuary of God. It had been all they could gather before Lucifer had launched his assault. Raphael looked up for a brief moment, his facial expression carrying a sense of urgency and immediate shock. Like an envelope of fire, fiery arrows flew straight into his ranks.

"The tower is ours." Mealiel beamed with relief. A company of angels had descended on the main gate and subdued the guards. Within the tower, Ashfalon made his way up the stairway slowly, pondering at his involvement with Mealiel. The two watchers had spent considerable effort arguing their positions on the war.

For all his wisdom, Ashfalon had followed Mealiel simply because he wanted to learn more. The further he had gone into the scheming, the more he had realized how so many angels had joined the rebellion against God. The more they had stayed away from the presence of God, the more tainted their minds had become. There could be no middle ground, and Ashfalon realized he had to make his choice now.

Vernon and Kionne, fellow watchers, had been subdued, and restrained inside the tower at the gate. Mealiel inspected the huge chains that bound them, fastened securely to a pillar. Ashfalon struggled not to make eye contact with them as he circled around them, following dutifully behind Mealiel. Reaching his side, he slowly tried to unsheathe a golden dagger and noticed the eyes on Mealiel's wings watching him. He paused.

"Ashfalon," Mealiel said beaming happily, "Our work here is done. I am heading to the guardian post of Elama to make my report to Lucifer. Are you coming?"

Ashfalon froze. "Yes of course, Mealiel, but go ahead. I will follow after you in a moment."

Mealiel's myriad of eyes opened inches wider. "You have something else to do here?"

Ashfalon bowed low, deftly moving his hand from the dagger. "No, Mealiel, I simply wish to question these two, especially on God's journeys outside the city. It may be that I will get some information that will earn me a higher rank and maybe ensure that I receive some form of reward."

Mealiel smiled. "I understand, good friend. Follow quickly but be careful. This tower is important to our cause."

"Yes brother. These two pose no threat to me. I will join you shortly."

"To victory!" Mealiel shouted as he spread his wings.

"To victory," Ashfalon responded.

Mealiel sped off with his legions, hurrying through the sky towards Elama, As soon as Ashfalon saw that Mealiel was in the distance, he began to hack at the chains holding Vernon and Kionne. Freeing the two guardians, Ashfalon sped after the now distant Mealiel.

Tessa's forces swooped in on Gabriel's attackers as Tessa grabbed Gabriel's hand, lifting him into his arms and guiding him to safety. As Tessa sped away with Gabriel, his party of angels encircled Deitriel and Succurel stopping their assault. Gabriel grunted weakly.

"Thank you, friend."

"Thank Michael. He sent me."

"Where are we going? The river?"

Tessa shook his head, his pale, glassy face grim. "No... I think they might have overtaken that by now. The closest sanctuary is the chamber of secrets." Tessa felt great pity for

Gabriel who had tears in his eyes.

"I was tricked and ambushed."

"God save us." Tessa muttered, his voice fading in to a tense whisper. "The heralds hold such high sanctity. I pray they aren't corrupted."

"Ah. The deception runs deep."

"We shall prevail."

"So be it."

"I see the chamber of secrets now." Tessa exclaimed with relief. "But there is an angel at the entrance."
Gabriel tried to turn and groaned in pain.

"Calm yourself. I think I recognize him. It is Bael."

Tessa landed and walked slowly towards the gate, carrying Gabriel in his arms. Bael simply stood with a strange smile on his face.

"On whose side do you stand?" Tessa shouted.

"Shh. Keep your voice down or you will put Gabriel in grave danger," Bael said moving towards them. "See? I am not here to restrain you."

Tessa was not convinced. "Stand back Bael! What is your purpose? Why do you stand like a guard of the King's secrets?"

"I am here to help. I have information for Michael."

Tessa stopped a few feet away from Bael as the two angels watched each other warily. "Information? What information? Have you been dabbling in the place of secrets?"

"No, but I am aware of Lucifer's plans."

"What is the price for the information you carry?"

Bael spread his arms and smiled. "A place in Heaven if the angels of God win."

"You cannot wager your decision. You must choose whom you serve. You seek to delay my path Bael. Either help me or get out of my way."

"Wait!" Bael said quickly stepping forward. "You are both in grave danger. Yes, I was asked to guard this entrance until an appointed signal, but I realize that I cannot give up my allegiance to God. I wish to help."

"You said we are in grave danger," Gabriel spoke up in concern.

Bael flourished his arm like a speaker before a great audience. "Lucifer has released Myesmoth."

"What?" Tessa almost dropped Gabriel.

Bael stepped forward, hands raised, and then placed a hand on Tessa's shoulder. "I cannot continue with this rebellion. It has taken its toll on me. At the end, I cannot turn my back against our King."

"How can we trust you?" Tessa countered, his voice filled with urgency. "You have consulted with the enemy and now, I must go back to warn Michael and the others."

"If the information I am giving you is accurate, then you can trust me. You can hide Gabriel in the chamber of secrets if necessary and head back to warn Michael but evil lurks close, watching our every move."

Tessa pondered for a moment. "That may be a good plan but I can't seem to grasp how Lucifer convinced the lord of forge to help him. Myesmoth can change the odds of this battle with his fearsome strength and weapons."

"That is true but the longer we wait for you to make a decision, the more danger you put Gabriel in." Bael said. "I do not mind giving you access to the chamber of secrets but note that not far beyond this chamber, Baeshedith summons Myesmoth at the quarters of the seraphim and…"

"That simply will not work. I cannot leave Gabriel unattended," Tessa interjected. "The only other potentially safe place closest to where we are is the main gate of the city with Vernon and Kionne. I have to hope that they have not been overrun. Will you go to Michael, Bael?"

"Tessa, I have been seen in the company of Lucifer and his minions. Do you really think I will get close enough to Michael to warn him?"

"So what do we do now?"

"We must decide quickly. I am sorry. I've also been trying to tell you that we are being watched. Above the top of the chamber is an angel called Narad. He will try to stop you."

Tessa heaved another sigh of dismay.

"Listen, I will carry Gabriel to the main gate far from the fighting. You can trust me." Bael extended his arms.

Gabriel looked at Tessa's face, grave concern etched on his face. "Trust? Who can we trust?" Gabriel said weakly.

"I know, Gabriel," Tessa responded. "…but we do not have much choice. Myesmoth will rout Michael's army from the rear. The only advantage he has right now is this information."

"But where is this Narad?" Gabriel asked Bael. "I do not see the angel of opposition."

"Behind me, on the pinnacle of the dome of the chamber," Bael spoke quickly without gesturing. "Narad stands watching us, biding his time to see what outcome will come from me confronting you."

"I cannot fight Narad while carrying Gabriel." Tessa was in agreement.

"I will gladly fight on your behalf then, at least to prove myself to you." Bael bowed slightly.

"You honor the King," Tessa said, his voice full of gratitude.

"It is my pleasure."

Suddenly Tessa looked up above Bael and he shouted. "Look out!"

Behind them, a myriad of deadly fiery darts whooshed towards them. Tessa instinctively swung Gabriel away from himself, pulling his bow out and firing a couple of arrows before pulling his sword and shield from his back in the same move. Almost immediately, Bael's wings spread forth in a shiny array of light as the angel leaped forward grabbing Tessa in a bear hug. His face contorted as the darts pierced through his back. Bael screamed in pain. The angels landed with a loud thud.

Bael grimaced. "Go! I will fight Narad."

"No," Tessa yelled, "You take Gabriel far from the battle till he regains his strength. I will deal with Narad and return to Michael. Thank you, Bael."

"Thank me later, brother." Bael sprang into action, spinning into a torrent of flame as he gathered momentum. He swept Gabriel into his rhythm and shot off like an arrow.

Narad swept in closer and closer, poised to strike. He clenched fiery darks in his left hand and a six-headed trident in his right hand. Tessa smiled grimly and stood like a mighty rock, his silvery hair buzzing with stunning electricity, sparks radiating from his frame as he waited for his foe.

"Come Narad. Let's finish this."

CHAPTER

—11—

CAPTIVE

The fiery ball that Mota started grew steadily, like a whirlpool of death as Adriel, Chesum and a few other angels watched in horror. With all of Mota's hate and malice poured in, the inferno grew from hundreds to thousands of angels, and towered over the few watching, bringing darkness and fear. Adriel stepped forward again, but Chesum restrained him.

"No. We can do nothing."

"Do nothing?" Adriel looked around wildly, a sudden weakness coming over him.

Tears gushed down his innocent face.

"God, where are you?" Chesum whispered.

The ball of fire suddenly spun upwards and then blasted southwards through the thick clouds towards the temple of God.

Gabriel took in his surroundings as they journeyed towards the main gate of the heavenly city. Around the streets made of gold were crystal panels standing like tall cellos, crafted to reflect the light of God around the city. The wounded angel watched as the crystal panels transformed the bright light into majestic explosions of color.

The colored lights revolved through spiral sockets set into the top of the gigantic beams, casting off a luster on the gold pathways. *At least, this place seems untouched by evil,* Gabriel thought and managed a smile. He would soon find refuge until he regained his strength. Suddenly, he felt Bael turning away from the planned path.

"Where are you taking me?" Gabriel asked. "This is not the way."

"Yes, Gabriel. It is necessary."

"I don't understand. Are we not heading towards the north gate anymore?"

"Not any more." Bael was now heading towards the east to Elama. Gabriel became tense as Bael smiled cheekily.

"You lied to us," Gabriel said slowly, realizing that he and Tessa had been tricked.

Bael almost laughed in delight. "You honor me. Indeed, I played my role perfectly."

"You foul, lying spirit."

"Obviously, you're in no condition for a little bit of genius. From what I have seen so far, Lucifer will win and I simply cannot be on the loosing side. So yes, I have chosen a side."

Gabriel's mind spun as he weighed his options. He would have to fight with every bit of his remaining grace to rid himself of Bael, but he knew he was too weak; so he waited helplessly in Bael's arms as he was carried into the waiting and eager arms of evil. He could do nothing but hope. For now, he had to admit that everything was about to go from bad to worse.

Narad was no feeble fighter and Tessa had to use every bit of craft he knew to withstand the angel. Ducking deftly to the left to dodge Narad's jab, Tessa swung his sword but missed his target. Narad then reliated with repeated strikes of his trident, bearing down heavily on Tessa for a winning blow.

Tessa's sword sparked with each clash, his arm straining with each blow, and his eyes lit with grim determination. He would not fall.

"Weak angel. You are weak," Narad said leaning forward, poised to strike again.

"I will defeat you, evil angel!" Tessa shouted, "This is God's kingdom and there is no room for evil."

"No, there will be no room for you when we are finished with you."

"Pity, you will not be missed."

"Really?" Narad retorted proudly, spinning his trident "We shall see." Tessa anticipated the blow but Narad was much quicker than he had expected.

The deviant angel fired his darts and at the same instant, threw his trident at Tessa. Unable to avoid the avalanche, Tessa attempted to dodge, but suddenly groaned in pain as a dart pierced his arm and exploded in a flame of fire. Narad had made his move, but now he had the advantage.

Tessa struck out through the flame and hit Narad on the chest. The enemy angel spluttered like a rag doll and hit the gates of the Chamber of secrets. Tessa was upon him in an instant, pounding away with his fists to his victory. Narad lay in a fetal position as Tessa rose slowly, clutching his wounded arm. He proceeded through the underground channels behind the hall of secrets and headed towards the crystal city of the Seraphs. This was his city and he knew every shortcut. At the end of the channel, the path spread out into a dazzling landscape, rich in jewels and glowing in a myriad of colorful lights.

Stretched before him was an ocean of crystal, amethyst and jasper. The citadel of the seraphim was immense and beautiful. Tessa paused to think. He had to decide whether to head back to Michael or move on to see how far Myesmoth had proceeded. He chose the latter.

The gate stood strong as Tessa approached slowly, weapons drawn. The once busy city seemed sullen and intimidatingly quiet. The heavenly creatures were nowhere to be seen, and where the seraphim with their golden harps would have welcomed his arrival, his own city was like a silent trap waiting to suck him in. Suddenly, a light blasted through the gate and it swung open.

"Ahh, welcome, guardian of the little ones."

Tessa strained his eyes open in dazzling light to see Baeshedith stepping forward from the entrance to the crystal city, his arms spread out invitingly.

"I see you are hurt," he said tauntingly.

Tessa stood his ground, his mind racing as he wondered where the angel of fury was. "This is not your place Baeshedith. Why are you here?"

"Overstating the obvious are we? You have your quarters in this city. I was merely visiting."

"I know whose side you're on. You are my enemy."

Baeshedith smiled, a hateful look splayed on his face. "It's not advisable to be my enemy considering the friends I've been making."

Tessa swayed on his feet as the ground under his feet shook. He knew it was folly to stand and fight. Baeshedith he could take easily, but this renowned angel who created the weapons of war would crush him in an instant. He pointed his sword at Baeshedith. "You will rue this war and suffer the consequences of your rebellion."

Baeshedith threw his head back and laughed. "We cannot lose. You will bow before us and serve us. Look to my left. Do you see the lord of the forge and the angels of the deep places?"

Tessa could see Myesmoth's frame appearing in the far distance. Behind him were more angels; a legion led by Astaroth inching towards the gate at a brisk rate. Tessa spun around and shot off like a dart as Myesmoth roared a mighty war cry in the distance. Baeshedith sped after him attempting to match the his pace.

Not too long after, Myesmoth emerged through the gates and chased after Tessa. His forces followed persistently, heading towards the grounds where the rear of Michael's army stood.

Michael watched as more enemy arrows struck Raphael's ranks.

"Lemuel! Lemuel!" Michael shouted.

"Yes, Captain Michael!"

"We must give aid to Raphael or they will soon be defeated!"

"What must we do?"

"We need a shield to cover Raphael's forces from Elzebur's arrows."

"I will go!"

"Go then," Michael commanded, and turned to his left. "I will defend the temple of God."

Lemuel suddenly stopped and gasped. "Captain, look to the west!" he shouted.

Sure enough, an angel in the far distance was hurtling towards them. Michael cringed visibly. Behind the lone figure, a much bigger angel pursued as a legion followed.

"Seems like Tessa. It's an ambush!" Michael shouted springing into action. "This must end now."

"What do you mean?" Lemuel asked.

"I must find the one who started this madness, the source of this insanity. I know now what must be done."

"Well how do you intend to find him?"

"That will be easy. I need to speak to him in person."

"What you speak of in itself is madness. You will willingly surrender to the enemy?"

"That is the only way I can get close enough to contend with Lucifer. I need to delay or restrain him long enough to get angels positioned within the outer court. We simply cannot allow them into our most hallowed place."

"That is not a good plan in my opinion." Lemuel said.

Michael looked around, seeing that they were in danger of being surrounded. "I have to do this!"

Tessa rushed towards Micheal, his face filled with dread. Michael grabbed his arms and looked into his eyes with a deep sense of urgency. He did not need to speak. Tessa's face went from despair to a strange calm.

"I understand, Captain," he said. "I will hold the gate for as long as I can. God speed. Come, Lemuel, we will go into the outer court and shut the gate."

As Myesmoth approached with his host of angels armed with choice weapons of power, Tessa's force sped towards the front of the gate of the outer court to defend it. Their backs turned in that moment, not one of them noticed Baeshedith slip into their ranks.

A distance from the battle at Raphael's fields, Lucifer stood with a few of his closest captains in the fields of Elama. He was brimming with excitement. Brooding over a crystal map forged in light, the great angel smiled lustily as he scrutinized it. His warriors stood about him, providing reports of the war's progress.

"We have taken most of the cities that have most value to our cause," Mescuriel, one of Lucifer's warlords proclaimed. "Soon we will take the fields, and then advance on to the throne."

"Do we have all the gates?" Lucifer asked as Mescuriel cringed visibly.

"Not all yet. We are still waiting on more reports. But the center... it will cave soon. The only place of intense resistance held by Raphael will soon fall."

Lucifer glowed happily and then assumed a more serious look, studying his map.

"My move, Michael. What's yours?" He grimaced, lost in calculated thought.

The map seemed alive with tiny replicas of the battling angels. Across the terrain of Heaven, he could witness his plan set into motion from his strategic position. His angels were positioned in a fine array of brute strength, itching to go into battle.

"Looks like we are gaining ground!" Mescuriel was slightly giddy as he peered over Lucifer's shoulder at the map. Lucifer did not respond. Instead, he focused on a tiny spec moving at great speed toward them over the throngs of angels lying in wait. Mescuriel turned to observe Lucifer's face. "Bad news? Lord Lucifer?"

"Be quiet, angel, be quiet." It was a grim chide from the huge captain of the hosts of enemy angels. "I have to think."

Mealiel, the wiry watcher angel captain, emerged behind Mescuriel and stood on Lucifer's left, bowing low in greeting.

"Master, the main gate of Heaven is ours. Ashfalon and I took it. He is very eager to please..." Mealiel paused when he saw what Lucifer was looking at. On the map, a strange speck of light continued at great speed towards their position. "Shall our angels shoot him down?" he asked.

"Yes!" Mescuriel let out a screech, which turned into a

squeal of pain as Lucifer burst into a torrent of fire and hit him in his mid-section.

"Nobody move! I think know who it is."

The angels stood uneasily, watching as the fiery light traveled at great speed in Lucifer's direction, far above the throng of angels. Mescuriel stood to his feet slowly, his eyes filled with hatred and fear. Shamed, yet proud, he took his former position, moving his hand close to the hilt of his sword as the great light moved towards them.

Mealiel stood still, waiting and watching. "I can't make out who it is, or what it is," he said. Over a hundred thousand of his forces watched tensely as the light began to descend.

Lucifer waited, a sneer on his face. "Calm yourselves." Lucifer said curtly. "It is going according to my plan."

Lucifer looked around at the hundreds of thousands of angels that had joined his rebellion. They were poised and ready for his command, willing to battle for every inch of the great city. *Let the great light come,* he thought. *Let Him.* They needed Him to get out of His holy place. Lucifer smiled.

"Yes, I am here!" he shouted. The light was within a few hundred miles. Lucifer's forces parted quickly as it descended. "Get ready!" Lucifer muttered quickly.

The light hit the ground forcibly, sending some angels tottering from the shock. Its glory faded slowly, revealing a familiar face. Lucifer's face suddenly expressed a look of disappointment as he recognized the intruder.

"Michael," Lucifer sneered with disdain. "It is only you. We were expecting... someone more important."

Michael rose up as the light waves bubbled about him, spiraling like wisps of fire. He stood tall among the enemy angels but it would take the unimaginable to defeat the mighty angels standing around Lucifer.

"Have you come to join my army?" Lucifer chuckled drily. "Foolish archangel. It is by my mercy that you were not shredded with a thousand fiery arrows of my servants. Had I known it was you, I might have commanded them to shoot."

Michael spread his arms, his face emotionless. "Thank you for your mercy, brother. I have come to reason with you... to talk."

With Michael on his mission, the war at the column of trees and around the river flowing from the throne room was a conundrum of angels in battle, sparing, shouting, and lashing out. A variety of weapons lay scattered about the once beautiful terrain. The angels loyal to God appeared besieged in their effort to maintain a defense of the highway to the temple of God. Tessa sped over the ranks of angels who stood at the ready, waiting for the advancing Myesmoth.

"How many do you reckon we have left?" Tessa yelled over the noise to Lemuel. Myesmoth was gaining quickly.

"A few tens of thousands still fight but with Myesmoth, we are surely outnumbered. My force is still ten thousand strong, sworn to the defense of the throne room." Lemuel's face suddenly lit up. "Let's get inside and shut the gate. That will keep them out and buy us valuable time while Michael is away."

"Yes!" Tessa nodded. " But we must do so now! They are almost upon us."

"But what about Raphael?" Lemuel said quickly.

"Brother, we either do this or stay here and be defeated. We have no choice. Raphael will retreat when he deems it necessary."

"You are right." Lemuel looked up at the tower. "Zuriel!" He shouted, "Open the gate!"

Zuriel poked his head outside the window of the tower. "Captain's orders. He said not to open."

"I am captain in his absence and I have no time for cheap arguments. Open up!" Zuriel and Lemuel stared at each other for a moment, and then Zuriel bowed slightly.

"As you command."

The gate sprang open and Lemuel gave the order. Immediately, his force of ten thousand dashed quickly into the outer court and stood in a fine array, weapons drawn.

Lemuel looked up at the tower at the gate of the outer court and yelled.

"Zuriel! Lock it down!" Zuriel appeared at the window again and nodded.

"As you wish."

Immediately, a fiery sheet of light spun across the top of the tower, creating a secure covering over the outer court. From their new position, the angels gathered in their ranks waiting for what seemed like a delayed but inevitable defeat.

Michael eyed the visual map of the war for a brief moment and then met Lucifer's gaze. "I must speak to you. Alone," he said, as Lucifer smiled brashly, enjoying every moment of their exchange of words.

"Why? You stand before my host and all the power and might of the ones who believe in my rule. You are beyond the realm of your safety. We have taken most of the domains that matter to Heaven and now press to crush the weak force you positioned outside the temple. Tell me, Michael, are you here for a share of our spoils or simply here to perish?"

Mescuriel took a half-step forward, weapon drawn, as Mealiel and a few dozen poised to attack. Michael understood now that his crazy plan depended solely on Lucifer's pride. He had to feed it.

"I must speak to you alone. A proposal. You know that you cannot enter the courts of the temple. Not with the gate shut."

Lucifer took a quick look at the map, scowled and then threw his head back and laughed, music bursting through the pipes laden in his wings. His captains laughed as well; only Mealiel kept full watch, trailing every move as Michael stepped closer to Lucifer and forced a half smile on his face.

"Like I said, I have a deal that will end this war and you will have what you have been scheming for without further destruction. However, I insist that we discuss this alone." Michael waited as the angel of music contemplated his request. If Lucifer gave an order to destroy, he would be overpowered; but Michael kept a calm face even as his insides burned with anticipation and dread. Lucifer smiled.

"Your bravery makes me dizzy with delight. We do not need to vanquish every enemy angel so I will listen to you. Come then...but no tricks. Otherwise, you end up like him."

"Like who? "Michael's puzzled look followed Lucifer's pointed finger as his captains parted ways, and then his eyes widened with horror. Strung between the pillars of the guardian's post at the top of the flight of steps of the field of Elama was an angel, his arms strung in fiery chains and his body bruised all over. Michael's voice broke.

"Gabriel."

Mealiel chuckled, moving quickly behind Michael in case the captain lost his mind and attacked them. Mescuriel ran up the short stairway and poked Gabriel's mutilated body with his trident. Gabriel screamed in pain, his body contorting as Bael and Ashfalon emerged on both sides of the pillars bowing low to Lucifer.

"You have done well, Bael," Lucifer said, slapping his hands together gleefully.

"Thank you, my lord," Bael responded. "but it was your plan. We are amazed at your wisdom, lord." Lucifer spread his arms wide enjoying the worship he was receiving.

A tear trailed Michael's face but he quickly wiped it off as his eyes met Gabriel's. The captive angel had a pained look on his face. Michael felt great grief knowing that Gabriel would be confused about what he was doing, seemingly thick in the counsel of the enemy. Surely he would wonder if he had turned against God. However, there was simply no way to answer his questions. He took a few steps up the stairway and paused. *Stay strong Gabriel,* he thought. *It will soon be over.* Michael had to stay true to his plan.

His eyes never left Gabriel's eys as he spoke. "Well then, no tricks. Shall we?"

"Come, then. Let us talk as you have requested." Lucifer stood beside Michael on the steps of the guardian's post, and Michael put a hand on his shoulder.

"Wait. No weapons."

Lucifer laughed heartily. "Are you afraid? You are scared you will meet the same fate? Very well, no weapons."

The archangels pulled out their weapons as Bael and Ashfalon stepped down to receive them. Ashfalon reached for Michael's sword and their hands touched briefly. Their eyes met for a moment as Michael released his weapon to the angel, wondering if he had found an unlikely ally deep in the enemy's ranks. He decided not to count on it. Mealiel stepped up, pulling out a sack with gold rims. "Here, put them all here." Michael looked down again, feeling the walls closing down on him.

Lucifer clapped heartily. "Good. Now all the formalities have been observed, I am keen to hear your proposition of surrender."

Michael put his right hand on Lucifer's shoulder as the angel put his hand on his, their eyes never leaving each other. They spread their wings as the other angels stood back. A ring of fire formed around them as energy built up around them and then the two angels blasted upwards above the field of Elama, a distance from the angels camped on the ground.

Below, Ashfalon and Bael resumed their positions beside Gabriel as their eyes followed the trail of light trailing the two archangels. Then, Ashfalon looked around quickly, observing that all the angels where looking upward; even Mealiel who was carrying the sack filled with weapons maintained his gaze on the two archangels. Ashfalon edged closer to Gabriel, his mind racing wildly, and he poked Gabriel in the side. The wounded angel groaned loudly. Mealiel did not break his gaze but a few angels did.

"Be quiet, Gabriel. Stop whining," Mescuriel teased.

In the clouds above, they could see the two angels in animated discussion; but none of them could hear what either angel said. Gabriel groaned louder, distracting the angels around him. This time Mealiel peeled his myriad of eyes away from the archangels' meeting to observe him.

"What do you want, Gabriel? Some fresh water from the fountains of Heaven to quench your thirst?" He taunted as some angels laughed.

"Or some manna to restore your strength?" Mescuriel taunted.

"Tell us, Gabriel, we are your humble servants." Mealiel laughed wickedly, moving menacingly towards the wounded angel.

The other deviants joined in, each with their own comments to taunt their once glorified victim. They were too engaged in the game of mockery to notice the moment that Michael attacked Lucifer.

CHAPTER

—12—

SEIGE OF HEAVEN

The elements erupted violently as Michael and Lucifer clashed above the mountains east of Topaz and El Dora, a great distance from the throne room of God. The angels' fury remained unabated as each parried and attacked the other. Lucifer fought with great craftiness, looking for every weakness in his opponent.

Michael had realized within the initial moments of the fight that he was battling for his very existence. Hate and ill will had lent a hand to Lucifer's fists, giving his blows added force; but he realized that Michael was no mean fighter. As he grappled with him, Lucifer soon decided that brute strength alone would give neither the advantage. "Weapons!" he shouted urgently.

Ashfalon saw Mealiel spread his wings and fly upwards towards the two captains locked in combat. Instinctively, he shot at Michael and hit him mid region. Mealiel's sack spilled forth as golden weapons created by the forge angels scattered about. Above them, Lucifer delivered a blow and used his knee to shove Michael's chest, freeing himself from his grasp for a moment.

"Ashfalon! You traitor!" Mealiel shouted and brought his two arms down heavily on Ashfalon's head, smacking the angel away. Ashfalon fell, his body dwindling in a fading light as it tossled towards Heaven's base. A moment later, Lucifer was armed with his sword and Michael immediately recognized that he was in grave danger. He had never imagined his powers to be used to attack one of his brothers, but he knew he had to act fast.

Lucifer was upon him in an instant with a golden sword in his hand, swiping and jabbing ferociously. The clouds of glory around them were torn and shattered, crystals and gold dust splattered about the warring angels. Smoke whirled around in a daze as chaos let loose over the natural order of the supernatural that had been contaminated.

Michael spun quickly and sped away, weaving left and right to dodge Lucifer's attacks. A peculiar glare caught his eye in the depths below, so he nosedived in a desperate attempt to escape; but to his dismay, he hit the grounds of Heaven, smashing into the enemy angels below. Wincing in pain as light erupted from his wounds, Michael bellowed a war cry that shook the elements, pounding the screeching warriors with his fits. He saw a discarded dagger and quickly grabbed it as Lucifer landed with a mighty thud.

"Leave him to me!" Lucifer bellowed to the throng of angels who had now surrounded Michael, as he ran towards his foe. "He is mine! Leave him to me!"

The angels backed off, dazed by the archangels' ferocity. Michael turned again to face his foe, his teeth gritting in pain, yet visibly calm.

"I serve the King!! You cannot defeat me!!" Michael shouted.

Lucifer almost ripped Michael's arm off with his blade but Michael's hand held grasped the dagger tightly. He countered the blow, though with less aggression as the raging Lucifer, which foreced him to the ground on one knee. Sensing the hilt of an abandoned weapon, he reached for it with his free hand, and with blinding speed, he cut a wide streak across Lucifer's face. Lucifer staggered a few paces backwards in shock.

Michael rose up, holding two daggers. He flailed the daggers about him, concentrating on the kill. He needed more grace to fight off this foe; if only enough to reach the healing pool. Nonetheless, he had to ignore the pain. Light revolved around Micheal's frame as Lucifer prepared to attack again, and that was when Michael noticed. The cut on Lucifer's face did not emit light as expected of angels of light; rather, it emitted a strange, greenish oozing substance. Lucifer didn't seem to notice Michael's shock.

The captain of the Lord's army had let down his guard. Lucifer brought his sword with so much force that the grounds shook vehemently, erupting the golden sands and spewing reckless destruction.

The pillars of Elama's guardian post were falling; golden monuments were disintegrating, and the vegetation was waning in the potent battles. Michael lost his daggers in the force of the attack, his glory ebbing away with each blow; his concern was growing for Gabriel as well.

It would be a desperate move but it would be enough. He had to make it to the healing pool and at the same time, lead Lucifer far from the throne room. He sped off like a rocket, with the raging angel of doom close at his heels and his deviant captains and warrior host in hot pursuit.

Myesmoth and the other mighty angel, Astaroth, split at the battlefield at Raphael's fields. The burly forge angel led a contingent force to finish off Raphael's troops while Astaroth stormed towards the gate of the outer court.

Raphael took one last look at the destroyed field and the healing pool. They had fought hard and long, but they had lost this vital piece of land. They could do nothing more but retreat. Raphael signaled to the remainder of his forces and sped westward, attempting to draw the enemy forces from the path to the sanctuary. Myesmoth was war-hungry and devastated that he had missed the better part of the fight.

"Cowards! After them! After them!" The huge angel walked to the healing pool and sat down on a ledge at its side while his forces chased after Raphael. Elzebur and his archers joined him shortly, securing the center of Heaven and the vital waters of healing. They were winning.

Zuriel rose from his chair and looked at the lever on the gate. It was his moment. He has to make his choice. He was the piece of the puzzle that would determine victory. He only had to reach for it and the gates would open, deactivating the shield of fire, and allowing access into the most sacred places in Heaven. The guardian remembered when he had welcomed Lucifer in the tower. He remembered their conversation. He also remembered his ordeal in Hades. Slowly, he reached for the lever and paused. Surely, a great reward would be given to him. He would rule and reign in the new kingdom.

Everything had happened just as Lucifer had planned. Their strategy had yielded great results, but everything hung in the balance of his decision. He still had the assets of choice and opportunity. He could resist the temptation and buy valuable time for God's angels, or he could follow through and give Lucifer his victory.

"Zuriel!" Astaroth yelled impatiently outside the tower. "Zuriel, it is time. Open up!"

Zuriel gripped his head in his hands. He needed to think.

"Well, what are you waiting for?" An angel stepped into the room.

Zuriel spun around in a daze. "Baeshedith! How did you?"

"That doesn't matter. Are you going to open or not?" Baeshedith probed, his eyes full of hate. Zuriel reached again for the lever and paused. Baeshedith walked towards him slowly. "What's stopping you? Open the gate!"

Zuriel turned slowly, his tears falling freely. "I cannot…"

Baeshedith let out a fearsome scream of rage, swung his fist and caught Zuriel in his jaw. The guardian angel hit the wall of the tower chamber thunderously. Grabbing the lever in both hands, Baeshedith pulled with all his might.

Tessa's watched, aghast and helpless as the gate of the outer court opened. Their last wall of defense was gone.

"Treachery!" he shouted, realizing that they had foolishly given strategic ground to the enemy. "Zuriel has let the enemy in! Defend the throne room!" Tessa shouted as his angels rallied around him. "Form up! Form up!"

The guardian angels outside the throne room quickly formulated a strategy to defend the gigantic room of the Presence. They stood side-by-side, shoulder-to-shoulder on three levels shielding off the attackers with their shields. Lemuel was grafted underneath two angels, his mind working furiously.

They had to hold long enough in case Michael returned victorious. Their arch captain had made a wise decision to lure Lucifer away from the throne room. The holiest place was far above the realm of the cities of Heaven and somehow, lesser angels, powers and principalities of Lucifer's order had been given access.

Tessa could not see Zuriel or the famed Myesmoth, but he imagined that the guardian of the gate had been in on the plot all the while appearing to be an ally to the angels loyal to God. He had never even seen some of their attackers before. The treachery had spread beyond the great city to deepest realms of Heaven. Astaroth and his legion rushed through the entrance and clashed with Tessa and Lemuel's forces.

They fought hard, their defense standing strong against the throng of enemy angels. The guardians of the holy place clashed with cursing and screaming rebels. At every moment an angel was cut down in his defense, another would step in immediately, holding his ground. This singular force depriving access to the invaders were ten thousand angels strong.

Thousands of enemy angels continued to pour in through the mighty gates, weapons gleaming with deadly purpose. Tessa battled with vigor, blazing a trail of fire as his sword smashed into a rebel's body, and then cut clean through another. The angels on his right and left shielded him in a circle of fire, averting off enemy arrows. A few of his warriors adopted his strategy. They could hold the outer court.

A few of the attackers backed off, wary of the astounding strength of the defenders. Realizing that they were gaining the upper hand, Tessa encouraged his forces to remain strong. Then, he looked up and saw something that startled him, causing him to recoil in despair.

"God help us." Tessa gasped.

"Yes, God help us." Lemuel almost dropped his axe.

Something was coming towards them at great speed, growing larger in size as it advanced. With reckless power streaking across the distant firmaments of Heaven, the gargantuan fireball swallowed the sky, darkening the heavens as it hurtled towards the entrance to the throne room, destroying all in its path.

Everyone paused to observe it. Tessa dashed back to the wall of angels, determined to wait for the inevitable end. The fiery ball of rebel angels continued to approach the outer courts at great speed, with no resistance in its path.

Michael approached the healing pool and in despair, he sunk to the ground a few feet away from the waters. An array of Elzebur's angel archers guarding the pool of healing had their golden bows pointed directly at him; and the enormous Myesmoth stood like a rock, beaming with delight. The light was fading from other angels loyal to God who had gone too close, their bodies strewn on the ground.

Enemy angels were plunging into the waters in droves to replenish from the healing pool, and return to attack the angels loyal to God. Michael's muscular knees hit the ground. The sound reverberated across the valley. His wounded hands stretched up like he was saying a prayer, as light seeped away from his frame uncontrollably. He heard the sound of Lucifer's landing behind him but he did not turn.

"Do you see now?" Lucifer taunted. "You should have joined me when you had the chance." Michael did not respond. There was nothing to say. Lucifer batted the back of Michael's neck with the hilt of his sword and Michael hit the ground thunderously. He did not move. He only waited.

"What a waste," Lucifer sneered. "Do you think I would not have given careful thought and great planning to my mission? Do you think me merely ambitious? You have fought and defended the One who has repressed you for so long. He gave you strength and glory for His purposes. He turned all of us into mindless creatures to serve His wit. Not me. When I am done with you, I will ascend up the great mountain of God and alight upon the very throne of God. It will be mine and all Heaven will worship me."

Michael lay flat on the ground wounded, yet unbroken. Pride had caused his enemy to become blind.

"I am good," he said weakly. "and you are evil."

"Was I not made by good?" Lucifer snapped. "Was I not created by a good God? If I am evil, Michael, how can good produce evil?"

"Good never produces evil. You were not created to be evil, nor did you create it. Evil is not a force or attitude that carries its own persona. It is not a gift or treasure. Evil is not a grace or intention. Evil is everything and anything that is anti-God." Michael spoke through gritted teeth, trying to buy some precious moments.

Lucifer had raised his sword to strike but he paused. "What?"

"Yes, Lucifer," Michael continued weakly. "You think He did not know? Evil abides only because you allowed it and what you have questioned in your mind does not justify the perpetration of your acts. You allowed yourself to stray from Him due to your pride."

"You blame me for my beauty? You blame me for my power? You blame me for my rank? I did not give those to myself. So who should you blame?"

Michael leaned on his elbows weakly. Everything was becoming a blur. He was drifting away. "The gifts of God are good, perfect, and just," he managed to say. "What you do with them… is another matter." Michael closed his eyes and waited for the inevitable.

Tessa staggered forward, distorting their defense as the boiling mass of fire towered right above them with a few moments left before contact. He watched wide-eyed at the circumference of the fiery boulder as it gathered momentum, a deadly whirlpool as big as a tsunami. "Hold!" Tessa screamed in desperation. "Shields!!!" Thousands of shields were lifted upward to guard from the new threat.

The angelic boulder sparked light, fire, and brimstone. It pulled lesser angels into its energy and the elements revolved around it. In an instant, the enormous ball of fire descended with blazing and raging energy towards the ranks of guardian angels - directly into the heart of their defense.

"You babble about the depths of God that you know nothing about," Lucifer said, now irritated by Michael's words. "You cannot change your fate. Maybe when I rewrite the books of mysteries, I will say God was defeated because we chose to rise beyond the mere knowledge of power to actually expressing power. He sought to restrain and restrict. I seek to set the angels free. Therefore my good must clearly be greater than His good."

Michael shook his head. "Maybe sometimes good is too gracious, it does not prepare adequately for evil."

Lucifer threw his head back and laughed. "Maybe good is weak. Weakness will have no place in my kingdom. The strong will always rule over the weak. Remember this, Michael, I have seen some of the scrolls of the mysteries of the kingdom. This God you worship and serve has been reserving the keys of the kingdom for another."

"What are you talking about?" Michael groaned audibly, looking up.

"What? You didn't even know about this?" Lucifer mocked. "Did you ever wonder why I went looking for Lurerdeth and the keys? Whoever wields those keys rules over us! I do not know its fullness but I will never bow to anyone again. The one who holds those keys will be given power to judge even us angels. Do you see now foolish angel? Do you see now?"

"Another will judge us?"

"Yes," Lucifer retorted in disgust. "Are we not good enough?"

"If that is the will of the King, who am I to question it?"

Lucifer shook his head and smiled wickedly, "No more vain-babbling. Good bye Michael."

Michael closed his eyes and waited again. Lucifer stood over Michael and brought his sword down in a violent and angry swing.

Tessa and the angels guarding the throne room were flung mercilessly in different directions as the boulder smashed through their ranks. Tessa crashed into the terrain, saved by the two angels who had thrown themselves over him. The angel above him was ruthlessly torn from his shoulder and ripped apart. Lemuel deftly made his way through the fire, deflecting arrows and swords in order to defend Tessa.

They had to hold on by all means. Tessa gaped for a brief moment as their defense disintegrated from the impact of the hit. Then he struggled to his feet, blocking a mighty arrow that almost pierced through his hand. He would keep fighting.

Mota detached himself from the fiery throng and raised his battle-axe, swinging his shield in a fluid movement and batting angels off mercilessly into far distances. He was strong, fearsome, and he could sense they were almost through.

With a fearsome cry, he pounded the Lemuel's knuckles and swatted him away with his war shield. Then, only the sure-footed Tessa stood in his way and the entrance to the throne room.

"This is madness!!!! This is madness!!!!" Tessa screamed.

Mota was not going to waste precious moments disagreeing with him. He raised his axe above his head, towering over Tessa like a mammoth fighting a pup. Tessa waited like a strident rod of lighting, poised for the glorious end. He had fought like his brothers for the King. If this was it, so be it.

At that moment, a loud and violent blast struck the angels, tearing through the realms of the heavenly city. Mota looked up to where the sound had come from. He knew that sound. It was his horn.

Lucifer staggered backwards. "Who blew that horn?" He said in a state of confusion. "Who is giving God perfected praise?"

He looked down quickly to confirm his kill.

The horn was in the hands of a herald standing on the pinnacle of the temple of God, his eyes focused on his task, big arms raised without exertion. The sound overpowered the noise of war and shattered through the clouds at the pinnacle of the temple of God. The blast shook the atmosphere and all of Heaven paused. He looked down, watching the angels for a brief moment and then put the horn to his lips again. The second blast shook the very foundations of Heaven, tearing angels off their feet and slamming them unto the ground. Smoke began to emanate from the holy place.

Suddenly, a sound waffled through the high places, strummed upon a harp of gold, music alive and full of purpose. Adriel stood firm beside the angel with the horn, harp in one hand, and flaming sword in the other. He and other praise angels had gathered above the clouds that resided above the temple. They knew what to do now. Chesum put the horn to his lips again and blew with all his might. Seven times, he blew the horn.

In an array, the angels revealed their instruments of praise. Tumborel began to pound on his instruments of rhythm. The cymbals crashed in resonance, whisking thunderously throughout the distorted ambience of heavenly Jerusalem. The angels strummed their harps and lyre. Suddenly, the light of God blasted through the temple as praise hit the city of Heaven.

The light was a force of God that the darkness could never fight or resist. Its very presence was the absence of evil. His goodness was a covering of glory and light, full of majesty; the very embodiment and expression of His awesome power. It was the reality of His might and the divinity of His sovereignty.

"For the King of kings! For the Lord of lords! For the Almighty!" Adriel shouted with all his might. The angels heard the powerful voice. The once meek angel sounded like a mighty warrior.

"God, the all-powerful!" Tessa shouted as Adriel descended with a thunderous shout in response. Angels continued along with blowing horns of praise. "There is none like Him!"

Lucifer looked perplexed as glory continued to stream from Michael's mutilated body. He had literally cut the angel almost in half but something he never anticipated began to happen. Light revolved around Michael as he slowly began to regain his form and his body began to heal. Lucifer gasped in shock, tightening his grip around his sword in order to strike again.

Suddenly he felt a surge of pain emanating from his hand. He looked down and saw that his own hand was bruised and a strange substance was slowly seeping from a bruise on his hand. When did this happen? Lucifer thought to himself. Lucifer started to cry out in agony as the light surrounded him, causing the wounds on his body to sting.

In place of light and glory, an unnerving aroma rose to his nose as the insipid liquid spilled from his wounds. The angels around him who had rebelled against God experienced the same thing. Thousands of angels screamed out in pain as the light of God's glory touched them. A change was coming in the heavenly city; something that had changed the tide of the war.

Michael rose slowly, covered by shimmering light - the very glory of God. His frame was booming with divine energy, his face full of determination. The voice of the Spirit of God had spoken and Michael received his instruction. He lifted his hands up, and bellowed, "Sons of God! Hear the Father of all spirits! The Lord is just and is the giver of dominion. This is the city of God and evil cannot dwell here."

Michael's eyes met those of Lucifer, who shielded his eyes as glory covered the archangel of God. Michael spread his arms, allowing the light to spill forth.

"I seem to remember you saying that you could win this war; that your glory was above the One who created us all. I recall you saying that the betrayal of the one who created us would allow for a new kingdom and a new order," Michael said and shook his head. "I pity you Lucifer. You were so beautiful and none could surpass you and yet, here you stand, having wasted it all for greed and pride. The evil you have accepted has corrupted and changed you and your followers irreversibly. You have been given a new name and will be referred to as Satan. The glory of God has departed from you, for God cannot dwell in iniquity."

Lucifer cowered along with his minions spread about the terrain, confused by the turn of events. Shaken by the fiercest revelation of the fervor of God's glory, the rebels became fearful. The goodness of God was powerful, forceful, and of much depth. It reeled around Heaven and the distant worlds like a vibrato of energy. They had never seen the ferocious anger of God.

The glory that Lucifer had once basked in now repelled him. He suddenly felt weak and lifeless, his mind pierced through with the power of the One he had defied. He staggered and fell to the ground as other enemy angels felt the same lifelessness. Those in the clouds fell, plummeting to the ground unable to resist God's might. The rebels on the ground were paralyzed, glancing around furtively in fear.

The music created by the worshipping angels was rich and powerful, extolling the King; and like a two edged sword, it rendered Lucifer and his minions powerless. Lucifer felt strange as he cringed in the presence of God's raw power.

A loud voice boomed out of the manifest Presence of God from the throne room.

"I am the Lord and I pronounce judgment. Iniquity has been found in you. Satan, you are cast away from my presence."

Stripped from the life of God, the once graceful angel's body became distorted, twisting in agony. Cut off from the divine light, a grueling darkness abolished his once smooth skin, replacing the crystals of light with an ashy scaly body. In astonishment, he stared in shock as his hands and bo became rough and ugly, unlike anything he had ever seen.

Even the angels of God gasped in shock at the transformation happening before their eyes. The enemy angels were becoming eerie creatures, slimy and reeking in their deformity. Once beautiful, the rebel angels became ugly beings, losing their original form and glory.

Michael felt no pity for the attackers as he stood, stoic like a tree, but he felt no joy either as the voice of God boomed across the landscape of Heaven. Every crawling and flying creature of the heavenly city heard the command.

"Cast them out into the darkness."

CHAPTER
—13—
REQUIEM

Screams of anguish resounded across the landscape of Heaven. The spirits screeched in their fear and vehemence, fighting the devastating feeling of lifelessness. The enemy angels, once filled with grace and glory, were dissected from the presence of God, condemned to be devoid of peace and goodness. The rebels screamed in the pain of their loss, for there was no longer any hope, or a counter-measure to break the spell of death. Some of the rebels became remorseful, pleading for forigveness as their wails rang around Heaven, but to no avail.

The angels of glory felt pity for their fallen brothers who were now being punished for their deeds. The rebels had become the embodiment of spiritual death itself, now lost and condemned to be in darkness.

Lucifer, once the most beautiful angel that God created had been transformed into the ugliest creature in Heaven. His hate and distaste for God's greatness had aided in his transformation. He alone had imagined the madness of his heinous crime, spread his cancer of evil, and tainted the meek hearts of others. Once the angel whose musical pipes had lit up the stratosphere of Heaven, and thrown the mightiest of celestial beings at God's feet, Lucifer, as all of Heaven had known him, was no more. He was now the lord of the dead, dying and ill. He was the devil.

What used to be the face of adulating light and glory had become ghastly. Lucifer had bacome a ghoul of gruesome form, writhing in the pain of the recompense meted to his sin. Death. He could feel it deep within. Cut off from the divine life of God, the former archangel lay in defeat; and in one dramatic moment, God himself declared judgment on he and his minions. The tragic result was the loss of their terrain in Heaven for all eternity.

As he lay on the ground, writhing and shielding his eyes from the bright light that Michael exucded, a myriad of thoughts plagued his mind. *What went wrong? I was so close to victory. Every single plan was meted out to perfection. What just happened?*

He grabbed his head, tormented by the battle he was fighting within. Maybe he had been wrong all along. Maybe he should have stayed where he was and remained content. Was it so bad that he had tried to take the throne of God?

"Lucifer," Michael said softly stepping forward with a hand outstretched.

"Michael." He reached out slowly, his bruised and gnarled skin covered with slime and puss. Suddenly he froze as his eyes squinted to observe Michael. "No!!!!" He screamed, "It's not over! It will never be over! I will have my revenge!"

"You remain defiant still?" Michael shook his head, filled with sadness. "The light of God is no longer in you. You are stripped from your title and rank. You are the devil; Satan, the adversary...and all your followers are now demons."

Satan said nothing. Michael sighed and shrugged slightly, raising his sword as millions of angels did the same.

"To the gates! Take them to the gates and cast them out!"

After the sentencing and casting out, the one now called Devil grabbed Bael outside the gates of the heavenly city, speeding off forcefully as he proceeded into the darkness with his minion. Around them, wailing and weeping demons pleaded for mercy as the angels threw them out.

"You said you have a map of Hades. The one you obtained from Zuriel. Show me," the devil demanded. There was no remorse from the fallen angel as Bael quickly observed. Even though he could imagine that the devil was reacting to his demise, he did not show his pain. Bael obliged him, looking around warily, though more troubled by the ugliness of the devil's transformation than even his own. The scroll he had obtained from Zuriel lit up like a flickering candle and the landscape of Hades spread out before them, just as Zuriel had drawn it.

The devil studied it for a moment and then waved his hand clearing the light. "I will take back what is mine. This is nothing but a minor setback."

"Well, I'm not sure anyone will be rallying to call you master just yet." Bael said wryly.

"And what about you?" the devil asked petulantly. He had not lost his pride or anger. His new look only added to the horror of the lesser spirit.

Bael gulped nervously and responded. "The earlier we get to Hades and claim that land, the better."

The idea seemed to calm the angry devil. "Lead the way."

Deceived. Myesmoth, Mota, Barachiel and Astaroth hid in the ashy dunes around the wall of Hades. Since Zuriel's return from the distant world, word had spread among the top ranks of Satan's rebel army of a world outside Heaven. Having lost Heaven, they knew the obvious destination of most of the fallen angels would be this fortress.

After all the rebels had been rounded up and pushed out of Heaven into the darkness, the gates of the celestial city had been closed shut behind them. The rebels realized that the life they had always known was now siezed from their grasp. Astaroth studied the dusty dunes with his eyes.

"Good thing we found Barachiel. I guess this is better than roaming around aimlessly. But why are we so far from the gates of Hades? Why do we skulk far from the entrance?" he queried.

Myesmoth, now a gigantic monster, turned around, his skin gleaming red with streaks of green and eyes full of hate. "Barachiel, you tell him."

"Because that's exactly where Lucifer will go." Barachiel responded. "Unless any of you are planning on taking him on."

"I intend to gather my warriors together and destroy that lying angel," Myesmoth replied. He then spun around in the direction of the muffled sounds ringing behind him. "Will you be quiet, Mota?"

Greenish, oozing tears matted Mota's face. Everything was lost and Mota, the angel who once led the heralds, was finding it hard to accept his new fate as he whimpered in despair. Nothing could compare to the wretchedness of being outside the presence and beauty of God. Now, he knew. They all knew.

Their once glowing skin had become a thickened maze of scales, drab and leathery. If that wasn't bad enough, the horrid smell of decay oozing from their body was an assault to their senses. Even their voices had changed, no longer did their voices sound silky smooth and pleasant; they were now harsh, and brimming with evil. They had been deceived and the price was steep.

Having lost their place of dominion, the fallen angels spread abroad the outer darkness wailing in the dusty dunes, consumed in their torture. They wandered about aimlessly for the very first moment in their existence. It was then that they realized they had no purpose, nor would they ever have the privilege of carrying out a divine assignment - a scathing judgment for their ills. Each one sought a place of rest from the torture that their bodies were enduring but were unable to, which filled them with even more rage and fear. Expressing their hatred for one another, they shouted all curses conceivable, and broke out in fights across the terrain of darkness.

Former lords of rank and might, former angels of the throne, watchers, heralds, and builders, warriors and poets; once nurtured in mansions with heavenly food, now lost, their recompense beyond anything they had ever sought to gain from the rebellion. They would never stop hating the one who had deceived them, nor the One who had cast them out. Everything was lost; and their pain was indeed great to bear.

Mealiel skulked far away from the wailing demons to seek out the one who had started it all. His eyes had become owlish orbs that shifted in opposing directions, full of anger and rage, and fueled by a desire for revenge. His arms were covered with oozing scabs. He had become a monster with huge, bat-like wings with contorted eyes all over his body.

Every promise from Lucifer that had spurred his choice to revolt had been futile. He wondered where Astaroth and Mescuriel were on the landscape of brawling demons. He searched restlessly with his now obnoxious array of eyes for Bael, or the former herald, Mota, or the gigantic Myesmoth. They were all scattered, full of fear and scathing anger.

Mealiel proceeded through the expanse of nothingness, looking out for angry spirits. The eyes on his back continued to scan the distances behind him. He could handle any of the lesser rebels but there was one he had to find at all costs. Alone in the darkness, he could only imagine that Lucifer's pride had been crushed and he was convinced that none of the banished angels would want to give him an ear to speak to. Lost in his wandering thoughts, Mealiel suddenly collided with another spirit.

An odious smell surrounded Mealiel before he saw the spirit crooning before him, arms raised in surrender. "Please let me pass and be on my way," the fallen spirit said.

Mealiel raised a gnarled finger. "What is your name?"

"Baeshedith. Please let me go on without trouble."

"I see. You were the one who did what Zuriel failed to do. You performed your duties. We are proud of you." Mealiel spat out words full of sarcasm and pain.

Baeshedith's face was sunken and deformed, two round whitish orbs for eyes. His gaunt wings now protruded from a well-built body laced with leathery, dry skin.

"Proud of me? This is a disaster," Baeshedith said. Mealiel sighed in agreement.

"Things did not turn out as planned," he said. "Everything has turned out to be a masterful disaster." Baeshedith shifted uneasily.

"I must be on my way."

Mealiel stood in the way of the fleeing rebel. "Why the hurry? We have all of eternity to live in perpetual grief and regret." Mealiel did not remember at first but then he recalled a rumor he had heard earlier. Something about a place of burning fire.

Baeshedith lifted up his hands, pleading. "I am simply looking for a place of rest like the others."

Agitated, Mealiel suddenly grabbed Baeshedith by the neck and squeezed with all his might. "Where are you going?"

Baeshedith spluttered the words. "Hades!"

Mealiel released the hapless spirit. "You are wiser than you look. Hades would be a prime real estate for anyone who controls it. Take me there."

Baeshedith knew better than to argue. Across the deep darkness, millions of spirits continued to wail and scream, finding no place of rest. They merely fought for the sake of it, now that there was no divine assignment to give them order. Descending through the darkness, Mealiel and Baeshedith charted course for the place of restraint - the land of death and fire.

"This way," Baeshedith said as they continued their descent.

Mealiel became increasingly weary. "How do you know the way?"

Baeshedith's wings fluttered with an eerie buzz as he stopped and responded. "I had one of ours among Gabriel's builders. His name is Barachiel. Besides, the lower we go, the more likely we will find it."

"Well, none of the others would have come this low except maybe one."

"Who?"

"You know who. Did you ever mention it to him?"

"Well, Bael had taken Zuriel's report to Lucifer. Surely, he must be there by now. I merely had a glimpse of the map." Mealiel felt some relief, yet was wary of seeing the devil. He had become the epitaph of shame and no one wanted to taste the wrath of his pride.

"Shall we proceed? " Baeshedith said hesitantly, his voice eerie and muffled.

Mealiel smiled bitterly. "Lead the way."

"Stop this pitiful wailing!" Myesmoth said to the teary-eyed monster that leaned on the wall of Hades. The scaly mass moved, and Mota shamefully turned to observe him. Myesmoth's face had become a ghoulish face of doom, a giant ogre with sunken lumps of skin, barely allowing his eyes to be visible. His feet were divided into what looked like hooves, horns protruding across his body. Mota turned away, wailing and groaning uncontrollably.

Throwing his hands in the air in frustration, Myesmoth walked away towards some of the demons that waited in hiding. Astaroth's eyes were beady, and orange. He stepped forward menacingly towards Mota but Myesmoth held out his huge arm.

"Don't do anything stupid," he said, blocking Astaroth's path.

"The fool will give away our position," Astaroth said, his eyes blazing like fire.

"Mota was one of the dominions over the heralds. They had closest access to God. He's taking this… transition… with much difficulty."

"Aren't we all?" The spite was evident in Astaroth's voice.

"He will come to. He is a fearsome warrior indeed. Besides…" Myesmoth pointed at the other demons, "We are few and we need all the force we can muster."

"Well, give me one moment with him. There is something I must tell him," Astaroth said, "just one moment."

"Fine."

Astaroth strode over to Mota proudly, and whispered in his ear with Myesmoth watching his every move. The weeping demon seemed to recoil for a moment and then continued wailing, louder than ever."

Myesmoth stomped forward in anger and grabbed Astaroth by the throat. "What did you tell him?"

Astaroth raised his hands. "I said to him: there is no salvation for us. We have no chance at repentance." His words were like the finishing blow. The weight of their actions seemed to smother him. Myesmoth released the fallen angel and slumped on the white dust, his affliction gnawing deep within him.

All hope was lost. They were bound to a fate of eternal punishment. They had tasted of the waters and food of

Heaven. They had seen God's glory and the intensity of His might and yet, they had defied Him. Astaroth was right. They were hopeless, unable to return or repent and receive pardon for their sins. Even if they could somehow find their way back to Heaven, there was no second chance; there was no way they could enter the dwelling of Presence in their God-forsaken form.

Myesmoth lay flat, allowing the heat of the horrid place to burn his skin. He would welcome madness if it would ease the pain but that too was pointless. The only reality that they had now was one of chaos and ill. There was nothing to fight or exist for - only to live on the edge of madness. Let the mighty Mota weep. He also would abandon himself to his grief and be consumed by it.

The gates of Hades stood imposing like a fortress of ill, sinister and vast. Mealiel and Baeshedith descended quietly into the dusty terrain that led to the gigantic gates. It was at that moment that they saw a flash of light.

"Welcome to my abode." The voice was silky and strong, an embodiment of strong essence, vibrant in its turbulence. Mealiel's multiple eyes opened wide in shock. Baeshedith almost tripped on the rough terrain. "Lu..ci...fer? It can't be..."

The light suddenly flattened and faded. The darkness around them showcased the silent whisper of doom. They could see his features now. Mealiel's face twisted with a tortured look, taken aback by the hideous face and contorted body of the one who had once covered the throne.

"Lucifer, it is you. How did you do that?"

The devil's face was filled with hate as he spat. "Don't call me that. Do I still look like the dawn star to you? Have you not heard my new title? Satan - the one who opposes God. Anyway, what do you want?"

"A resting place, just like you." Mealiel's face darkened.

"There is none here," the devil said, turning in disgust to point at the towering gate that loomed over them. "He won't let us in."

"Who won't?" Mealiel cast a dejected look, weary of his demise after their casting out. "Which angel has claimed this land?"

"Ask him!" The devil stomped off sullenly towards the gate. Another spirit stood by in the darkness across the plains outside the gate of Hades. The sandy terrain was white and ashy, hot to touch.

Baeshedith knew who it was immediately. "Bael must have led Lucifer here."

"Just as we feared." Mealiel turned to his companion, who had taken a few steps away from him. "Who is lord of this land?

"Lurerdeth holds charge of the keys of Hades," Baeshedith responded, staring as Lucifer flexed his fists and pounded the gate repeatedly.

Mealiel was not satisfied. "What else do you know?" he probed, facing Baeshedith.

"Well, before the fighting began, Adriel did tell Lucifer that the keys were not made for any angelic being to control."

"What?" Mealiel's eyes rolled in wonder. For a moment he pondered, lost in thought, and then he looked towards the devil who was berating the guardian of Hades with all his malice. "Lucifer has gone mad."

"What are you going to do?" Baeshedith asked.

"We wait here and rest, for now. Well, until he finds his reason."

"We? I answer to no one anymore. I am lord of myself." Baeshedith frowned hatefully.

Mealiel strode to an ashen boulder and sat.

"I do not dispute that. You are lost and without purpose just like all of us. Besides, most of the angels know of this place from the babbling Bael so we can expect a major showdown soon."

Elzebur had allied with a band of angry spirits who had been quick to follow him after he wittingly promised them directions to Hades. As one of the devil's closest captains, he had told them he would lead them to a haven of rest. Many of his archers remained loyal to him, and others joined them as well.

From a distance, the band of spirits watched as Satan pounded on the gates of Hades.

"I think we should attack him now. We have the numbers," Deitriel said. A few other spirits nodded in agreement.

Elzebur was not too convinced. "Even in his fallen state, he is still dangerous."

"He is not representative of light nor rank. They have given him a new name - the one who opposes God. Accuser and Slanderer – Satan, also referred to as the devil."

"Regardless, he is dangerous." Elzebur spat out sulfur.

"Do you prefer to wander around aimlessly without purpose? This is prime land, and whoever controls it will be lord of the lower realms." Elzebur looked around as more of the angels grunted in approval. Deitriel was not even a part of his force and had been of lesser rank in Heaven; yet he was winning the argument. Elzebur made a mental note to deal with the meddling spirit later.

"I do not dispute that." Elzebur raised his hands, "I'm only expressing caution."

"I say let's attack," another spirit said.

Deitril's hand burst into a flame of greenish fire. "We take the gate and hold it until such time as we can find a way in." The demons cheered.

"Look!" Elzebur shouted, pointing. "Other spirits are attacking!" The demons looked down to see a huge wave of spirits descending unto the terrain of Hades, fire and sulfur spluttering about as they attacked the spirits at the front gate.

Deitriel grabbed Elzebur's arm. "Let us attack now. No other group will claim our spoils."

Elzebur nodded as the war-thirsty lot cheered. Deitriel spun as red smoke billowed around him.

"Take the gate!" he shouted before Elzebur could give the command.

The demons shot like arrows into the heart of the fight at the gates of Hades.

Lurerdeth sat behind the gate hearing the screams, curses, and fighting across the open terrain before the main gate. Face in his palms, the guardian of the keys learned the heavy truth. Satan and his minions had been banished and sought a place of refuge. Returning to the heavenly city had been his greatest longing but now, locked behind a wall separating him from fighting angry demons, he sobbed while quietly singing the praises of God.

In the melee of the fight, Satan became desperate, having successfully beaten off many of his former followers, yet he faced an onslaught of demons as more of them poured in. Without knowing who or what they were fighting for, the spirits tore at eachother, even as they advanced towards Satan. Then, he spotted Mealiel and swiped his huge fist across the demon's face, smashing him unto the white dust.

"Align with me!" he commanded, yet his huge red eyes looked almost imploringly at Mealiel.

Mealiel struggled to stand as Satan continued to fight, screaming a ferocious war cry that reverberated across the terrain. As the spirits fought, many of them tried to stay out of his way. Then, they heard a sound. A loud thumping sound hit the valley as a huge demon stepped in from the east side of the wall. The demon matched Satan in height.

"Lucifer! Satan! Liar! You will answer to me!" Myesmoth shouted. The devil looked up in dismay. Behind Myesmoth emerged two other demon warriors, Astaroth and Mota. Satan decided it was time to beat a hasty retreat. "Come with me," he shouted to Mealiel, stretching a gnarled hand. "They think you are with me anyways."

Mealiel thought quickly and realized that Satan had a point. He reached out as Satan grabbed his hand and burst into a column of fire, blazing a trail away from the ground he had once claimed.

The demons in front of the gate of Hades screamed in fiendish delight as Myesmoth saw his chance to claim some form of power.

"Rally to me! That liar led us to our demise. It is time to claim this place," he shouted. "Help me take this city. Break down the gate!"

The demons turned towards the gate, releasing all their vehemence and anger on the looming tower. But even with their relentless barrage at the gate, they could not break through, which frustrated them the more.

"Let me lead you and you will find me a better leader!" Astaroth screamed over the din.

"And I suppose you have a way to get into this place. Tell me, do you secretly possess the keys?" Myesmoth responded seething with rage. "I am stronger than most. I shall lead you all."

Many of the demons that had once been heralds rallied around Mota.

"No! We select Mota to lead us," one of them said.

"What?" Myesmoth said incredulously, "You pick that weakling, that sobbing relic?"

The insult stung Mota beyond what any of the demons could fathom. He released a fiersome cry and leaped forward, catching Myesmoth by surprise with an onslaught of heavy blows. Immediately, the demons loyal to Myesmoth attacked those who had joined forces with Mota. Astaroth's forces joined in, as the exasperated demons began to fight each other again.

A safe distance away, Satan and his new aide, Mealiel, continued on, the watcher demon acting as a guide through the darkness.

CHAPTER
—14—
CREATOR

At first, there was nothing; only pitch darkness in the outer realms far beneath the city of God. God proceeded through the void, set in His sovereign purpose to continue His divine work. A great distance from His manifest Presence, a company of warrior angels, cherubs and Seraphs were positioned across the lower channels at the foundations of the heavenly city. Michael allowed a small smile as he turned to observe the angels who stood behind him. He nodded to acknowledge Raphael who smiled back.

"Glad you are here, brother," Michael said quietly.

"Wouldn't miss it for anything," Raphael responded, "and our friend, Adriel, is here as well."

Michael reached out and greeted Adriel, almost chuckling at the beaming angel. "Heaven is grateful for your loyalty, Adriel. I am glad that you are past the horrors you faced."

"Thank you, captain. Heaven is peaceful and beautiful again. Everything is back as it should be."

"Is it?" Michael responded solemnly, "Nothing will ever be the same again as long as evil lurks. Yet, God continues His work and we must continue ours."

"Pay no mind to Michael," Raphael said playfully, "Allow us a moment to enjoy what is good."

"Still, we must remain vigilant," Michael responded. "I cannot help but feel that our inaction must have aided our fallen brother's cause. That mistake, we must never again repeat."

"You are right brother," Raphael said, "and I agree, our good work must not cease because evil abides."

Michael scanned across the opening expanse to the pitch-dark void, watching and waiting. Then he saw a flicker of light.

"Do you see that?" Michael said.

"Over there," one of his aides pointed.

Michael turned quickly to one of the watcher angels. "Can you see who it is?"

"It's Gabriel. He is signaling that the lower channels are clear. No demons lurking about. He is approaching."

"Good," Michael said. "It is about to begin."

In the clear expanse of space, God began His great work. The angels waited and watched with great anticipation and a lingering patience, knowing that they were about to behold a mighty wonder. There was a moment of quietness where everything in existence seemingly became mute. Then it began.

It started with a deafening roar as light revolved around the Creator. Blasts of light marooned the blank space, spinning wildly as lateral lines appeared, creating a blueprint. God set forth boundaries, forming a transcendent expanse beneath which He framed the foundations of a new world. At the base of the blueprint, God put in place the soil foundations of the earth, matted out in perfect order as He had pre-planned. Through the material of earth, water sprung forth across the expanse, bubbling cantankerously through channels God that had pre-formed into the earthen base. The ravenous water blossomed like a colossus of spiraling torrents, gradually rising in the shapeless void. The waters cast off a mournful, hollow tone as they became calm, tepid, dark, and then unmoving and lifeless. Channels of the heavenly paths were framed in perfect order, stretching for millions of miles above the shapeless mass. The waters covered the soil, its composition full of potential in its very makeup. As the waters calmed, the Spirit of God settled above the watery expanse, still in the darkness of the new world.

Then God spoke. "Let there be light."

Suddenly light materialized, activating the framework of visibility. The immaterial came into existence, illuminating the expanse of waters. Though lower in its intensity, compared to the light of God, the physical light lit up the entire expanse. God basked in the midst of it all, carefully inspecting it before drawing the light upwards at an angle. From the edge of the light, darkness manifested. The physical world was set and ready. Fully satisfied at His work, God called the light day and the darkness night.

The angels simply gawked with feverish delight as they watched from a great distance. Gabriel sped through the new heavens at blinding speed to reach Michael.

"All clear Michael, no trouble from any demons around here."

"What about the deeper places close to Hades?"

"I did not venture that low." Gabriel responded.

"Well, take a few warriors with you and secure the deeper places."

"Is this really necessary?" Gabriel asked, bemused.

"Ah, let them see the wonders of God," Raphael spoke up before Michael could respond. "Let them see and tremble."

"Nonetheless, we must be vigilant. I will go with you Gabriel if that gives you comfort," Michael said, as he turned his attention to the new planet before them. "So now, the heavens and the earth have been made. Amazing. Raphael, I leave you in command. Come, Gabriel, let us go."

"Lead the way, Michael" Gabriel responded as they both burst into light and descended.

The space above the earth was empty, but suddenly, the hand of God dropped with angst into the still waters and began to move in a circular motion. In response, the waters roared and began to swirl around at the base. God elevated the mass of water as it roared thunderously and He placed the waters far above the earth, setting the frame for the sky. The waters then morphed into minute drops, which congealed into a new structure, white and fluffy. And in that moment, God created the skies and the firmament.

A trio of demons lurked in the deeper places far beneath the circumference of the new earth, watching with great agitation as the wonder of creation came into its full swing. God was creating a new phenomenon that was fascinating in every respect. A scheduled order ruled by light to measure the passing of time. According to their findings, the new system of daylight had been two earth days. Bael and the other two demons watched, taking in as much as they could see from their hiding place. Sooner or later, they would have to move closer and risk being attacked to see the fullness of the astute wonder of what God was doing.

Oblivious to the enemy at the fringes, Michael's troops watched, transfixed by the detail of the new world. With great fortitude, God continued his work of creation and forcefully shifted the waters, causing large walls of liquid to form on the earthen base. Eventually, the base cleared as waters trickled off to the sides, revealing a hardened mass of soil – land. God framed the dry land in different sizes and shapes, casting a layer of heaps of terrains and plains, valleys, and hills.

"Do you see that?" Michael asked in awe as Gabriel kept speed with him. "Every bit of created mass was strewn together from the tiniest particles."

"Amazing workmanship…" Gabriel responded, quietly soaking in the wondrous sight. The wonderful terrains stretched throughout the planet blanketed by oceans and river ways, forming beautiful waterfalls and landfalls. The waters enveloped some portions of immense land, causing islands to emerge. Throughout the earth, channels of waters passed through the underbellies of the earth, set in perfect motion.

Michael shook his head in silent awe. "He speaks and it comes to pass."

"It is indeed amazing to behold. God is all-powerful," Gabriel responded and then pointed. "Look!" he said, 'It is a new earth day and He is speaking again."

God spoke again, and sure enough, vegetation, plants, and trees, each after its own kind, materialized. Multiple species of trees sprung out tall, their pines and diverse vegetation beautifying the earth. God was pleased with what He saw. Then with great articulation, He framed every single plant and tree into seed form, and scattered the seed across the earth in their predetermined locations. Even beneath the oceans and seas, God worked meticulously to establish what He had pre-imagined, putting in place the ecosystem of the new planet.

The angels heard a booming sound. Lights surged in jolts of energy, echoing across the expanse of the newly created universe. A convoluted body of lights spread in their framework, as even more body masses with lights of diverse sizes emerged from smaller, gaseous matter. The angels could not hold back their sheer excitement and some shouted praise and cheered as the universe lit up in a canvas of sparkling lights. Constellations of stars were born, and arrayed numerous galaxies; planets spread across the gargantuan universe, each with specific instructions given by their creator.

"Do you see what I see?"

"Lights," Michael nodded, wide-eyed at the spectacle before them. "Come with me." Michael beckoned to Gabriel.

"Do you not wish to scout the lower depths anymore?"

"I do but I must see these sights." Michael responded as the two captains proceeded through the new cosmos. Surrounding the angels were orbital lines that created a path for the lights God had made. The complex network of lines had been fused into a grand blueprint that God had established. Michael grinned. "This is interesting."

"I know," Gabriel responded, touching a portion of the celestial body. "They seem to come in pairs overlapping in perfect sequence."

"A new mystery. Their composition is stunning, but we will understand their make-up soon…and their purpose."

"Well, it's body is made of a different nature though we can see its spirit, or its source"

"The immaterial births the material." Michael said.

Gabriel saw the hand of God moving, and alerted Michael immediately. "Another wonder in the making. Look!"

At a great distance beyond, God began to form an immense ball composed of light and intense heat that was bigger than the earth itself.

"It's the Sun," Michael said.

Gabriel half-smiled. "You have seen the scrolls. Some of these things seem close in nature to what He has made back in the city."

"Yes, though I wonder which of us will govern this new world."

"Ah Michael, you are the very best of us. Surely the keys of this kingdom will be handed over to you."

"Will it? If this is indeed what Satan discovered in his search, then maybe not."

A look of curiosity spread over Gabriel's face. "I don't understand what you mean."

"Well," Michael said as more stars spread about the galaxy and planets were released into orbit, "he sought the keys of the kingdom so he could seize dominion. He said it was reserved for another."

"New angels?"

"I do not know, Gabriel. Regardless, I am content serving His will."

"We will find out soon…" Gabriel paused. "Michael, do you see that?"

A strange greenish light flickered in the distance beneath them. "Demons!" Michael muttered under his breath. "Do not let them know we have seen them."

Not far from the jubilant archangels, Bael watched fastidiously with his minions as Michael and Gabriel basked in the wonders of creation.

"Fools," Bael spat, "if they had come a little lower, they would have found us."

"Shall we retreat then?" one of the demons asked.

"No, how can we miss this? There is new terrain that we may have the opportunity to inspect soon. For now, they are distracted and we must stay and observe for as long as we can."

"We can hardly see all the wonders of His creation," another demon whined.

"Yes indeed. We must find a way to get closer. The knowledge we get from this is far too important and I would rather be here than fighting spirits aimlessly," Bael muttered. "There are six of us. We need a diversion."

With an evil smirk, Bael pointed at two of his minions, "You two, go attack the archangels and then head west when they chase after you."

The two demons hissed in frustration at the task but bowed and spread their gnarled wings. They pulled out their swords and sped upwards towards the archangels.

The galaxies were a complex array of celestial bodies that showcased God's perfect craftsmanship. Though dark and void in its original form, the new world was now lit like a dazzling canvas of glory. The universe was rich with diverse bodies of light; graceful light-bearing bodies radiating their luster and expressing the glory of the One who had made them.

"Light, be," He had said, and the universe obeyed. Multiple galaxies were set in their pre-made locations, established millions of light years apart. God framed the locations of frost and the inter-relationships of the elements forming newer compositions and crafting new chemical reactions.

The angels saw the workings of the spirit of the wind above the clouds, forming an assorted circular diagram. The orifices of the wind sources were placed at the four corners of the earth to usher in the movement of air and sound. Within the earth itself, God set the center of gravity, creating a force to hold all things to the foundations of the earth.

At the north end of the earth, farthest in its orbit around the sun, the wind encountered a strange cold atmosphere that was seemingly devoid of the heat of the sun. The whole environment was glazed in ice as the clouds began to form into snow that cascaded downward towards the closest portions of the earth.

Within that day, the orbit of the earth around the sun birthed the seasons and the times while underneath the earth, the water settled low. As the galaxy of the earth crooned and began to move in its first moments, God made other planets across the different galaxies of the universe and set them in motion, each to its own kind as He had intended. As evening settled into the new dawn, God's spirit stepped unto the earth again, sweeping through the clouds of the new earth.

"After them!" Michael bellowed ferociously swinging his sword and narrowly missing one of the demons that had attacked them. The whimpering demons sped away as the archangels pursued through the lower depths of the galaxy under the orbit of the new planet. As the archangels flew into the distance, Bael revealed himself moving closer to witness the wonders of creation that were before him. Bael's plan was working perfectly.

On the fifth day, God tirelessly continued the work of creation. The far distant galaxies exhaled with life and expression, a kaleidoscope of countless lights and reflections of lights. The glorious display was a majestic painting that appeared to be still from afar; but the gaseous balls of light were anything but static. All of them flashed across their paths in perfect harmony. God looked around and determined that the new world was finally ready for life.

He spoke again and Raphael and the angels heard a sudden flutter of wings break the silence as diverse species of winged creatures filled the air. The clouds disintegrated as life filled the heavenly skies and the creatures of flight spread their wings, spiraling around the glory of God. They spread into a mighty tower around the life force of God's presence, basking in His glory.

Beneath the winged creatures, the waters of the ocean began to bubble over and then, creatures of the deep spilled forth from the waters. From the largest to the smallest, the fish and other water creatures canvassed around God's glory. God looked at His work and blessed it; and then millions of water creatures set forth in different directions, exploring their new habitation.

"We're losing them," Michael shouted dejectedly as the fleeing demons increased the distance between themselves and the archangels.

"What earth day are we witnessing now?" Gabriel asked, turning his attention to the now distant planet earth.

"The fifth day is just about ending."

"At least, the fallen are far from the awesome work of creation. But I wonder how much they have seen and what they will try to do with the information"

Michael signaled and the two angels stopped, hovering in mid-space.

"Look, Michael, look!" Gabriel exclaimed.

In the distance, a gigantic dragon-like creature spewed fire on fleeing demons. In the same instant, a company of demons swooped in, swiping at the huge demon. The angry spirits brawled, spitting and screaming curses as more joined the fighting from different directions.

The two angels watched in abject shock as the third heaven was covered with fighting demons.

Michael turned away. "Let us get away from here while we can."

"Yes."

Michael and Gabriel sped away towards the earth, putting some distance between themselves and the third heavens.

CHAPTER

—15—

ADAM

On the sixth day, God said, "Let the earth bring forth living creatures after their kind: cattle and creeping things and beasts of the earth after their kind." The earth erupted with a cacophony of sound as creatures sprung from the earth at God's command. Diverse animals emerged from the soil of the new earth and cried out in praise to the Creator.

Tall, small, and even minute creatures came into existence, each carefully crafted. Each kind had their own intelligence, instincts, and unique abilities.

God inspected his work with the attention of a skilled appraiser and He nodded, pleased with the results.

The Author of Life basked in the beauty of the earth, inspecting His work. God set His laws to guide every single particle and their inter-relations with other particles - a well thought out colossus of inventions only made possible by a supremely intelligent being.

Fully satisfied with His work, God turned His attention to a very special task. He said, "Let us make man in our own image, in our likeness and let them have dominion over every creature…"

"Come quickly," Mealiel said urgently to Satan as the last of their attackers fled. "You need to see this."

"How can we go any closer if these puny demons keep attacking us?" Satan grunted, "and what about Michael and Gabriel?"

"They have returned to the earth. I'm not asking you to go witness creation. I have sent Bael to spy out what is happening on the earth. Those two you attacked were with him."

"How was I supposed to know that?" Satan spat out sulfur. "I thought they were attacking me."

"Nonetheless, there is good news. Most of the warring factions have migrated from the gate of Hades since creation began. It will be the safest place to hide for now. Most of the faction leaders have lost interest anyway. As long as those gates remain shut, no one will attempt to fight over Hades. Shall we return?"

"I grow tired of wandering in the darkness. Let us return and begin building our army again. I hope that Bael's report will be useful."

The glory of God filled the atmosphere as the Creator made a creature that was fashioned after His likeness. God, in His fiery essence, reached for the soil with hands in the likeness of wisps of light, entrenching them deep into the earth. Poised like an artist in His immaculate benevolence,

God molded the frame of the being. Slowly, carefully and intricately, God made the one He called Adam with every organ and tissue according to their specific purpose - a nose, a mouth, hands, legs; the Creator had carefully thought out His creation.

Michael and Gabriel rejoined the angels as they watched the beauty of creation. "Come, brothers. Come and witness this amazing wonder of God," Raphael said, welcoming them with open arms, "...but was there any trouble below?"

"You have no idea," Gabriel responded quietly. "Demons fighting demons. Chaos."

"Hmm," Raphael sighed and then smiled almost immediately. "This seems like the grand finale. Look! A new creature made in the image and likeness of God."

"Must be the ones who have been promised the keys of the kingdom from the foundations of the world," Adriel said. The three captains turned to observe him.

"Continue," Michael said.

"Well, they are to extend God's dominion in this realm. The very hands of God have written this before time began." Michael and Gabriel exchanged glances. "Mankind. Made from the soil of the earth."

"This is remarkable," Raphael exclaimed. "Made from dust."

The angels watched in the distance with abject awe and wonder. The lifeless body lay upon the earth as light covered the expanse of the land. Leaning over the man, God breathed into the body and immediately, the organs in the man's body came to life. His chest began to heave upwards and downwards, and in that dramatic moment, he came to life.

The man opened his eyes and had to cover them immediately as the light of God canvassed in front of him. God withdrew for a moment as the first man lay in the dirt of the ground awakening to his new home. Fully intelligent and aware, he tried to sit, up transfixed by the presence of his maker. God smiled with unreserved joy and love.

"Welcome, Adam."

Adam acknowledged the greeting and wanted to kneel down in total surrender. Instinctively, he knew he was before God, his creator.

In that instant, the angels behind Michael let out a shout of praise. The angels chorused thier cheers, singing and shoutin, and releasing torrents of lights and tremors throughout the heavens. Michael raised his hand quickly.

"Oh let them shout!" Raphael nudged Michael and laughed heartily, "Let them give praise."

"Yes! You are right, Raphael. The existence of evil must never cause good to be silent." Michael pulled out his sword and lifted it high, "The Lord is just and mighty!"

"The Lord is strong and mighty!" The angels chorused in unison.

> *The Lord is strong and mighty*
> *The Lord is just and gracious*
> *Great and mighty is He*
> *He made the heavens and the earth*
> *And released the lights into the universe*
> *He made the sun, the moon and the stars*
> *The greater to govern the day*
> *And the lesser to govern the night*
> *He made the creatures of flight*
> *And the creatures of the waters*
> *The crawling and creeping*
> *Both the tall and the short*
> *He made them all*
> *For His glory*
> *For His good pleasure*
> *His abundance has been made manifest*
> *His love abounds over the earth*
> *Creation displays His majesty*
> *He made man from the soil of the earth*
> *And put His breath in him, the very breath of life*
> *And man lives, a living soul*
> *The Lord is mighty*
> *The Lord is great."*

"Your name is Adam," God said lovingly.

The knowledge of God filled the man's heart as he trembled at the intense power around him. Yet, the light did not hurt him. It warmed his body and covered him, slowly guiding him to his feet. Light wrapped around Adam like a sheet of silk, embracing his frame until he began to glow with the very light of God.

"Welcome to your home," God said. "This place, this world, I have made for you to live in, and to thrive." Adam simply nodded as he began to attempt walking; suddenly he wanted to try everything. God laughed as Adam ran around the level plain jumping and leaping, doing a merry dance of joy.

"Come. We have work to do." God said.

"Okay, Father," Adam responded as he watched the animals walking around, acknowledging his presence. Across the skies, the birds fluttered around, as everything that drew breath seemed to be drawn to the aura of God. God measured out a portion of land as Adam went to explore one of the rivers closest to him. He leaned close and touched the water as he saw different species of fish swarm around his hand. They were beautiful indeed, and he wasted no time in stepping into the water, slowly at first. The water warmed his ankles as he went deeper. He was lord of the rivers and everything that God had made on this planet.

Bael and his minions blinked feverishly watching the new man as everything began to fall in place in his mind. So this was the creature. Bael was amazed at the innocence of the man, and the immense authority he carried. Creation seemed to acknowledge his every move. The animals honored him and the waters caressed his frame as he bathed in the river.

At the other side of their position, oblivious to their presence, the angels continued to render praise to God. Bael almost squealed from the nagging pain he felt in that moment. The more he watched, envy rose within him. A greenish tear trailed down Bael's face. Why did God dote over this man with such intense love and care? The very expression of divine love that the angels had never experienced was being poured out over man. Bael could not understand it.

As Adam busied himself in the water, God began to plant a garden. He caused the trees to grow from the soil, accelerating the process of their growth. Diverse types of trees and plants sprung forth from the soil in an instant. Their fruits glittered across the beautiful garden. Adam arose from the water to the amazing sight. Mouthwatering fruits in diverse colors, shapes, and sizes surrounded him.

"Come eat." The hand of God carried Adam and placed him in the garden. Adam needed no second bidding. He dashed towards a tree and took one of the fruits, sinking his teeth deep into it. Its sweetness seemed to explode within his mouth, tantalizing his senses and rendering him giddy with delight.

Strength coursed through his bones, giving his body energy and life. He grabbed another fruit from a different tree and tasted it. An entirely different taste filled his mouth, yet just as precious a taste to savor as the former. The creatures of the earth came in mass around the Father and the man, drawn by the aroma of the fruits of the garden.

God then led Adam into the heart of the garden. In the center, there stood two trees that looked slightly different from the other trees in the garden. One of the trees was white with huge, strong, green leaves, and light shimmering around it from its top to its roots.

"This is the tree of life." God told Adam. Adam observed the tree, as it stood majestic and strong, towering over the other trees around the sacred grove. Birds spiraled like a column of moving mass around the top of the tree. The foliage around the roots of the tree glimmered with the light from the tree, their leaves rich and colorful.

"It's beautiful." Adam exclaimed.

The fruits of the tree were whitish, casting off the look of orbs of light. Spread across the branches of the tree, the fruits were arrayed like flickering flames, beautiful to behold.

"Adam," God spoke the name in a silent whisper. "There is something important that you must remember." Adam nodded, as the light of the sun created beautiful rays of light that protruded from the branches of the trees.

"Of every tree in this garden, I have given to you for food." Adam smiled, happy and content. "But this tree...," God continued as Adam shifted his gaze to the tree that flanked the tree of life. Its trunk was equally wide and strong, and its branches stretched out like huge, flailing arms.

The fruit of the tree were almost a translucent color, connected to strong twigs. This tree cast a light that moved in cinders of tremors, powerful and strong. "This is the tree of the knowledge of good and evil. You must not eat of this tree for in the day that you do, you will surely die."

Looking up at the tree, Adam did not perceive that there was anything sinister about the tree. "Good and evil," he muttered, taking a step back from the tree. The glory of God surrounded his frame as God lovingly guided him from the grove. As they walked, the sun set across the west, and the nocturnal animals chorused with different sounds. God showed Adam a bed of wool under a group of low hanging trees. The hanging vines made for a warm place to sleep. Adam crawled in as the leaves around him warmly caressing his frame.

"Tomorrow, I will bring the animals to you so you can give them names."

Adam nodded. "Yes, Father." Content, fulfilled, and joyful, he and God discussed the detail of the work he was to do. The Creator and the created enjoyed each other's company, talking about the earth and the many wonders of creation late into the night. Adam eventually slipped into his first sleep, and the Spirit of God ascended from the earth.

Millions of miles beneath the earth's foundation, through the darkness of the deep and the outer shell of the heavens, Bael and his fellow spies descended unto Hades, whipping crazily through the channel of the stars and the constellations of the mighty celestial lights. They journeyed to find Satan and Mealiel, who had returned after the fighting factions had moved on in search of other places of rest.

Seated beside Satan outside the gate, Mealiel pounded his fists in disappointment. "Took him long enough."

Satan moved forward, "What news?" he asked, rudely

shoving Mealiel aside. "What news, I said?"

Bael's greenish eyes lit up with a strange light. "You should see it," he said, spreading out his arms excitedly. "It is beautiful - this new world. This Earth." He was giddy with delight.

"Will you stay still and speak?" Satan was not in the mood.

Bael's face glistened slightly as a star passed by in the far distance "You have to see it for yourself," he said, spreading his arms wide. "I tell you this. It is different. The whole cosmos... the very universe with lights... new spirits..." His voice trailed off.

"Like us? Do they speak?" Satan asked, hanging on to every word.

"They carry light like God, a special kind of course. These beings are fiery and huge, like gigantic balls of gushing flame and heat. They are obedient to their purpose." Bael paused to see how his audience was taking in all he was saying. He reveled in his newfound knowledge.

He continued with pomp like an orator, "I have seen the lights, the firmament, the sun and the moon, the earth filled with a new type of creature, Man. We witnessed it, from a distance of course, but who can hide such beauty? The elements are not made of the same framework as we are, though they seem a prototype. There are similarities."

"A world of shadow and mimic," Satan grunted. "A physical world."

Mealiel turned to observe Satan. "What do you know of this?"

"There is a place where a powerful force called wind exists..." Bael was not about to lose the attention he was getting. "I have seen where it is born, and begins its travel through the earth, and yes, there is a schedule of heat and cold, all working in tangent to bring about the will of their Master on the earth."

Satan turned away sullenly, and then smiled bitterly. "An ancient plan, timeless in its working," he crooned, almost chuckling. "He is proceeding without fear of interference." Satan looked upwards, beholding the distant lights moving across the galaxy. "Who is the proud one now? Answer me, Lord of Light! Who is the proud one now? Have you learned nothing yet?"

Mealiel was exasperated. "Who are you speaking to?"

Satan became quiet, a yellowish tear slowly streaking down his contorted face. "Where is Baeshedith? He is with us, isn't he?"

"Still scouting what is now called the third heaven for recruits. He has sent two to me. You have to realize rebuilding your army will not be easy. Astaroth has gone far away with his forces and Myesmoth has set dominion in the far east of the dark realms - a poultry force. There are others scattered into smaller groups but there is no clear leader."

"Chaos." Satan said.

"There are many who seek revenge against you," Bael said bitterly, upset to have lost his stage. "Best you stay in hiding."

"I am not afraid," Satan sneered. "No one dares fight me."

"That would be every one of the fallen," Bael said. "You deceived us all."

"No, you chose your path and now you suffer the consequences. I have no intention of justifying or explaining my actions to you. The most important thing right now is finding out what God is doing with His creation. I must see this new world and learn all its secrets."

"I will go with you," Mealiel said, stepping forward. "It is boring and hot here. Besides you need me to watch out for your enemies."

Satan nodded flatly. "Bael, you may stay here if you wish, and keep rebuilding our forces with Baeshedith."

Bael nodded, content for the moment to be under Satan's charge. Unlike the others, regardless of the tragic results of his failed rebellion, Satan had a deep cunning that could prove useful in the near future.

Days after his work of creation, God entered the garden to meet with Adam.

"Father," Adam said heartily as God's frame extended a hand and enveloped Adam's hand.

"What have you been doing?" God asked.

"Look around, Father, I have been working as You asked. I have also been giving names to these beautiful animals as you bring them to me." The glory of God covered Adam, drawing him close.

God smiled. "Come my child, I think it is time that you got some help. It is not good that you are alone."

The two proceeded through the garden, as God led him

through a path to a clear expanse. God touched Adam's head and guided his body to the ground as Adam fell into a deep sleep. It was time to make Adam's companion - a woman.

CHAPTER
—16—
ETERNAL
CONSPIRACY

*"*Why did we worship? What was the qualification?"
Satan asked pointedly. His once silver eyes were now
yellow and sickly as they watched, a great distance from
the garden. "Did we not render words of adulation based
on His glory and the majesty of His Presence? Now you say
He has made two beings with ability to relate with Him on
a deeper level. Are you sure this is what you are seeing?"

"I tell you, these creatures are communing with him. They seem like they are in deep conversation like… like friends." Mealiel responded dejectedly. "This is a greater slap than the recoiling visage of our bodies."

"A divine affront to our existence," Satan sneered back. "He is not only trying to humiliate us with His new pet project. This new Earth; this new world! This new being... Man." The fallen lord spat the last word out with disgust and rage. A sore repugnance had grown within him as he saw the beauty of the earth.

"Better to dwell far from them… from objects of love that give us such grave pain. See how He spends time talking to them." Mealiel's multiples eyes wafted in different sizes as he took in the sight.

Satan shrugged defiantly and took a step forward. "I must draw nearer to see this. First, one; and now He makes a second. Soon they will spread abroad this new world. I would go closer though I fear they must be well guarded."

"Hmm. My eyes see no guardians, nor warriors of Heaven."

"Impossible!" Satan was shocked. Mealiel turned one of his large yellow eyeballs to observe Satan's repulsive face. "No angel can hide from my sight. I have not lost my powers or skill from preceding purpose."

"It is a trick!" Satan bellowed with impunity. "He seeks to lure us into a trap!"

"Quiet! Keep your voice down." Mealiel warned. "Wait! I think… He is leaving."

The glory of God's divine presence rose quietly from the beautiful garden. Creatures bowed in acknowledgment of their Maker as He rose from His fellowship with Adam and Eve, returning to the heavenly kingdom, emitting a formidable and sprightly radiance. God disappeared from the sight of the man and woman, who held hands as they beheld the wondrous sight. Their skin glowed with the residue of God's presence.

Adam held Eve's hand and then he playfully swept her off her feet. Her eyes were like pearls framed from jasper, and her hair was like a verdure of rich, silky black, cascading like a stream around her neck. When she laughed, it was like the sound of the rivers flowing east of Eden. He loved her and she loved him; and all was beautiful and peaceful.

When he had woken from his sleep, he saw her and was speechless. He knew immediately who she was. "Woman," he had said. She was beautiful to behold. Adam had reached for his side and smiled. "You are the bone of my bones, and the flesh of my flesh." Eve had blinked, staring into his eyes with a quiet smile appearing on her face as she observed the man. Adam had looked towards God and said, "She will be called Woman, because she was taken out of man."

Together, they proceeded towards the north of the garden where Adam had found pleasant flora that spread its wooly leaves over them. This was home and their garden responded to their every move. They held each other, enjoying the music of the sweet dripping rivers and watching the distant stars twinkle merrily in far off galaxies. They loved this life as they drank in the nectar of life. Slowly, in fullness of health, life and joy, they slept.

The slits of the evil one's eyes moved feverishly. He had finally summoned enough courage to come much closer. No guards. No angels with flaming weapons. No meddling cherubs. With his ever mercurial attitude, the devil crept closer and closer until he could see them covered up in the gigantic leaves of the Teribinth tree.

Light shone forth laxly around them as they rested in blissful sleep. They had the blessing of God. There was security, peace, and divine alignment with the order and purpose of God. They were favored; lords of this earth in direct dominion of everything God had made. They had a fellowship and a deeper relationship with the Father than any angel had ever even imagined having.

Satan moved closer to the garden as he pondered. Who were they to deserve such? Who were they, in their pale frailty, to enjoy the very unique and singular Presence of God? The concept was intriguing like a reckless gambit, or a sincere error. How could He allow them to live alone, knowing that fallen angels abounded in the third heavens? Knowing that he, Satan, still skulked around.

Satan pondered on the thought. There had to be a catch. It seemed all too simple. He had to figure out what God's plan was for these beings called 'Man'. He had to understand the divine purpose for their creation, which, at that moment, he could not fathom. For now, he was content to simply watch them and hate them for their peace. They had a precious beauty he could never have again.

Mealiel, the demon watcher, stayed far from the garden to ensure there would be no ambush by guardian angels, or the archangel Michael himself. All the while that Satan stayed close to the man and woman, there was no single intrusion. A few of the banished spirits flew around occasionally, but none came close to the vicinity of the new earth. They hovered mainly in the third heaven, wailing and cursing, yet their chaos was distant from the peaceful scenery of love that was before them.

Mealiel himself felt no loyalty to the humbled Satan. Because of him, they were now disconnected from the God of life. Their punishment was enough to drive them mad and indeed, it seemed madness that the ever-scheming evil one was trespassing into the hallowed grove where the new creature, made in the likeness of God, dwelt.

Mealiel myriad of eyes blinked voraciously as they protruded out of charred, leathery skin. His hatred of himself and Satan helped him to stay sane. They had been subjected to a living death – a state that was entirely inconceivable in the moments when they walked the streets of Heaven, but this had become their reality for all eternity. He half-wished a few angels, mighty and powerful, would suddenly appear to hinder Satan but nothing happened. That night, as the sun receded and the moon appeared, Satan and his watcher lurked in the garden's environs, studying their fascinating prey. Fascination mixed with jealously. Their hatred was enough fuel for their little game of espionage.

The two fallen angels learned more about the man and woman without a moment's pause throughout the next day. They had risen early and gone to the river. The man had jumped in recklessly and the water embraced him, massaging his frame, with a bubbly torrent rejoicing at its master. The woman had also joined him and they seemed lost in the sweetness of their companionship. After bathing, Eve gathered fruits for their morning feast. They sat and ate, biting gratefully into the juicy and healthy fruits, allowing the fresh aroma to fill their nostrils and the juice to stream down from their mouths unto to their necks. They were filled with energy for the day's tasks. Eve began to care for the animals while Adam headed northwards of the garden to tend the plants. He untwined figs, and straightened limbs, carefully preparing the moist and living earth to take in new seed to expand the garden.

"How close can we stay when He comes?" Mealiel asked Satan, later that evening. He seemed unconvinced. "I don't like it one bit. What type of creatures are they?"

Satan paused before answering. The two spirits proceeded across the distant plain mountains. There was new vegetation here and there, as they highlighted upon a hill with red sand and revealed their forms. Satan leaned and sniffed about, deep in thought as he manipulated the soil. He observed the particles for a moment.

"A few things I have learned," he said. "They possess a body that is necessary for living in this particular planet, but they are spirit like us on their inside."

Mealiel nodded. "Yes... yes... I noticed. They seem docile."

Satan sprang up as if stung startlingly by the giant watcher. "Yes! Docile. Peaceful... good. The very expression of His goodness; untainted, unspoiled, holy, clean..."

"Something we can never be... again," Mealiel said sourly, regret heavy in his tone. The beings eyed one another feeling hate and envy. Mealiel continued, his tone soaked with regret. "You brought this on us, you foolish angel."

"I was tricked!" Satan growled. "Do you think I saw this coming?"

"You challenged Him! You challenged the One who holds all..."

"Shut your mouth!" Satan bellowed, his eyes bursting into flames of light, and his torso expanding into a ball of fire with sulfur spewing around the edges. "This isn't over! The war is not over! I will cause His most treasured, most loved creation to hate Him. I will influence their will and steal their power. I will drive them to insanity and corrupt their goodness. I will taint their connection to Him and sever them from the hand of God. I will bring ill, death, and pain to them. I will drive them mad enough to curse their maker."

Mealiel skulked back, far from the raging spirit, the incarnate spawn of doom. There was no reasoning with his pride and anger when he was provoked. Lightning struck across the sky and Mealiel watched in the far distance as the glory of God rose from the earth and ascended into the heavens. He had ended His visit and was leaving them for the time being. Mealiel looked down in amazement. Satan was pounding his wings heading towards the garden again. In mute horror, Mealiel spread his eroded wings and plunged down the hill after him.

Mealiel caught up with Satan at the edge of the garden. Satan turned to him. "I'm going in."

"Are you mad?" Mealiel responded.

"He put the tree in there."

"What?" Mealiel asked.

"You slow witted creature," Satan spat. "He put the tree of the knowledge of good and evil in the garden."

"That is not possible." Mealiel responded in disbelief. "To what purpose? Why?"

"Either a game of cosmic proportions, or the biggest folly of eternity." The devil stepped forward, moving slowly through the garden towards the center. "But, we shall find out."

"It makes no sense at all. Pause to reason before you land us into another disaster."

Satan paused and glowed with pride and anger yet again, but he remained tame. "No, this is simple, really. They have to choose."

"No." Mealiel remained unconvinced. "This is more of your madness."

Not far from the two evil spirits, Eve chased Adam around a huge tree. He ran through the green foliage past her trailing arms as they laughed heartily.

"I am not mad," Satan turned again with a cruel gleam in his eyes. "I have a plan." Satan touched the tree of the knowledge of good and evil and looked at the fruits hanging from it. All around them, other trees bore fruit as well, ripe, luscious, and beyond any doubt, sweet and nourishing to taste.

"This tree," Satan said, caressing the trunk of the tree, "poses a crossroads for the man and woman. He has asked them not to eat of its fruit. The only condition He has given to them."

"And the tree of life?" Mealiel asked.

"No, they have access to that even if they have not eaten of it yet. I mean, of what use is that when they have no fear of death or pain?"

"So that's your big plan." Mealiel did not hide his sarcasm. "You get them to eat the fruit."

"From a tree he has marked as forbidden?"

Satan cast a weary look at his companion. "I do not have to explain myself to you."

"No you don't... but I have been your closest ally from the beginning of this war and I will stay close to you because of those irritable marauding spirits."

"You will be well rewarded."

"Your plan is filthy and useless. You get them to disobey God and then what next?"

"I do not know but I would trade anything to see what He does when He realizes His new creation is not worth the value of the angels He has lost through my uprising."

Mealiel tapped Satan's arm. "Let us leave. Our presence sours the grove." Sure enough, many of the animals in garden sensed darkness around the center of Eden and stayed away.

Satan finally turned away. "We will come back when I finalize my strategy." He paused. "Wait! Baeshedith mentioned that we could not handle the power of the keys."

"Yes, they are reserved for a special being."

"I have questions for the keeper of secrets."

"He will not open Hades to you." Mealiel shook his head. "What makes you think he will speak to you?"

"I will have to try," Satan said and paused as light filled the grove, piercing the darkness as the moon loomed silently in the sky. Adam and Eve stepped into the center of Eden.

"Ah, the forbidden tree. Now, I understand why even the animals do not come near it." Eve said smiling. "Come, Adam. Let us go to sleep." Satan groaned as the man and woman left.

"Did you feel their power? So much authority," Mealiel said, struggling to stand. The light from the man and woman had burned them both, just as they had suffered at their casting out from Heaven. Satan recoiled at the expression of raw power that the humans emitted. The grace of God covered them like a fiery enclosure, impossible to penetrate. He could see that they embodied their Father exactly, even in frame and form. They even personified His authority and dominion. Satan clasped his chest feeling a sickening depression as he remembered his former glory. Without even trying, the humans' elicited more respect than that which he had once received from angels.

Mealiel spread his wings. "I am getting out of here. It is too dangerous."

Satan did not respond immediately. He just walked quietly with his head bowed, deep in thought as smoke emanated from his charred body. At the edge of the garden, he finally spoke. "How do I speak to them? All I need is a way to communicate directly with them."

"Maybe you need a more beautiful face before you approach them." Mealiel said, ducking quickly as Satan tried to swing a blow at him. Mealiel raised his hands in surrender but at that moment, Satan looked past him and quietly brushed him aside.

"What's this?"

Mealiel's gaze followed Satan's gnarled finger as he pointed towards the ground. He gasped. Peering up at them intently was a beautiful creature. Its eyes were shiny, round orbs embedded in the sides of its slim head. It had scales that shimmered, reflecting the soft light of the moon. The beautiful creature slithered on the ground, and then it stood erect on the rear tip of its body, looking in their direction with a strange calm. Satan met the creature's gaze. It reminded him of a part of his character that he could not really place.

Mealiel whispered urgently to Satan. "Does it want something?"

"He obviously cannot see us, unless..." Satan responded moving closer.

"No, do not reveal your true form," Mealiel cautioned.

Defiant but quick witted, Satan knew his assistant spoke the truth. "Can you see the creature's composition?" he asked. Mealiel nodded warily. The devil was standing directly in front the creature's face. "Let me see if I can interact with it from this realm," he said, reaching stealthily for the creature.

The serpent simply stood waiting, its eyes blinking. Satan touched the serpent, expecting the creature to resist his evil but it did not. Slowly, he drew it close to himself, blending with its frame and merging his essence with the creature. Suddenly, he could see through the eyes of the serpent and control it's movement. He now had his perfect cover to interact with the man and woman.

"I don't understand at all." Mealiel looked on in shock. He looked at the serpent as it looked directly at him; then he saw Satan's eyes and knew immediately. Satan had done the unthinkable. "You are within its core?" he asked.

The serpent's mouth opened and spoke with a hissy, raspy voice, "Yes, I am within it. You can say I possessed it. Stay away, but keep a watchful eye in case our enemy visits."

With that, Satan, in his new form, crept quietly through the garden, seeking an opportunity through which he could speak to Adam and Eve.

CHAPTER

—17—

SIN

⬡

The days turned into weeks and Adam continued his work of naming the animals as God brought them to him. Adam and Eve were always fascinated by the animal's antics. Each was unique, and diverse beyond description. From the docile lambs to the larger creatures - immense beasts of the field, yet loving and tender - each enjoyed the company of the man and woman. The animals acclimated to the earth, finding and creating habitations for themselves, and eating of the fruits of the trees.

There was abundance and absolutely no lack. The man and woman had peace and tranquility as they enjoyed all that God had put on the planet for their complete satisfaction. In the evenings, Adam and Eve would visit the rivers and bathe in thier waters. The dolphins would leap through the surface of the waters; and in the distance, the gigantic whale would occasionally shoot up horrendous torrents of water. Sometimes, Adam and Eve would throw fruits into the waters, watching as the fish leaped out to catch them.

They were very fond of each other. They would wander through the forest with God as He taught them and showed them different things. They would ask questions and He would lovingly answer. God showed them how to plant seeds in the earth. It was almost an instant process in the garden as within hours, life would spring forth from the seed and the plant would begin to blossom. The divine energy around the planet was strong and responsive.

Everything grew and waxed strong, without any delay or contamination. There was no sickness, no pain or fear, and no doubt or anxiety about anything. As the days passed, Adam kept himself busy, cultivating and tending the garden as God had taught him. Adam and Eve would take long walks during the day but they always knew where to meet their Father once the morning was over.

As the new day came, God would descend into the garden and commune with them. Adam and Eve would bow before Him and talk to Him. God would teach them about the secrets of the planet and He would laugh when Adam named the animals. Whatever he called them was what their names would be.

"You must pass this knowledge and wisdom on to your offspring," God said.

"What will they look like?" Eve asked, winking at Adam.

God smiled. "I made you in my image and likeness. You are my representation. Your offspring will be just as you are, only they will be small at birth and they will gradually grow to become like you as the days pass."

Eve nested her head on Adam's chest as they sat under a huge poplar tree while God taught them.

"Everything that has life in this world produces according to their kind. I have made it so. The animals produce their kind and you will produce your kind. Ensure that you give your children names as well. Whatever you name a thing is what it is. Be mindful of the names you give your offspring."

The man the woman listened aptly, soaking in every word from God.

Eve placed her hand on her stomach. "Life carrying life," she whispered, lost in thought. She looked upwards at Adam's face but he had dozed off. The glory of God faded from her sight. She could see the stars twinkling through the leaves of the tree.

Eve stood up quietly, taking great care not to wake Adam. She walked through the grass and played gently with the plants as they leaned towards her to feel the tip of her fingers while she brushed past them. She looked up at the stars, numerous and uncountable. She wondered at how big the stars were. God had told them that some of the tiny, shiny things were large in size than their world.

She was amazed by the awesomeness of their planet and what was in store for them. Full of curiosity, she formed a circle with two of her fingers and peeped through to see the stars. She kept looking up as she walked until she suddenly felt moist soil at her feet. Eve realized that she had walked towards one of the rivers that flowed through the Garden of Eden. She stooped at its edge, curling up to enjoy the calm waters, and she laughed gently at the far away glow-fish that spiraled in the water. It was a beautiful sight indeed. A drizzle of rain began to fall quietly, through the garden and beyond. Suddenly, Eve looked up and around. She thought she had heard something peculiar.

"Eve."

"Adam?" She called out. She smiled. "Adam, where are you?" Getting up, she ran through the garden, expecting Adam to appear and playfully grab her. When she had reached the center of the grove, she stopped abruptly. "Adam, where are you?" she called out a second time. She surveyed the area with her eyes, and then, she saw a creature slithering down the trunk of a tree.

"Oh," she muttered to herself, "I thought I heard my husband." She was about to turn away when she heard a mysterious, raspy voice.

"It is I, not Adam."

Eve turned in surprise. "One creature that speaks at last! Why did you say nothing when God brought you to Adam to be named?"

"I was in awe and speechless in His presence," the serpent responded, moving closer. "We lesser creatures must know our place."

"Know your place?" Eve said laughing. "What do you mean?

"What? God hasn't told you this? Has He told you nothing of power and might?"

"Father has told us many things."

"Apparently, He reserved some of the good information."

"Like what? I don't think that is true. He has taught us many things."

"Oh yes, I know, but I am privy to much wisdom and knowledge. I have learned many things and I can show you."

Eve began to feel slightly uneasy, but she kept a straight face. "Well, I have to return to Adam."

"I'm here," Adam said, stepping into the moonlight. "I wondered where you went." He said putting his arm around Eve as he observed the serpent with great curiosity. "You speak?" Adam asked, surprised.

"I was surprised as well," Eve said, spreading her hands.

"Yes," the serpent said, moving towards the two trees in the center of the grove. "Did God actually say not to eat of any tree in the garden?" Adam and Eve followed slowly uneasy that the serpent was going towards the forbidden tree.

"Of course we may eat of the trees of the garden, however God told us not to eat of that tree, not to even touch it or else, we will die." Eve responded pointing to the tree of the knowledge of good and evil.

The serpent flickered its forked tongue as it hissed. "You will not surely die," Satan said through the serpent. "God knows that your eyes would be open and you would be like Him, knowing good and evil. You will become wise."

Adam gasped as the serpent slid around the trunk of the tree. Eve looked towards the tree, and then at Adam. Then, she took a step away from him. The tree of the knowledge of good and evil stood strong and tall, its branches bearing precious fruits that radiated with beautiful colors. It looked desirable indeed. She thought about what the serpent had said. They could actually become wise. She contemplated the idea, imagining what it would be like to understand the depths of the mysteries that she and Adam had simply stood in awe of from the beginning of their existence. She reasoned within herself. *It would not hurt to be wise like God.* Finally, Eve stretched out her hand out slowly towards the fruit of the tree as Adam held his breath.

"Eve," he muttered, as her hand touched the fruit. Adam remembered God's initial warning about the tree. He looked around, wondering if something would happen to them abruptly. Nothing. They could only hear the constant singing and chirping of the animals.

The serpent paused as well, anticipating an onslaught of the angels of God, swooping in through the skies to save the man and woman. Nothing. Eve looked at the fruit again and wondered at their beauty. The more she gazed at them, the more the thought of being wise took root within her heart. Adam wanted to step forward and stop her. He wanted to question the speaking creature.

"Eve, do you feel anything? Are you okay?" Adam asked, concerned.

"I am... okay," Eve responded reflectively. "I'm fine."

Slowly, she plucked the fruit and gawked as the serpent's words rang in her ears. Adam watched silently, the feeling of dread growing in his heart. He attempted to console himself. Maybe God would be pleased that they desired to become wise, he thought, watching as Eve slowly moved the fruit to her lips.

"So, this will make us wise," she said, caressing the fruit. "Look, Adam, this fruit will make us like God. Doesn't the thought appeal to you?"

"Yes it does... but I am concerned that Father may be displeased with us," Adam responded.

"To be wise is good," the serpent hissed. "That, after all, is the only thing that He keeps from you. True knowledge. Why do you think He made you in the first place? Or even more importantly, why is this tree here? Surely He could have found a safer place to hide it."

"I quite agree with the serpent," Eve said. "And look, I'm holding it and I am still alive. It looks delicious too."

Adam looked into Eve's eyes as she stood excitedly, staring at the fruit. "Eve..."

"Adam, we're going to be wise." She put the fruit to her lips and bit into the fruit. Instinctively, Adam took a step forward and he suddenly paused. Nothing happened. Eve was still alive.

"Eve. Are you sure you are okay?" Adam asked, wondering if she would suddenly drop to the ground lifeless; but Eve began to chew the fruit and swallowed it.

"Here, eat. I do not feel different," she said to Adam as he slowly took the fruit in his hands, looking into Eve's eyes.

"Maybe it does nothing."

"I felt something that I've never felt before," Adam said gratefully, "I was afraid I would lose you."

"I'm still here," Eve said, " I feel perfectly fine."

"Just like I told you," Satan said through the serpent. "Eat."

Adam wanted to protest, but Eve clasped her hands around his as he held the fruit. "Do you feel wiser?" Adam asked softly, looking into Eve's eyes. He enjoyed her beauty, yet his heart was full of questions.

"I honestly don't think it does anything." Eve chuckled as the serpent stared at her wide-eyed, almost like it was waiting for something to happen. She looked at Adam lovingly as he placed the fruit in his mouth. He smiled uneasily and slowly bit into the fruit.

In a sudden moment, the man and woman gasped in utter shock, awakened to the reality of the horror of their spiritual death. Their authority and innocence was corrupted as the glory around them faded, dissipating callously until they realized their identity of Godlikeness had been severed. Adam and Eve suddenly realized they were naked and gasped. Satan smiled wickedly basking in the glow of light that bubbled around him.

They held each other closely, and for the first time, they felt deep fear and loss. Doubt crept upon them like a cloud of doom, marauding their senses and filling them with a torrent of shame. They had died a spiritual death and their dominion had been stripped from them. Adam and Eve ran from the tree; stomping deep into the garden, fear gnawing at their hearts.

God descended into the garden quietly, moving through the trees and fields of green. The beautiful landscape of the garden reveled in the hallowed grace of God but everything had changed. Full of sorrow and anguish at the sin of the first man and woman, God began to call out for Adam.

"Adam. Adam, where are you?"

Adam and Eve hid in a foray of bushes as the light of God filled the deepest crevices of the garden.

"He's here," Eve whispered to Adam, her voice full of fear. "He's here. Oh what have we done?" Their faces were matted with tears. They could not fully grasp it, but the very presence of God that they had loved and basked in now seemed fearsome and terrible.

"Adam," God said again, softly. "Where are you?"

Adam slowly let go of Eve's hand, his mind working furiously. He had tried to stop her. He had done everything God had asked him to do. He would not take the fall for it. He had even made clothing for them from fig leaves that they had strewn together after realizing that they were naked. Adam stuttered as he spoke slowly stepping out of his hiding place to face the inevitable,

"I heard you coming into the garden and I was afraid because I am naked so I hid myself."

There was no going back. The Holy One had settled it. Sin had brought death and things would never be the same again. Yet, filled with love, God moved with purpose through the foliage of the garden. El Elyon communed deep within Himself, and with great grief as well. Nothing was too much to give; nothing was too great or grave to give for mankind. The Holy One paused as He came to the place He had planned for this moment.

A flock of sheep acknowledged the presence of their Creator, and gathered around Him. The Almighty took His own creation, love guiding His hand, to plant a seed of the ages. He was making the first move of redemption that would restore man back to Himself. Everything He had made was silent in that moment; only the ragged breathe and wailing of a sheep was heard as it laid flat with its blood pouring out unto the earth.

A few moments later, God clothed Adam and Eve with the skin as clothing.

"You cannot stay here, otherwise you will eat from the tree of life and live forever in your sinful state," God said. "You must leave."

A storm broke across the earth and lightening flashed across the skies. The heavens began to thunder and the rain

pummeled Adam and Eve as they ran out of the garden through the east entrance as God drove them out. When they looked back, they could see the light of a cherub with a flaming sword guarding the entrance to the garden. They would never be able to return.

Adam held Eve close under the thick growth of a tall tree and they wept bitterly, lost and afraid. His mind flashed back to what had happened in the instant when they ate the fruit from the tree. They had suddenly realized that they were naked. The light that had covered them had faded, leaving them feeling uncovered and empty. In that instant, their state of innocence, strength, and honor had been lost. For the first time since their creation, they had felt a strange feeling of fear and doubt. The garden around them still remained beautiful but the animals had turned aloof and wild.

Adam and Eve had hidden themselves when God visited after they had sinned. When God called for him, Adam had responded, his voice full of shame and despair. There was no point hiding, he had thought. Adam bowed low, cowering in shame. "It's the woman you gave. She gave me the fruit and I ate," he had said weakly, hoping to find mercy and some pity from the Father. The words that God had said to them as He sent out still rang in his ears. He could only imagine what Eve was feeling. Full of grief, Eve mused on the words God had said to the serpent.

"Because you have done this, you are cursed beyond all livestock and all the beasts of the field. You will crawl on your belly and eat dust. I will put enmity between you and the woman, and between your offspring and her offspring; he shall bruise your head and you shall bruise his heel."

Eve wept. She felt the horror of her actions, but even though they had been kicked out of the garden, God had clothed them. Everything around them had lost the luster of light and tranquility. As the rain calmed, Adam and Eve continued to wander far from the garden, looking for a suitable place to rest.

Adam turned to Eve and spoke quietly. "He said we can use a certain type of soil and the wood from the trees to make ourselves coverings to live in."

She nodded and burst into tears. "Adam, I am sorry." She leaned in towards Adam as he put his arms around her. The two held each other, weary and spent; yet they found solace in one another.

"I know He will not abandon us forever," Adam responded. "He told me about how we should bring offerings to Him. He will keep us safe."

Eve detached herself from Adam's embrace. "We abandoned him and now any children we have will be borne in pain." She said through fresh tears and then she suddenly exclaimed. "Look!"

Above them, the sun had risen to its highest point in the sky and shone brightly, emitting the first rays of light since their fall.

"It is beautiful indeed… and so powerful. I can hardly look directly at it," Adam said. "Come, let us keep going, till we find a proper place to settle."

They could finally see the surrounding terrains and distant mountains as the sun shone radiantly above them. The thrushes and weeds had become wild; and the undergrowth was filled with thorns. Though still in awe of the creation around them, Adam and Eve were weary of the wild beasts that cried out in the distance. The storm had torn down the branches of some of the trees, so Adam skillfully made rough staffs to aid their journey. As the sun dried up the plains, the man and woman followed the edge of a river they had found. Eventually, they settled at a point on the riverbank and began to gather stones, twigs, and leaves for their new home.

CHAPTER
—18—
DOMINION

A fiendish howl of delight resounded across the expanse outside Hades, full of hateful relish.

"He's done it! He's done it!" Baeshedith landed in the ashy terrace of Hades and stopped in rude shock. The gate was wide open and a company of angels was lined in fine array inside. A legion of demons had also gathered, shouting threats and curses, but not engaging in battle as they taunted the angels.

Baeshedith flinched as he observed the contrast between the angels and demons, and he almost felt sorry for himself; but it was too late. They all knew that there was no consolation for what they had done. They had seen His majesty and turned their backs on Him. The demon walked slowly, careful not to meet the steady gaze of the angels he had once called brothers. Looking past the gate, he could see Hades buzzing with activity. Angels proceeded through one of the doors, preparing some sort of otherworld.

Everything in the ashen world had changed. Satan's work had produced results at last. The heavenly world and the cosmos were abuzz with news of the sin of the first man and woman. Satan's move had handed them a decisive victory. They had lost Heaven but somehow, with a stroke of genius, Satan had tricked the man, made in the image of God, full of authority and light, to disobey their Maker. With a masterful stroke of genius, Satan had weakened them with their rebellion, lending them a similar fate as he and his demons – cursed, and cut-off from their father. Earth was now fair game for Satan and his minions to rule. Mankind no longer had authority. The repercussion had been swift as justice was meted out.

In a chamber deep in the lower regions of Hades, Bael consulted with the demon lords on their strategy for managing their newly found dominion. Myesmoth, Mota, Astaroth, and other demonic leaders had gathered, summoned by the scheming devil that had delivered on his promise this time around. One by one, they had come to pay homage and pledge their loyalty to Satan's new rule. Finally, they had some form of responsibility in the happenings on earth. Mealiel had placed Bael in charge of the organization of their hierarchies in the lower heavens.

Giddy with delight, Bael spoke with pomp as the gigantic figures watched him impatiently. They had expected to meet with Satan but the imp before them continued to berate them about unity, strategy and the quest to retake Heaven.

"Why doesn't he come to address us? Why did he send you?" Belial, who was once called Roawen, asked insolently, "Anyway, I already chose a dominion. I want the eastern heavens."

Bael spat out greenish ooze before speaking. "Satan determines who holds dominion and where." Bael waved a parchment around with his gnarled hand. As he laid it flat on the table, an oozy, dark, and putrid smoke bubbled over the scroll. Out of the smoke, a faded, ashy light beamed from the scroll.

"Reach in," Bael said, spreading his wiry wings like a graceful benefactor. "Pick your destiny." One by one, the strongest demons reached into the smoke as their rank in Satan's kingdom became visible on their palms. Some of them shouted curses and some others reached for their weapons, exclaiming in dismay as Bael tried to back away from the fracas.

Myesmoth pounded the table with his huge fists. "I contributed much more to the rebellion and deserve more." The enormous room was on the verge of total chaos when a blast of fire erupted through the doorway, startling the demons. Satan appeared at the doorway, a grim look on his face.

Seeing some of the captains who had fought against him after the casting out, Satan met their worried looks with a determination to drive his point home.

"Look at the lot of you, acting like the feeble insects on earth. We are on the verge of unprecedented history and you fight over nothing!"

"You summoned us here," Astaroth retorted, "but you sent this worm to speak to us instead."

Bael bowed as Satan stepped in front of him. "My attention was needed in the throne room."

"You were granted access?" Astaroth was surprised

"But I am lord of the earth now. They call me the prince of darkness and prince of the earth and why not? I welcome the name. They also called me Accuser when I laid my accusations against the man and woman."

"I do not understand," Myesmoth said, "Did you not trick them into the sin? And were you not cursed?"

"Tricked? No," Satan said smiling. "I merely presented an opportunity and they took it. I revealed the truth that they have the choice to determine their own destiny. If they are not mere puppets but creatures of choice, then what I have done is set them free."

Mealiel stepped into the room clapping his hands. "A masterful stroke, indeed. With Satan's act, he not only aided in their fall, but also gave them the pathway to sin, to rebel against God. Not only that but the keys of Hades are now under our control. Masterful indeed."

Bael stood right beside his master. "You see? While you were all trying to amass your forces against Satan, we have been busy." Some of the demon lords shouted curses back at him.

"Enough!" Satan shouted. "It is time for a new era but there is still work to be done so we must be united in strategy. There are millions of demons still scattered in the outer darkness. We must gather them together and unite using the platform of this new world. There is something in their future that we can use against Him." Satan glowed with a yellowish light, his eyes peering with hatred at the twisted and smelly warriors before him. "He has blessed them and commanded them to be fruitful and multiply. They will be our playthings and we will rule them now that they have been introduced to fear, doubt and shame."

With Satan's order given and ranks assigned, the demon lords proceeded out of Hades to find the rest of the demons scattered across the outer galaxies of Heaven. Mealiel turned to Satan when the last demon lord had left. "I always wanted to ask how you escaped from the garden."

Satan had a look of glee. "He did not even know it was me. I fooled Him. He cursed the serpent and didn't even address me directly. But we must be watchful of the seed of the woman just in case. I will personally take care of this, though."

"The seed of the woman?"

"Yes. Something He said that we must watch out for."

Outside Hades, the principalities, powers, and dominions worked with a renewed zeal towards their new purpose. Evil had found an anchor, and drove a wedge between God and His beloved creation. Yet, as Satan watched the new order of things starting with the stolen dominion over the earth, he tempered himself with caution.

Hands on the table, Mealiel at his side, he mused on what God had said to the serpent. "Bruise the serpent's head..." He muttered.

Mealiel gave Satan a look of respect as he spoke. "A masterful stroke, lord, you need not concern yourself. If indeed she does produce her seed, we will destroy him just as well."

Satan turned slightly, as if waking from a trance. "Leave me." Mealiel bowed low and stepped out, shutting the doors of the chamber.

As soon as he was alone, Satan collapsed to the floor and grasped his head with both hands as his gigantic, horned wings furled around his body. Around him, a thick sulfuric smoke billowed. A myriad of ideas about what God's words to the serpent could mean raided his mind like sharp daggers. The dread of it built up slowly, almost choking him. There was something in the curse on the serpent that filled him with fear. What was the plan? God had killed an animal to clothe them and He Himself had understood the concept of remission of sin through the shedding of blood - the life of the biotic creatures. A sacrifice had been required to atone for Adam and Eve's disobedience, and allow them some form of access to God.

Shrugging helplessly, Satan rose up and stepped out of the chamber slamming the door shut behind him.

In the central hall of Hades, the second door had been opened slightly and the angels were arrayed in front of it. In the land of the dead, it seemed a special place was being reserved though most had no idea who it was being kept for. Lurerdeth, Michael and a company of warrior angels inspected the beautiful terrain and headed towards the entrance.

"So this is the place where those who are good and righteous will reside when they die on the earth." Michael said, starring wide-eyed at the expanse of land and caverns of water and colorful mist. "What is it called?"

"The name of one not yet born upon the earth." Lurerdeth responded, "Abraham's Bosom."

"Who is that?"

"I do not know."

"Simply remarkable." Michael responded, "Our God knows all."

"Yes, and the other side is for those who commit evil upon the earth." Lurerdeth said somberly, "and Michael, I never told you this but even I had my doubts during the rebellion. I could not understand His purpose until He revealed it to me."

"Oh I struggled as well. Many of us did and in truth, everything has changed. Brothers, we must be on the alert and always ready." Michael spoke grimly.

"I was compelled to open the gates." Lurerdeth said, as they went through the narrow crevices of the heated stones towards the central hall. "Something changed when the man and woman fell."

"It is no fault of yours." Michael responded, "Man has fallen but this is not over by any chance. I am glad that Gabriel reached you on time."

"Yes, I sense a greater part of our purpose is about to be revealed. Without question, the handiwork of evil changes things; yet we stand confident of a bigger plan."

Michael nodded. "Absolutely. You are privy to many of these things, Lurerdeth. No offense, but you can understand why He wants me to escort you back to Heaven. By the way, Satan was there earlier, you know?"

Lurerdeth stopped abruptly, his eyes flashing a fiery tone of red, "What did you say?"

"Yes, it's unimaginable. God allowed him into His presence where he blatantly accused the man and woman, demanding destruction and God's judgment on them."

" He is such a manipulator."

"We presented him with his new title – Satan, the accuser," Michael responded prodding Lurerdeth to continue walking. "But the blood-letting of the slain animals served to cover their sins. God has not and will never abandon them, weak and frail as they may seem."

"You have seen them?" Lurerdeth asked, pushing on the golden bar enclosed in the framework of the door leading to the alcove. The gigantic room was abuzz with activity, but the angels paused to acknowledge the entrance of their captain. Far south of the alcove, demons watched the angels warily, full of hate and envy. Michael paused at the center of the dome before answering.

"Yes, Lurerdeth. They are a spectacle, even without their former glory."

"This indeed is remarkable."

Michael turned suddenly and gripped Lurerdeth 's arms. "Cast away your sullen look. All is not lost. All is never lost with Him who was before all things and who is after all things. They will be redeemed at the set time. As for this place, Tessa will take lead and protect those who are to come to the place of peaceful rest."

"Let us go then. Take me far from this place of woe and darkness."

"What is this? Come to honor me in my new abode?" A voice intruded.

Michael did not turn around. "Yes, I imagined only you would attempt stopping us."

"Imagined? You actually use your imagination?" Satan scoffed. "Puppet. Isn't that what He has given to the new earth creature? Imagination. What do you have Michael? I have a whole world. I have taken it. By guile, it is mine. All the castaways will answer to me and my army will soon return to full strength."

"We have His light, Accuser. We have His glory, and we have the heavenly city." Lurerdeth chimed in, repulsed by Satan's ghastly form which was fully visible at close range.

"Oh, keep those!" Satan spat on the ground insolently. "We have great power indeed. Have you not seen the potentials of this earth? It is ripe for plucking, for building my empire. And you coward, Lurerdeth, with all your knowledge, you could have been a great asset to my cause, yet you ran away. You know I could have given you a share of my spoils? My new servants will pay homage to me. I will be their god. They will burn incense on my altars and worship me."

"They will reject you and choose God." Lurerdeth said, taking a step towards Satan, his eyes blazing with fire, "You forget that they are creatures of choice and you cannot have those who choose Him."

Michael put a hand on Lurerdeth's shoulder restraining him. "Say no more. He gets the message."

"Do I?" Satan was not finished with his taunting. "So then, keeper of secrets! Keep hiding while we play the final round of this game, but I will have them all. I will."

Michael's warriors formed a circle around Lurerdeth and himself, spreading their wings. Violent rays of light erupted from their wings, spinning in a chasm of power as they took flight. Satan stepped back, bubbling with anger as he covered his eyes. He watched as the angels ascended at blinding speed towards Heaven. He thought he had heard Michael say something about the man and woman's seed, but he could not be sure. Whatever the angels knew, he would be ready. His victory could only come if he was a step ahead; and so, he was convinced that he had to study the timing of God's move using the very secrets buried within the created beings themselves.

"Restore them?" Satan shouted, shaking his fist in the air. "We shall see. We shall see."

Lurerdeth gripped Adriel's arms outside the hall of secrets as the smaller angel welcomed him. Beaming happily beside them, Michael clapped while a few warrior angels stood cheering. In front of the entrance, a group of angel scribes stood in honor.

"Welcome back, Lurerdeth," Adriel said. "It is good to have you back. Welcome home."

"Ah yes, Adriel, we have much to celebrate." Lurerdeth looked around, enjoying the luster of light that covered the divine landscape. Angels were busy rebuilding the heavenly city. "I have longed and pined for my chambers. I have been absent for so long."

"We would not have you return to see a mess." Michael said, "Let Adriel show you what we have done with your chambers. I must return to the throne room."

Lurerdeth smiled, "Thank you Michael. I surely will join you soon at the appointed time."

Michael nodded and sped away with his warriors as Adriel pointed with a flourish. "Welcome keeper of secrets."

"I am filled with joy."

"Lurerdeth, I have always wanted to know. What happens now... that man has... sinned?" Adriel said as Lurerdeth stepped into the chamber and beamed with delight at his throne and table. The lord of secrets trailed his hand around the edges of the table. Behind them, the angel scribes proceeded inside and went about their duties.

"Adriel, This is what I know. I know that everything is now focused on the man and the woman. They hold the key to the full expression of God's love. I know. That in itself is more of a question than an answer but it is what I know. More will be revealed in time."

"Yes, but it does seem a heavy blow to our cause to have them sin. Oh the deceptiveness of evil, the cunning of the devil."

"Adriel," Lurerdeth sat and raised his hand, "sin is no match for God's love. You will see in the fullness of time."

"As you have often taught me, I will remain patient and see the wonders of God," Adriel responded.

"Yes, of course. Who leads the heralds now?"

"Chesum." Adriel smiled slapping his hands on the table. A fiery effigy of Chesum appeared on the table. "You should have seen him. When Mota betrayed God and formed a huge fiery ball big enough to tear apart the heavens, many of the heralds joined his cause. See? We couldn't even go near it. It was too powerful and their plan was to destroy everything in their path to the throne of God."

As Adriel spoke, the flames formed into a huge fiery ball descending towards a replica of the angels fighting in the inner court.

"Here stands Tessa and Lemuel, captain of a host, in the frenzy of battle for our King and for our kingdom. In the moment when everything seemed lost, when all seemed hopeless, it dawned on us. Perfected praise."

"Who would have thought?"

"Yes, Lurerdeth, perfected praise for our King silenced the enemy. Now, order is restored, at least to heaven..."

"Excuse me," One of the angel scribes interrupted Adriel and Lurerdeth.

"What is it?" Lurerdeth asked.

"Zuriel is here to see you." The angel responded as Lurerdeth and Adriel exchanged a glance.

"Zuriel," Adriel nodded. "He was supposed to open the gates to the outer court givine significant advantage to the enemy but he refused. He is a hero."

"Interesting."

"But why would he come to see you?"

"Yes, we shared... an experience in Hades." Lurerdeth said with a wry smile. "I am happy to know that he is still here as strange as that might sound. Send him in."

"I will take my leave, Lurerdeth," Adriel responded bowing. "And surely return later to share other details of the war with you."

Lurerdeth nodded and rose up slowly, a slightly bemused look on his face as he remembered what had happened when Zuriel had visited Hades uninvited.

CHAPTER

—19—

THE WATCHERS

Far south of Eden, beyond the confluence of rivers, the community of men had grown. Adam's settlement had migrated further south through the distant terrain, seeking better pasture; and his sons, Cain and Seth, had established their own settlements. Customs had been introduced, as knowledge of the earth increased through learning and discovery. Fathers passed down their understanding of nature and of how to till the ground to future generations. The traditions of marriage, and rules for society were already taking shape.

Zuriel and Gabriel took it all in as they flew through the clouds. The people below were concentrated around the eastern and southern borders of Eden, though thousands of miles apart in some instances. Man thrived. They had established a settlement where Adam had taught them how to engage their world. Adam and Eve had learned how to build altars of fire to sacrifice to God for their sins.

"Teach your children and your children's children to observe this," God had told them. "I will respond with fire from Heaven when your offerings are accepted."

There had been whispers in Heaven when Cain was born. Gabriel would never forget it. The woman had nurtured her son in her belly for nine months and, in great pain, endured his birth, the first ever of its kind. God's presence had been strong in the room where she labored, guiding Adam as he tenderly and tearfully aided her. Gabriel had understood early on that man was a creature of choice. He would always have to choose. A painful reality the angels had endured when Cain had killed his brother Abel because God has accepted Abel's offering and rejected Cain's.

"I said it didn't I?" Zuriel said, "I told you Satan had plans for Cain. We really should have seen it coming. After all, he is the first seed of the woman; consider how he was corrupted."

"I agree, Zuriel, we should have seen that coming and done better." Gabriel smiled bitterly, and then chuckled slightly at the Zuriel's eagerness to make his point. "There is always a plan. I mean, look at you. You were faced with a choice as well. And you chose right. Here you are, promoted to lord of the watchers and now with your first earthly assignment. I am proud of you Zuriel."

"Thank you, Gabriel. Thank you." Zuriel said, his eyes misting slightly. *If only Gabriel fully knew what had happened,* he thought to himself. "You should have seen Lurerdeth's face when the lord of secrets returned and I went to see him."

"I can only imagine. How did that go?"

"Slightly awkward I must admit," Zuriel said and laughed. "He's convinced his actions saved me from the fate of the devil and his minions. I really don't care. I'm just happy to have survived my ordeal."

"We are grateful to call you brother."

"And I as well," Zuriel said smiling, "I am also grateful to be trusted with such a mission."

Zuriel had noticed and reported of Satan's keen interest in Cain as the years had passed since their birth. "We must guard him, or else the devil will have him," he had proclaimed in the council of the sons of God. Ever mindful of the dark fate he narrowly escaped, Zuriel was grateful. He often thought about the moment when it had all come down to opening the gate during the war. It was like a second lease of existence. That choice had paid off tremendously for him. His promotion was one of the many honors he had received. The angels had worked tirelessly to rebuild the city, restoring it to its former glory and beyond. There were new assignments and promotions.

Since the creation, the angels had witnessed it all, watching as God visited earth's first family ever so often. Adam had taught them how to worship, as he had learned it first hand from God. When God spoke to them, they heard Him clearly and were not afraid, nor appalled by His visits. Heaven's work and attention were devoted to the earth.

Meanwhile, the devil and his demons worked tirelessly, laying pitfalls for the seed of the woman. Satan's objective was clear - Cain had to defy God just as his parents did, and then, all would truly be lost. If this was the seed of the woman that would crush his head as God had said to the serpent, he would destroy him first. The first murder on the earth had been a win for the forces of darkness.

"Can you see any spot where we can set up a look-out?" Gabriel asked as Zuriel smiled distractedly, pulling away from his thoughts.

"Yes, I am searching," Zuriel said, "And you should know I am excited about this new mission."

"Oh yes," Gabriel responded, "I knew you would be."

"It's an exciting planet. I can't wait to explore and enjoy this new adventure," Zuriel beamed as he took in the beautiful landscape of the earth.

"...and to give aid to mankind," Gabriel jokingly added.

"Of course, Gabriel, of course," Zuriel responded.

Zuriel and Gabriel scouted the mountains of Nod, as they quietly flew over Earth's hills and valleys.

"Do you see any demons?" Gabriel asked the watcher angel.

"Not one," Zuriel responded, his wings unfurled. "This is the city that Cain built after he killed his brother Abel and was cursed. What about that mountain over there beyond the city of Enoch?" Zuriel asked pointing.

Gabriel looked down. Far beneath them, the city thrived with activity, thousands of men and women preoccupied with their lives. Cain had moved east of Eden and married and began building a city that he named Enoch after the name of his son.

The earth was an amazing sight to see from the angels' viewpoint. From the first man, to thousands upon thousands of men and women developing cities, cultivating traditions, communing, singing, and worshipping. It was a beautiful world.

Gabriel assessed the mountain as the hovered over it. "I don't think so," he responded to Zuriel. "Looks like this is not a good enough vantage point. Let us scout southward."

"As you wish," Zuriel nodded and headed south after Gabriel's lead, watching carefully for enemy forces.

Later on, the two angels settled on a mountain called Hermon and transformed into their earthly bodies. Gabriel touched the soil and smiled. Breathing in the air of the earth, he walked towards the edge of the mountain and watched the expanse of land far below, and abroad. From this high point over the earth, Zuriel and his host of watchers were to observe the activities of Earth, and in turn, report to Heaven.

"Do not tarry before I hear from you. You may summon Azazel and your other forces," Gabriel said, "but do not forget that your mission is not open war but to provide information to us, and aid to the people of earth when they cry out to God."

"I understand completely but to have the forge angel with us on this assignment gives me great comfort. We would hope to do our work unhindered by the forces of evil." Zuriel smiled as he struck the ground with a pole of fire. The pole split at the top, releasing a blazing glow.

"Heaven will miss you brother," Gabriel continued. "Be careful of Satan and his minions. They are deceivers and corrupters seeking to destroy everything that is good and God given." He locked arms with Zuriel.

"I will; and it will not be long before I send mission reports. I also hope to see you again soon."

"Oh, I'll come often with messages - not just for you, but for the people below as well."

"For the King, brother," Zuriel said.

"For the King." Gabriel nodded. Their marker in place, he flew back into the heavens and beyond to the city of God.

Zuriel stood, waiting and watching. He wondered if any

demons would dare interfere. So far, they had seen none. The clouds seemed normal for a brief moment and then a few seconds later, a couple hundred of angels descended like orbs of fire down unto the Earth following the flaming marker. Zuriel waited for their arrival, full of excitement. Once they settled in, they would be God's direct messengers on earth, observing its affairs and fulfilling Gods commands as they related to man.

A farmer had been tilling the ground beneath the mountain, humming a tune when the clouds darkened. Alongside, his son and two daughters stood in abject shock as the heavens parted and light blasted through the sky unto the top of the mountain. Seconds later, orbs of fire began to descend in multiples unto the top of the mountain. Afraid, the family huddled close to each other as the light faded a few minutes later, and the dark clouds disappeared. They abandoned their work and retreated back to their tents, each one marked by what they had seen, and yet having no explanation for the visitors that had just entered their world.

Azazel beamed with delight as he inspected his forge tools. The angels had set up station on the mountain as they acclimatized to the earth.

"I saw no hesitation in your demeanor when you were called upon," Zuriel said, as he approached Azazel. The forge angel turned and made a face.

"Hesitation? The action is on earth. Heaven has enough weapons of war. The whole city is in a frenzy about building new cities and creating mysterious instruments and symbols of prophecy. Not that I mind but my talents, as I have discovered, are now in creating instruments of force."

Zuriel laughed heartily, "Hope we will not disappoint you my friend though I quite doubt that we will fight many battles here. Our work must be done under Heaven's authorization only. We only exert force when the name of our God is called upon. Such is the way. Such is the structure of things in the universe now."

"And who's to complain? We are indeed fortunate to be called upon for this. There are many angels who wish to be this close to mankind."

"You do have a point there but we all have our assignments."

"I understand, but I must say that I am eager to see mankind at closer range."

"What?"

"You heard me Zuriel. How can we give Heaven adequate and accurate information if we do not go among them and learn of their ways and see the wonders closely? It's something that has been on my mind since we were given the details of our mission."

Zuriel laughed again, this time with a hint of caution. Azazel, we are watchers. We have depth of sight, and need not go close to them. Maybe only under the most extreme of situations. I would not want to go against the directives given to us from Heaven."

"But Zuriel, we are far away from Heaven. Are you insinuating that you will not interact with them? You will not learn of their ways and their customs?"

"No," Zuriel said walking away slowly, "That was not my commission. We are not to reveal ourselves to them nor influence or interact with them except by authorization. You will do well to remember that Azazel. There is a reason why you were sent here. Do not forget that."

Azazel raised his hands. "Zuriel, wait. You speak as if the thought never crossed your mind."

"It has."

"Then come with me, just once. Let us go among them and see if we can find any that are loyal to our God. What is wrong with that?"

Zuriel turned and wringed his hands in frustration. "Azazel, do you forget that they cannot see us?" Zuriel's eye's opened wider, "You mean to reveal yourself?"

"Yes." Azazel stepped forward and placed his hands on Zuriel's shoulders, "Yes, brother. Just once. Let us go among them and see what angels long to see and understand. I really want to know."

"Know what?"

"Why He loves them so much. The first man and woman sinned yet He did not destroy them. He clothed them. Cain killed Abel and pleaded for his life. God put a mark on him so no one would kill him. They are weakened in their fallen nature and yet He does not cast them into the fiery place beneath Hades that you saw. Instead, He sends us here to care for them, to protect them, to shield those who worship Him. Tell me you do not seek to understand even a fraction of this love. We have never experienced it in this capacity, never."

Zuriel turned away again and looked down the mountain. His eyes grew wider as he scanned the distant cities around the mountain.

"What you say is true but…"

"Come, you and I, let us go down," Azazel said quietly. "What's the worst that can happen? Two travellers visiting for a few days…"

"One day." Zuriel said reluctantly.

"Just one day? We need at least two days."

"You have given your word and it shall be so. Two days it is and then we return."

"That is fine with me." Azazel beamed with delight.

"Do not stay too long or we will come looking for you," one of the watchers said jokingly.

Azazel changed form. Apart from his height, he looked like a man. "No, we will not. How do I look?"

"Dashingly handsome by earthly measures," a fellow watcher said.

The angels laughed as Zuriel stood tall with his hands akimbo as he enjoyed the admiration of his fellow angels. His frame was strong and tall, his golden hair bound behind his neck. Draped around his mid region was a belt of gold and he donned a flowing white garment with silver linings at its hem. Azazel transformed into a man clad in fine linen with a gold sash around his head and waist.

"Are you ready?" Zuriel said.

"Oh yes I am, Zuriel" Azazel responded with excitement. "Let us go and mingle with men, and learn of their ways. This will aid our cause." The forge angel and the watcher stepped unto the rocky terrain and began their descent from the mountain.

The other watcher angels cheered as they descended, each longing to follow them and hoping that they would have the same opportunity to interact directly with the men and women of the earth. They had come in fire and tempest. They had come with their knowledge and powers. The world would never remain the same. The watchers had come.

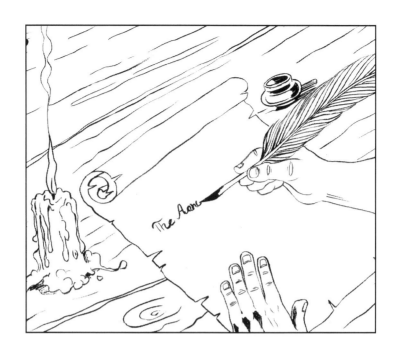

CHAPTER

—20—

ENOCH

❈

A sweet melody filled the crystal-like room where the angels were gathered. Michael and Raphael watched with keen interest as Shelan worked the huge furnace. Ever since Myesmoth's expulsion from Heaven, Shelan had been given the responsibility of completing the projects that he and Azazel had started.

Crystal beams lined the chamber, forming a curved pyramid layered on every side with choice rubies. The jewels sparkled teasingly through the embroidery of the drapes that adorned the sides of the chamber.

At the corners of the room, the forge angels had made smaller furnaces and each worked tirelessly at their stations crafting instruments of worship or whatever else the Spirit of God asked them to create.

In the center of the room, embedded in its own frame, a wheel spun within another wheel, releasing sparks of feverish light. Around the wheel was a spectral wisp of light in full motion, and one angel in particular observed the lights as they moved. The door of the room burst open suddenly.

"Chaos! Utter Chaos!" an angel announced, taking long strides to the center of the room. The meek faces of the angels in the room gave way to amazement at the angel's words and demeanor. Gabriel was not often disgruntled.

"What do you speak of?" Michael looked up with concern.

"Chaos!" Gabriel spread his hands. "The watchers' offspring corrupt the earth. They have bred giants who are demolishing the earth."

"Our own angels," Michael gritted his teeth. "Our own brothers again betray the King."

"The height of that which is forbidden. It has been hundreds of earth years since they were sent on their mission. First, they stopped communicating with me. And now, they marry? And they have not only married but are producing offspring!"

"Zuriel and his brothers err against God," Michael said grimly as the other angels gathered around him. "We must proceed to the throne room and receive instruction."

"Is the scribe coming with us?" Raphael asked, pointing to a man who had been watching and listening to them.

The angels turned and observed the man. He appeared small and frail compared to the angels. He was bearded and lean, filled with awe as the light of Heaven caused him to squint at all times. Adriel stepped up.

"He is under my charge and the Most High wants him to write certain things down."

Michael shook his head. "No. Wait here. We will return shortly from the throne room after we have taken the cries of the earth to God, and then, we will reveal those things which must be written."

Adriel bowed slightly as the angels took their exit, and then turned to the man. "Come Enoch, there is much within these walls that I have been commanded to show you."

Heaven was abuzz with activity. Standing in the midst of the great company, Enoch observed all with rapt attention. His face, set with grey eyes, wrinkled as he struggled to keep his eyes open. He could never get used to the light of Heaven. His clothing was made of linen and the light of God - alive and full of joy, glazing around his body tirelessly. In his few hundred years of life, he would never forget the first day he began to see visions. His father, Jared, a sixth-generation descendant of Adam had thought him mad. Unlike all men on the earth, Enoch had a very special relationship with God. He often heard things that men could neither hear nor understand. The Spirit of God would often visit him and they would converse in the quiet pathways of the forests, sheltered from the activity within his settlement. At times, Enoch would be gone for days; but every time he returned, he would gather those who would listen and tell them of God's ways.

In the large forge and armory of Heaven, diverse weapons beyond number lined the sidewalls, and in the center, a battalion of angels began to assemble, ready for battle. Adriel walked with Enoch, explaining the things he saw.

"The earth has cried out to its Maker," Adriel said, pointing to the gathering army. "and we are God's response to the earth's plea."

Through the huge glass doors, Michael, Raphael, and Shelan, the new lord of the forge, emerged with a stunning radiance encircling their bodies.

"I believe all is ready," Michael said to Adriel and acknowledged Enoch's presence. "Enoch, God has commanded judgment upon the watchers who left their posts and cohabited with the daughters of men. We have made our case before the Lord, our King. We have told of Azazel's sins of disclosing the secrets of Heaven on the earth, and how the watchers have taught sorcery, the mixing of species, and the movements of celestial bodies. We have told of their offspring, of the giants and their grave sins upon the earth. We have numbered them and reported their names. There will be recompense. The King has pronounced their judgment." Michael turned to the angels as Enoch scribbled furiously.

"Let us go. It is time."

The angels descended with their swords drawn and fire in their trails. For a second time in their existence, brother would fight against brother. The clouds parted as the host, led by Michael, plowed the heavenly pathways as the firmaments gave way, releasing a thunderous storm upon the earth. With his arm firmly around Enoch, Adriel descended behind the army.

The angels whizzed through the skies like light beams from Heaven and alighted on the top of the mountain where the watchers had first arrived. In a short time, they routed the watcher guards, and then descended from the mountain and sped off in groups like fiery darts through the settlements, fortresses, and towers in their paths. They rounded up the watchers, one after the other, and brought them back to the mountain.

In their angelic forms, the hapless defectors knelt down as Shelan restrained them by locking chains of fire around their wrists. Michael's forces surrounded the hostages, standing in a circle with their weapons drawn. They made way as Michael approached the captive angels, Gabriel following closely behind him.

"You gave no fight so I imagine that you did not care about the warnings of the righteous scribe," Michael said, pointing at Enoch, who was standing beside Adriel.

"We are at your mercy," Zuriel said, bowing his head as he lifted his hands imploringly. "We are not like Lucifer's minions. We have made a grave mistake but seek the mercy of God. We have not turned from Him."

"But you have greatly offended Him and His creation. Zuriel, you have offended the earth. You have offended mankind. You have offended the beasts and animals. Your offenses have brought far worse corruption to the earth!" Gabriel shouted.

"Do you know that you have created evil spirits all around the earth?" Michael bellowed, fiery sparks blazing around his frame.

Zuriel bowed his head, his heart burdened with remorse.

"But it was… it was Azazel who convinced us to do this. I wanted no part of it."

"Still you complied. All of you," Michael retorted.

Azazel groaned, an angel's sword at his neck, "We only sought to serve God by getting close to them."

"You took the daughters of men as wives!" Michael stomped towards Azazel, "What madness induced you to do such? What did you think would happen?"

"Michael," Azazel said imploringly, "we have made a grave mistake but seek forgiveness. Surely, God forgives men. Why does He not extend such to us? These are the things that we sought to understand."

"You disappoint me brother," Michael said, "Hear the judgment of our God. He is just. God is putting every sin on your head. You are the scape goat, Azazel, and you and all of these watchers are condemned by the hand of God."

Out of desperation, Zuriel turned to Enoch. "Scribe of righteousness, will you not make a plea for us? Will you not speak to the Most High and speak of our repentance?" Other angels joined in pleading with Enoch as he watched quietly, Adriel's strong arm around his shoulder.

"Silence! A place of judgment has been reserved for you all." Michael towered over them and gave the signal. "Take them to the dungeons."

"Tell me, Michael, tell me." Zuriel struggled with his captors, "How long shall we be restrained?"

"I do not know." Michael shook his head solemnly. "Take them."

"Wait," Azazel shouted, "Michael! Michael! Remember me brother and all I did for Heaven during the rebellion. Without me…"

"Silence Azazel! You were rewarded and now you are rewarded again. If it does any good, this gives me no pleasure. We have held you and Zuriel in the highest regard until now. You should have known that no good would come out of marrying the daughters of men, not to mention having children by them."

"Gabriel, will you say nothing?" Zuriel pleaded, attempting to reach for Gabriel's hand. Gabriel turned away as a tear streaked down his face.

Michael spread his wings and gave his command, "Take them to the dungeons of Hades."

With two hundred captive watcher angels in their company, the angels began their descent from the mountain to the lower dungeons beneath Hades, where they would be held until the day of their final judgment.

As his forces led their prisoners away, Michael turned his

attention back to the earth, surveying as men worshipped idols, and performed acts of immorality. The giants, offspring borne from the unions of between the watcher angels and the women of Earth, were busy building and expanding their kingdoms. In palaces where the watchers had been seized, pandemonium had already broken loose. The watchers had been reigning as gods on the earth. Michael motioned to Gabriel.

"Come, Gabriel. Cause the giants to devour one another. Give them no rest till they are wiped from the face of the earth."

Gabriel nodded and sped off with a smaller company of angels, fully committed to their task. Alone, Michael returned to the top of the mountain and sat. There had to be a plan in all of the chaos. God always had a plan but yet again, he could not understand it. This world. This project. It had all seemed so good at the beginning. It had all been so beautiful, just like Heaven; but in that moment of man's fall, everything changed. Death now reigned in the world because of Satan's corruption. This time, however, Heaven's own angels had initiated far greater evils on the earth. They had mixed the blood of man with that of angels in human form. The archangel sensed an evil presence alight on the mountain and slowly reached for his sword.

"Peace, Michael, I come in peace."

Michael's blade was out before he responded. "Ah, Satan. I imagined you would have sent one of your weaklings to restrain us."

"Ah, but I have come myself." Satan said, smiling. He had come in human form. His cloak was made from rich wool, with etches of crystals.

"What are you here for?"Michael demanded.

"Simply to gloat, old friend. For all my existence, to imagine the worst insult to God would come from your brothers. Especially that coward, Zuriel."

"They are being punished," Michael retorted, lowering his blade yet he remainded alert. "I do have one question however."

"No need to ask," Satan said smiling wickedly. "You wonder why we did not interfere? Why would we? Though I would never have thought about it in the least bit, Zuriel and the others have done the unthinkable. We are simply reaping the benefits. Men worship us, and we fulfill their deepest, darkest desires. Those lustful angels have achieved for me what I would never have imagined in all my supposedly evil ways."

"Your time will come soon enough," Michael spread his wings as light bubbled in tremors around him.

Satan stood back, his eyes filled with hate, "Well now that the seed of the woman is all but tainted, how will you and your God respond? I do not command a meager force of demons. You cannot take us all! We are not weak and mindless, like Zuriel and his puppets."

Michael ascended from the mountain without a response as evil relished a laugh. As for him, he had to return with his report. God would deal with the prince of this world in His own good time.

Adriel led Enoch through a separate pathway, far from the activities on Mount Hebron. Lemuel, who had been reassigned to guard the celestial lights, lit a pathway for them through the concourse of the sky, and then through the waters to the deeper realms beneath the foundations of the earth. "Enoch," Adriel said, "I will show you the fountains of the deep and what must happen in the course of time when your grandson, Noah, is born."

Beneath the slightly humid clouds, a giant clasped his hand around a huge horn and blew into its mouthpiece. One could hear the horn as far as the distant plains of the unexplored lands of Nod. In the distance behind him, the terrain trembled as giants thudded through fields and plantations, fighting battles to expand their territory. Tribesmen from the northern hills had deserted their lands and sought higher grounds and caves to hide their women and their young from their gargantuan invaders.

As the giants increased in number across the earth, men had fought to maintain ownership of their lands. Others had pledged fealty to the giant kings who ruled with impunity. Their strength was matched by no other earthly beings. They had built vast weapons of diverse types, and ruled their lands with fear, thereby amassing great wealth.

"Kill them all!" the giant bellowed menacingly. In the next moment, a huge spear abruptly pierced his temple as he turned. Behind his flailing body, other giants grappled about, shouting chants of war and slashing their opponents with brute force. The fighting had dragged on for days and men with their cattle had begun to migrate to escape from the bloodletting.

Observing the melee from the skies above, Gabriel spun around in a circle and headed upwards towards Heaven. The sun cast a red light as it faded over the horizon behind him. Darkness was coming.

Hundreds of miles from the battle of the giants, a small colony gathered about a small fire. Having returned from his latest vision, Enoch rejoined his family at their campfire and broke bread, giving thanks. They had kept vigil through the dark days, their sons and brothers taking turns to watch for intruders. As the fire crackled, Enoch observed their faces, which were now wearied and darkened with soot. They had passed through the low lands unobserved but they occasionally had to fight off beasts and vagabonds. Their once beautiful Earth had become an open grave of death.

They were the righteous, living amongst brute giants and corrupted men. For the most part, man no longer sought communion with their Maker to learn of His ways. Rather, they resorted to the evils introduced by the watchers to appease their insatiable cravings. Men became sorcerers, chanting dark sayings and spells to enforce their desires on the earth. They participated in orgies and human sacrifices, and consorted with demons in the darker places of the earth.

Men had mastered the art of war and enslavement, and became evil scientists of sorts, conducting experiments to mix animal species, even to the extent of cojoining the human bloodline with that of mammals. The more corrupt the earth became, the more the land suffered until food became scarce and life, a struggle.

Enoch raised his hands. "Let us be thankful that we are alive and still together." He noticed the quiet sobbing of one of the women as he passed out rations of bread to his family around the fire.

"We are alive, but for how long Grandfather?" Lamech asked.

Enoch observed his grandson's troubled face before responding. "I know what I have seen. Judgment is coming."

"I am afraid," Lamech said, nibbling gently on the bread.

"There is nothing to fear. God has spoken. He has shown me what is about to happen."

They turned as a twig snapped a few paces away. "Father, are you still filling up my son's head with your visions?" Methuselah emerged with two men holding torches and spears.

"My son," Enoch reached for Methuselah and kissed his forehead. "How is the road ahead? Come. Sit. Share the warmth of our fire."

Methuselah sat and reached for the roasted venison on a spit over the fire. "The road ahead seems clear of danger. Our only focus needs to be on getting east of Eden as quickly as possible to bury our great father."

"I know. Adam our father has gone to his rest and I would travel faster if possible but for the younger ones."

Methuselah nodded and settled down as he stuffed his mouth with the cooked haunches of a roasted lamb. "It seems God is sparing him the horrors of this earth."

"And God will soon sweep upon the earth and save us from them all," Enoch said, his eyes misting.

"Save us? How? The seed of the woman has been tainted. Corrupted! Even the animals," Methuselah said angrily, startling one the suckling babies. The baby woke and began to cry as his mother pacified him.

Enoch nodded. "I know how you feel. I feel the same way, however, God is planning something historic."

"Historic or not, we best keep on moving at first light." Methuselah spoke and then winced slightly when he realized the harshness of his tone. "Father, I do not mean to..."

"Peace, son," Enoch reached out his hand and touched Methuselah's shoulder. "Help me up. Let us walk and talk because I cannot sleep."

"Lamech, make sure everyone is comfortable and most importantly, quiet," Methuselah instructed as he stood, offering his arm as a support for Enoch. Lamech nodded in response and watched on glumly as the two men walked away.

The moon had appeared and cast a mournful mood on the landscape. "A full moon," Enoch mused quietly.

"Surely you do not believe in the tales of wolves and

men." Methuselah shook his head. "Father..."

"Save yourself the trouble," Enoch responded, prodding the ground beneath them carefully with his staff. "I know the things that I have seen. You don't have to believe me."

"I believe you." Methuselah's voice was a hollow tone. "I want to believe. I want to know that when you seal your tent for days that you indeed see the things that you say you see. The things you write are beyond anything I can understand. Yet, we have survived thus far."

"How will you protect what I write if you do not believe in them?"

Methuselah did not respond. With one hand firmly around his spear, he cautioned Enoch. They had descended quietly down the hidden grove to a narrow lake. "Fresh water," Methuselah whispered. "We went north, so we missed this. Wait! Do you see that?"

At the edge of the drying lake, a creature drank of the water. It looked like a boy from the distance but the hair around its upper body was dark and wooly, almost like that of a young lion. Suddenly, the creature turned to observed them and bared its teeth angrily.

Methuselah gripped his spear tighter, ready to attack. At the same moment, Enoch's face suddenly began to glow with a strange light." Methuselah threw caution to the wind. "Father! No, not now." The creature growled and began pawing the ground, blood fresh on its breath. Methuselah could make out the carcass of a young goat lying behind the beast.

"Stay back!" he yelled at the creature and deftly caught Enoch's body with his other hand as he fell to the ground. "Father, this is not the time for one of your visions!" Methuselah cried. He grit his teeth, anticipating an attack, and then groaned when he realized the creature was not alone. Behind the beast, a fiend, almost bigger than a full-grown man, leaped across the narrow drying lake.

Disadvantaged and concerned for their lives, Methuselah flailed his spear around menacingly. The larger of the creatures stepped forward and put a hand on the smaller one, as if to guard it. The creature looked up and let out a howl as the larger creature's claws sunk in the soil. For a moment, the fiend held Methuselah's gaze.

Methuselah lowered his spear slowly as he realized that the beast's face could have passed for that of a man, just like that of the smaller creature. Its eyes were roundish but intelligent. Turning, the larger creature grabbed the dead goat, and with its claws firmly clasped around the smaller creature's neck, it trudged off, fading into the darkness.

Not long after their encounter at the lake, Methuselah urged his family on as two men carried Enoch's body on a stretcher made of reeds and cloth. His mind was cloudy and full of grief concerning what he had seen. His right hand man, Elkan, rode beside him while Lamech rode with the men behind the women and children, their camels saddled with their luggage.

"May his sons be born in better times," Methuselah muttered under his breath.

Elkan nodded. "Yes, indeed."

"Both of us were born in despairing times, but father speaks of Lamech's future son as a child of rest. Father says many things that are beyond normal, but on this one, I indeed pray to God that we find rest and comfort."

"Amen, this is my prayer as well," Elkan responded and sighed. "This creature you saw, it was a man. No?"

"Not a man but some form of evil... an abomination! The world has become hopeless."

"Yet, one must only hope for a better future."

Methuselah grit his teeth. "The world is hard and painful. Young men die and old men live on, too weak to fight and yet too strong to die. We see the times and seasons pass through the bitter winters and the dry summers and yet, we linger on. We stay because we must, and our days are filled with pain and anguish. Yet, we live on, seeing our children birth their children to the third and fourth generations. Leave me to my thoughts. Maybe tonight, I will say a prayer and offer a sacrifice. I do not know of anything else to do."

A tear trailed on Methuselah's cheek as he spoke. They cleared the forest pass into the valleys, and through to the final stretch of their journey.

Three days after, Adriel returned with Enoch. When he realized that his family had gone far beyond the hill pass and the drying riverbed, Enoch arose with excitement, his face full of light.

"Where is Lamech?" he questioned. The family had camped with one day's journey left to their destination. Lamech hurried into the tent as Enoch grasped his arms. "Listen to me, God will visit with judgment. When your son is born, you must name him 'Noah,' for the Lord Almighty will bring rest and comfort."

"Noah," Lamech mulled over the name. "It means rest. My father will be pleased to hear this. I also, I'm glad."

"Good," Enoch said. "Now listen. You will keep all my writings safe and give them to your son. Do you understand?"

"Yes, grandfather. Yes."

"Good. Now fetch me my staff."

"Are you going somewhere?" Lamech asked puzzled.

Enoch held Lamech's shoulders, "Keep the writings safe. You are a good boy. Walk in the ways of your fathers who have worshiped God. The one true God. As for me, I am going on a long walk. God is coming to talk to me. Now, go find me my staff."

Lamech stepped out of the tent, shielding his eyes from the glare of the sun. Noah. His grandfather had named a son he had not even conceived. Noah it was. Lamech would wait and pray. "Rest and comfort," Lamech muttered to himself. The sound of it made him smile.

CHAPTER
—21—
THE CURSE

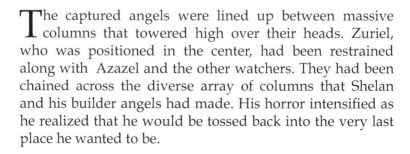

The captured angels were lined up between massive columns that towered high over their heads. Zuriel, who was positioned in the center, had been restrained along with Azazel and the other watchers. They had been chained across the diverse array of columns that Shelan and his builder angels had made. His horror intensified as he realized that he would be tossed back into the very last place he wanted to be.

Zuriel had wrestled with his captors throughout the journey, shamelessly pleading as he and the others were chained in the lower recesses of Hades. He was once again at the mercy of his own choices.

The other captive watchers had spared no words in condemning Azazel who remained defiant all the way. Secluded in a corner, Azazel had passed his time initially without much grace, often scheming and inciting a few of the watchers to attempt futile escape plans but as the earth's days turned to months and then to years, the captive angels struggled to adapt to their chains until one after the other, the reality of their demise dawned on them.

They eventually accepted their fate, and all grappling ceded. The silence itself was the only solace they had. Left to their thoughts, and oblivious to the changing world far above them, the angels came to understand that there would be no escaping the judgment of God for what they had done.

"How remarkable," Bael muttered as he stepped into the lower recesses of the dungeons quietly. The angels seemed like buried relics, huge statues blending in with the dark and dusty prison. Bael stood in the center in front of the central columns.

"Well, what do we have here? Angels chained while we roam around free?"

The voice stirred the captives who rose slowly, wondering who their strange guest was. A large frame shifted, with dust and ash dancing in the atmosphere in response to the movement. Zuriel opened his eyes.

"Where is Zuriel, my old friend? It is I, Bael."

"What do you want, demon? Here to gloat?" Zuriel queried.

"Gloat?" Bael raised his hands in mock-humility. " No, Zuriel, I did not come here to gloat."

"Then what do you want? Have you come to set us free? "

"I have not come for that either. Haven't you tried to break your chains?"

"We have all tried countless times," Zuriel responded. "There is no freedom for us."

"You poor and pitiful fool," Bael crooned, sliding his hand slowly down the huge chains as Zuriel sat. "No one can remove these except by God's mandate."

"What do you want? Leave us in peace. Our punishment is painful enough."

"Do you not want to know how things fare on the earth?"

"Pray, tell," Zuriel said quickly. "We have not had visitors for hundreds of years. I am passed counting."

"There is too much to tell but I must know something first."

"What?" Zuriel responded full of suspicion.

"A simple question, really. How does it feel to be an angel without His glory, and yet not be disfigured like us?"

"If I answer that question, will you share with me what has been happening on the earth?"

"I can answer that." Azazel said from his corner.

"Oh Azazel, betrayer," Bael said smiling wickedly, "I am impressed that Myesmoth has not come down here to torment you. He will never forgive you for what you did."

"Nor I," Azazel grunted, "He left me out of Lucifer's plans after everything we had accomplished together in that forge. He left me no choice."

Bael shrugged. "You should have told Michael the truth behind your reason for helping him. That would have made it an even more interesting spectacle."

"Did you come seeking me or Azazel?" Zuriel spat with disdain.

"Oh, why, you of course. So, will you tell me what it is like?"

Zuriel frowned. "I most surely will."

"I am listening," Bael said and crouched in front of Zuriel.

"This is enough to drive lesser creatures mad. We have dwindled and faded into grey and ash, shadows of our former selves. Without His glory, surely we have become a forgotten thing, a by-word."

"Interesting. Quite different for us, eh?"

"What happened after we were taken?" Zuriel asked.

"Well, first your sons began to wage war. Utter chaos. Gabriel saw to it and giants began fighting, destroying, and killing one another. Blood soaked the earth. Men destroyed their children with fire, giving them up as sacrifice to you. There were all kinds of evil, and then God caused a flood to destroy the earth."

"What?" Zuriel blurted out as other watcher angels expressed their shock as well.

"Lemuel released the fountains of the deep and the bowels of the clouds were emptied. Whoosh!"

"He destroyed everything with water?" Azazel groaned audibly from his corner. "We built wonders upon the earth.

We taught them all kinds of amazing things. We were worshipped."

"But, He preserved one family - Noah, his wife, his three sons, and their wives. After it rained for forty days and forty nights, the waters covered the Earth and every living thing upon the face of the earth died. Your offspring and corrupted sons perished, their spirits wandering aimlessly across the earth, finding no peace, no resting place. They were lost, but… " Bael leaned closer towards Zuriel and whispered, "your seed lives."

Zuriel's eyes opened wide, "What? What did you say?"

"In weakened form of course, much smaller yet mostly twice the size of regular men."

"But you said…"

"They survived beyond the flood. Maybe Noah should have been more careful about the wife he picked for one of his sons. We have been very strategic in our operations."

Zuriel was downcast. "Why have you come to me? To give me hope?"

"Hope? No. At least not for you. Your offspring serves Him at the moment. He has become a mighty warrior before God, bent on destroying all living giants from the earth. His name is Nimrod. I want him."

"Why do you come to me?"

Bael smiled invitingly, "Because, you must release your dominion to me. That is, as always, the order of things in our realm. I will wrench him from Gabriel's will and set him to Satan's purpose - a one-world kingdom and power will be established and I have been chosen to herald it. They will worship me and make sacrifices to me in temples built to honor my name."

"So the war continues then…"

"What war?"

"The war between good and evil. You seek to help them in fulfilling anything but God's will."

"I'm glad you get the picture, but back to the subject of Nimrod. Release your dominion to me and you will rule through your descendant. We will build a monument that will touch the heavens. The people will gather to our might, our majesty, and our power. Our dominion will cover the Earth and our rule will be established for all time. All worship on earth will be ours and mankind will remain a constant source of abhorrence to God."

"I want no part of this conspiracy," Zuriel said. "Look

where my actions have gotten me."

"Sheer bad luck, Zuriel." Bael turned with flourish and observed the other captive angels who watched on with keen interest. "You and your lot can rot here for all eternity, but give me what I ask and you will not be forgotten."

There was absolute silence.

"You should take his offer," Azazel said drily. "What else do you have to lose?"

"The last time you said that," Zuriel turned and glared in Azazel's direction, "...see what has become of us."

Bael rose impatiently.

"Listen, you all. You will be deities - demigods worshipped and revered through the ages. Statues will be made to honor you. Stories will be written and told to future generations of your greatness and your deeds. I only make this offer once."

"Take it!" one of the watchers shouted, and a few chorused their approval as well.

"Like I said, take it," Azazel said again, stoically.

Zuriel nodded slowly, "I cannot use my dominion from here. I do hope you will keep me informed about how Nimrod fares."

"I will, most definitely."

"Bael, all my earthly interests, and the dominion that I attained through my rule is yours. We release our authority to you."

A strange smoke spread across the lower dungeons as Bael reveled in the powers the angels released to him.

"I will be back," Bael assured. "Just so you know, those who pray to you call you Zeus. They believe you are the father of the gods. You see? Your legacies are not forgotten."

As Bael strode off, Zuriel shouted, "What do they call you?"

"Me?" Bael shouted from the distance. "Baal. They call me Baal!"

The sun cast a dazzling glow over the mountain as Noah and Shem arrived at the base of Mount Hermon. Meanwhile, their clan of servants, soldiers, and wives had stopped at a point that was almost a full hour's journey from the mountain. Noah had cautioned them to be vigilant and his warning was needful given the times they were in. As they waited on a queue of excited travellers at the base of the mountain, a score of guards inspected each traveller and their possessions.

"And here we are," Noah said. "Ham's warriors must have been alerted to our presence. My son definitely knows that I am here. I do hope our journey will not be in vain." Noah looked back at the path they had followed to the mountain. The forests were assembled on all sides of the mountain, making it a centerpiece of sorts.

"How can we hide thousands of sheep and men, father?" Shem half-smiled as he dismounted his horse and walked towards his father. "Steady, father. Let me help you off your horse."

"Thank you, Shem. As for his men, I am not afraid of any of them. I'm here for my estranged son."

"I don't think he will be pleased to see you, father," Shem said as he steadied Noah's body. "I don't think he has forgiven you for what you said either. Actually, I do not think that he will ever forgive you."

"What was I supposed to do? I was angry."

"And drunk, father."

"Yes, that too, but we must look to the future. He will always be my son."

"That much is true," Shem responded as one of the warriors stepped forward.

"Welcome Noah, son of Lamech, and welcome Shem, son of Noah. Your son, Ham, has been expecting you." He motioned with his head to a fellow warrior. "This man will lead you up the path to the top of the mountain."

Shem nodded and whispered to Noah. "So far so good, father."

Noah smiled. "Lead the way."

The warrior guide urged Noah and Shem forward through a rocky stairway of sorts that spiraled through trees and stones up the mountain. As they journeyed, Noah and Shem observed peculiar insignia hewn into stones that were lodged in precarious locations throughout the mountain – emblems of demigods of the past.

"What are those?" Shem stopped and asked the guide, pointing to the signposts.

"They are signs of the gods who once walked the earth," the guide responded. "People come from far and near to buy houses so they can live close. They hope to see the gods again."

Shem and Noah briefly locked eyes as they continued on through the ragged path. .

"Around the mountain and mostly other portions around these paths are settlements." The guide continued, "More people come by the day. Come, let us proceed."

The three trudged up the mountain, listening to the sounds of the diverse creatures that lived in its recesses. Occasionally, docile animals passed by them but the greater part of their journey was without event.

"At dawn," the guide resumed, "devotees and priests approach the top of the mountain of three peaks to invoke the rising sun. They lavishly spill oil carried by fair maidens to honor the great fire that lights up the world. They believe the darkness is a curse, and they tell the young ones to honor the light."

"That is indeed remarkable; that the things that happened before the flood have influenced so many people today," Shem said, lost in thought. The path continued, winding upwards until the visitors reached a point where they could see the distant lands. At this height, the sun shined brighter, forcing Noah to squint.

"See there, the lands of our people, spreading abroad." Noah said.

"Yes, father, there is so much to see from here; though many find it hard to believe when you say that everything was once covered by water."

Noah tugged at his grey beard slowly, his grip tightening on his staff. "You were so young then… and scared."

"We were all scared father, including you."

"Me?" Noah feigned defiance for a moment and then smiled. "God was faithful to us. He did not forget us."

"Yes, and the rainbow, we will welcome it forever," Shem said quietly as they took in the wondrous expanse of land beneath the mountain. "Many often take the three-day journey to see the ark that housed us during the great floods though most of it had fallen apart, due to the elements."

"Now, it seems they come here looking for a sign of the supernatural." Noah sighed. "Nothing has changed in man's thirst for power."

"Indeed father, the ark has become a memorial of sorts. Sojourners visit but few have rarely found the courage to climb up the mountain where it rests to touch it."

"The sun will begin its descent soon," the guide warned, struggling to conceal the urgency in his voice. "It is better to climb Hermon when the light rules. Let us find a place to take shelter."

He stopped a few paces away, sighting a location to build tents for the night but then realized moments later that Noah and Shem had continued on without him. "We will not stop. Not until we see Ham," Shem said when the guide caught up with them.

"Very well. We must simply follow the signs and carvings of the priests etched in stone."

A few travelers passed by the trio and some pitched tents on even terrains they found on the sacred mountain.

"Can you hear that?" Shem asked.

"The sound of debauchery and revelry," Noah responded weakly, gritting his teeth. "We are close."

Not long after, Noah, Shem and their guide finally reached the top of the mountain as the ground beneath them became less treacherous. The top of the mountain spread unevenly for miles and was abuzz with men and women, animals and all types of priests.

"Wait here, I will tell your son, Ham that you have arrived. He resides in that tent. Wait here till I come to get you." The guide said and stomped away towards a company of tents.

"Father," Shem put a hand out to steady Noah, "why have you brought us here? This is not merely because of Ham, is it?"

"Because I wanted to see it for myself."

"To see this? Men worshipping their idols?"

"They are hoping to see the sons of God again, the very ones who brought abomination and grave sins upon us. They disappeared mysteriously you see?

"And this is where they first landed?"

"Yes," Noah said, watching as the people danced wildly shouting obscenities. "According to the writings of my great grandfather, Enoch."

"But father, what madness is this?" Assembled before father and son, the worshippers danced in a frenzy, cutting themselves with knives. An aged and frail man dressed as a priest sparked a fire amidst a pile of sticks. Following his lead, the worshipers added wood to the fire, and tended it until it became a proper flame. In a concerted effort, they suddenly began to implore the sons of light to appear.

"Madness," Noah said. "They worship what they do not know. Your brother must have told them about this place and the events that preceded the flood."

"Do they not see the destruction the giants have caused? And how sad that we still have them today."

"I know." Noah found a patch of soil to sit on while Shem knelt beside him. "Ham's son... Canaan," Shem muttered the name as the guide stepped outside the tent nonchalantly.

"Ham will see you at the end of the sacrifice," the guide announced, flashing an uneasy smile.

Noah looked at his son and nodded, his countenance reflecting his grief. "Come now, Shem. Let us find a quieter place to speak and I will tell you about my great grandfather's visions; and of the sons of God who landed on this place."

Bael soared in the skies above the mountain, watching the festivities keenly as a priest clad in a red hooded cassock held up a knife to his chest and cut his skin. He proceeded to cut his arm, letting the blood drip into the fire as the people around him followed suit. An eerie, red glow began to emanate from the burning pile. It was time. Bael swooped into the heart of the fire, causing it to roar and rise above the worshippers, his voice expressing guttural tongues and uttering curses.

The flames rose, unnaturally swept up by Bael's hands. The demon spun around basking in the glow of the chanting and revelry of the people. Bael smiled wickedly watching the ruckus with deep hatred.

"Enough of this madness!" Shem rose suddenly as the people cheered, dancing dangerously close to the fire without getting burned.

"Shem!"

"Wait here, father," Shem said, and forcefully shoved his way through a group of dancers towards the tent. A few of Ham's guards tried to deter him but he elbowed through to the tent's entrance, almost ripping off the covering of the tent's entrance. "Ham, you coward! Show yourself!"

Inside the tent, an organized gathering juxtaposed the chaos of worshippers that thronged the mountaintop. Ham sat at the head seat of a large round table surrounded by his company, a glorified elder amongst his hardy men. The company stood alert, hands reaching for weapons in the event of an attack from their unidentified intruder. Shem eyed his surroundings quickly and observed Ham, Canaan, and a giant with a few others.

Ham stood slowly, his hand lifted to pacify his crew of men.

"Calm down. Calm down, all of you," Ham said, and spread his arms. "Well, brother, join me and my sons. Join our counsel."

Shem looked around the table. He could recognize Cush, Canaan, and Mizraim but the sight of the huge man gave him the greatest concern.

The trio nodded. "Uncle. You are welcome always," Canaan said.

Shem stepped closer to the table, but did not sit, noting the sarcasm in Canaan's tone. His gaze remained on Ham.

"Father is old and full of years," Shem said. "We have travelled through treacherous land to see you; and the giants in our path added even more difficulty to our journey, but here you sit in cohorts with one of them."

"Shem, brother. Welcome. My sons, Mizraim, Cush, Put, and Canaan greet you. Nimrod you do not know. Cush's son," Ham said with a forced smile. "I am pleased to know that father has sought me out. After all, he cursed my son, Canaan; and now, he misses us." Ham seemed indifferent to Shem's grievance. Like Shem, he was full of age. He was frail and wrinkled yet his eyes sparked with a strange ferocity. Ham had become a hardened man. He leaned forward.

"You are silent? Ah! Do you know nothing brother? The curse I could bear but the giving of good land to you as your inheritance leaving me nothing worthwhile… that I could not take. Do you know what hardships we have endured? Do you know?"

"Father wants nothing more but to reconcile with you before his time ends," Shem responded, toning down the anger in his voice.

"Sit down brother," Ham said curtly.

Shem assessed his surroundings a second time; and then, he sat slowly as Ham eagerly continued the discourse.

"Now," Ham said, slapping his hands together, "Father's curse is the reason why we are gathered. For a long time, I tried to reason through his purpose for cursing me. I could find nothing to justify it. He drank too much wine and became drunk. The great Noah laying in his own mess, drunk and naked... What did I do to be labeled accursed? What was my crime? Shem, these lands, we have claimed. My sons and I will not leave these lands. I know they are yours by right, but Nimrod here has gotten rid of many giants. This is God's will. We have been His instruments in ridding our land of His enemies; and now, we are here to claim the good land."

"Ham," Shem spoke, struggling to muffle his anger. "... this land was given to me and my sons according to the lots that father cast. They have nothing to do with the curse. You were to move beyond these parts. My lot apportions Lebanon, even towards Egypt, to me and my sons forever. Beyond the Nile is yours, brother."

"We are not going anywhere. We have as much right by conquest to these lands. Look at this map, brother." He motioned towards a map spread over the round table.

Shem studied it, remaining alert. He knew quite well that he was in the company of hard men who lived by the sword and who had no love for him for that matter. "What are these red marks?" Shem asked.

"Those are the fortresses of giants. Nimrod leads my armies against them. He is the only one that has killed the most giants. We are planning our strategy, and when we wipe out God's enemies, the curse will be reversed. So tell father that I need not see him unless he comes to bless us. After all, we have been doing his work."

Shem shook his head in defiance and retorted, "There is no blessing after what you did. You saw your father's nakedness and did not cover him. Regardless of father's error, you know quite well the symbolism of what you did. What you did... is best left in the darkest crevices of our minds. Take your punishment well, brother. Leave this unholy mountain. You and your filth are passing children through the fire of desecration and corrupting God's Earth with your savagery and idolatry." Canaan pounded the table and reached for his sword.

"Peace!" Ham shouted, his greying beard vibrating as he shook with anger. "Canaan, peace. He is your uncle. Now, you listen to me Shem. My sons and I have lived under the shadow of your wealth and arrogance for far too long. Our hands built everything in this city and on this mountain. We have worked hard and long to achieve everything we have done. This is a holy mountain. Many in my family have their roots here. The god of fire visits us so do not blaspheme against those who believe in him. Leave us, brother. You and father. Leave us! Be grateful that I let you leave unharmed. My sons do not have the same patience I do, or bonds of love that we share."

"You will all suffer the same judgment of God if you do not leave." Shem rose up and stomped outside the tent, tears streaming down his face.

"Well, what do you have to report?"

"They are misguided fools," Bael said to Satan as they soared in the skies, watching as Shem and Noah began their descent from the mountain. A group of high-ranking demon warriors surrounded them all about. "They serve us, yet they do His will by waging war against the giants."

"This Nimrod, you say?"

"Yes, he is a mighty warrior. At least, they will not leave Shem's inheritance. That is a victory for us."

"An incomplete victory," Satan sneered. "Getting Noah drunk was good but only a piece of the fullness of my plan."

"What do you mean?"

"We cannot rule the affairs of men if they are divided and eventually scattered abroad. It will weaken our control and influence. So, yes, it is good that they plan to stay in the blessed land. It is good that they corrupt it with the dark arts, and the sexual depravations we have introduced. However, we need to unite them under a one world leader. Not under factions and divided cultures, but one man that will rule with an iron fist and enforce our will and influence across the earth."

"How do you reckon we will achieve that?" Bael asked furtively. "The giants, who would have been great enforcers, and have already established great civilizations, will soon be on the verge of extinction if Gabriel's pawn, Nimrod, has his way."

"Then our target must change from Ham to Nimrod."

"What do you mean?"

"We must get him to do our will. He has the heart of a king. He is a ruler that can enforce our will through a united force of leadership."

"Yes, my lord, I agree," Bael said. "...but how do we get the people to follow him? It seems slaying giants is not enough."

"We need a spectacle. Something grand. A project. Something that will inspire and motivate people to come together around a common cause," Satan said. "What brings people together? What unites them? What sets them to purpose without complaining and whining?"

"A whip and threats of lashings!" one of the demon warriors said.

"Yes?" Satan responded, as if waiting for more.

Bael glared at the demon that had spoken. "Baeshedith, enslaving people is not the same as inspiring them. But what if..."

"What if they built a fortress for themselves...for all people," Baeshedith countered quickly. "Do you see the throngs who visit Zuriel's mountain hoping to see a return of the watchers?

Before Bael could respond, Satan clapped his hands together.

"Good thinking! I have a plan already set in motion and I will need you, Baeshedith. Gather around closely all of you and listen to my genius."

Bael scowled sullenly as Baeshedith smiled with glee, seizing his opportunity to shine. The demons flocked around their master, a sinister darkness consuming the expanse where they gathered.

CHAPTER

—22—

BABEL

The watchman of the city of Nod hurried quietly towards the huge expanse where the night's festivities rang. The people of Nod had doused the fires on the watchtowers they had built so that they could watch out for intruders. The reveling that was characteristic of their celebrations had barely begun. The women danced and the men drank. Warriors sat here and about, enjoying the pleasantries of the night; and the newly appointed king of Nod, Nimrod, laughed brazenly while seated on a throne overlooking the festivities with his priests and counselors standing by.

A large pyre, upon which a tumultuous fire burned, had been built in the center of the large arena where the people celebrated.

"He is Nimrod, slayer of giants! Nimrod the mighty," the priests chanted as the people reveled. Across the festival grounds, they had made smaller fires where they roasted the venison from their hunt. On one side of the raised stage where they had placed Nimrod's throne, musicians played flutes, tambourines, and reeds. The spoil from the warriors' conquests littered the campus grounds, displayed with abandon amongst the thousands who had gathered.

The watchman almost fell twice, maneuvering through the wild crowd. His breathing was hoarse. He had run for miles without rest from the city gates, and would have collapsed into Nimrod's laps if one of the king's guards did not shove a shield in his chest.

"Stand back, man!"

The musicians continued to play their instruments as the women danced around the pyre. The men cheered even louder. Nimrod looked down towards the watchman, who was now sprawled out on the ground before him, trying to catch his breath. He was trying to say something, but it would be impossible to hear with the din.

Anerbar, Nimrod's right hand man, leaned towards the king. "Drunk already; and we just started."

Nimrod observed the restrained watchman. "This one... is not full of wine. An urgent message perhaps?" The watchman nodded in between choked gasps of air. "Yes," Nimrod said grimly. "A message, it seems."

The king stood with a menacing look on his face. His armor was strapped to different parts of his stately frame, glinting as it reflected the light from the pyre. At the base of his throne as a giant's skull with a huge helmet decorated with flowers and petals. The helmet itself could fit six heads of fully-grown men. The watchman rose to his knees to catch his breath. At the same instant, Nimrod bounded down roughly shoving the guard aside, he grabbed the watchman's shoulders as their eyes met. Nimrod studied the man's face and realized what was coming; and he welcomed it. Turning slightly, he looked at the helmet and smiled bitterly. Before he could speak, the ground shook.

Nimrod squared his shoulders and let out a war cry. The music stopped abruptly as his warriors tried to gather their wits. Nimrod knew what the watchman had come to tell them.

"Giants!" Pandemonium broke loose as the men drunkenly struggled to find their weapons. The ground beneath their feet shook as they rallied around to grab their weapons.

"Archers!" Anerbar yelled, running down the elevated platform. As the men gathered together, they heard screams from afar. Nimrod stood firm, waiting and watching, his face set as flint, and his right hand gripping his huge hunting spear. His head was adorned with a golden torc grafted on its edges with the horns of a wild bull he had hunted down.

"How did they get this far?" Anerbar yelled as he waved for their horses. Nimrod smiled and pointed to the skull on the platform.

"We killed their brother. What do you expect?"

"I imagined we had all but wiped them out."

Nimrod turned to observe Anerbar, "No, the few that remain have fled far beyond the Nile, even beyond Egypt. I do not know how many attack us or how they got so close without being seen."

"Neither do I Nimrod, but if we do not vanquish them, how do we claim the blessing and this good land?"

"We will rid ourselves of this curse no matter what. Let us deal with the enemy at our gates first."

Nimrod bounded from the podium and stepped into his chariot, which had arrived with his aide. "To war!" he shouted, and spurred his horses forward. His warriors responded in like fashion, flanking him on both sides as they charged on towards the city's exterior. Archers raced after them throughout, as they approached the burning city gates.

"They are strong and mighty," Nimrod shouted over the din, "but they are large and greatly exposed."

Easy to kill, Nimrod mused as he sped past the houses and fields towards the city gates. The vast cities in the distance had yielded rulership to him, but there were still cities and settlements to conquer, especially the few where some giants remained. Men still pondered on the giants' history, and how they had survived the great flood that had killed all of mankind, except the eight that escaped in the ark that Noah built.

The great ark's remains stood grafted atop Mount Hermon as evidence of the flood's occurence, yet the only existing recording of the giants' history remained with Noah. Their great father, as many called him, had the words of his great grand father, Enoch, who had great insight into how the giants had first come about.

Nimrod himself had lived on Mount Hermon. He had seen the place that the priests called sacred - the landing place of the gods where the angel watchers had first come to the earth, prior to bearing giants as offspring. However, he was now God's instrument to rid the earth of them after the flood. God wanted them dead.

Just outside of Nod's gates, Nimrod's troop saw a giant smashing through the towers, destroying the oil depots used for the catapults.

"How many do you see?" Anerbar shouted, endeavoring to keep pace with Nimrod's chariot. Nimrod did not answer. Eyes on his target, he raised his spear and declared, "Tell the archers to fire at will." Before Anerbar could respond, he charged ahead through the burning gate.

The giant stood stout and strong, clothed in large breeches made of fine leather. His face was masked by a bronze helmet, revealing steely eyes filled with hate. He set his gaze on Nimrod as his men raced through the city gates, and their eyes met.

"I see you, giant hunter!" he bellowed. "Now you die!"

Nimrod bellowed a war cry, spurring his horses forward. He realized that this creature was the great giant king, whose son's skull now adorned his throne. This fight was personal.

The giant flexed his hands, "You betray your kind, and hunt down your brothers. I tried to ignore your ills but you have killed my son and today, you die."

Nimord stood firm as flint, his right hand hoisting his war spear as his chariot charged towards the giant. "I only do God's will," he shoulted intently.

"We know of your wager. It is a waste of time. God will never accept you and your fathers. You are mere pawns."

"You lie!" Nimrod thrust his spear at the giant and stealthly pulled out two shiny daggers from his back. The giant king bellowed in pain as the weapon sank into his thigh. He grasped the weapon and slowly pulled the spear from his thigh. In that instant, Nimrod struck his daggers deep into the giant's leg, forcing him to kneel in pain. Going for his kill, he steered his chariots close to aim at the giant's head - another ornament for his throne.

But as Nimrod passed, the giant swung his arm at Nimrod's horses, killing them instantly. The sheer impact flung Nimrod's body off the chariot and unto the dry terrain.

Back at the burning tower, a score of archers waited on the order to fire at the giant, but Anerbar would have nothing of it.

"Hold!" he shouted. "Nobody fire until our king is clear." Nimrod rose, his face contorted as he shouted. His eyes were alive with a strange fire. The giant had risen, struggling to ignore the pain as he towered over Nimrod with deadly intent.

"Die!" he giant shouted as he swung an arm at the giant killer's body, but Nimrod was quick. Swinging to the right, he escaped the giant's blow. The giant rounded on him sensing the kill.

A great distance from fighting, Noah and Shem arrived at their camp and family. Shem put his hands around his father's body, guiding and consoling him. Noah wept bitterly. There was no going back. He would never be able to change the course of the future get his son's forgiveness.

"We must leave here father," Shem said. "It is not safe."

"Yes indeed," Noah responded, "I felt the ground shake as well. I only hope Ham is safe."

"They have the giant slayer. Surely, they will prevail. Come father. Let us leave this place. Whether or not these lands are mine, I do not intend to contend with my brother forever. Someday this land, the promised land, will be ours forever."

"Yes, my son. Yes indeed. So shall it be."

The giant could sense that victory was near. He swung his arm, catching Nimrod slightly on the jaw. Nimrod's boody shook and smashed haplessly unto the ground.

In the distance, Anebar bellowed his alert. "Save the king!" He dashed into action, running through the burning gate with a few warriors at his heels. "Attack!"

Nimrod lay on the ground, his eyes focused on the giant king, who now towered over him. "Finish it," he said through bloody teeth.

As the giant went for his final blow, an archer's arrow

pierced his arm with fire. The giant king wialed in pain. Seeing his opportunity, Nimrod struggled to rise up, his breath coarse and his blood boiling. The giant turned away for a moment and stomped on the ground causing some of his attackers to fall. Anerbar dashed forward with his men, his gaze set on his target.

With the giant's back turned towards him, Nimrod saw his moment. He ran towards the giant and leaped on his back and raced towards his neck, steading himself with the leather fastening on the giants garment.

"Nimrod!" Anerbar shouted, and threw his dagger towards the giant's face. Nimrod caught the dagger and sunk its blade into the giant's neck. The giant swayed unsteadily for a moment and then slumped thunderously to the ground as the soldiers cheered.

They poured out of the city, shouting and chanting Nimrod's name. Wounded and bloodied yet full of pride, Nimrod stood on the dying giant basking in the honor of his men. "Hail, the slayer of giants, the ruler of the world," they chanted.

Anerbar ran to embrace Nimrod, his head only reaching Nimrod's mid region. "Another victory for the lord of the earth. God has given you another victory."

Nimrod's face darkened. "He? This victory was not of God. If indeed we can buy the blessing with our blood, have we not given enough? No, He has turned from me. I do not slay the evil spirits for Him like I once did. Not anymore. Now I do it for myself. For everything we have done to rid the earth of his enemies, the curse has not been lifted. Ham was foolish to believe in this."

"Regardless, today is your victory. Noah and Shem will be grateful."

"They should be. They wish us to spread abroad the earth, to leave this good and desirable land to find another? No. I want to bring men together, to one place, to one king, to one way of worship. What is wrong with that? No. God and I are no longer in agreement."

"So what is next, our king?"

"Put this giant's head on a spear at the pass of Nod and Morhan. Let the bards sing of my kill and let the distant lands hear of my feats. And gather the people to me; let us build a tower that will touch the heavens. When men look up, they will look up to us. We will rule the entire world. We will be as gods among men and maybe even throw down those who dwell up there."

Anerbar's heart pumped with excitement, his eyes grew wider as soaked in Nimrod's words. "Your words are my will."

"Everyone will work together to build this tower. It will be one that history will always talk about. It will touch the heavens, surely."

"Touch the heavens," Anerbar mused.

"Yes, the gate of God. Babel..." Nimrod smiled. "And get me another chariot. We must find the land where we shall build."

As the men returned to their festivities, a dark sinister force sped away from the kill, unbeknownst to the men below. It's mission completed. Baeshedith sped towards a consternation of demons following a path to the area of his dominion. Yes, let them gather in one mind and build. Let them build. The gate of God would be a phenomenon that would shake all of Heaven.

Baeshedith joined the dark mass of demons cheering his effort with Bael at the elm. He had shielded the giant from the sight of men, allowing the Nephilim to pass through the preceding cities unannounced. The giant had taken the bait, lured by the opportunity to exact revenge on the giant slayer. Baeshedith had used his opportunity to encourage Nimrod's thirst for power. Their conqueror would build a pathway to the heavens where men would attempt to fight their Maker.

Days after their visit to Mount Hermon, Noah and Shem built an altar to God as they paused to rest on their journey. Shem had listened intently to everything his father told him through the long nights as they journeyed. "I know," Noah said to Shem as they gathered their belongings. "I know that you wonder how he was taken by God."

"Yes, father. I do very much."

"His face was often covered with light because of the great things of God that he had seen."

"But you were not born then," Shem reasoned.

"No," Noah smiled. "I was not. But my father gave me his writings and I myself have often heard God."

"I know father," Shem said, helping Noah on to this horse. "We would not be alive if it were not for you."

Noah spurred his horse as they continued their slow journey. "We have seen wonders, haven't we? The animals as they came in twos, the violent beasts calmed by angels, the waters as they sprouted out of the ground and the rains that the heavens poured; the screams and shouts of the people who had once doubted as they raced towards the ark and the roar when the angel of the Lord shut the door and sealed it. The fear we felt and the peace we knew because God had promised us He would fulfill it."

"Ah, and what of the rainbow?" Shem smiled.

"Stunning, vibrant, peaceful." Noah responded, "an eternal covenant that the earth will never again be destroyed by water. Shem?"

"Yes father..."

"You know this earth will one day return to how it was in Eden?"

"That would be great, father. That would be great."

Their words faded into silence as the company of men and animals journeyed east towards home. In the skies above them, two guardian angels journeyed with them, protecting and covering them. The Spirit of God lingered far after Noah's camp had moved on. The expanse of land spread across hills and valleys as the earth slowly regained its vegetation and color. The terrains had changed and many ancient monuments had been lost. Fossils and treasures were buried deep within the earth as God washed off the corruption that had stained the earth.

God's presence filled the expanse as Noah and his men passed through the ancient path not knowing that thousands of years after, one of his seed through the lineage of Judah and David, the begotten of the Father would walk through this path, up a hill called Golgotha to the place of the skull where God would give His ultimate sacrifice to redeem lost mankind. No one could foresee it at this point in time, except the Most High.

A few years later, the Spirit of God proceeded northwards and descended, watching the men below. "Come, Michael. Come, Gabriel. Do you see what the children of men are doing?" God said.

Tirelessly, the people worked, mounting stone upon stone, as their tower rose steadily. Without so much as a quick rest, the men worked feverishly, using a steady flow of water, lumber and rocks from the stone pits. All men, women and children worked.

The tower had risen tall and wide. Nimrod's tent flashed a dainty red, sporting the helmet of his most recent giant kill hooked at the top. Beneath the covering, Nimrod consulted with his trusted men. More men than he had expected had come from the distant lands to build the tower. The news had spread quickly and men gathered to see the spectacle and to labor alongside.

Unabated by title, class or family name, the men worked through a schedule system sorting by strength so that the builders and climbers could work and live at different levels of the tower. The women carried straw and pitch mixing it by walking around the huge mixing baths. Some others carried buckets of water from the wells ensuring that there was a steady supply of food and water throughout the tower.

In the distance, Michael, Gabriel and Lurerdeth watched quietly. Arms folded and grim faced, the angels watched as travelers came from far distances to the tower through which man would touch the heavens. Since the flood and the few giants that surprisingly emerged through the lineage of Ham, the earth had witnessed no other spectacle as this. "Why spread about without cause?" Nimrod had proclaimed, "Let us make a name for ourselves. Let us unite as one."

"See what they begin to do," God said, "and nothing will be kept from them."

"It is only left to wonder how they constantly go against your will. You expressly commanded them to be fruitful and multiply, and cover the earth." Michael said solemnly.

"There is another power at work here," God responded, "but my purpose will still stand."

"What should we do?" Michael asked, his angels poised, waiting for their instruction.

"Go down and confuse their speech," God said.

The angels descended as one, swooping down upon the

tower and its people, changing their languages. Man turned to his neighbor, seeking to be understood but to no avail. Pandemonium reigned. Abandoning the work, people sought for those who spoke their own language, which created clusters of people groups. Those who understood Nimrod's speech amassed to him as even more began to argue in diverse tongues.

"What is gong on?" Anerbar yelled. "They have stopped working! They are speaking difference languages."

"Send men to gather those who still understand our tongue."

Nimrod gazed upwards to the heavens, wild eyed and confused. Anerbar stood dutifully by his side as officers worked tirelessly into the night to gather men who could understand their words. "We will not have enough to complete this work from the number of those who understand our words," he said. "I do not understand how this happened. One moment ago..."

"Our enemy, God, has made His move," Nimrod said dejectedly, pounding his fists together. "However, we must leave this place. There may be those who will come to claim the tower." Nimrod walked forward as if in a trance. "The tower of confusion," he muttered regretfully.

Anerbar turned to the soldiers, "Gather what horses you can find. Gather your families and let us depart to the Euphrates till we have rebuilt our forces and our kingdom. Then we will return and finish what we have started."

The darkness over the terrain faded as the last of the people dispersed. A mild rain washed the earth as the once busy valley became as silent as the grave. Nimrod stood on the gigantic stairway that led into Babel, gazing at the remains of his thwarted plan. The people had abandoned their work; and as the days passed, only very few dared to approach the valley before continuing on in fear of the place called Confusion.

Leaning on a pillar, he observed the direction of the wind as a tear rolled down his face. They had made openings for sunlight in the first floor of the tower. The glow of light beamed through the windows as he observed quietly. An idea began to form in his mind, a plan of revenge that only he could mete out against the Creator.

The seed of the woman would suffer. He would pass her seed through the fire and have the people worship the gods of death. He would reign upon the earth as lord of the world, and unite the kingdoms again under his rule. Nimrod pulled out a blade and pressed it deep into his left hand, cutting into his flesh. He then cut into his thigh and marked his chest as the light of the sun basked over him in the center of the room.

Reborn in his hate, his eyes glowed red as blood dripped unto the floor. He would be king of kings and he would find those who worshipped God and destroy them. The darkness returned as a myriad of whispering voices filled the room. Nimrod spread his hands, welcoming them. The idea of a new world order to defeat the King was born and he was the chosen one to bring it to pass. The war had only just begun.

CHAPTER

—23—

THE ANGEL
OF THE LORD

"So you will simply give up and give in, son?"

"Mother," Nimrod stretched his hands and welcomed the woman clad in red, who stood at the entrance of the hall within the abandoned tower. He could tell that she had been crying but there was a strange glare in her eyes.

"Far from it mother, but I have lost this fight. God has dealt me a heavy blow."

"Why do you stand here sulking? The people who have stayed to follow you...they need their leader. You must rise up and be their king. The gods I worship have promised to strengthen your rule. They came to me last night through the fire and told me of things that will happen."

"Mother, you never quit do you? You have the heart to rule over many kingdoms."

"It is a mother's love. You know I will do anything for you." Semiramis rested her head on Nimrod's chest as he held her close.

"These gods you worship. What do they say of my future?"

"My son," Semiramis said as Nimrod looked down, searching her eyes. "your enemies will try to kill you. Shem is your enemy and you must kill and enslave his seed. They are dangerous and they oppose our cause. My gods demand this."

"Ham would not have it."

"You speak of a man whose time is past. Shem, Ham, all of them. Their times are past and it is your moment, your chance to rule the world. The whole world will come under your rule and your whims and we will rule for all eternity. The people need a god that they can see and worship. I know many secrets of the universe and we must indeed share this sacred knowledge with those who follow us."

"You speak wise words, mother."

"We are entering into a new age of knowledge and power. There will be a rising tide of hunger for truth beyond our world but we can shape thought and culture. We have an opportunity to define how men will interact with the supernatural, with the gods I worship."

"I have felt their power. I have heard their voices. I am their servant. I will be their warrior's hand on the earth." Nimrod smiled as he leaned slightly and swept her into his heavy arms.

"Come, let us go from here," Semiramis said. "We must get to work quickly before everyone else leaves you. And there is something they have requested you and I to do. I will explain later."

"As you wish, mother."

In the distance east of the tower of Babel, the evening fires burned brightly, dancing with the gusts of the whistling wind. Weary travellers spent the night eating and resting after their journey from the tower as their tethered horses grazed in the neaby grounds.

A sullen Nimrod stomped through the encampments as his soldiers bowed towards a huge red tent. He stepped into the tent and paced around, ignoring his man at arms and the other warriors who sat, feasting in chairs covered with sheepskin.

"Welcome our king and champion." Anerbar rose, bowing as the men in the tent followed suit. Nimrod offered no greeting but immediately grabbed a roasted rabbit's haunch. Continuing to pace, he bit into the savory meat, allowing its juices to soak through his beard.

"Nim…"

"I don't want to talk about it," Nimrod said, as he continued to pace. "I still cannot believe we got that far and now our glory lies unfinished, a home to wild beasts and vagabonds. Even our offering of silver for workers was turned down."

"Great king, men do not need to speak the same language to build, but the people call the tower cursed and refuse to go near it. What are we to do?"

"My mother, Semiramis. She knows what to do and yet she counseled me to lead you all away from the tower. Where is she now?"

"I had her tent made closer to the top of this mountain. I thought it best till all the chaos dies down. She continues to offer prayers and sacrifices. The people gather to feast, drink, and dance around the fire."

"This is no time to feast, men. We must send riders out to seek those who speak our tongue. We must unite those we can. I am sure that there are more! Also, we must make slaves of those who do not speak our tongue. They will serve us."

"As you command."

"Tell me," Nimrod said. "How many stone masons have you gathered?"

Anerbar stiffened. "We have fourteen from my last count."

"You have fourteen?" Nimrod walked menacingly towards him. "Do you know how many people we had building the tower? Do you know? Now you sit here feasting. But that's the very problem isn't it? You have no ambition. I'll rather be cold and dead in a grave than become an obscure figure, forgotten and lost in history."

Anerbar nodded slowly. "I understand."

"Do you?" Nimrod retorted quickly, "If you did, you would realize that our greatest assets are the masons."

"You wish to continue building the tower?"

"No, Anerbar. No." Nimrod leaned close, towering over the men seated about him, who remained silent. There was no arguing with him when he was disgruntled. "We are going to build a city that is bigger and more magnificent, full of glory and wealth. Kings and rulers will come to my throne and bow at my feet. We will channel the Euphrates to water our fields and tame the beasts of the fields to serve us. I will create a kingdom such as never has been seen in all of the earth. My Babylon."

The men cheered heartily as Anerber pounded the table with his silver goblet.

"We stand with you until death takes us."

Nimrod's face began to glow eerily as he spoke. His followers leaned in, caught in the rapture of the moment, and lost in the words that spilled effortlessly from his mouth.

"I will rise in glory and power and my influence will reach the ends of the earth. All those who oppose me will perish by the sword and fire. We will erect statues of our gods and give them new sacrifices regularly. As for Shem and the others, we will enslave them. Their daughters will be our slaves and their young men will work tirelessly to build out cities. We will rule this earth. My glory will cover the earth. My dominion shall cover the seas!"

The room darkened mysteriously and the men looked around furtively as dark voices filled the room. Through the night, the strange light from the tent drew men and beasts towards it as Nimrod's voice rose through the starless night carried by the spirits that aided his cause. At the top of the mountain, Semiramis reveled with the men and women worshipping at the peak of the mountain, uttering dark words and committing illicit intimate acts.

At dawn, they would begin their work of building the foundations of Nimrod's city, and the gathering of the stonemasons were to form a secret order that would live through the ages.

"Things are in motion, my lord," Bael bowed low before Satan who was standing, accompanied by Mealiel and a dozen of Satan's captains. They stood listening as Bael gave his report. Nimrod's men had begun their descent into the fertile land to begin building their new city, oblivious to the dark spirits around them.

"Your reward is to rule this new kingdom," Satan said. "I give you the kingdoms of Nimrod. What will you call it?"

"They already call it Babylon, gate of the gods," Bael responded, smiling with glee. "I have led them to a fertile plain between the Tigris and the Euphrates rivers. They will be a wonder of the world. We will begin building from the land of Shinar."

Satan nodded.

"The woman, Semiramis, she has proved an asset beyond anyone else, " Bael continued.

"She is only a tool to be used for our desires but my concerns are that I do not know what He will do next. As long as Shem's seed remains, there is a glimmer of hope for our enemies. You must convince Nimrod to send out warriors to find them and kill them all."

"As you command, my lord." Bael bowed low, struggling to hide his scowl.

"Now I must turn my focus to the land of Mizraim, Egypt." Satan said.

"The lands of the Nile will prove a great asset to our cause in the coming years," Mealiel spoke up quickly.

"Yes indeed, people have begun to gather together as well across the Nile. This is where I will establish my throne and rule the world but first, Astaroth will go as my forerunner."

"And what about me?" Mealiel asked, as the demons turned to observe him. "You distribute power and leave me out?" The demons turned their gaze from Mealiel to look at Satan, wondering how their leader would respond or react. Satan spread his arms disarmingly.

"Mealiel, you have stayed with me and I can never forget. What I have for you is far bigger than these puny cities. I place you above all my principalities and powers across the heavenly realms. I will personally focus on finding and destroying the seed of the woman while you manage all our affairs. Do you accept this honor, friend?"

Mealiel bowed, "I am yours for always."

Satan clapped his hands. "Good. Gather our forces. It is time."

Mealiel nodded and gave a signal. Another demon sped upwards releasing a greenish flame. In an instant, hundreds of demon principalities, captains, and dominions began to congregate around the area.

"This is where we shall begin to build the new Jerusalem," a voice resounded through the thick smoke. "I will give you details every step of the way. This is very special to my heart. This city is for a peculiar people, a holy nation."

"Yes, Lord." Shelan responded meekly, bowing low. The builder angels knelt quickly, paying homage.

"First we will lay foundation of the city and then the walls. You may proceed."

Full of purpose and excitement, the angels sped to action propelled by the force surrounding the cloud of glory that kept close vigilance as they worked. Four angels sped across the terrain at blinding speed, measuring the land in different directions. Everything had to be done according to the plan they had received. As soon as they reached the set limits, they erected a pole of fire giving the signal the other angels were waiting for.

Standing in front of the square expanse, bordered by the poles of fire, the building angels cheered heartily relishing the excitement from their new assignment. They worked in groups, taking turns to create the foundations of the new city.

"Stunning work!" Shelan beamed with delight. "This is beautiful." The angels had built the first foundation entrenched in an open space as they worked through the final details of the their work.

"Michael and Gabriel approach," one of the builder angels announced. The angels parted ways to allow the archangels to step into the newly built construction.

Shelan spread his arms joyfully. "Welcome Michael, and Gabriel."

"You have progressed at great speed," Michael responded. "This is indeed fascinating and beautiful."

"This is only the beginning. Neither Myesmoth's rebellion

nor Azazel's for that matter could put an end to this work."

"Yes, Heaven thrives under the leadership of its new appointees," Michael said. "Lemuel has charge of the earth and the lower places. Vernon now sits in the tower at the gate of God's temple."

"The thought of Zuriel's acts still plagues my thoughts," Shelan frowned and then smiled. "How are Chesum and Adriel?"

"Yes, Chesum leads the heralds now. Quite befitting if I must say. Adriel cares for the righteous on the earth, an important task," Michael said as Gabriel stepped forward.

"Putting you in charge of the forge was definitely a befitting reward for you, Shelan," Gabriel said as he hugged the angel. "Greetings from all creatures of good. This new city will be great indeed. It is remarkable that you build it within Heaven. A city within a city."

"You have to ask our King," Shelan said, turning to the glory cloud, but he realized that the cloud had disappeared.

"Another mystery," Michael chuckled. "We shall know the purpose of this city soon enough."

"How about this, then?" Shelan asked teasingly, "There will be 12 foundations for the walls of the city. It will be made from the purest jasper. Yes, the city itself will be made from pure gold, as clear as crystal."

"So even the foundations will be well laced with all types of precious stones," Michael said, studying their surroundings.

"Absolutely. Symbolic." Shelan laughed as he watched the archangels' excited gestures. "We have just completed the foundation of jasper. Their is still much to do. Let me show you more."

"Please do," Gabriel responded eagerly as Shelan revealed a scroll. The blueprint of the city lit up immediately with sparkling trails of light and energy.

"See? The city will have twelve gates with names I am not familiar with. Three gates each on the north, east, south and west."

"This is amazing. Indeed we see these things first before they happen on the earth."

Shelan scratched his bearded chin. "I do not think that this is meant to remain in Heaven."

"What?" Gabriel expressed his surprise. "What do you mean?"

"I don't know. It is a hunch. Another heavenly expanse is

being prepared for mansions. We shall have a great many living here in Heaven at a time I do not know. All we can do now is prepare for that time."

"Remarkable," Gabriel said, "He will not leave them in Hades forever. The righteous will be with Him."

"Or maybe He will go to them first." Michael mused, deep in thought. "What is this city called?"

"Jerusalem," Shelan responded quietly.

"Are you ready to do your duty?"

"Yes."

"Good." Lurerdeth rose slowly from his chair and walked to the array of books lined neatly in the shelves across the room. The shelves were huge, each containing an uncountable number of scrolls, parchments and bound books. The books glowed, casting off different colors. "Here is what you need to study. Some of these are prophecy and are yet to be revealed on the earth. Do you understand Adriel?"

"Yes, I do."

"That is good. Evil is gathering again. They are coming together in unity with a central goal, a common cause - the corruption of mankind." Lurerdeth pulled out a book and then paused to observe the quiet Adriel. "I sense that you are even more excited about your new role than the details of the mission."

"I am excited to serve God."

"I know, I know." Lurerdeth smiled empathetically, "You are eager to jump right into the heart of evil but it is important that you understand the state of the earth."

"I am listening."

"Good. Satan is rallying his forces for a singular purpose – to destroy anyone who opposes his agenda. He seeks to control how men believe and whom they believe through the establishment of religion. There are those who have begun to call upon the name of the Lord, and so, more than ever, he fears that Shem's lineage will produce the seed that will crush his head. He is closing in on them and they must remain protected." Lurerdeth pointed to a name in the book, "One young man in particular...Terah. He does not call on the name of the Lord but he is important to our cause and must be watched closely. His soon coming child has been singled out to do great and mighty things. Here, Adriel, look at this."

Lurerdeth picked up a scroll on his table and opened it.

"Here are the first set of missions and remember, some of them will require being the hand of God's judgment on the earth. I wish you and the others success."

"Others?"

"Yes, Adriel, there are two others who will go with you. Come with me."

Adriel followed Lurerdeth closely into an inner room in the Hall of Secrets. There were two men waiting inside the room, which shocked Adriel.

"Surely you didn't expect that you would go in angelic form." One of them said as the other smiled.

"Ashfalon, I can't believe it," Adriel beamed, wide-eyed, and then saw the face of the second man and stood, stupefied. He began to feel a dread and it suddenly dawned on him to fall flat on the ground in worship.

"My God, my King."

"Rise," the Man chuckled though the words carried a life and light that made the angels dizzy with the raw power He carried. "I will be going with you. I will not be far from my people, and this will one of many visits."

Adriel rose to his feet slowly and looked at the Man. "What shall we call you?"

"You may call me the Angel of the Lord."

"You must really love these people. Surely, even with how prone they are to rebellion, you do everything to be reconnected to them."

"I love them," the Angel of the Lord said with a strong determination expressed in his tone. "Come let us go. We go to establish Salem, and one called Melchizedeck as king and priest before me forever."

In the dungeons of Hades, Zuriel suddenly sat up and listened, wondering what he had just heard. A few other watchers stirred as well.

"Do you all hear that?"

"Someone is coming," Azazel responded.

"It is I," Myesmoth stepped into the lower dungeons of

Hades, a strange light buzzing around him. "Zuriel, I have come to announce to you the new age."

"What new age?" Zuriel asked as Myesmoth stomped into the center of the gigantic dark prison.

"The age of dominion," Myesmoth said proudly, "The time of gods and kings. The propensity of mankind to worship is powerful. They have the capacity to move God's heart and yet they pray to the things He has created to serve them. It is utterly ridiculous I tell you."

"Wish I was there to see it," Azazel said, "Do the giants prevail?"

"The traitor dares speak to me. You betrayed me, Azazel. I remember the great instruments we built together and yet, you conspired with Michael and made weapons for our enemy."

"Is this why you have come...the great and powerful Myesmoth has come to whine and complain?" Azazel responded with scorn.

"You have always been a betrayer...a cheat and a liar. Did you ever wonder why I never involved you in my plans? I could at least have tried to get you to be part of our mission but I knew you could never be trusted."

Azazel smiled bitterly. "I do not regret for one moment that I helped Michael. I do not. You are right, my motivation was one of revenge against you for taking up a commission with Satan without involving me."

"Now here you are, a pitiful fool bound for all eternity."

"Are you two quite finished?" Zuriel interjected, gritting his teeth. "Since we have very few visitors, what can you tell us of the happenings on earth? How do the giants fare?"

"Azazel's weapons of death are being upgraded. You will be amazed at what they have developed from the things you taught them but to answer your question, the giants are depleted."

"No thanks to Zuriel's seed," Azazel said as Zuriel glared at him and rose up slowly.

"Myesmoth, lord of the forge. Why are you here?" Zuriel asked, trying to hide his disdain.

"Lord of the forge? It has been long since I have been called that. But oh, it is my place to be here," Myesmoth responded with a chuckle. "I have been given charge over this abyss. I am now the king of the pit, Apollyon, as they now call me. We will forge weapons of fire and destruction in the hidden places."

"What of Bael?"

"Bael has made a quite a name from himself with the people of the earth. You gave your authority to him. Your offspring, Nimrod, serves him or shall we say his mother... who is now his wife?"

"What madness do you speak of?"

"It matters not. Bael is called Baalzebub. They have erected statues to him and offer incense to him, calling upon his name, Baal. Deservedly of course since he led the building of the abandoned tower of Babel, and oversees the building of Nimrod's empire, Babylon. Many sins and much blood will soak the lands of this new kingdom. Its very existence will be a scourge to everything that is good and godly."

"How is Nimrod doing?"

"He contends with tShem's seed. I do not know what will come out of it just yet. What we know is that God is preparing a special people called to Himself who worship Him alone. We do not have all the details yet, but we continue to work on this. No matter. Now to my real purpose. A new prison has been made underneath the Euphrates River and a request has been released from the throne room to move Azazel and three of his cohorts whom God deems most dangerous."

"From the throne room?" Azazel asked, "What do you mean from the throne room? Do you now take orders from heaven?"

"No, but we are willing to oblige. We of course must sometimes pretend to be diplomatic. You mean nothing to us and besides, Azazel you have been nothing but trouble, even for us. Your whispers of escape and scheming are a thorn to all. You are one dangerous angel."

"But why move us to further seclusion? Who defends my case? I am as opposed to God as you are? Why did no one argue on my behalf?"

"That is totally besides the point. Have you forgotten what I just said? You were the one who gave Michael and his angels a chance to defend themselves. How can we ever forget or forgive that? No one will speak for you or represent you in the courts of Heaven."

"I wish to be free. What trouble is that?"

"You, above all else influenced us and caused us to sin against God." Zuriel could not hold back any longer, "I simply concurred to marry and love the woman I selected; you chose to teach them about weapons of war, the mixing of creatures and sorcery. That was your doing, Azazel. You deserve worse than what is coming to you."

Producing a key, Myesmoth said interject. "God has imputed all of that sin to you. Come now, no fuss."

A dozen demons stepped into the prison brandishing weapons.

"You are in charge of the new prison also?" Azazel asked. "No," Myesmoth responded smiling in an evil manner, "Lemuel and his forces wait in the great hall of the dead. We will hand you and the other three to them."

Zuriel leaned against one of the pillars he was chained to as Myesmoth and his forces led the hapless prisoners away. It would be a long time of waiting for his final judgment but he would wait. He had no choice but to allow himself a weary smile. He remembered his tower at the gate of the outer court of God's sanctuary. He remembered Lucifer's first visit. He remembered the confusion amongst the angels, and his first visit to Hades. He remembered the war and the casting out. He could see the faces of his brothers and friends, singers and instrumentalists, now warriors and captains either for good or for evil. He remembered the glory of God and the countless moments shared in the throne room, basking in His presence.

All of existence had been changed forever. Innocence, purity, and holiness were things that man would now have to strive for. They were no longer innate. Death and pain had become real; yet there was something about it all that brought Zuriel comfort. He thought about it and almost smiled. God had a plan. He could sense that through all the madness that now plagued the world, God had an ultimate purpose that was still unfolding. Something monumental and historic that would change the course of human existence in its totality was going to happen. It began to dawn on him that if God was Alpha, He also knew the end of all things. This revelation brought him joy, a feeling that had evaded him given his current plight.

Zuriel closed his eyes and allowed himself to drift away as he allowed the comfort to calm his mind. In those precious moments, he forgot his restraints and began to hum a song of worship to God.

AN EXCERPT FROM
FATHER OF SPIRITS
BOOK 2

— / —

THE BOOK
OF
DOMINION

— / —

BY

ROTIMI
KEHINDE

I
EMMANUEL, GOD WITH US

Gabriel sped through the colorful expanse of the firmament, watching carefully for demon patrols in the third heavens. The angel's mission was of the gravest importance and as such, he was quite tense, knowing the danger around him and the need to remain concealed.

The city of Nazareth, in Galilee, a city created over two thousand years after the Tower of Babel was before him as he proceeded. Gabriel did not linger as he advanced into the city getting closer to his destination. The dusty city was spread out in a complex network of houses, markets, garrisons and synagogues.

Conquered by the Roman Empire, the Israelites had been forced to serve the Romans, but were allowed religious freedom in their places of worship. The emperor had craftily put the provinces and cities under governors to uphold Roman law and justice.

The market of Nazareth was like a coliseum with stockpiles of produce from distant lands. North of the market was the temple and the quarters of the Chief Priest. Occasionally Roman patrols marched and happily sorted out the few local disputes but primarily, the priests provided their own brand of justice to their people.

Standing tall near the central market square through a paved road with the statues of Roman gods and legends stood the parallax with a golden eagle at its top- the center of justice of the governor, Herod. Two huge demon guards were standing on the marble frame of the linings of the roof watching the activity below them as the people went about their business.

"Do you see that?" One of them spoke pointing.

"I see nothing." The other grunted, attempting to observe where his partner was pointing.

"A holy one perhaps." The demon was persistent.

"I'm not sure but I can almost swear that I saw an angel."

"There are always angels among them on assignment, so what of it?"

"This one seemed different. He moves like an archangel if I am correct."

The second demon was interested now. "You think God is on the move? Something important is about to happen?" He asked enthusiastically. "If what you say is true, we must speak to Baeshedith immediately. I only hope you are correct because nothing of note ever happens here."

"You are right," the first demon conceded. "We cannot report this if we are unsure. Let's go check."

The two demons pulled out their weapons, unfurling their gnarled wings. They descended from the mantle of the building speeding through the air towards the housing communities of Nazareth.

"Do not be alarmed." Gabriel stepped into the dimly lit room as light flooded the small space reaching into the crevices. Mary was startled but she kept her composure.

"Who are you?"

"My name is Gabriel and I am a messenger of God. You are highly favored. Blessed are you among women."

Mary's confusion was evident at Gabriel's words. "Do not be afraid Mary. You will bear a son and you shall call Him Jesus. He shall be great and be called the Son of the Most High. God will give to Him the throne of His fore father David. He shall reign over the house of Jacob and of His kingdom, there will be no end."

The words of the angel sank deep into her heart as Mary knelt mulling over what Gabriel had said. Still full of wonder, she thought about Joseph, their coming wedding, and what people would say. A strange peace flooded her heart but she could not fathom how it would happen. "How shall this happen?" She said, "I am a virgin."

Gabriel smiled, his voice rich and melodious yet full of

power and awe, "The Holy Spirit of God will come upon you."

Not too far from Gabriel's location, the demon guards scoured the streets of Nazareth seeking the intruder. Oblivious to the presence of spirits, the people continued their lives not knowing that a long established prophecy, passed from generation to generation, was being initiated at that very moment. The promised deliverer was about to be born.

Gabriel left Mary's house on a dirt road, his sandals raising the dust of road through the streets of Nazareth. Very few noticed him as he pulled his garment over his head as a hood, appearing as a mere traveler going about his business.

A few houses from Mary's, a demon landed on the roof of a house, his greenish eyes filled with hate at the people of God. Something important had transpired but they did not know what. As they stood on the roof, the suspicion grew deeper in their hearts. The thought that an important messenger had come, and there was no telling what message or who it had been given to, made them nervous.

"But why here? This city isn't important. I would have expected somewhere in Jerusalem but not this dusty smelly town." The demon guard said. "We must report this." His companion said. "We have no choice. If something big develops from this, our punishment will be unbearable." The two demons unfurled their distorted wings and sped off.

Gabriel waited till they were gone, his apprehension great, having sensed their presence as he left the house. Gabriel faded from the physical world, as light covered him, he sped off into the heavens. It was too dangerous to come in spiritual form so the angels would have to find another way to communicate with the humans. Time and secrecy was of prime importance with the mission of heaven. There could be no mistake. The salvation of the human race depended on this mission. They had to protect the woman at all costs and the seed that was already forming in her belly.

God had chosen the perfect and most dangerous plan and only few of the angels understood. God was going into the world as a man through the lineage of King David, a technicality that seemed important to God. The angels watched the proceedings carefully as heaven stepped into the affairs of earth in an epic move that would change everything. God had picked Mary, a woman betrothed to Joseph who was of Bethlehem of Judah. They were engaged with wedding plans were fully underway.

Gabriel looked down for a brief moment. In the far distance in the firmament, he could sense the woman's movement. She was gathering her belongings. It was as God had told Him. She would visit her relative, Elizabeth who was Zechariah's wife. Gabriel himself had visited Zechariah who had been selected to enter the holy place and burn incense to the Lord that year.

Elizabeth had been barren and Gabriel had appeared to the priest telling him that his wife would bear a son. "You will call his name John" Gabriel had told him. "He will be great before the Lord, he must not drink wine or strong drink and he will be filled with Holy Spirit, even from his mother's womb. He will go before Him in the spirit and power of Elijah. His mission will be to make the people ready for The Lord."

Zechariah had looked stunned. "How shall I know this? I am old and my wife as well." Gabriel's face had flashed anger. He never understand how men could be so faithless while God was so divine. Through the years, Gabriel had watched men fail to trust in the word of God, choosing to trust in the physical world that they were experiencing. The words of men were full of power and there was no way he could take that risk. "You will be mute until my word is fulfilled because you did not believe." Gabriel had told Zechariah. Some days after, Elizabeth got pregnant just as Gabriel had said.

The messenger of God exited the outer heavens knowing that everything was in motion. Gabriel had been there, from the fall of man to the removal of the evil seeds of the watchers to watching the chosen people of God delivered from Egypt; he had watched them sin and continue to grow in sin. Wars had been fought and blood had soaked the foundations of the earth. Yet in all the chaos, the earth thrived. Faith was alive. God's people held that singular hope that God would not forget them; that He would send a savior.

They did not know when or how but they knew that God would deliver them. However, God's plan of deliverance was much different from anything they could ever imagine. How could they know the plan was global and would affect all of mankind? How could they see beyond being delivered from the might of Rome that had enslaved most of the civilized world?

The angels of God watched from afar as the demons began canvassing and galvanizing their troops on the earth below. Something was happening on earth that was unique and special. God was making His move finally and they had to be ready.

Far across the consternations of the stars, Lurerdeth released a gigantic star, and a mighty sound marooned the far heavens of the galaxy. The star began its movement towards to the earth as a sign. A message for those who would look out for it. Angels and demons alike were focused on Nazareth and Judea. The biggest showdown in history was about to take place.

The palace was a dazzling edifice of glory. The very luster of its marble floors glinted with the colorful array of crushed crystals pressed into the detail by the stone masons of Rome. Herod had made sure of it. Being sent to govern the cities of Judea was no promotion and Herod's pride had been hurt.

In the throne hall, on stone tables covered with hand-woven silk, the high lords and tribunes ate and drank from silver plates and goblets jesting about the glorious days of war, fire and retribution. The world had bowed to Roman law and the Romans ruled with an iron fist.

The servants kept their wine jars filled and the musicians played a merry tune as the festivities continued. Watching with a quiet uneasiness, Herod watched the visitors who had come from far across the desert lands. They seemed wealthy and well fed and different indeed but he had not travelled very far in his lifetime yet they fascinated him. "A star you say?" Herod asked for the third time each time looking slightly to his left to the captain of his guard, Galeo.

An interpreter stood behind one of the men, leaning close to repeat Herod's words in a strange tongue that irked Herod rather than amuse him. "Yes," the interpreter said, "we followed it and it led us here." Herod observed them. "Magis" He mused almost to himself, "magicians are you not?"

"Some refer to us as that but we are mere humble

students of the stars" Another wise man responded through their interpreter. "We have never seen anything like this before."

"I'm sure they have not" Herod said to Galeo, "They are here eating my good food and talking about moving stars." Herod was ready to play his part content that this was better amusement than the lot of the tribunes and generals drinking and making sour jokes. "Tell us" Herod said struggling to smile, "What is the significance of this star? Why has it brought you so far from your home?"

The interpreter spoke again as Herod put a goblet to his lips and drank, fantasizing about beheading the interpreter. "The star is unique, different from anything we have ever seen. It represents the birth of royalty. A king has been born."

Herod's eyes opened wide. A couple of his captains heard the words and turned to observe the interpreter. "Say that again." Herod said. One of the wise men smiled, his face thin, skin dark and tanned from the sun and travel. He beckoned to the interpreter who wrote on a parchment.

Handing over the parchment to Herod, the man smiled. "This is why we here," He managed in the common tongue. Herod did not smile as his captains came close to the table standing behind him. Galeo spoke before Herod could respond. "A king will be born here?"

The wise men seemed to understand his question. One of them repeated the word "King," nodding profusely.

Herod rose up as the musicians stopped playing. "Clear the room." He bellowed. "You stay Galeo and you Livius."

Spreading his arms on the table like a benevolent lord, Herod looked at the puzzled faces of his guests and whispered. "Where will he born?" The interpreter spoke cautiously. "We do not know. We are unsure the exact location but the star has led us towards the city before your soldiers led us here."

Herod forced a smile, "It is Roman courtesy to welcome important travelers such as yourselves. Excuse us a moment. Enjoy your food."

Herod walked towards the open window attended closely by Galeo and Livius. "Galeo, see to it that our guests are properly entertained and with proper lodging for the night. Livius, get me the chief priests and scribes immediately. Go now." Livius saluted "Yes my lord."

Herod gripped the base the window his fingers

crunching into the stonework; he winced in pain and calmed himself. He was Herod and he was in control. Everything depended on time now. There was no time to waste. He had to move fast to destroy the new king.

Behind him, Galeo led the wise men to their chambers leaving Herod alone in the room. The flames of the torches created shadows on the walls as Herod looked around gripping his head in his hands filled with anger. He felt an evil pressure around his neck, like a tightening noose snuffing out his life.

Hearing voices, Herod fell on the ground, happily waiting for his torment to cease. All he could see was blood and his head was filled with screams of little children. Somehow, he knew what he had to do now.

Astaroth released Herod watching with disgust as the governor of Judea crumpled to the ground sobbing like a baby. The demon looked down and laughed scornfully knowing that Herod was at his mercy. Rising like a gigantic bat, the demon rose up to the top of the room, wings spread across the gold chains holding the candle edifices. Herod rose slowly and struggled to stand. He knew that by his decree the newborn had to die.

Outside in the courtyard, the first of the chief priests arrived with the scribes. Livius had made no idle threats on the consequences of lateness. The one word that Livius said was "Bethlehem."

Astaroth sped from the room like an arrow, skirting the city upwards till he reached a vantage point. Looking up at the sky, the demon released a flame of fire spiraling upward and thundering as it went. In the far distance, a huge wall of angels saw the signal, concealed and hidden; they had shielded the star from view until the appointed time. Across the spirit realm, thousands of demon warriors began their journey towards the signal to the land of Bethlehem in Judea.

"I have to go in again. I only managed to get Joseph and Mary out of Bethlehem in time." Gabriel said with apprehension as Michael tried to reassure him.

"No, send another to warn the wise men through a dream. Do not give a target to the enemy."

Gabriel pondered about their options, which were less than few. "Lemuel, go in my stead to the wise men. Warn them in a dream not to return to Herod."

"Herod's anger will be unabated." Lemuel said, "Who will protect Joseph and Mary?" Michael's face glistened with light as he spoke, "A few of my best travel with them. We cannot draw attention." Gabriel turned away as Michael reached out to him. "I know. You and I know what Herod will do. We know the prophecy."

"Yet we do not stop him." Gabriel retorted, fire licking up his hands as he spread them wide in frustration.

"A voice is heard in Ramah, mourning and great weeping, Rachel weeping for her children and refusing to be comforted, because her children are no more." Michael said grimly.

"I know the prophecy." Gabriel said.

"Then you understand we must pick our battles; the Lord Jesus Christ must remain in Egypt until Herod is dead. So is the nature of our mission."

Far beneath them, a donkey trudged through the dark and dangerous roads towards the land of Egypt, a company of angels covering their escape. In the land of Bethlehem, a scream was heard as Livius and his men began to fulfill their instruction from Herod.

Astaroth and a company of demons reveled in the darkness as the spirits of children born within two years rose up into the heavens.

"So you are the One, the One everyone has been writing and talking about. The Savior. The Son of God," said the hooded man as he walked cautiously towards the man lying on the dusty ground. The body of Jesus had grown lean and frail; his lips parched and skin dry as he continued in prayer. In the sandy wilderness, He had spent forty nights in prayer giving no thought to food or drink. Jesus looked up and shielded His eyes. "So you have come."

"I have, have I not?" Satan sized up his enemy. Here He was, the One who had turned water into wine, a clever trick for a man who was supposed to deliver His people. Was this the precious seed of the woman finally here to face His eternal foe? Satan wondered.

If He was so full of tricks, how about He prove it first. "So then, if you are the prophesied One, the Son of God, why not turn these stones to bread and eat. Surely you need strength. Your body is weak and you won't live very long without food."

"It is written," Jesus said the words slowly, pausing to draw breath. "Man shall not live on bread alone but by every word that comes out of the mouth of God." Satan winced. He knew those words; remembered them clearly. He would never forget what God had said "The seed of the woman…"

"Well," Satan said spreading his hands benevolently, "You have spoken well. You do know the writings of the prophets. I'm impressed to say the least. Do you not care for your physical body?"

Jesus sat up steadying Himself refusing to comment. Satan turned his head to the side observing everything, watchful as He tried to find a leverage to win their war of words.

"Ah surely, you must believe yourself protected somewhat from the dangerous elements of this world. Come, if you would, let me show you something." Satan waited to see if His enemy would take the bait.

Jesus stood.

"Come then with me to the pinnacle of the temple, let me show you something." Satan said cunningly wondering if Jesus would comply. Jesus nodded. Slightly puzzled but eager to win, Satan smiled. This was going to be easier than he had imagined. The next instant, Jesus was standing on the top of the temple.

Satan leaned over looking down. "Well then, if you are indeed the Son of God, throw yourself down. For it is written, "He will command His angels concerning you, and they will lift you up in their hands, so that you do not strike your foot against a stone."

Jesus turned and observed the devil, knowing the evil angel had quoted from the holy writings. "It is also written," Jesus responded, "Do not put the Lord your God to the test." Satan was enraged but struggled within himself to remain calm. "We are speaking from the writings aren't we? Well then, away with that. This world you have come into; do you know that it is mine? Let me show you my many kingdoms."

Satan's words spilled forth like a proud lord showcasing his collection of wealth and war trophies as he led Jesus to a high mountain. "Look." A strange light buzzed around Satan as he revealed the splendor of the kingdoms of the world.

Jesus looked around seeing the wealth of the world and the emerging industries, dazzling inventions of mankind. "All this, I will give you," he said, "if you will bow down and worship me."

Jesus turned away as the light melted. "Away from me, Satan" He spoke, his voice full of power and authority. "For it is written, "Worship the Lord your God, and serve Him only." The relentless vibrations of power in the words of Jesus stung the devil forcing him to cower. Satan skulked away realizing he had been defeated. Suddenly, the light of heaven busted forth as angels descended to minister to the needs of Jesus.

The devil retreated brooding deeply on his next plan of action. If indeed, this was the Son of God, he had to act fast. They had not been able to kill Him as a child but he needed a plan. Satan proceeded into the third heavens. He would summon the council of his principalities and powers. They were at war and God had made His move.

Waiting in the third heavens, Mealiel waited impatiently hoping for good news. Behind him, a few demon captains waited but when they saw the sullen figure of Satan ascending to meet them, most of them skulked away knowing he had failed in his mission. Mealiel did not budge. He wanted details.

"Lord, how did you fare?" Mealiel asked bowing.

Satan brushed past him proceeding through the company of captains. "Listen to me, You remember the first man and how he was made to spite our very existence. You remember because I do. Yet, I took my time, studied my enemy and struck where it mattered most. We are no strangers to waiting just as He does." Satan paused for his words to sink in before continuing. The demons gathered closer and closer listening to his words. "There is another Man down there who carries dominion and raw authority.

He has come to challenge us. He has been sent to tarnish our work and claim that which is rightfully ours. Shall we allow this?"

"No," A few demons murmured unsure if Satan indeed wanted an answer.

Satan spread his hands like a skilled orator. "God interferes in our world as He has done time and time again. But this time, it is personal. He sends His son to taste our wrath and judgment. Brothers, God has come to earth. Let us go kill Him." The demons cheered gleefully laughing wickedly as they began to curse and cheer.

Stepping away from the ruckus, Satan mused within himself. His minions were ready but he needed a plan. Mealiel watched Satan warily as the hapless creature schemed. There was something forming at the edge of Satan's mind. The ruler of darkness turned suddenly and motioned for silence.

When the demons had quieted down. Satan smiled like a mother hen crooning over her chicks. "The grave will have a visitor soon and it must be ready to hold Him. My plan is foolproof. We have unknown allies in the very priesthood and religious powers of God's people. His own people will soon spit in His face and we," Satan smiled evilly, " must make ready the new prison where we shall hold Him for all eternity."

For the casual observer on the earth, the clouds seemed calm and beautiful, a spread of an astute expression of creativity but no one could imagine the evil that hovered over the earth. Plans were being set in motion to cut short the life of the Man who now walked towards the waters of Capernaum seeking to call His first disciple, Simon Peter.

II

THE SEED OF THE WOMAN

"Let me handle this." Bael said shifting uneasily in one of the silver chairs that adorned the chambers in the circular conference room of Hades.

"What makes you think you will be more successful where others have failed?" Baeshedith retorted drily. "The Son of God makes short work of our forces every time."

"Those puny evil wandering spirits are nothing compared to our real force. Besides, this is not about a show of strength."

"I suppose you have a plan this time. Remember how your philistine empire was crushed by the children of Abraham."

Bael spat. "And I suppose you assume that we have forgotten your failures in Egypt as well. Ten plagues and your glory came crashing down."

"Oh you are nothing. You have no legacy."

Bael stood brimming with anger. "My statues still stand. My worship still continues. The people still fear my fearsome power."

Baeshedith stood as well with a wicked grin on his face, "On this planet? When last did a mortal mention the word Baal? When?"

Satan stood quietly and looked from principality to principality as they continued their tireless argument of their conquests and their empires. Other powers and thrones simply sat and watched, no one willing to join the exchange of words.

The days had turned to months which turned to years after Satan had tempted Jesus. The atmosphere around Judea and its environment had become too dangerous to dwell in. Not too long ago, Jesus had released his disciples into the neighboring towns and villages empowering them with His name and authority. It felt like the days of the fall all over again. Satan's body was wounded and sore all over and he had retreated further after suffering the shame of falling from his encampment in the third heavens over Rome.

By the hand of uneducated fishermen, Jesus had shamed him. They marched brazenly from city to city declaring boldly the good news. They stretched their hands to the sick, healing the lame, blind and the ill. Evil spirits were banished and people were set free. The people he had plagued for so long were being liberated, one by one, man, woman, child, the Savior of the world made good His Name.

As the shouting spirits continued their tirade, Satan slowly walked outside the chamber towards the heated grounds of hades. Across the distance, he could see Abraham's bosom where those who had been accounted as righteous resided.

He hated to punish himself this way but he had nothing better to do today. He could tell who they were in contrast to the spirits of the unjust who wailed and screamed in anguish in their never-ending torment. Satan remembered their days on the earth and their defeats. Abraham, Isaac, Jacob, Joseph, Gideon and Deborah. He remembered the feats of Sampson and his eventual demise at their plans.

Satan would never forget the works of Elijah and Elisha. He would never forget nor forgive the love God had for David. He could never understand or grasp why God would love a man who had murdered another man and married his wife. Grace. Satan hated the concept of grace and mercy, not to mention the prophecies of the prophets. To him, it was a cheaters card to turn the odds in the enemy's favor. Satan spat in disgust.

Slumping on the burning ground, Satan almost smiled at the torture his minions had meted to the prophets of God through their own people. They had corrupted the will and minds of the people turning them against God's servants. Many of the prophets had been tortured, burned or stoned through the ages. Yet, the Word of God prevailed. The Word lingered and now, the Word dwelt amongst men. Men were receiving a deeper knowledge of the mysteries of God that defied reason.

As the months had passed while their gravest enemy

had released so many of those they had bound. The evil lords and principalities busied themselves with scheming and planning hoping that they could make a comeback and be rid of Jesus.

"Lord."

Satan turned impatiently. "What?"

Bael bowed low. "Forgive my..."

"Speak quickly imp."

"There is word from Mealiel above."

"I am listening." Satan said sullenly.

"We have an insider. A man by the name Judas Iscariot, one of the disciples of Jesus."

"What about him? The petty thief."

"He is considering betraying Jesus to the chief priests."

Satan's greenish eyes opened wider. "So what's the issue?"

"He's considering. We have planted the thought. We need to push him to go through with it."

Satan stood, gazing at the splendor of the other side of Hades, his mind working viscously. Bael had a puzzled look on his face. "You are going back up there aren't you?"

Satan brushed Bael aside with a flick of his arm. "Who else can see anything to completion? Who else? Eh? Our biggest opportunity yet to be rid of our tormentor and you think I'll leave this to you blundering fools?"

The devil stomped through the courtyard towards the gates. The angels guarding Abraham's bosom watched unsure of what was happening. Satan seemed to have found his stride and pride again. Satan paused for a moment at the gate and turned to observe them. The evil smile on his face gave them great concern as the ancient dragon laughed lustily.

"Prepare! Prepare the deepest dungeon of the grave! Prepare Oh Death! Prepare! Victory will soon be ours." Satan spun into an inferno of fire and shot upwards towards the earth where Jesus sat in a dimly lit room breaking a piece of bread and was handing it out to His disciples.

Consternation reigned in the room when Jesus said the words. It was unimaginable; bordering on treason- that one of them would even consider such a thing. The three years of the ministry and work of Jesus had culminated in this historic moment when their Teacher had said, "One of you will betray me."

Sitting around the table, the disciples murmured to each other, their hearts confounded with the thought as they questioned themselves. Self-righteous to the point of defiance, the disciples claimed their innocence.

"I'll follow you no matter what."

"I'll die for you."

Peter watched Jesus closely. "Master, how can you say such a thing?"

Jesus looked up and met Peter's eyes. "One who shares this cup with me shall betray me." Sitting close, Judas Iscariot almost sank into the ground. His heart torn in two by his hidden agenda. He had returned from a meeting with the chief priests and was bound to an oath of 30 pieces of silver. However, Jesus was different. There was something awe inspiring about Jesus and the love He had shown them. Judas himself had witnessed such raw power flowing from his touch when he chased out evil spirits from the bodies of tormented people. He had seen miracles and had learned at the very feet of the One he was selling out.

Judas willed Jesus to pick him out, to expose him, to display his weakness for money in front of the other disciples. Anything. Anything but having to seat through the ordeal of betraying Jesus. *Surely Jesus knew everything so why did He say nothing.* Judas froze. Jesus was looking at him.

A dark aura filled Judas's heart causing him to sit uneasily. Satan waited, listening to every word that transpired within the room. A distance away, in the courtyard of the high priest, Mealiel, Bael and Baeshedith worked tirelessly speaking lies and uniting the priests against Jesus.

The captain of the guard Xadus had gathered his best soldiers in the courtyard, their weapons and torches ready. All they needed now was the arrival of the disciple who would lead them to Him. This had been the perfect plan. There was no way the priests could detract Jesus in the open, not with His wisdom and wit, or miracles. They could never take Him in the light but darkness provided an opportunity, even if temporary to brand Him as a criminal before the Romans.

The time was short and the feast of Passover was at

hand. They would never have a better opportunity now that many travelers and visitors from outside Judea had gathered for the feast, many of whom would be happy to have some form of distraction.

Satan forced his mind back to the activities in the room. Jesus was looking at Judas, He could sense it. Judas himself looked flustered as Jesus passed the cup to him. He expected a chiding, or strong rebuke from the One who had called them all.

Jesus had called the tax collectors, fishermen, men who had no social standing or love among the people, to be his disciples. Surely it would have been assumed that the promised Savior would have kept company with the elders and chief priests, living in the quarters of the high priest with a royal guard.

Surely the Savior would have raised an army by now and overthrown the tyranny of Rome. The people of Israel would have been liberated and they would have sacrificed many bulls and goats to honor God. The minstrels would have written psalms and the prophets would prophecy the blessings of Abraham.

The glorious days of their fathers in the Promised Land would be reborn. The people would call on Yahweh and observe His laws from generation to generation teaching His statutes to their children and their children's children.

However, none of this was the case. Jesus had focused His mission on teaching men, women and children about the kingdom of God. It had all started with John the Baptist and his words "Repent, for the kingdom of God is at hand."

Now three years after, Judas could not understand where the kingdom was. Even John the Baptist had been confused sending a message to Jesus when he was arrested. John had asked Him if He was the promised One or if they were to wait for another. Jesus's mission simply did not make sense to those around him.

It was all well and good for Him to heal people and teach with authority. It took a lot of guts to stand up to the Pharisees and Sadducees but what about the promised kingdom? Judas imagined. What about it? When were they going to rule and reign?

"Is it I?" Judas asked.

Jesus leaned close across two of his disciples. "What you must do, do quickly."

Judas rose up quietly and left the room. A few disciples

looked puzzled at his exit. The evil presence within him gave him great speed. Judas ran across the dusty roads towards the house of the high priest. The hour had come.

Many hours later, darkness reigned. The clouds had retreated as the enemies of God swooped into the earth reveling in the taste of their soon coming victory. The Son of God was stripped down, covered in blood, carrying a wooden cross. The only interference they had faced was the few angels that had comforted Him in the garden of Gethsemane where His closest disciples had slept at the late hour.

Jesus had been in deep anguish as He cried out to God. "Father, let this cup pass from me, but not my will but Your will be done." His pain had been real as He prepared Himself for the worst.

Satan had tried to anticipate His every move but the Son of Man had shocked them all. The demons had expected every force of heaven to be unleashed upon them, but so far, it seemed that God had abandoned Jesus upon the earth.

Surely, His work on the earth was to save all of mankind and now, as they paraded Him and derided Him, Satan relished the moments. Lash after lash, the Roman soldiers tore his flesh to the bone. Beaten to a pulp, wounded and battered, blinded by His own blood yet dedicated to the mission, Jesus began His journey to Golgotha, the place of the skull.

Many of the women covered the eyes of their children as the throng pressed on both sides of the road leading to the hill where the Romans made examples of criminals and rebels, the ultimate punishment meted out to remind everyone of roman rule and power.

Mealiel loved a gruesome crucifixion. It was ghastly indeed. The soldiers would break the spirit of their captive by forcing him to carry the very instrument of death, their shame on their backs before their hands and feet were nailed with massive nails.

Standing at the top of a high building overseeing the procession, Satan almost smiled. God must have never seen this coming. The very people He had thought to save had turned against Him. Again, like His prophets of old, the special One was carrying the object of human shame up the hill to His death. The earth would be fully his again.

"We will wipe them out. We will start from His disciples and enslave all those He has healed and freed." Satan shouted as the demons cheered. Mealiel was not convinced. Shouting plans and goading the demons on, the ancient watcher demon looked about furtively still puzzled why God had not acted. Maybe when the nails hit his flesh, maybe then God would react.

Jesus collapsed again, his sore body filled with pain, flesh blood stained the streets as He struggled to stand. Livius turned on his horse and groaned waving for the centurion tasked with the crucifixion. "We'll never get this done today."

"And it's dark already." Verus agreed, "Yet, you chose to come."

"I would have it no other way. This is a historic death one way or the other."

"Why do you say that?" Verus asked.

"Look at this." Livius said, lifting up a wooden plaque.

Verus shook his head, "The King of the Jews. Yes, this will be historic indeed."

"Let us get it over with shall we? Get some help for Him. Otherwise, you will have a corpse before we reach the top of the hill." Verus saluted and turned. "You! Yes, you! Help him with the cross."

Atop the hill, the soldiers gathered Jesus' clothing and spread them out. A small contingent of them laid the three crosses on the ground. Then they stretched Jesus out on the cross.

Beside Him, two other criminals endured the same fate. Livius stood by watching grimly as Jesus winced when his back touched the rough shaven wood. Livius could only imagine the irony- a carpenter's son on the very thing that He had worked with all His life.

As a soldier held down Jesus' hand, another put a nail into His palm raising a huge hammer poised to strike. Livius wanted to look away but He was a soldier. There was something so wrong about what they were doing and yet though he harbored no love for the Man, there was something meek about Him that was unique; almost like He was at peace with His death.

He had witnessed a few crucifixions but nothing compared to this one. Most of the people had come out to observe. Some laughed and mocked while some wept. Usually, the people would plead for the lives of their people regardless of the crimes they had committed. Yet for all the miracles, Livius' spies had reported to Herod and himself, he was shocked that his own people wanted Him dead.

He could understand the politics of it all but when Jesus had the chance to defend Himself, He had said nothing against those who wanted Him dead. Livius had to see this through. He was a soldier, trained in the Roman way and sentiments had no room in his heart. Jesus was here to die and he had to ensure it happened.

Jesus groaned audibly in uncontrollable pain as the nail went through his hands and feet. The women screamed and cried distracting Livius. He turned slowly seeing their faces. The women who had followed Jesus, cared for Him; the disciples who had travelled with Him, the people who had eaten the bread He had given them, the healed, the freed, the saved and the Pharisees and Sadducees; the mob.

They stood there, each with his or her emotions, with their beliefs and convictions. With each strike of the soldier's hammer, the suffering One convulsed in pain struggling to breathe letting out whimpers to manage His pain.

Fastened to the woodwork, the soldiers ensured the base of the cross was grafted into a hole they had dug earlier. Slowly, they began to lift up the cross, as the body of Jesus rose from the ground displayed for all to see. There He was, the One who loved mankind, the One who had been sent to redeem the house of Israel, the only begotten of the Father. There He was with His body broken, His blood streaming down, bearing the injustice of those He had come to save.

Satan was giddy with delight. "I cannot believe what I am seeing." He shouted. Mealiel finally allowed himself a bit of happiness from what he saw. "It is happening. Our enemy is defeated." Satan turned to Mealiel. "Send your forces. In fact, send the fullness of our warriors to await Him in hell. I will lead them myself." Mealiel nodded and then flew off shouting out orders. Satan himself took one last look, a satisfied smile on His face before heading after Mealiel. He could taste the victory already.

Jesus looked down from His vantage point. He could make out the faces of those who looked at Him. Using the remainder of His strength, Jesus focused His attention on His mission, loving humanity to His last.

Suddenly, He felt a darkness creep over Him. Like a sheet of ill, the weight of sin, shame and death came over Him. The damnation that had covered man and the curse came over Him. Like the clammy claws of a monster, sin latched onto Him netting over Him causing His Spirit to reek of evil. Jesus could see it all through the eyes of His Spirit.

Every rape, murder, lie, theft, drunkenness; every fruit of the fallen nature of man drenched Him like a cold bath. Like bees, they stung causing the Holy One to become unholy in that moment.

It was worse than the pain from the beatings. It was worse than the shame of being stripped and spit upon. It was worse than the taunts from the soldiers or the jeers of the mob. The weight of sin pressed Him down and He screamed when God turned away from Him.

The connection was severed. The eternal Word was left upon a hill sinking into a pit of damnation. He carried it all in that moment, the committed sin and the uncommitted sin. He took it all- the ultimate justice for sin and disobedience. He accepted His fate and fulfilled His divine work.

Livius looked up at Him as the soldiers drank and played dice over the clothing of Jesus. The Roman tribune could not simply sit down with them. Something of epic proportions was happening on the earth. The clouds had darkened and the elements seemed to be at war as the skies thundered and lightning struck across the land.

He could not figure it out. Jesus was telling one of His disciples to care for His mother. He had even refused the wine he had offered to Him to ease His pain. What kind of Man was this? Livius wondered. Jesus had screamed something in Hebrew moments before. Then Livius heard something that shocked him to his core.

"Father, forgive them, for they know not what they do."

Livius gasped. The world around him seemed to pause in that moment as Jesus said, "Father, into your hands, I commit my Spirit." Then, Jesus died.

"Seal the gates!" Myesmoth bellowed as the remainder of the demon warriors entered into Hades. A flag demon at the helm of the two towers of the gate repeated the command..

Immediately, lesser demons began pulling on the huge chains of the gigantic gate as it moved slowly back in position sealing off the land of the dead. The great detail of demon soldiers lined themselves in the gigantic ashen landscape before the huge gate.   The huge glistering door that led to Abraham's bosom had been sealed shut. Even the angels that guarded it where nowhere to be seen. Satan had sought them out first when he arrived back from the earth.

Their greatest enemy was locked in a huge dungeon. The holding cell had been prepared and planned out to the minutest detail. The devil was careful with his strategy of containment. Myesmoth trudged quickly into the lower corridors and pathways to the dungeons below hades. A few guards acknowledged him as he passed.

They had invited the strongest and the fiercest demon lords, who had strategically influenced earth events at diverse times. In the inner chambers, Myesmoth made his report to Satan. Standing in the room, Astaroth, Bael, Mealiel and a few others cheered. "We have finally won." Myesmoth said, clapping his huge scaly hands together, "Our strongest warriors are guarding within and outside the gates."

"Good," Bael said, "We have Him. Do our scouts report any angelic activity? Some rescue operation in the making?"

"None." Mealiel said. "Baeshedith continues to encircle the earth and Elzebur's archers are positioned at the outer walls, their fiery darts at the ready in case of an attack."

The demons in the room rejoiced thunderously except Satan, who sat at a corner deep in thought. "We have Him." Mealiel tried to reassure Satan but the evil lord would hardly look up.

"Do we?" Satan said as if troubled by something he saw, "He took their sins."

"How does that work?" Mealiel asked scratching the top of his head.

Satan observed Mealiel for a moment before responding, "It's almost like He wanted to die... strange but until we had killed Him, I did not fully understand it."

"But He had to die," Bael said stepping forward, "He simply had to die. You all know of all the havoc He caused on the earth. Our work can continue on the earth now that He has been removed."

Some of the demons nodded but Satan remained unimpressed.

"Fine, we did foresee Him coming down here but the legality remains true that the ultimate payment of sin is death and thus, He has died and in His sinful state, shouldering the sins of mankind, He had to come here but why so willingly?"

Bael's eyes widened as looked at Satan. "You're saying He wanted to come here, into the grave... but for what?"

"To what end?" Mealiel chimed in looking from Satan to Bael.

"Thinking back now, there was something that was written," Satan said, "about not allowing His body to see corruption."

Mealiel waved it off. "We have a contingent guarding the tomb. No surprises there. The stone cannot be easily rolled away."

"But if indeed the sins of the world that was placed on Him brought Him here which is your legal right by ownership of the dominion you took from the first man," Bael clapped his hands together suddenly, "then, through Him, He is bound to the will of him who holds the keys of death and the grave... unless..."

Satan jumped up fire swelling across his torso, "By what right?"

Bael shouted, "The keys! We must protect the keys!" Satan bolted towards the door.

Satan flew down through the lower channels heading to the lower dungeons where they kept Jesus. Satan's demon lords thumping hard after him. Satan knew it was already happening as he reached the huge recess of the lower dungeons. Demon guards had been flung across the heat and melting ashes.

The oozing sulfur had buried the frames of wounded warriors who had guarded the lower levels. Through the huge cataclysmic hole with fiery chains, Satan looked down and saw nothing. Jesus had broken loose. Satan shouted in anguish as fire engulfed the space around him. The demons cowered at the might and anger of their lord. "Find Him!" He shouted as the demons sped back upwards. "Secure the keys! Secure the keys!" Satan shouted in a panic. Immediately, a horn was heard. The demons had raised the alarm. An escape was in progress and they had to shut it down.

"You've been played for a fool."

Satan turned. "Who said that?" Through the dimly lit cells, whitish pillars stood in parallel lines across the space.

"You are a fool." The voice said again.

Satan pulled out his sword and walked slowly into the darkness and then stopped. "It's only you, Zuriel." Satan said sheathing his sword.

Zuriel leaned forward as the grim lightning revealed the restrained angel. "Yes, He spoke to us. Just before He routed your puny guards."

"Did he...?" Satan said walking towards the bound angel. "What did he say?"

Zuriel smiled bitterly, "He proclaimed who He was and His mission. He told us. Yes, He did. His death is only the beginning. Through His death and His carrying of the sins of mankind, you have unwittingly released the very embodiment of the Holy Spirit of God into this place."

Satan gasped. "I don't understand."

Zuriel almost laughed pitifully, "You really do not know. Who could have imagined it? You have always assumed yourself to be a student of His mysteries. Corrupter. His purpose is hidden in the word 'Liberty'. He came to set mankind free, not for this moment only but for all eternity to reconnect them back to their original state as at the beginning before you tainted them."

"But how does He intend to achieve this?" Satan inquired nervously.

"By the blood of God, the holy lamb slaughtered to erase sin once and for all."

Satan groaned audibly as Zuriel continued, "You see? His death was necessary to fix the bridge between man and God. The link is restored again and His holy seed has been birthed into a glorious holy lineage of God's children spreading across the earth establishing His kingdom. Do you see now? His death is your downfall."

"He had to die." Satan said in a daze as he felt his knees getting weaker.

"Did he?" Zuriel retorted drily, the other restrained angels looking on, "You have paved the way for God-carriers to cover the earth. A new divine bloodline of God expressing His glory and Kingdom rule upon the earth."

Satan clasped his head with his hands. "He had to die.

He was healing the sick, delivering the oppressed and raising the dead. He simply had to die."

Strung to the pillars, the angels who had left their estates and married the women were restrained. Some of them nodded as Zuriel continued. "You killed Him without thinking about the consequences. For that, you are indeed a fool."

Satan leaned close to Zuriel's face and satisfied his pain and pride by smashing his fist into Zuriel. The angel buckled over groaning. Satan grabbed Zuriel's faded hair, "You went in to the women of the earth and spewed forth giants that tainted His creation. You had everything and threw it all away and you call me a fool. I am free to roam, as I will. I lead an army of warriors. I have dominion over the earth. You are bound forever or until He decides what your final fate will be. Who is the greater fool?" Satan shouted in Zuriel's face. "Answer me! Who is the greater fool?"

Gripping him by the neck, the angry spirit executed a forceful and violent twist as he turned away. Zuriel sunk propped up by chains holding his wrists and waists, gasping in excruciating pain. Satan pulled out his huge sword. "I will go settle this once and for all. Then after, I will visit you again Zuriel and add to your pain and suffering." Satan dashed out of the prison of pillars and made his way upwards to the Spirit of Jesus and war.

Judas skulked through the dark streets covered in a hooded garment. Mostly everyone had retreated indoors except for the hopeless drunk or the homeless. He did not want to be seen.

"You killed him." The voice said repeated again as Judas clasped his head with his hands, fresh tears streaming down his face. "He trusted you and you betrayed Him." Judas almost convulsed at the thought.

The guilt covered him like a blanket of gloom as he staggered through the streets. He could see the face of Jesus as he was tortured and beaten, his body laced with wounds and stripes, his hair matted with the mesh of mockery and pain. His master had taken it all. Judas felt so much remorse.

If only Jesus could see how much he was suffering for

his mistake. He could never fit in with the other disciples. How would they accept him back? They had all traveled together, sat at his feet, had their feet washed by Him, eaten with Him. He had taught them about the coming kingdom of God and asked them to wait in Jerusalem until they had been ensued with the power of the Holy Spirit. Then, after all the great things he had seen and tasted, he had betrayed Jesus.

"For what?" the sinister voice said again. "Thirty pieces of silver. You sold Him for thirty pieces of silver." Judas leaned on the wall flailing in anguish, beaten senseless by his own conscience.

His very existence had become a story of shame, the legend of the one who sold out His master, the one whose greed had condemned a good man to die. There was no getting past that type of record, no escape from the repercussions of his actions. There was no purpose for living.

Judas continued through the dark roads avoiding the few people who passed by till he reached the open field. He knew this place and understood what he had to do. Judas stepped into the field towards the vegetation and trees.

"End it." The demon whispered to him. Looking up, the tormented man reached to touch the tall tree standing in the field knowing that he would take his own life.

"Where are my warriors?" Satan burst into the upper alcove of the dividing doors of Abraham's bosom and hell. The majestic door had been flung open. No one responded to his question as demons scampered about in fearful daze. The once awe-inspiring line of defense had been broken and pandemonium reigned. The demons had been routed.

Suddenly a light burst overshadowed the huge space originating from the door to Abraham's bosom. The blast caused the demons to fall flat tumbling to the ground in thousands and Jesus stepped out. The glow around his bodily frame was reminiscent of the raw divine energy that covered the manifest presence of God in the throne room.

It was the kind of power that induced worship. Satan

cowered under the feverish light as Jesus walked stepping over the demons that were in His path. In His hand, He held a great chain that restrained Myesmoth and in His other hand, He held the keys. The gigantic lord of death had been subdued and was being paraded before the saints. They poured out like a mighty army.

Adam, Eve, the patriarchs of old, the mighty men of valor, the righteous ones, those who had served the one true God, those who had done good and received the award of right-standing before God, Jesus led them out and then it finally dawned on Satan. He had made the biggest mistake of his existence.

The blood of bulls and goats had merely covered their sins so that God could connect with them but this death, the death of Jesus had completely taken away their sins.

"Now you have lost your claim to mankind. I have completely removed the record of their sins and their dominion has been restored. I have defeated death and the grave. Man is reconnected back to the Father through Me. I am the bridge."

The words shot forward like flamed arrows of light striking the demons causing them to bow forcefully at the violent power of Jesus. The meek man that had been beaten was no more but here He was in the full power of God Almighty, united back in Spirit. Myesmoth fell to the ground releasing a cracking thunder and Jesus stepped on his back and then turned to the great ocean of the spirits of men.

Jesus turned to the great countless rows of saints. "I will return to the earth and then ascend to my Father. You may ascend as well and those who wish to show themselves to their loved ones, it is permitted." Jesus said, smiling lovingly. The saints cheered as the great company full of gladness and joy.

Jesus stepped forward full of power and raw light. Reaching the main gate of Hades, Jesus opened the doorway and flung it open. In one move, He had conquered death and hell. The saints pressed forward, a mighty army stepping out and heading to heaven for the very first time in their existence to be with the Father. Outside Hades, a great company of angels awaited them as Gabriel led them upwards to the heavenly kingdom where glory, bliss and the goodness of God awaited them.

Michael headed into the earth, at full speed, towards a company of soldiers guarding an enormous stone covering a tomb. In a split second, he smashed into them scattering them forcefully and almost blinding them. Then putting his hands on the stone, Michael rolled it away and sat on it. Jesus was alive! The grave could not contain Him! He was alive!

The soldiers had returned claiming that the chief priests had relieved them of their duties. "That is all that Caiaphas said?" Livius asked the centurion.

"Yes sire."

Livius had seen the fear etched in the man's face, like someone who had seen a ghost. This was a soldier of Rome and they were not easily fazed.

Livius looked around the pavilion where he sat with two of his tribunes. "Come with me." He said. He wanted to get to the bottom of it. As he walked with the centurion, Livius tried to pry away the truth. "Now tell me. I am your commander. What happened out there?" The centurion suddenly stopped breathing heavily as if under a spell. Livius became irate. "You are a roman soldier. Take hold of yourself and speak. What happened? What is your name?"

"Verucious."

"Verucious, you will tell me what happened or I will have you flogged." Livius clasped the man's shoulders.

"You won't believe me."

Livius released the soldier who sank to the ground. What had he seen? What had made him loose his wits?

Livius knew the answer already. He was sure of it. Slowly, he walked away musing to himself. Was it possible indeed that the Man had risen from the dead? Was it possible? As he reached for the door, the centurion spoke like a frightened child.

"He's alive."

"Who else knows this?" Livius asked turning.

"We told the priests and they paid us to be silent and said to say his disciples stole his body."

"Stole his body though the tomb was guarded by Roman soldiers?" Livius said aghast, "You must indeed be silent. Word of this must not get to Rome. I will seek out his followers so that I might learn the truth. There is a young man, son to a friend, called Saul from Tarsus who might be able to help seek them out. You are dismissed."

Livius stood for a while lost in thought. It was unimaginable yet as bizarre as the story was, the past few days and Herod's actions in the many years prior had left Livius dumbfounded. There was something powerful happening in his time and he would try to get to the bottom of it.

III

THE RISEN ONE

"You think we will see Him again?" Peter said, pinning the edge of his fishing net to a large hook, as James followed suit on the other side of the boat. "I pray so brother, I miss His words and acts. I wonder how things will be now."

Peter heaved and grunted as he and James threw the net into the water, images of Christ's appearing fresh on his mind. After they had seen Jesus the first time, Jesus had appeared again allowing Thomas to even feel the holes caused by the nails and the spear. Those special moments were forever engrafted in his mind.

The disciples had gathered around the room, shadows of their former selves, sad, teary eyed and confused. Most of Jesus' followers, after the crucifixion, had been too scared to be publicly affiliated with Jesus. Peter had looked about the room from a dark corner feeling guilty for denying Jesus. He had been so verbose about his faithfulness and Jesus had prophesied it. It had happened just as Jesus had said.

"I let him down." Peter remembered his words. He had said it more to himself but it only pushed some of the women to weep more. "We all did." John had responded curtly, "but what Judas did is beyond words."

"What about me? I am no better than he. When I was asked if I knew Jesus, I denied Him. Not once, three times." Burying his head in his hands, the disciple had let out his pain, as did the others.

It was at that moment that Jesus had appeared in the room. Shocked and afraid, the disciples shouted and cowered but Jesus spread His arms. "It is I," He said. "Just as I promised, I have risen again. See my hands and see my side."

Peter stood by the elm of the boat a slight smile on his face.

"Why do you smile?" John asked slightly puzzled.

"Remember when He asked us to pull out to the deep after we had caught nothing."

John nodded profusely. "I could never forget."

"We had toiled all night" Peter chuckled drily, "but He asked and I obeyed. The amount of fish we caught almost drowned us."

"Glad that we had faithful companions."

"We are blessed, truly blessed to have met such a One as He. We didn't always understand Him but He loved us. He taught us many things."

"You speak as though it is all over."

"It is, is it not? He came to show us the way. Three years, John, of power and change."

"Somehow," John replied, "I feel deep within me that we are only at the beginning. Look!"

Peter leaned over and saw the net teaming with fish. "Ah! Just as the man at the seashore said!" Peter exclaimed as they busied themselves with hauling in the net.

John turned quickly excitement building into his voice, "It is The Lord." Peter turned releasing the net as James reached quickly grabbing the net. The boat rocked unsteadily forcing the disciples to grab the keel. "Haul in!" John shouted as James rushed forward to grab the sinking net. Heaving up, the net jacked upward as James pulled upwards.

"Peter, help!" John yelled but Peter was in the water already swimming with heavy strokes to the shore.

Sitting on the seashore around the fire, the disciples sat with Jesus as He spoke to Peter. They were amazed that this time Jesus ate with them, yet there was a sense of finality about Him. "Come, do not doubt," Jesus said. "See my hands and feet, touch them for a spirit does not have flesh and bones. Come."

Jesus reached out to them and they came slowly bewildered but happy that Jesus was indeed alive. "Come. These things have been written, that Christ should suffer and on the third day, rise from the dead, and that forgiveness and the repentance from sin should be preached to all nations in His name. You are witnesses to these things."

Jesus smiled as they gathered around him. John touched His hand and felt around the lacerations of the healed wounds that Jesus had borne. "Listen, I am sending the promise of my Father upon you. But stay in the city until you are clothed with power from on high."

Full of anxiety after His death, here He was sitting and eating with them. Yet, within their hearts, they knew a phase of their lives was ending. He had come at a time when they could never have imagined doing the amazing things they had done. In three years, they had traveled across the land, speaking, healing and changing lives. They had been hungry, tired, full and happy, going through the earthly ministry of Christ as brothers, as students learning from their great Master but He had prophesied it.

Jesus had told them, "I am going to the Father and will prepare a place for you and I will ask the Father and He will give you another Helper to be with you forever," much to the chagrin of the disciples. Thomas had asked Him, "Lord, we do not know where you are going so how can we follow?"

Jesus had said to him, "I am the way, the truth and the life. No man comes to the Father except through me." The disciples had been stunned at His words. They were full of power and life yet confusing.

Here was He who was the son of God declaring that they would do greater works. It was unimaginable that He was talking about leaving them. For the many who had expected a king, a revolutionary, it was unfathomable that in His coming, and His mighty acts, He would leave so soon.

"Greater works" they had mused. Yet it was compounded by the fact that Jesus told them "If you ask me anything in my Name, I will do it." The disciples began to see a pattern, a divine discourse of epic proportions. God had come into the world and empowered them through His begotten Son. The unlearned and uneducated were receiving divine power to showcase His power to the world and reconnect them to the Father.

As they feasted on bread and roasted fish, the men were lost in their thoughts. Peter thought about the great things they would do now that Jesus was back, happy at the thought that though he had denied Jesus, the Master still loved him and had chosen to come visit and eat with him. It was a love that was beyond comprehension.

Peter slightly turned to observe John's face. The other

disciple always had a rapturous delight and distant look when he was around Jesus. John himself had questions but he was content to wait till the right moment. Jesus had told them to wait until power had come from on high. "The Helper, the Holy Spirit, whom the Father will send in my Name, He will teach you all things and bring to your remembrance all the things I have said to you." Jesus had said.

Peter shifted uneasily and signed, as a familiar picture flashed in his mind- the servant girl, the fire, the mob, the soldiers, the elders and priests, the night when all hell broke loose. The night he lost every sense of grace and loyalty, vehemently denying knowing Jesus.

The guilt was building again slowly like a rising tempest, Peter almost groaned audibly but then a clear light seemed to fight the darkness as Jesus put a hand on his shoulder. "Simon, son of John, do you love me more than these?" "Yes, Lord, you know that I do." Peter responded.

"Then, feed my sheep." Jesus said to him. Peter nodded, slightly agitated when Jesus asked him the same question a second and third time, puzzled as Jesus rose. "Come, it is time."

The company of angels waited patiently in the third heavens overlooking the city of Bethany as Jesus took His last walk with His disciples. Michael and Gabriel stood at the fore of the arrayed angels waiting to welcome the One who had conquered all things.

It was all making sense now and the way things had played out caused Gabriel to smile. From the death of Jesus to the victory in hell, the angels had come to understand the mystery of Christ's mission though they still could not fathom why God had so much love for mankind.

After the veil had been torn, and the bridge to God reconnected through Jesus, the people of the earth had continued in their ways oblivious to the historic incident that had brought liberation to the world. The darkness had been forcefully removed and dominion restored but it was unimaginable that millions of people still lived blind to the truth through their ignorance.

Like the disciples, they could understand if Jesus stayed

longer to convince the world of the truth about their planet, their new status, and their freedom. Yet, He had promised them the Holy Spirit of God.

"The kingdom of God has come to mankind." Michael said watching the proceedings on the earth carefully. Gabriel nodded in agreement, "Yes, his disciples are His representation on the earth now. They are light and we will help them. I sincerely hope that their eyes of understanding are opened to see what God has done for them."

"Yes, it is our sincere hope." Michael said, "Come, Gabriel. It is time, let us go."

The two angels descended in a trail of light.

The disciples looked around wondering what would happen next, their hearts calmed by the promise of God's Spirit. One of them had asked if Jesus would restore Israel, as had always been their expectation of the Savior yet Jesus had been patient with them, pressing them to focus on the coming of the Holy Spirit. "Do not forget," Jesus said, "you will receive power when the Holy Spirit has come upon you, and you will be my witnesses in Jerusalem, in Judea and Samaria, and to the ends of the earth." As He spoke, a light came from the sky spiraling in undulating tremors and encapsulated Jesus lifting Him from the ground.

Lifted up, Jesus spread His arms in a loving fashion looking down upon them, His love crying out for them. They stood mute looking upwards, each with his flaws and weaknesses, yet bolstered by grace and the experiences they had shared with Him.

Jesus went upwards and they stood looking at the One who had come prophesied by the prophets and John the Baptist. They would never recover from it. The One who had called them and empowered them. He had taken them from their ordinary lives and given them a global mission, giving them a new life.

He had picked them ignoring the learned priests, elders, the wealthy and the educated. Jesus had come for the lowly and the weak, the hurt and the broken, the wounded and the shattered. Jesus had come for the captives and the oppressed. He had come to seek and save the lost.

He had defied the traditions of His generation and

established a new law of love. "Love your neighbor as yourself!" He had shouted on the dusty ledge in the crowded street. He had spoken in the temple, on the mountains, hills and valleys. Jesus had taught about the coming kingdom of God, the rule and reign of God upon the earth where the dictates of the King of Heaven would prevail.

He had faced-off with the spiritual leaders and rulers of His time, countering their religion with truth, exposing their lies and self-serving doctrines. He had come against the tide of tradition breaking into pieces the ugliness of religion that had ignored God and put traditions before love.

Jesus had changed everything. The dead had lived, wounded healed, diseases and infirmities had melted and evaporated; blinded eyes had been restored and weak limbs made strong.

Joy, hope and life had entered the earth and a people who had once lived in spiritual darkness had seen the light of God enter into their midst. The only begotten Son of God had made quick work of unclean spirits commanding them to come out of those they had possessed.

He had set people free culminating in His death and resurrection- the earth was no longer the same. He had taken the fall, accepting the humiliation and beating. The very creatures He had made had mocked him. He had borne it all to the cross where in dying, He had carried the sins of the world once and for all, eternally restoring a lifeline to the Father.

The historic coming of the seed of the woman prophesied through the ages had finally come to pass and though hell had fought forcefully and aggressively, He was the victorious One, the undefeated Champion, the Lord of life and the keeper of the keys. He had restored dominion back to man through His sacrifice.

Jesus ascended in light and glory finally fading from their eyes as they squinted and struggled to keep their gaze. Suddenly, two angels appeared by them as men in white robes. "Men of Galilee, why do you stand looking up into heaven? This Jesus, who was taken from you into heaven, will come in the same way as you saw Him go into heaven."

The disciples rejoiced at their words as they worshipped God. "Come, brothers, lets us return to Jerusalem and wait just as He asked us to." Peter said.

Gabriel and Michael watched as the disciples departed from the place where Jesus had ascended. Arms folded, Michael forced a half-smile. "It is only just begun. A new era is beginning and a new season has come."

"Yes, indeed," Gabriel responded, "the lineage of God will thrive as it has. His people have suffered much from the enemy. From the days of old, they have suffered violence but the violent always take it by force. We have always come back to win."

"We have endured. God's people have endured. Through slavery, pain and death, yet..."

"We have thrived." Gabriel smiled as the last of the disciples faded from view.

"The life of God cannot be shut down. Hidden in the strangest places, through the strangest people, God hid His lineage up until now and now has opened a supernatural rebirthing for those who believe who will be His children and He will be their father."

"Did you ever see this coming?" Gabriel smiled smacking his hands together.

"No. Often times, I thought we had hit a dead end." Michael said, "Come, let us walk a while."

The two angels walked slowly reminiscing of their experiences since the creation of the earth and the first man.

"You know what, Michael, when it all comes to it, these mysteries are so simple. They have been right before our eyes. The salvation was not for the people of Israel alone. Jesus died for the entire world."

"The entire world," Michael mused as they continued through the open vegetation spread across the farmlands and the paved roads to Bethany. "In fact, the prophecy was not for them alone. Through this, anyone can become a child of God, if only they believe."

"I believe that is indeed the point. They must believe, be born-again and be baptized."

"That is true, the difficult work has been done through His death and resurrection but so many have veils covering their eyes. Their eyes must be opened to see the truth."

"I believe the disciples will do well."

"I pray so, Gabriel, for the sake of the entire world, I pray so."

EPILOGUE

T he room seemed to erupt as a sound of a mighty wind filled the room where the disciples and other followers of Jesus were gathered, obeying Jesus' command to remain in the city. Suddenly, like a fire, different tongues came upon them and they began to speak in different languages expressing the mighty works of God.

Their voices loud and strong, the noise carried through to the streets as people began to gather around wondering what the commotion was. The disciples with the people that had gathered with them had been filled with the Spirit of God. Peter stepped from the room, full of boldness, his timidity removed. Empowered by God's Spirit, he stood as some people mocked them, while others expressed their astonishment that they could each hear their languages that were native and diverse tongues from distant lands. The promised Spirit of God had come, in power and might.

Reserved for those who believe, who accept the sacrifice of Jesus, the divine Spirit of God came as an indwelling Spirit. Resting on and staying in them, he gave them the fullness of their status as sons and daughters of God. They had been delivered from the kingdom of darkness into the kingdom of light.

They had been given the enabling power of God to express kingdom rule and reign upon the earth. Peter stood responding to the people who had mocked saying they were drunk and began to speak. The one who had once denied Jesus stood damning the fear of the scribes and chief priests. They had thought to cut off the head and thus deal with all His followers. But they were wrong.

God's move was the ultimate gambit of glory. He had sent His begotten son as a seed into the earth, in His death, burial and resurrection, the concept of seedtime and harvest had been fulfilled, the harvest was the people who now bore His Spirit upon the earth.

God had direct influence through His people on the

earth now. Through the death and resurrection of the last Adam, a people had been born that would carry the very life of God to the very ends of the earth. The body of Christ had been conceived and the earth would never be the same again.

God was on the earth through His children and they would spread the knowledge of the King across the earth attacking the demonic strongholds and exacting the full recompense for the evil the devil had brought upon the earth.

A supernatural army had been born with the insignia of faith, armed with raw divine energy through the expression of faith, they would take nations, subdue kingdoms, enter new lands spreading the love and mercy of God across the earth.

The seed of the woman was victorious. Heaven had come through. That historic day, as Peter spoke like an oracle of heaven, like a learned spokesman of the mysteries of God, everyone knew that something had changed.

These were the no names, the unknowns, the people without influence who suddenly spoke words of fire leaking into the crevices of their hearts and destroying their idols, traditions and chains. Humanity was experiencing freedom, true freedom for the first time. Jesus had not come to bring a revolution against the romans. He had come to lead a revolution against the devil and the darkness that had covered the world and He had won!

The kingdom had come and many people knelt receiving salvation; no longer required to spill the blood of bulls and goats, the access to God had been fully and eternally restored for those who would believe.

The Father of life had given His best - Himself - for mankind and would now reap millions of people spreading His love, influence and light across the world. He was indeed the source of all life, the eternal One who had called forth out of nothing.

He had made the heavens and the earth, the luminaries and stars, the land, animals, vegetation and man. God had made the entire universe and everything that would relate with man's existence. He had created everything out of His wisdom and might for His good pleasure.

In due time, His love would spread across the earth passed down from generation to generation, a mighty army of children who would extol Him and worship Him in spirit and in truth. Grace had been poured out over the earth. Mercy was being carried through the winds. His children would gather in multitudes praising Him, speaking of His love across the world. People of diverse colors, backgrounds, and languages would take the good news to the ends of the earth.

God was pleased. There was so much work to be done but He was directly engaging the planet now through His people, His 'called-out' ones. Through them, He would spread His love to a dying world and bring relief, comfort and peace through them.

He was the Father of life and existence. All things began by and through Him. He would defend His creation. He had died for His creation. Love was fulfilled because love had given all and through Jesus, He could now receive all back to Himself.

He was the source of all things and the Father of Spirits.

SCRIPTURAL EMPHASIS

I understand that not everyone who reads this novel will be a person who believes in Jesus Christ or the Bible so feel free to send me an email with questions/comments at **rotimi@fatherofspirits.com**. *I encourage you to open your mind and study on the subject of God, existence, angels, creation with a fresh pair of eyes. Mostly those who believe in the Bible will see the relevance of the texts provided below.*

Because this book is based on a true story, I have determined that it is important to provide some key references to aid your understanding of the truths contained therein. This is very important because knowledge shapes thinking which ultimately influences our lives, families and society at large. If indeed these things are true, you can imagine the impact this book will have around the world. The fact that there is a spiritual realm that influences what happens in the physical natural world, and vice versa.

Understanding the past, our collective origin or source helps us as humanity to dissect the truth about the future. This has important ramifications for everyone, indeed. If this world was simply an act of chance or moreso, regardless of your faith or bias, the creative and planned work of a genius mind, this book helps you to begin your journey in finding truth.

Are we mere victims of an evolutionary state born by a progressive mutation of elements or where we made by a superior and supreme being? No one should answer these questions for you. I believe that everyone alive at some point in their lives should seek after truth, regardless of the family you were born into or the religion your family offered you. The answers are the very keys to existence. If we are to exist in our physical state on the earth for a set of years and then step into unkown world of life after death, studying our existence should be important to you. That's the relevance of the book you have just read.

A great part of the scriptures provided here will focus on angels. For a full account of creation, read Genesis Chapter 1 of the Bible. For the full account of the watchers who visited the earth and married women, read the book of Enoch*. The Bible touches on this briefly in Genesis Chapter 6.

---

*The book of Enoch is a pseudepigraphal text or Apocryphal writing. It is not to be treated as the authoritative Word of God. It however gives some valuable insight into events referenced briefly in the canonized text of the Bible.

1 When man began to multiply on the face of the land and daughters were born to them,

2 the sons of God saw that the daughters of man were attractive. And they took as their wives any they chose.

3 Then the LORD said, "My Spirit shall not abide in man forever, for he is flesh: his days shall be 120 years."

4 The Nephilim were on the earth in those days, and also afterward, when the sons of God came in to the daughters of man and they bore children to them. These were the mighty men who were of old, the men of renown.

(Genesis 6:1-4)

Jude and Peter wrote about these angels refered to as Sons of God in their books. I find it remarkable that canonized books have references to uncanonized books.

And the angels who did not stay within their own position of authority, but left their proper dwelling, he has kept in eternal chains under gloomy darkness until the judgment of the great day. (Jude 1:6)

4 For if God did not spare angels when they sinned, but cast them into hell and committed them to chains of gloomy darkness to be kept until the judgment;

5 if he did not spare the ancient world, but preserved Noah, a herald of righteousness, with seven others, when he brought a flood upon the world of the ungodly;

(2 Peter 2:4-5)

ANGELS

There is much to be explained in the discussion of the existence, purpose and description of angels. Most of the texts below focus on scriptures that serve as foundational theology on angels. However, as stated in my introduction, I used creative freedom in the formulation of names and descriptions.

12 Then he said to me, "Do not be afraid, Daniel, for from the first day that you set your heart on understanding this and on humbling yourself before your God, your words were heard, and I have come in response to your words.

13 "But the prince of the kingdom of Persia was withstanding me for twenty-one days; then behold, Michael, one of the chief princes, came to help me, for I had been left there with the kings of Persia.

14 "Now I have come to give you an understanding of what will happen to your people in the latter days, for the vision pertains to the days yet future."

(Daniel 10:12-14)

A good text that supports the physical description of angels can be found in the book of Daniel. The same scripture also gives us some insight into the organization of the spiritual realm. You can safely deduce that the devil's kingdom indeed has heirachy and structure. The spirits who rule over different regions of the earth are called princes. As can be expected, they often work tirelessly to disrupt the missions of God's angels and thus, impact their good influence on the earth.

Most often than not, in the Bible, angels would tell the humans they appeared to not to fear. This showcases the visible might and splendor of these angelic beings. Seeing them would make anyone afraid. Unlike their counterparts who perpetuate evil, God's angels do not want to be feared or worshiped.

There are more texts to support the description, temperaments, emotions and conversations of the angels but the few below, at the minimum, will serve as guide for your exploration into this interesting and mysterious world of good and evil angels.

DESCRIPTION OF ANGELS

5 I lifted my eyes and looked, and behold, a certain man clothed in linen, whose waist was girded with gold of Uphaz!
6 His body was like beryl, his face like the appearance of lightning, his eyes like torches of fire, his arms and feet like burnished bronze in color, and the sound of his words like the voice of a multitude...
(DANIEL 10:5-6 NKJV)

ANGELS WITNESSED CREATION

4 "Where were you when I laid the foundation of the earth? Tell Me, if you have understanding,
5 Who set its measurements? Since you know. Or who stretched the line on it?
6 On what were its bases sunk? Or who laid its cornerstone,
7 When the morning stars sang together and all the sons of God shouted for joy?
(JOB 38:4-7)

6 You alone are the LORD; You have made heaven, the heaven of heavens, with all their host, the earth and everything on it, the seas and all that is in them, and You preserve them all. The host of heaven worships You.
(NEHEMIAH 9:6 NKJV)

THE WATCHERS & GIANTS

1 When men began to increase in number on the earth and daughters were born to them,

2 the sons of God saw that the daughters of men were beautiful, and they married any of them they chose.

3 Then the Lord said, "My Spirit will not contend with humans forever, for they are mortal; their days will be a hundred and twenty years."

4 The Nephilim were on the earth in those days – and also afterward – when the sons of God went to the daughters of men and had children by them. They were the heroes of old, men of renown.
(GENESIS 6:1-4 NIV)

After the angels sinned by marrying and copulating with human women, they bore them gigantic hybrid children. The Bible calls these offspring nephilim, the "mighty men of old, warriors of renown" (Gen. 6:4). When they appear again later in the Scriptures, they are called by a variety of names, including Rephaim, Zumim, Emim and Horites (Gen. 14:5), Anakim (Deu. 2:11), Zamzummim (Deu. 2:20), and Avim (Deu. 2:23).

37 "But as the days of Noah were, so also will the coming of the Son of Man be.

38 For as in the days before the flood, they were eating and drinking, marrying and giving in marriage, until the day that Noah entered the ark,

39 and did not know until the flood came and took them all away, so also will the coming of the Son of Man be.
(MATTHEW 24:37-39 NKJV)

And the angels who did not keep their own position, but left their proper dwelling, he has kept in eternal chains in deepest darkness for the judgment of the great Day.
(JUDE 6 NRSV)

For indeed God did not spare the angels who sinned, but cast them down in chains of darkness into the low regions and delivered them to be kept for the judgment of torment.
(II PETER 2:4 Magiera NT Peshitta translation)

19. . . He went and preached to the spirits in prison,

20 who formerly were disobedient, when once the Divine longsuffering waited in the days of Noah, while the ark was being prepared, in which a few, that is, eight souls, were saved through water.
(I PETER 3:19 NKJV)

Let not the dead live, let not the giants [repha'im] rise again: therefore hast Thou visited and destroyed them, and hast destroyed all their memory.
(ISAIAH 26:14 DRA)

ANGELS EAT

Man ate of the bread of the angels; he sent them food in abundance.
(Psalms 78:25)

JUDGEMENT OF THE ANGELS

Do you not know that we are to judge angels? How much more, then, matters pertaining to this life!
(1 Corinthians 6:3)

There will be more scriptures on our website. For example, the description of Hades was gotten from the parable of the rich man and lazarus. Also, the story about the death and ressurection of Jesus.

There are other aspects of the book that we may not have covered but over the next few months and of course, through the next two sequels, I'll be able to answer more questions and write based on the questions and cconversations that come from this first book.

In the sequel to this book, **Father of Spirits, Book2: The Book of Dominions**, I will delve more into stories of angels who visit the earth in earthly form with special missions. There will be more resources to aid your journey on our website: **www. fatherofspirits.com**. Especially if you visit the forum, you will be able to engage in discussions with others and learn even faster.

On a final note, I hope you enjoy your journey of truth. Finding truth is vital to truly living. The truth indeed sets free. The truth changes how we think, how we react and ultimately the type of life we live.

Thank you for reading this book.

Rotimi Kehinde

THE VALLEY OF DEAD DREAMS

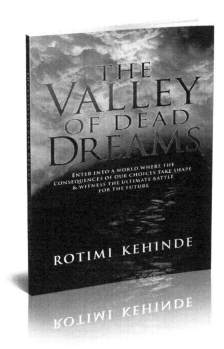

The Valley of Dead Dreams is an inspired revelation of a world where dreams go when they are unfulfilled in the real world. This powerful story is told with captivating and riveting imagery, visionary detail and narrated in first person. Enter into a world of dreams, fascinating landscapes, and realms within realms. See the battle of life unfold before your very eyes; the valley of dead dreams will expose the truth of the spiritual realm and showcase a reality where our actions and inaction meet the truth of consequence.

Available on Amazon.com

Rotimi is the founder and chief executive officer of GodKulture, an organization that builds creative platforms to engage and empower individuals, organizations and businesses through an integration of creative expression and art.

He has worked on hundreds of visual design projects and over forty book design and development projects for clients over four years through his creative agency.

He hosts a monthly creative workshop called Advance and mentors many creators and innovators in the city of Chicago on their purpose-fulfillment journeys. Rotimi also convenes an annual conference called FireStorm that attracts hundreds of attendees every year. He is also a leader at ReNew Phila, a church in Skokie, Illinois.

Rotimi and his wife, Aramide, currently live in Chicago, USA.

Contact Information

You can contact Rotimi Kehinde. He would love to get your feedback.

ROTIMI KEHINDE

815 630 9890

@RotimiKehinde

facebook.com/rotimikehinde
E-mail: **rk@rotimikehinde.com**

Please include your testimony of help received from this book when you write.

You can order additional copies of this book at
www.Godkulture.org
www.rotimikehinde.com
www.fatherofspirits.com

Godkulture ministry is a conglomerate of kingdom-driven men and women. We are creative spirits with diverse vocations who have a burden to express God's love to our world. Likewise, we are devoted to using our gifts, talents, and resources to glorify God and touch lives. In every endeavor, Godkulture's core purpose is to establish kingdom culture on the earth.

www.Godkulture.org